NO PLACE LIKE HOME

NO PLACE LIKE HOME

A NOVEL

SUSAN WACKERBARTH

Boatyard Press

No Place Like Home
Copyright © 2020 by Susan Wackerbarth
All rights reserved

Cover art and maps by Lisa Bade
Author photo by Reed Takaaze

First Edition
Printed in the United States

ISBN-978-1-7341095-0-4 (print)
ISBN-978-1-7341095-1-1 (ebook)

Library of Congress Control Number:
2020909836

For my children

CONTENTS

Author's Note   *ix*

Map of Hilo   *xi*

Map of Hawai'i Island   *xiii*

Part One: Made of Straw   1

Part Two: Oil Can   111

Part Three: Put 'Em Up   191

Part Four: Beautiful Wickedness   299

Part Five: Ruby Slippers   379

Acknowledgements   407

Discussion Questions for Reading Groups   409

Additional Resources   411

AUTHOR'S NOTE

THIS IS NOT A BOOK ABOUT HAWAI'I. I AM NOT QUALIFIED—NOR do I wish—to write such a book. This is a story about people who, for a number of reasons, happen to live there.

During my long residence on the Island of Hawai'i (aka the Big Island), I have developed a deep love and appreciation for the land and culture, particularly for East Hawai'i and my hometown of Hilo. As a *haole* (white) person writing in a still actively colonized Hawai'i it was important to me that I not presume to speak from the perspective either of native Hawaiians, or of local people with roots in the plantation era, out of respect for cultures that are not my own. Instead, I have written from the perspective of *haole* immigrants to Hawai'i, misfits trying to make a home in a place they may not really belong.

While many of the locations in this novel are real, my depiction of them is fictional. I have taken liberties with Hilo geography, with the Palace Theater's architecture, and much more. The production of *The Wizard of Oz* in this novel is not based in any way on the actual 2007 Palace show. My fictional Hilo police force also bears no resemblance to the real one.

This story makes light of many serious things, and especially pokes fun at *haoles* in Hawai'i, both "grown" and "flown." No offense is intended.

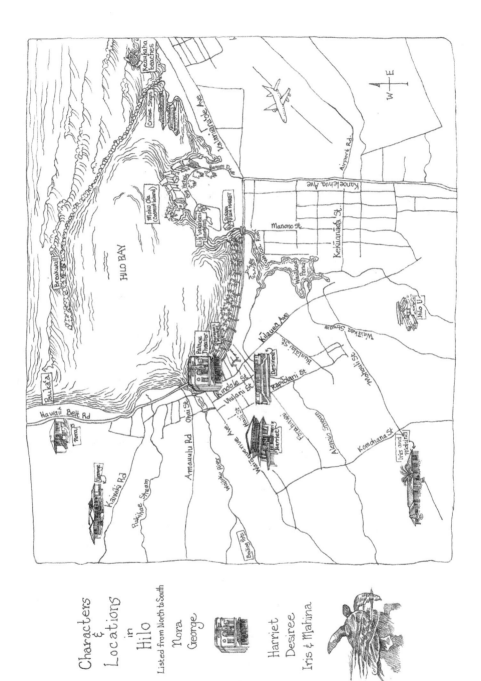

Characters & Locations in Hilo

Listed from North to South

Nora
George

Harriet
Desiree
Iris & Mahina

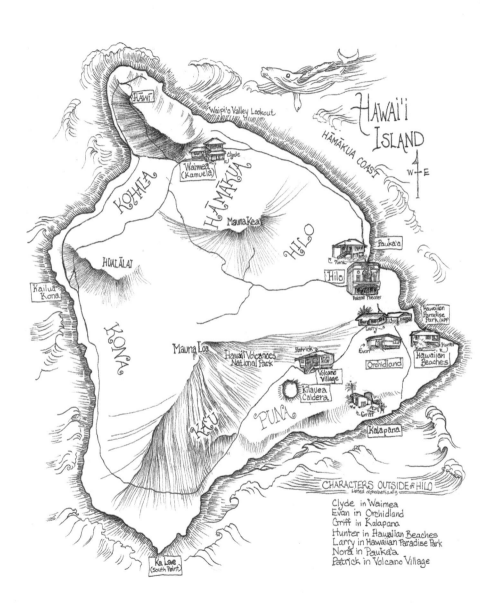

Hawai'i Island

Hāmākua Coast

W — E

Hāwī

Waipi'o Valley Lookout

Waimea (Kamuela)
Clyde

KOHALA

HĀMĀKUA

Mauna Kea

HILO

Pauka'a
Nora

Hilo
Palace Theater

HUALĀLAI

Hawaiian Paradise Park (HPP)

Kailua Kona

Larry

Evan
Orchidland

Hawaiian Beaches
Hunter

KONA

Mauna Loa

Hawai'i Volcanoes National Park

Patrick

Volcano Village

Kīlauea Caldera

PUNA

Griff

KAʻŪ

Kalapana

Ka Lae (South Point)

CHARACTERS OUTSIDE OF HILO
listed alphabetically

Clyde in Waimea
Evan in Orchidland
Griff in Kalapana
Hunter in Hawaiian Beaches
Larry in Hawaiian Paradise Park
Nora in Pauka'a
Patrick in Volcano Village

"I despise no one," she said, "no one. Regret your own actions, if you like that kind of wallowing in self-pity, but never, never despise. Never presume yours is a better morality."
~Aunt Augusta, *Travels with My Aunt*, Graham Greene

"My, people come and go so quickly here!"
~Dorothy, *The Wizard of Oz*, L. Frank Baum

PART ONE
MADE OF STRAW

CHAPTER 1

Dusk tips swiftly into dark in the subtropics. Nestled into a scoop and a knob on the windward coastline of Hawai'i's Big Island, which dangles at the end of the island chain, the town of Hilo accepted the natural scheme of things and went to bed early most nights. Along the bay front, palm fronds rustled in the breeze drifting off the Pacific, and sodium streetlights cast an orange glow on weathered storefronts.

In August and September, even the cooling trade winds brought scant relief from summer's heat, leaving greenhouse air thick, warm, and wet. At night, mosquito dentists drilled for the brain. Coqui frogs chirped and pinged in a deafening chorus, like tiny, demented bells.

During these steamy months, some folks set up camp at the beach, or moved upcountry to take refuge in cooler climes. Not so the East Hawai'i Community Players, gearing up for the annual fall fundraising musical at the historic Palace Theater—this year, the iconic, crowd-pleasing theater-packer, *The Wizard of Oz*. They needed a sure thing.

The night before the first read-through, the director and cast slept fitfully—or not at all.

⤳

THE WIZARD, GRIFF, SAT AT HIS KITCHEN TABLE IN THE ONE-room house he'd built himself on twenty lava and scrub-covered acres in the Puna district southwest of Hilo, eating a late-night snack of cornflakes and listening to *Shore to Shore a.m.* on his battery-operated radio. He smacked a mosquito on his neck and looked at the blood on his hand. It reminded him of 'Nam.

"The first time I was abducted, they gave me a sex-change operation," said a caller. "I went to sleep a girl and woke up a boy with a big ole penis." The caller chuckled. "I screamed, and they dumped me right back in the dirt outside my house."

Griff rinsed his bowl and spoon and set them in their storage rack. He had one of everything. One fork, one knife, one plate, one frying pan, one towel. The only luxury—and security breach—he permitted himself now was the internet. He'd jerry-rigged a radio connection from his nearest neighbor's house when they went away on vacation one year.

"What happened the next time they abducted you?" The radio host, Buck Leary, sounded concerned, interested.

"Well, Buck, they took off my pants and probed me, that's what." The caller's voice hit a high squawk. "It tickled like a sonofabitch. I was hootin' and hollerin' till they went and put a gag on me."

Griff made a mental note on dialect and inflection, in case he ever played a hillbilly. He had always liked playacting, especially if he had lines to memorize. It soothed him and quieted the voices. He was already word-perfect for Professor Marvel, and the Wizard's lines were close behind.

Griff lay down on the sagging garage-sale couch that doubled as his bed and drifted off for a moment. He woke again and slapped his head as a posse of whining mosquitoes made a meal of his ears.

"The path of the comet nearing earth's orbit has changed into a straight-on collision course, according to some experts," said Buck Leary. His voice sounded lower and richer than before.

Griff sat up straight. It was The Voice. He hadn't heard It in years.

"Callers say Energy Centers around the world are being activated. Something big is happening, folks. We need to pay attention and stay in tune with the harmonic waves."

A hundred little lights sparkled in Griff's brain. A commercial for erectile dysfunction followed, and he switched off the radio. He paced across the rough floorboards he'd pieced together from scrap lumber. After years of silence, The Voice had spoken directly to him again through the radio waves as It had years before when he'd been hunted and on the run. Why?

An Energy Center had sprung to life in the Palace Theater. He'd felt Its vibrations, but hadn't had a name for their source. Until now. The comet was hurtling through space, either a threat to life or a power for transformation.

Griff felt a quickening in his chest.

⌣

ABOVE HILO TOWN IN UPSCALE SUNRISE RIDGE, MAHINA (AKA Dorothy) sat propped up in bed with her laptop and phone, cruising Facebook and texting. She uploaded a new profile picture—close up headshot, angled, and cut off on one side. Hot and edgy.

Ding.

A comment already!

You look good enough to eat, my pretty.

Mahina didn't recognize the sender, BomBoy. Not one of her friends. He (or she) must have read her postings about landing the leading role in *Wizard*. What a creeper.

She shrugged. Mahina's mother was always insisting that she change her privacy settings to avoid just this kind of thing. But how else would she be discovered?

Ding.

A new comment popped up.

Where's your little dog?

Mahina looked around, then leapt out of bed. Her toy poodle, Ziggy, usually nestled in the covers with her. How had she not noticed he was missing? Iris, her mother, was already asleep down the hall, so Mahina decided to be thoughtful and not yell.

She swung open the French doors, switched on the outside light, and stepped barefoot onto the rough, nonslip terra cotta tiles of the *lanai*. She didn't remember letting Ziggy out, but maybe her mother had. Mahina had been exhausted after watching Judy Garland's *Wizard of Oz* performance in preparation for the read-through tomorrow. Dorothy basically never shuts up. So many lines to memorize—so much attention!

She smiled, then frowned. Hadn't Ziggy watched the movie with her? He would be a perfect Toto. She would insist on it. She'd definitely brought him home from the video store. The little dog always hopped into her bright red Honda Civic and sat on Mahina's lap, licking her face as she drove. Iris would have a fit if she knew— probably take her sixteenth birthday present back again.

"Ziggy, come boy." Mahina heard rustling in the gardenias across the wide expanse of lawn. The coqui frogs stopped chirping.

"Meow." Pounce, the neighbor's fat tabby cat, rubbed against her legs, then sat down and began to wash his face.

"Ziggy!" He was never gone this long. Mahina shivered as a slight breeze pressed her thin nightgown against her body. Here she stood in a spotlight, while some pervert was probably watching her with Ziggy's mutilated body at his feet.

Just then, the little dog ran into the light. He held something in his mouth.

Mahina knelt down and wrestled out a slimy, gnawed chicken drumstick.

Ziggy growled and gave a few sharp yaps.

"Gross. Who gave this to you?" Mahina threw the bone as far as she could over the hibiscus hedge bordering the neighbor's yard and wiped her hands on the grass. She picked the dog up, his small, fluffy body squirming in outrage.

"Dogs can't have chicken bones, silly." She kissed his muzzle. "Where have you been?" She buried her face in Ziggy's puffy top-knot, and he licked her fingers.

She and Ziggy heard the sound at the same time: footsteps crunching on the gravel path alongside the house that led to the street.

Ziggy gave a savage yap and strained to get away, but Mahina held him tight and leapt back through the doorway. She whirled around, slammed the doors behind her, slid the bolts, and switched off the light. Then she peered through the slats in the lowered blind. Was that a shadow?

Mahina hurried across the polished wooden floors of the dark house and checked all the outside doors to be sure they were locked. She wouldn't wake her mother. Iris was already far too focused on her only child. She'd want to do a purification rite. She'd want to work with Mahina to dispel her negative energy. No, Mahina would deal with this herself. If she'd already attracted a stalker in Hilo, she could only imagine what New York would be like when she was a Broadway star. She'd have to hire a bodyguard.

Mahina drew a big, gleaming knife from the wooden block on the kitchen counter, and rummaged under the sink for one of the housekeeper's hidden bottles of bleach solution. (Iris disapproved—poison!) She would not hesitate to spray it into an intruder's eyes. Serve him right if it blinded him. She retreated to her room, Ziggy trotting behind. She climbed into bed and pulled the covers up to her chin.

Just try it, buddy.

The little dog sprang up and snuggled into the curve of her back. A surge of anger warmed her to her toes.

⌣

ON HILO'S NORTH SIDE, 2,000 FEET UP THE LUSH SLOPE OFF Kaiwiki road, the director, George, awakened, sweaty and startled, when his boyfriend Cal flung an arm across his chest and moved in to snuggle.

"Christ," George hissed. "I'm trying to sleep." He pushed down the covers to let the muggy night air wash over his body. He'd considered springing for a house on the dry side of the island after he'd sold his personal injury firm to an up-and-coming young litigator and escaped from the East Coast. But real estate on the leeward side was overpriced, not to mention overrun with tourists. However miserable the climate might be, especially at this time of year, Hilo was a genuine place unburdened by the need for pretense.

"Sorry." Cal rolled over and curled up in a ball on the far side of the bed. He'd been so moody lately, so needy.

George lay on his back and stared into the darkness, trying not to second-guess his casting. He'd know more after the first read-through tomorrow. This had to be the best show the Palace had ever put on, or the theater could end up shut down, boarded up, and used for storage again, damp, rat-infested, and unloved.

George held his breath and pushed down on his sternum to quiet his heart's loud thumping, a method he'd read about on his favorite medical website.

He couldn't explain the fierce attachment he'd formed to the old theater, but it had been immediate. He'd felt it the first time he walked up Haili street to watch an art film and saw the gaudy old marquee blazing against the night sky, its name a gap-toothed smile: P _ L A C E. Perhaps buildings were easier to love than people.

There was still "evidence of vagrancy and drug activity," as the building inspector's report had phrased it just last week—and so what? Every downtown business struggled with the homeless epidemic. You could live on the streets of Hilo year-round without freezing to death, and food actually grew on trees, as well as in trash bins stuffed with tourists' leftovers. All efforts to get rid of the folks who had taken up residence in the potholed alley alongside the Palace had failed. They just kept coming back to shelter from the wind and rain.

Petty vandalism was a mere pimple compared to the metastasized cancer of structural decay. The county had threatened to condemn the building unless the Friends could shore up the foundations and put on a new roof. A million dollars. An impossible sum.

George swung his legs over the side of the bed and stood up, wincing as a spasm shot through his back. He shuffled to the kitchen to pour himself a nightcap.

⌣

A SHARP DESCENT FROM LOFTY SUBURBIA, DOWNTOWN HILO'S crowded, low-rent district bordered the tsunami evacuation zone. The Good Witch, Desiree, lay on her back and stared at the ceiling of her tiny bedroom through the half-light, as dark as her room ever got with the damned streetlight outside. She'd finally calmed the children down and herded them into the makeshift bunk beds she'd crammed into the other tiny bedroom of their rickety apartment on Kapi'olani Street, an oversized twin shared by the girls, Kolea and Malia, with a narrow bunk above it for Nakai. The walls shook whenever a big truck roared past and disturbed the cockroaches, who scuttled and scratched and sometimes whirred into flight.

Desiree had seen the call for auditions in the Palace window the week before, after one of her regulars, Patrick, the IPA connoisseur, had told her he was trying out to be the Scarecrow.

She passed the Palace every day as she walked from her apartment through narrow alleys and scuffed-up streets to the Aloha Bar & Grill on Kamehameha Avenue. For years after Kama split she had left her kids in the apartment during her night shifts, with the TV on and an elderly neighbor as backup, but after they'd almost burned the place down trying to roast hot dogs and marshmallows over the gas burner she'd switched to daytime, which meant no more solo beach days—and lousy tips. Another sacrifice of motherhood.

The Wizard of Oz would be the Palace Theater's fall fundraiser this year, proclaimed the poster in the big display window. Desiree had stopped, captured by the sparkling green Emerald City shooting its spires into the sky. Auditions for all parts would be held that weekend: women, men and children needed. Munchkins. Desiree's mind started to tick.

She remembered her glory days in high school, back when she thought she had a future in show business. Before she ran off with her boyfriend to the next Kansas town, big whoop. Before she dropped out of school. Before her never-supposed-to-be-permanent career as a bartender began. And long before she took an exotic vacation to Hawai'i and fell into her new life, still bartending.

Staring at the sign, Desiree felt something flicker inside. Since she didn't work nights anymore, they could all try out. A family activity. The kids could be Munchkins, and she could be—well, not Dorothy, obviously, even though she still felt like Dorothy sometimes, in a long, long wait for ruby slippers. The Wicked Witch of the West? Or the Good Witch, Glinda. Wasn't that her name?

Desiree closed her eyes for a moment, and the cracked sidewalk disappeared. She stood in a warm glow of light, dressed in a glittering white gown with a big poofy skirt, a tiara on her head, and a sparkling wand in her hand. Glinda the Good.

Desiree turned over in bed and the image vanished. She needed some real magic in her life to cover the rent, for starters. Kama always paid his child support, but it wasn't enough.

She closed her eyes and saw her ex's smiling face. Sexy as fuck. She could never stay mad at him for long. Revved up car engines and the occasional drunken shout soothed her to sleep like a lullaby.

CHAPTER 2

SATURDAY MORNING AT THE PALACE THEATER IN THE HEART of old downtown, just up Haili Street from the bayfront. In the theater's heyday, from the 1930s through the '50s, Hilo had a full-blown Mouseketeer's Club. Photos in the lobby featured hundreds of grinning children in mouse ears, many of them offspring of Japanese, Chinese, Filipino, and Portuguese sugar cane plantation workers. Every Saturday morning, the theater played the *Mickey Mouse Club* on the big movie screen, with a sing-along afterward led by a dapper host enthroned on the shining white organ podium. A real community event. But by the 1960s, after the second tsunami had devastated downtown Hilo all the way up to Kinoʻole Street, the Palace had become a warehouse. By 1982, it was boarded up and abandoned. After a decade of fundraising, lobbying, and hard physical labor, the Palace had reopened in 1998, ten years ago.

Now, on the morning of the first read-through, the *Wizard of Oz* cast gathered. They flowed in through the side alley door, their voices loud and excited. Some laughed and hugged, while others watched, hoping they, too, would achieve such intimate hilarity with those who were still strangers. Regardless of their connections, or lack thereof, the cast arrived united in purpose: to save the theater and put on a hell of a show.

Among other things.

⤚

"WELCOME, EAST HAWAI'I COMMUNITY PLAYERS, OLD AND NEW." George's voice boomed out into the vast recesses of the auditorium where his cast sprawled in the cramped theater seats and fanned themselves.

To chorus member Nora's critical eye, he looked rather like Toad of Toad Hall from *Wind in the Willows*, which she had just finished reading aloud to her twins. She could see him wearing driving goggles and a long scarf. Poop poop.

She stifled a giggle. Dust motes danced up-current in the steamy late morning heat, and she wiped a trickle of sweat off her forehead. She twisted against the wooden armrest of her seat to peer behind her. Her children must have gone exploring, which she was dying to do herself.

George's voice broke through her thoughts. "For maximum audience appeal, we'll perform the movie version of the play that everyone knows and loves."

Cheers and foot stomping.

"Our assistant director and stage manager, Fred Moon, will pass out the scripts and rehearsal schedules while Enid Takeshita shows us her mockups of the costumes. Never too early to start collecting what you need. Then, Harriet Furneaux will show us preliminary drawings of the sets. Yes, Harriet the

Wicked Witch is also our set designer. We'll all help out with set building later on."

Fred, a stocky man in his forties wearing a baseball cap, waved and gave a toothy smile. Then he bustled around thrusting photocopied booklets into everyone's hands.

Nora noted the people who seemed acquainted already. They leaned in, talking and laughing, even while George cast his penetrating gaze on them like a spotlight.

"Get these dates into your calendars, folks. We open Friday night, October seventeenth, nine weeks from today, and close Sunday November second."

Enid, a tiny, impeccably turned-out woman of indeterminate age, her hair a sleek silver bob, revealed beautifully painted renditions of the costumes, many constructed around pieces they could find at home or at the thrift store, she assured them: pants, boots, dresses, etc. She would then dye, alter, and gussy up their findings with trim and sequins.

Harriet, tall, middle-aged and heavier-set, with a dark pageboy and swooping brows, draped an easel with set designs painted on large sheets of newsprint. The set pieces were reversible and had parts to fold out or in for different scenes.

Ingenious, thought Nora.

George thanked Harriet and Enid and continued his speech. "I also want to introduce Belinda Hudson, our choreographer, with whom you'll all work closely."

A blonde, curly-haired twenty-something bounced up out of her seat in front, turned, smiled, and curtseyed. "Hello everyone." Her accent was some variety of southern.

Fresh off the plane, thought Nora. She felt almost like an old-timer after just over one reluctant year on the island, which would never be home. Never.

"Belinda is a dance instructor at Hilo U. She comes to us all the way from Oklahoma with a strong background in theater."

Scattered applause.

Nora looked around for someone to talk to. That was the whole point, after all, getting to know people in her new community and making friends.

Iris, the New-Agey real estate agent who had found Nora's rental house—and purified it with burning sage before they moved in—had told Nora her daughter Mahina was trying out for Dorothy. She'd suggested Nora and the twins try out, too.

So here she was, a newly minted Munchkin townsperson and Ozian. Her eight-year-old twins, Miri and Oliver, were Munchkins and Flying Monkeys.

George introduced Larry, the music director, a tall, gangly man with frizzy, greying hair pulled into a ponytail.

He said a few words about chorus rehearsals and working with the principals on their solos and ensemble pieces. The orchestra would come in later in the rehearsal schedule.

Nora craned her neck to look around the other side of the theater, and her heart gave a little lurch.

Oliver and Miri sat with their strawberry blond heads touching, as they did whenever they wanted to block everyone else out of their twin world. Even their mother. Or perhaps especially their mother. Did they blame her for the divorce? It was always the mother's fault, even when it wasn't, which was absolutely the case in her situation. Could survival ever be the wrong choice?

Nora squeezed her eyes shut. She'd read an article recently about a new therapy tested on people with OCD, in which they visualized a stop sign whenever they felt the urge to perform their repetitive behaviors.

STOP. The bright red sign touched the corners of her brain.

"Okay." George clapped his hands and motioned behind him to a circle of ancient metal folding chairs set up on the stage. "Come find a seat, and let's start reading."

⌣

ONLY TWO PARENTS HAD BROUGHT THEIR MUNCHKINS TO THE read-through, thank goodness. Harriet, the Wicked Witch, had always found youngsters trying. Terrorizing them would be enjoyable.

The woman playing Glinda—Desiree?—let her three boisterous kids run amuck. They soon swept into their wake the pale, red-haired twins who belonged to a pretty young woman in the chorus. The gang of children ran up and down the aisles of the theater and played a noisy card game in the lobby. Glinda's three broke into squabbles their mother chose to ignore, ignoring also Harriet's pointed glances. Harriet tsked inwardly.

The cast eyed each other over their booklets as they took their seats onstage. They were a motley assortment wearing shorts and rubber slippers in the stuffy midday heat. Harriet recognized Dorothy, a sultry teenager named Mahina, who had brought her toy poodle along. Mahina's little dog had already taken a dislike to George, who was clearly not an animal lover. More to the point, Mahina was a student in Harriet's Beginning Drawing and Painting class at Waiānuenue High this semester. She sat in the back corner of the classroom, surrounded by a posse of nervous girls who vied for her approval. Harriet had her eye on them, ready to crack down.

Oz was a strange, nondescript man in his sixties, named Griff. He didn't speak a word the entire time except to read the script, which he did flawlessly, his voice rich and expressive. Harriet met his eyes once and had to look away first.

She knew the Scarecrow, Patrick, a community theater regular who sometimes subbed for her at the high school. He looked type-cast, a lean, loose, good-natured man, although possibly of weak character.

The Tin Man, Evan, was a slick-looking young stud, saved from insufferability by his slight hesitation. Not a Hilo type. Actually, he reminded her a bit of her own son, Luke, who lived with his boy-friend in San Francisco.

Harriet knew Merle, the Cowardly Lion, another theater regular, by reputation. He threw back his mane of thick, curly, unnaturally dark hair and flexed his powerful shoulders, bombarding the twins' mother and the choreographer with a series of sexy smiles.

That's right, she thought. Go for the new blood. All the better if it's young and fresh. Harriet frowned as she remembered the night before.

Restless before bed, she had floated through the cooling night air of her garden, a wraith in the soft folds of her loose, sleeveless nightgown. The grass lay cool and damp beneath her bare feet, while trees and plants formed dark shapes against the stone wall.

So far, her Wicked Witch of the West laugh had been half-voiced and experimental. She wanted to try it at home in the darkness before letting loose in front of the cast the next day, but the neighbors were too close. Just blocks above the theater, her gracious old Haili Street house stood only several paces away from their open windows. The elderly couple went to bed early. During the day, she heard their television and voices. They were kind and sometimes brought her homemade sushi or miso soup. The husband even cut the grass in her front yard with his little push mower.

Perhaps they saw her as an emotional invalid in need of care, the woman whose husband had left her. The *haole* returnee after decades on the mainland, trying to come home again.

"Ha ha ha." The harsh whisper caught in Harriet's throat, and she coughed. She and her black cat, Salome, rattled around her castle by themselves now, without a broom or a monkey, unless you counted her unruly students at Waiānuenue High School. Teenagers were more monkey than human.

Who would grow into adulthood if they knew what lay in store? Old age and incipient death. She dug her toes into the lush grass and spread her arms wide. You assume life will just go on as it is, even though you're surrounded by evidence that it won't. You're so surprised when everything changes, when everything you thought was your life just disappears, as if it never was. And you're all that's left.

"Ha ha ha ha ha ha." A little louder this time.

A light went on next door.

She dropped her arms and tiptoed stiffly across the damp night grass, hunched and witchlike, and slipped into her house.

Now Harriet smiled. It was time to embrace her cronehood. She waited for her first entrance, ready to begin.

⌣

"Let's take a break, folks." George closed his book and stood up. "Get some food, and we'll meet back onstage in fifteen."

Finally. Nora's bottom had gone numb from sitting on the hard chair.

Intermission came after the poppy field scene. Glinda, who sat next to her, had almost missed her entrance. She obviously hadn't paid attention to the script after her big opening scene—too busy sighing and twirling her hair and fidgeting.

George had cleared his throat during the long pause, and Nora had given her neighbor a nudge, pointing to her lines on the page.

Now the cast swarmed around a folding table set up below stage with sushi, triangle-cut deli sandwiches, fruit, cookies, chips. A cooler of iced soda cans and water bottles sat underneath.

"Compliments of your director." Fred gestured toward the display.

George bowed with a flourish.

As Nora filled two little plates for Miri and Oliver, the Good Witch—Desiree, that was her name—cut in line next to her, grabbed a piece of sushi, and popped it into her mouth. Nora watched out of the corner of her eye as she chewed with gusto. Desiree pulled back her long blonde hair, ends bleached white from the sun, and twisted it into a bun. She stuck a pencil through the bulging mass and pointed to the spam musubi Nora had put on the twins' plates. "Watch it. You know what's in those?"

"I do, alas." Nora shuddered. "But the children love them."

"They're a local delicacy." Desiree grinned. "Hey, thanks for saving my ass up there. I totally spaced."

"No problem." Nora felt her chest tighten as it always did these days when someone was kind to her, or even just noticed she was alive. Nora still could not believe she was a single mother living in the tropics. This could not be her life, a nice Canadian like her.

She blinked her watery eyes and forced a smile. "This is as close to adult activity as I've had since the twins and I moved to Hilo three months ago, after my divorce. I homeschooled Miri and Oliver up in Waimea, which really just meant they stayed home and played."

"Wow. I'd go nuts." Desiree's eyes wandered.

"I really need to get a job, though. Child support isn't cutting it." Nora spoke in a rush as she picked the bright pink imitation crab out of her sushi. She took a tentative bite. Desiree looked at her. A point of connection, perhaps? "My ex-husband got a job as a software engineer at one of the telescopes. When we moved to Waimea from Canada, everyone told us the public schools were terrible. The local kids just beat up the white kids and—" Nora's voice trailed off as Desiree's eyes narrowed.

"Yeah, my kids have a tally going on the wall at home. We have quotas they have to meet before they get snacks." Desiree broke into raucous laughter. "I had you going there, didn't I?"

"I'm so sorry." Nora felt the flames of her redhead insta-blush. She hesitated. "But you're not—"

"Local?" Desiree snorted. "White as bread, sister, from Kansas. My ex is part Hawaiian, so my kids are *hapa*. You know what it means?"

Nora shook her head. "I've heard the term, but no, not really."

"A local term for half something, usually *haole*—white—and half Asian or something else. Most local people aren't actually Hawaiian, or maybe just a tiny bit. They're Japanese, Chinese, Korean, Portuguese, Filipino, Pacific Islander, or whatever. Usually a big mix of everything."

As Nora turned her head to look for her very pale twins, a chord reverberated up to the ceiling. Everyone stopped and stared.

The Wizard, Griff, sat at the organ podium, which rose high above the last section of seats on the left below the stage. He started to play "Follow the Yellow Brick Road," segued into "We're Off to See the Wizard," then into "Ding Dong the Witch is Dead," and ended with "Somewhere over the Rainbow."

He's a whole orchestra in himself, Nora marveled, remembering the children's school field trip she'd chaperoned just over a year earlier to hear the Vancouver Symphony play *Peter and the Wolf.*

From his seat at the pipe organ, Griff called up the flute, clarinet, trumpet, tuba, violins, and cellos, xylophone, drums, and cymbals to sing and dance together. All in the space of about two minutes.

Nora realized her mouth was hanging open, and shut it. People around her murmured in wonder.

Just as abruptly as he'd started, the Wizard stopped and shut down the organ. He hopped off the podium and disappeared backstage.

Fred, the stage manager, hustled down the aisle waving his arms. "We're not supposed to touch the organ. Only the Hilo Organ Society can play it—a priceless antique! Parts of it survived both the tsunamis in '46 and '60. This organ has travelled all over the islands and finally come home again at huge expense." He gazed around the room, wringing his hands. "Who was playing?"

Larry responded. "Our Wizard, Griff, and I think we should bring the organ into the production. It's brilliant." He held up his hand as Fred began to sputter. "Don't worry. I'll talk to my guy on the board, Phil Peterson. You remember him from auditions, right? He's a real supporter, very interested in the play. He'll love the idea." Larry patted Fred on the back.

"I am the King of the Foreh-eh-eh-eh-eh-ehst," boomed a resonant baritone voice. All heads turned as one to see the Cowardly Lion striking a pose in the entry hall, his arms outstretched.

So theater people really are like this, Nora thought. Wow.

He caught her eye and winked, then growled. "Put 'em up, put 'em up."

Everyone laughed, and all the children, including the twins, swarmed around and punched at him. He roared and pretended to punch back. They screamed in delight.

Nora folded her arms, but couldn't stop grinning.

"What an attention hound." Desiree sidled up next to her. "But the kids love him. Women, too, I bet." She nudged Nora, who flushed.

I need to loosen up. Even Glinda the Good thinks so. Nora shook her hair back from her face and fluffed it up off her sticky neck. She'd have to learn how to twist it up in a pencil bun, like Desiree's.

⌣

GRIFF LEFT THE ORGAN AND HIS STUNNED AUDIENCE BEHIND, unaware of their response. He walked down the hallway left of the stage, which doubled as a makeshift dressing room. He passed the wall of mirrors and lights, with stools shoved up under a narrow shelf running its length, and stopped before the main doorway which opened to a covered area called Actors' Alley. A larger dressing room on the right side of the stage opened to another alley and the parking lot. The Palace had been built as a movie theater, and the Friends had retrofitted it for stage productions as best they could with limited space.

Griff pulled out a key he'd taken from Fred's big key ring. He'd copy it and slip it back on at the next rehearsal. He unlocked the narrow door, nearly hidden under the thick conduits that brought wind from the blower in the basement to the pipes in the chambers overhead, then felt his way down the cement stairs, groping for the light switch on the wall. A naked fluorescent tube illuminated a wide, low room with a rough cement floor. The ceiling's wooden beams were broken only by the trapdoor onstage. The Wicked Witch would melt through it at the end of the play.

At the entrance, a thick steel cylinder as long as a man lying down and at least three feet in diameter housed the organ blower. Hidden within, given voice through the organ, pulsed the Energy Center. Griff rested his hand on the metal, which vibrated beneath his touch, warm and urgent.

Griff had gone online after The Voice had spoken to him through the radio announcer last night. Energy Centers were much discussed. The main theory held that a kindly alien race had planted centers all over the world in human gathering places where disaster had struck, to protect humans from further harm. They were activated when a threat approached, which was happening now as the comet headed for earth.

The internet was rife with debates about the comet, too. Some predicted the world would come to an end when it struck. Others argued it would change course again and spare the earth. Still others claimed it held a time capsule created by an earlier, space-travelling human race, launched into orbit to reveal the secrets of our former glory, when we were ready to take them in.

Griff had discovered the most valuable website shortly after he first rigged his contraband internet connection: a special site for veterans. Multiple passcodes and encryptions protected each member's identity. He wasn't the only one in hiding. This was his true community, knit together by the twisted bond of combat and hidden behind the mask of code names. His was Chimera. Discussions ranged over every topic imaginable, but members seemed especially drawn to conspiracies and the paranormal. Griff tended to hang back, always careful not to reveal too much, but he paid attention to the conversation, especially when a new member, AdVisor, offered a rare, cryptic comment.

Last night, AdVisor had sent a private message to Chimera: *The girl will play a part in the coming struggle.* He always spoke as though his words were an oracle.

What girl? Griff kept his posts short.

Think. More to come. AdVisor signed off.

Griff supposed he must mean Dorothy. She was the most prominent girl in the Palace production. But if AdVisor knew about her, it must mean he knew who Griff was, too. Did he live on the Big Island? In Hilo? Could AdVisor also be in the play?

Alerts sounded in Griff's head. The voices began to speak, low and harsh, but he pushed them down. Something greater was happening now which took precedence over his own safety and secrecy. He had been called to aid and protect. He was the keeper of the Energy Center, the only one who knew Its true purpose. It would speak to him again, maybe through the radio, maybe even through AdVisor, and he would know Its voice. Griff had felt the connection when he played the organ, its music given life by the Energy Center.

CHAPTER 3

THE READ-THROUGH HAD SEEMED INTERMINABLE UNTIL HIS first entrance, and then Evan, the Tin Man, had come alive, thrilling to the script's iconic lines. It was over in a flash afterward. Now, late on Saturday afternoon, Evan and Belinda, the choreographer, drank Bud Light at the Red Ginger Saloon, a low-lying wooden building nestled beneath a huge banyan tree on the banks of Waiākea Pond in the middle of town. The basement of the saloon was actually submerged in brackish water.

Not a good place to be when the next tsunami hit, Evan thought, but the beer was cheap, and the place stayed open until midnight, even on weeknights. As he had found after his move from Iowa six months before, Hilo closed down early.

Belinda widened her eyes at him and smiled, showing all her teeth. Wow. Her parents had sprung for first-rate orthodontia. They probably still gave baby girl an allowance. Evan smiled back and raised his glass. "To new friends."

They drank. The two had already exchanged pared-down life stories during the break, before Griff's unexpected performance and the Cowardly Lion's grandstanding.

Belinda, at Hilo U since January, her first professional position, struggling with the transition from Oklahoma.

Evan from Iowa, financial advisor who transferred to a small branch of his firm in Hilo, for a change, an adventure.

Both in the prime of young adulthood, blond, athletic, attractive, and single, they were among the only people their age in the show. Their eyes had met across the crowded circle of chairs, and a spark had flashed—or perhaps a distress beacon.

Evan was lonely. That was why he had tried out for *Wizard* when his most demanding client, George, had mentioned at one of their frequent sit-downs that he was directing the Palace fall fundraiser.

It hadn't taken Evan long to figure out why he'd been given such a high net-worth client on his first day at the firm. No one else would touch George. Apparently he'd hopped from one Hilo financial firm to the next, leaving scorched earth in his path. But Evan was hard to scorch. For six months, he had listened patiently each time George raged. He'd then suggested a sane course of action, to which George usually agreed, even if he insulted every part of it. He must have been a holy terror as a lawyer.

Evan turned to Belinda. "Why do you think there are so many *haoles* in the show? Definitely out of proportion to the general population." He'd recently discovered that the local term for white people didn't have to be derogatory, so he tried to toss it into conversation whenever, just cazh.

Hawaiian music twanged in the background, *'ukulele* and falsetto voices in harmony.

When George cast him as the Tin Man, Evan had been elated. He imagined a free and easy theater group full of potential friends and lovers. Now, here he was with a beautiful, talented woman after the very first rehearsal.

"Maybe they're all like us, feeling out of place and wanting a community." Belinda moved closer on her stool, so their shoulders touched. "I've never lived anywhere before where I was a minority. It's weird, isn't it? Almost like a foreign country."

They giggled, glancing around at the other Red Ginger patrons, all some variety of local, which meant some shade of brown. Several sat alone at the bar, staring into their shot glasses. A loud table in the corner threw down cards and roared with laughter as the green beer bottles mounted up. It didn't feel like America.

Maybe because it wasn't supposed to, Evan thought, remembering the history of Hawai'i he'd read before the move.

"I feel invisible sometimes." Belinda drained her glass and lifted it with a quick grin at the bartender. "Or like another species." She shrugged. "Maybe it's just the university. Everyone has either known each other and their mothers' aunties their whole lives, or they're really weird and reclusive. Some people are friendly, but there's this invisible barrier."

"I feel it, too." Evan picked up his fresh beer. "The local people at work have this whole busy life with their extended families and lifelong friends. There are a couple of new guys like me at the office, so we hang out sometimes, but they're surfers, so it's a whole different scene. I guess I should try it."

"We could take lessons together." Belinda turned her wide smile on him.

Evan smiled back, but her loneliness was starting to repel him, mirroring his own. He had been through this many times before. Somehow, his relationships never seemed to stick. He liked women but he just wasn't passionate about them. Belinda for example. Pretty, perky, needy, obviously panting for it, but underneath the surface flirtation lay the unquenchable thirst for love. It was always love, in the end, and that he didn't seem able to produce.

After three beers, Belinda leaned toward him. "I'd say your place or mine, but it had better be yours because I share a house with two people, and they're not friendly either. Silly me, thinking it would be like college again—besties with the roommates." She laughed and fluttered her eyelashes at him, pushing her hair up with one hand and fanning her neck with the other. "Whew, muggy."

"Well, mine then, if you don't mind driving out to Puna." That was quick, Evan thought. "You can follow me." He leaned over and kissed her. So soft. Wasn't that supposed to be good?

They each left a twenty on the bar. Best to start out as you mean to go on. Evan was no one's provider.

⌣

THE SCARECROW, PATRICK, WENT HOME ALONE. HE TIPTOED into the house after the long drive up the hill to Volcano Village, which bordered the national park southeast of Hilo. He hoped Cindy was asleep.

Feeling restless and keyed up after the read-through, Patrick had caught an action flick at the Kress dollar theater two blocks away from the Palace. He sat in the dark with a host of Hilo families seeking low-budget entertainment during the late afternoon heat and munched on popcorn. His shoes stuck to old soda spills on the floor as larger-than-life action flickered on the screen above.

When he reentered the outside world, it was dark. Images of car chases, exploding bombs, and gorgeous starlets burned against the night sky for a few brief moments. They faded as he jaywalked across Kamehameha Avenue to the bus station parking lot where he had left his trusty old Mazda that morning.

"Patrick, is that you?"

No luck. He stuck his head through the doorway. Cindy had just switched on the bedside light, every sleek black hair on her head falling in line. Her delicate features looked peevish.

"Sorry I woke you. I'm just going to have a beer and unwind. I'll be quiet."

"Please. I have to get up early." She switched off the light and Patrick eased the door shut.

He took his home-brewed IPA out to the *lanai*, feeling rather than seeing in the darkness his three acres of lush fern and *'ōhi'a* forest, interspersed with white ginger. He'd been lucky to buy this place back when Volcano real estate was cheap. He could never afford it now. At 4,000 feet above sea level, the air was noticeably cooler than down in town. He breathed in the delicate scent of ginger, imagining the space around him, the solitude.

An illusion soon shattered.

"I can't sleep now until you come to bed." Cindy perched on the porch swing next to him and began to rock back and forth with her tiptoes. Patrick felt a throbbing in his temple, but put his arm along the back of the swing, just touching her shoulders.

She twitched.

"How did it go today?"

He could feel her tilt her head and look at him. It was a wifely question, like one his four brothers' sturdy Eastern Washington farm wives might ask after the grapes had been harvested and delivered to the local wine co-op. When had his life become so mundane? He was artistic. He'd escaped the hot summers, harsh winters, and marital expectations of his youth. He brewed his own beer and lived on an active volcano in the middle of the ocean, damn it.

Patrick imagined the substance of solitude draining away through a grate below him, silvery and viscous, like mercury. Bloop.

"Rough. Lots of lines." The Scarecrow would be a challenge. He would have to start working on the floppy, loose-jointed walk, the controlled clumsiness.

"Tomorrow's a Volcano day for me." Cindy hardly missed a beat. "I've got sessions with Mariko, Val, and Kenji." Cindy was a massage therapist, which was how they'd met. She'd developed her own special blend of techniques and had a devoted client base to whom she travelled, massage table, towels, oils, and soothing music in hand.

Patrick rarely felt her firm, therapeutic grasp on any part of his body these days.

His own bowl-turning business had never made enough money to pay the bills. He subbed for the Department of Education, landing jobs at least a few days a week, and sometimes for several weeks at a time. Once for an entire semester when a teacher was out on medical leave.

"What are you going to do tomorrow?" Cindy was like the energizer bunny, but without a flap for battery removal. He could feel the undercurrents of mixed expectation and disapproval in her question.

Patrick picked up his empty bottle and rose from the swing. "I think I'll trim the *hāpu'u* and do some weed-whacking, and start learning my lines." He thought of the unfinished mango bowl sitting in his workshop. He'd been thinking about it for weeks.

"You should have a go at that mango you started. It's been drying long enough, hasn't it?" Cindy stood up and patted his back. He held absolutely still. "Back in the saddle."

"I'll know when I'm ready." Patrick gritted his teeth until she finally moved away. He was fond of Cindy, and she of him. They were just in a transitional period. At least she paid her way, which most of his previous girlfriends hadn't.

"We have dinner with Mac tomorrow night, don't forget."

That blowhard bon vivant. Patrick resented Mac, a trust-funder whose artistic success was due more to his relentless marketing drive than to talent. His bowls were predictable and repetitive, and his house was straight out of Architectural Digest, with a Polynesian twist. He'd even put in a circular drive to accommodate vans full of Japanese tourists.

Patrick sighed.

"Oh, come on." Cindy looked back at him. "It's the least we can do after he gave you that big chunk of monkey pod. And he's lonely. Crystal only left him a few months ago."

"He just wants to drool over you." Patrick stretched and yawned. "But at least he can cook, the pretentious foodie. Too bad he has to bore us with each ingredient's origin story."

"I think it's sweet." Cindy took Patrick's hand. "Come to bed now. I need to sleep."

Patrick closed his eyes. He saw himself leap into a Maserati and screech out, bombs exploding in his wake as he roared down the road to his next adventure.

Was this really the best he could do?

CHAPTER 4

ONE WEEK AFTER THE READ-THROUGH, DESIREE SLAPPED another glass of locally brewed Humpback Blue lager down on a cardboard coaster and flashed a smile. "Here you go, darlin', Hilo's finest."

She worked a lunch shift at Aloha Bar and Grill between Saturday morning Munchkin rehearsal and evening principals and chorus rehearsal, and she intended to make the most of it. The palm trees outside the big plate glass windows stood still, and the ocean spread to the horizon like a broad blue sheet, with hardly a ripple marring its surface between the beach and the breakwall. A real scorcher. Desiree banished sensuous visions of burrowing her rump into the sand as she lay supine, her skin soaking up the sun until she was so deliciously hot that she rose and plunged into the cool, velvety waves. Lower tips were not the only price she paid for giving up her night shifts.

Desiree's red uniform T-shirt was tight and showed her cleavage, especially when she leaned over the bar. The tips would follow. The Humpback Blue guy was kind of cute, actually, nice muscles, and he seemed to be sizing her up. Desiree whirled around and grabbed a martini glass and shaker, nearly colliding with the new girl serving tables. What? Who trained this moron? Rule number one: never, *ever*, come behind the fucking bar.

"Watch it, honey. Servers on the other side, remember?" Desiree smiled with laser eyes. The girl held up her hands and backed away.

A baseball game played on the big TV screens around the restaurant. End-of-season playoffs were close, so the place was packed. Be nice if the boss hired for skills, not just looks.

Desiree shook the flask and strained the liquor through the ice with an upward flourish at the end, then stuck in a skewer with olives and set the glass down in front of the silver-haired man who'd ordered it. Grey Goose, of course.

"Thank you."

"My pleasure." She could feel his eyes following her as she made two margaritas for the young couple at the end of the bar, after checking their IDs—on the rocks, not blended—and mai tais with all the fruity trappings for a group of obese sunburned tourists wearing matching aloha shirts.

"Can I get you another?" She smiled and leaned her cleavage toward Silver Hair. Was he sniffing her? Kinky.

"That was the best martini I've had in years. Yes, please." His lips were thin, but he was clean-shaven and his eyes were bright blue, like a Bombay Sapphire bottle. Colored contact lenses?

Desiree flushed with pride. She was not only fast, she had mad skills, as her children would say. During her long tenure as a bartender she had taken pleasure in perfecting the classic cocktails, as well as developing new ones, some of which the Aloha had adopted, like her popular lilikoi-mango whiskey sour.

When she picked up his check and two twenties—he hadn't waited for change—she found a business card: Hunter Craddock, Craddock

Enterprises, Inc. She smiled and tucked it into her apron pocket. He looked wealthy, his crisp, ironed white button-down a contrast to the usual Hilo male attire of T-shirts for casual and reverse print aloha shirts for business. And he ran his own company. That would make a nice change from her working-class dates, even if she did like a muscular body in bed. She could get used to fancy dinners and a cruise.

The big glass door to the street swung open to reveal Patrick, who sauntered over and slid onto the barstool vacated by the Grey Goose martini man.

"The usual, Scarecrow?" Desiree grinned and held up a chilled beer glass.

"If it please your majesty." Patrick bowed his head in mock obeisance. "And an order of fish and chips with extra tartar sauce." He grimaced. "Cindy put us on a raw food diet and my body is craving fat."

"One extra cold Surf Rider IPA coming up." Desiree set the foamy golden pint in front of Patrick, and he took a long, grateful pull. "You're lucky you have a woman who cares about you, buddy."

She typed his food order into the machine, then leaned against the bar. "I hardly ever cooked for Kama. Maybe that's why he dumped me, not the cultural stuff." She shrugged. "I hate cooking, so shoot me." She pointed at her head and beamed. "But now I'm Glinda the Good, and I get to wear a tiara."

Patrick snorted, a foam mustache on his lip. "And I'm basically the star, even though people don't always realize that, especially with the Cowardly Lion pulling focus all the time. The Scarecrow embodies all the qualities the others are searching for: courage, heart, *and* brains."

"Oh, get over yourself," Desiree scoffed. Patrick was such an egotistical jackass. Weren't all men? But he was sweet in a goofy way, and he tipped well.

"I need three pinot grigios and a Jack and Coke." Another pretty young server stood waiting at the counter, tapping her foot.

Desiree whipped back into action.

⌣

USUALLY A NATURAL DANCER, PATRICK STRUGGLED WITH HIS Scarecrow routine at the evening rehearsal. The two beers he'd downed in quick succession at the Aloha hadn't helped his mental clarity, and the fish and chips sat heavily in his gut. Torrents of sweat poured down his body. Even with the side doors propped open for a cross draft, the theater was sweltering.

Patrick told himself he wasn't fumbling because he felt outclassed by the Cowardly Lion, not to mention Oz. He'd been in shows with Merle before, but always in a subordinate role. This time his role was equal—no, actually higher up the scale than Merle's, which made him nervous, like he had something to prove. The Scarecrow was the heart of the show, Dorothy's most stalwart supporter. Was he up to the challenge? He would have to dig deep into his shallow soul.

Griff was a newcomer, but obviously a seasoned performer. Offstage he shut down, Patrick noticed, just sort of sucked his energy back inside and disappeared, spoke in monosyllables or went off by himself. Strange guy. But onstage—wow. It was all there, like he was channeling Dick van Dyke or something. His Professor Marvel was full of flourish and expression, and his Oz showed a range of pitch and emotion Patrick would be hard-pressed to emulate.

He hated to admit how important his roles in these plays had become. At forty-five, was playing the Scarecrow in a community theater production of *The Wizard of Oz* his lifetime achievement? No one was ever going to name a bridge after him, that was for sure.

"Here, try this." Belinda demonstrated a series of floppy shuffles and a mock stagger, arms waving in the air, then gave him an open-mouthed smile with wide eyes. They were onstage, the chorus clustered around Larry at the keyboard below, learning "Ding Dong the Witch is Dead."

Patrick tried it. Much better. Attractive girl. No! Too young. After a disastrous liaison with a twenty-five-year-old less than three years ago, Patrick had resolved to stick to women thirty-five and up. More baggage, but also more perspective. His passion for Cindy may have died down—and let's be honest, hers for him—but they got along well enough. Although not so well lately. But maybe it was time to settle, said a small voice he was hearing more frequently these days. Patrick grimaced. This was not the stuff the Scarecrow was made of.

"Okay Dorothy, Scarecrow—places." George gestured, and Larry began to play.

Patrick warbled the Scarecrow's song in his pleasant baritone voice. He felt the music and tried to let it flow into his body. What were those moves again? He faltered and nearly tripped.

"Loosen up, Scarecrow. You're not playing the Tin Man."

Patrick pushed away George's negative energy. He visualized the warm blood flowing through his limbs and relaxed, shuffling and vamping, imagining he was held up by an invisible string attached between his shoulder blades.

"That's it."

George looked grudgingly pleased. Mahina gave Patrick a big grin and a thumbs up. Strange girl. Toto jumped out of her arms and ran offstage.

While George turned his attention to Mahina, who rolled her eyes, Patrick let his gaze wander offstage. Something drew his eye to that new woman in the chorus—Laura? No—Nora. The pretty redhead with the twins. She was staring at Merle, who lounged up against the stage talking to Desiree, who was standing a little too close and tossing her bleached-blonde hair around, laughing.

Toto started barking and ran up to George, leaping at his ankles.

"Ziggy!" Mahina scooped the dog up again.

"If you can't keep that mutt under control we're going to go with the stuffed dog, Dorothy." George glared at her. "He's becoming a real—"

"Oh, please Miss Gulch. You can't hurt Toto!" Mahina interrupted in a malicious falsetto.

Everyone laughed.

"Ha ha ha, Dorothy." George managed a smile. "Okay, back to business."

Moving into position, the Cowardly Lion shifted his gaze, feeling the intensity of Nora's stare.

She dropped her eyes and turned away.

Patrick watched this mini-drama unfold in a matter of seconds. God, he loved theater.

⌣

"ALL OZIANS ONSTAGE."

Still warm from her eye contact encounter with the Cowardly Lion, Nora waited her turn to mount the stairs. She could feel him looking at her. What on earth was she doing, engaging in this ridiculous flirtation?

Nora watched Belinda inspecting the group as they walked onstage, assessing how they moved. Several large women were already panting from the exertion of plodding up the stairs. A couple of lanky men jerked and bobbed. A few short, compact women moved together, like a school of sturdy fish, taking economical steps with minimal body movement.

Remembering her childhood ballet lessons, Nora willed herself to walk fluidly, with rhythm and grace. As she turned to face the house, she caught the Cowardly Lion's eye again, and a full-body blush swept over her. She wrenched her gaze away and watched the last few Ozians bring up the rear: a few stocky bordering on paunchy men, one with a rollicking gait.

Below stage, Larry struck up the opening chords, and the chorus burst into song.

"Ha ha ha, ho ho ho, and a couple of tra-la-la's."

Nora tried not to wince at the discord around her.

Belinda showed the chorus members how to weave in and out, linking arms and giving a little kick. George wanted movement and music learned at the same time—a holistic approach, he claimed.

"Sit on *top* of the notes, people. Don't scoop, and don't sag. Lift the pitch," Larry called from the keyboard. He jabbed his finger in the air. "Men, you're not singing melody here. Learn your part." He played the low harmony line twice through, and the men sang it back.

Raggedly, thought Nora.

A gust of fresh air wafted in from the side doors, open to the alleys. A moment later the rain hit and played a deafening drum solo on the roof.

"Any notes, George?" Larry shouted above the din.

"Timing, people. That's what theater is all about." George stared at one of the large women, who was loud and behind the beat. She didn't seem to notice. Instead, she made a comment to another woman next to her, this one so thin and tanned she looked like beef jerky. They laughed. "And smile when you're singing, folks. You're supposed to be happy." He grimaced and did a little dance.

The Witch looked up from her conversation with the Cowardly Lion and pointed. He mimicked George's dance and Nora choked back a hoot.

Larry played the opening chord again and the Ozians, who were giggling and talking amongst themselves, straightened up.

Nora pulled her shoulders back and took a deep breath.

"Right foot first, remember," chirped Belinda.

Larry called, "From the top, people. Let's get it right."

Maybe this was a good idea, after all, Nora thought as she wove and kicked. As long as she could keep her hormones under control, that is. She hadn't sung for years, other than in the shower or car or with the children, and now her voice rang out with joy. Her whole body radiated with life and dripped with sweat. Clyde hadn't liked dancing—he had no sense of rhythm—so that part of her life had also shriveled during their marriage, along with so much else. She looked out and saw the Cowardly Lion staring at her again. This time, she flashed him a big smile. He beamed and waved.

Nora had first stumbled across the Palace Theater on a Saturday morning shortly after her move to Hilo, before she had figured out the cross-streets of the Mamo Farmer's Market, and had parked what felt like miles away in the steamy heat. In those early days, she was still very strict about sunblock and hats, which the twins hated and tore off at every opportunity. If June was this hot, as opposed to its cool, rainy counterpart in Vancouver, what would real summer feel like? As they trudged along the baking sidewalks of old downtown Hilo, not even a hint of breeze wafted in off the flat blue expanse of water down the hill.

In search of shade, Nora and the twins ducked down what seemed like a side street but was actually a well-used thoroughfare: Haili street. The theater marquee jutted out above the lovely, weathered, neoclassical façade of the building. Nora slowed to look at the movie posters in the showcase windows and saw that a rather obscure art film she wanted to see was playing that weekend. No way would the children sit through it, though, even if she could afford the tickets. They would have to check out the Kress "dollar theater" offerings several blocks away and smuggle in their own snacks—then hope a cockroach didn't crawl up the wall next to them and take flight, prompting screams from the audience to punctuate the movie soundtrack. The Kress was their main source of entertainment outside the house. At least it was air-conditioned.

Miri pulled on her arm. One of the doors to the theater was propped open, and Oliver had already squirmed through. Nora followed him into the dim, deserted lobby. A few couches and over-stuffed chairs were arranged in seating groups along the walls, punctuated by potted palms, with tables near the snack bar.

"Oliver," she called. "Get back here."

He turned and grinned, then ducked through the maroon velvet curtain, which screened the theater auditorium from the lobby.

Miri moved to follow, and Nora grabbed her hand.

Where the lobby was cool, the auditorium was warm and stuffy, its high ceiling a dark dome overhead. The only light came from behind the stage. Someone must be working back there. Nora had read that enthusiastic community members had come together to raise money and awareness, and to restore the theater to its former glory as a hub of neighborhood activity and entertainment. It looked like they still had a long way to go.

Someone coughed just ahead of them, and Nora stopped.

A middle-aged man with a shiny bald head had opened one of the side doors, illuminating the aisle that bisected the auditorium. His face creased into a big smile, his teeth so white and perfect Nora was sure they were dentures. He wore stained coveralls with tools hanging from loops around his ample waist.

"Hello there." She smiled back. "The front door was open, and my son slipped in, and—"

"Guess I forgot to close it, careless of me." He bounced up and down on his toes, his grin still in place.

"Are you with the Palace Friends? You must be doing restoration work or something?" Nora kept smiling, too.

"That's right. I'm on the board. Name's Phil." He walked closer, until his body blocked the entryway. "The theater is closed now, so you'd best be on your way. Safety regulations."

She called into the theater, "Oliver, we need to go."

Her son's head popped over the railing from the seats above. "This is cool, Mom. Miri, you should come and check it out." He saw Phil, and his head disappeared again.

"Right now, Oliver!"

While Miri struggled to escape her mother's grip, Oliver came skipping down the hallway.

"No tours today, son," said Phil. "Obey your mother." He scratched his smooth scalp. "Kids." He shook his head and winked at Nora. "Hey, you should all try out for the fall musical—fun for the whole family."

"Do you live here?" Miri stared at Phil.

"Oh no, missy, I'm just a caretaker." He laughed, a high-pitched, jolly sound.

Nora grabbed Oliver's hand and hustled the children back into the lobby.

"Sorry about that," she called over her shoulder. "We'll close the door on our way out."

But when she looked back through the curtain, he had vanished.

Nora was wrenched back to the present as George's enraged howl echoed through the theater.

"Dog shit on my script." He held out the book by its corners, a lumpy brown pile in the middle. "That mutt had better not show his face in this theater again."

A few guffaws broke the shocked silence. Nora saw Desiree and Patrick snickering below stage.

Mahina clutched Ziggy and glared at George. The little dog gave a sharp yelp.

One of the stagehands, Moku, walked over to inspect.

"That's not Ziggy's poop, boss—it's about five times too thick." Moku held up a circle with his thumb and finger. "Look how small he is. His little poops must be like tootsie rolls."

Everyone laughed, and Mahina smiled in triumph.

Harriet spoke up. "It must be the ghost again, George. You know what they say about this place." The rest of the cast murmured. She gave them a broad wink.

"Fred." George turned and yelled at his stage manager, holding out the offending book with stiff arms. "Do something with this."

Fred hustled over and took it, keeping the book level so as not to spill the contents. The long bill of his cap hid the expression on his face.

～

"YOU THINK I'M JUST A SUPERSTITIOUS OLD WOMAN," SAID AUNTY Em, who looked at least ninety years old to Mahina. "But there really is a Palace ghost—more than one, actually." She leaned in, nearly losing her balance. "Some are nice and some are nasty." She grinned, showing yellowed teeth. Eeew. "Some people say the ghosts are spirits of people who drowned in the theater during the tsunami and couldn't find their way into the afterlife."

The old woman had teetered up the steps to where Mahina sat with Moku, her new ally, waiting to rehearse the yellow-brick road sequence. Again. Mahina still clutched Ziggy, ready to defend him from George's rage.

"Come and sit, aunty." Moku jumped up to help her into his seat on the aisle and gestured for Mahina to move down.

Mahina widened her eyes, tilted her head, and made a "cuh" sound, but Moku just nudged her along.

Growing up with her mother's random collection of New Age beliefs, Mahina was impatient with the paranormal—yet the Palace did have a distinctly weird vibe. And what else did she have to do right now, while Belinda worked with the Ozians onstage, except hang around and keep Ziggy out of George's way before he got violent? What a hater.

"When I was a girl, we used to come to the Palace every Saturday morning." The old lady settled back in the aisle seat, her legs spread apart. "The corner store sold two sushi for a nickel, and daikon with it."

Big mistake. Boring alert. Mahina pulled out her phone and started texting.

Moku elbowed her. "Have respect. She's our *kupuna*."

"Chill out." Mahina put her phone away. She wondered what Keola was doing.

"...and one Saturday morning when my friend and I climbed high into the balcony, a little girl was already sitting there." Aunty Em paused and turned to look at Moku and Mahina, who had slumped down in her seat. "We sat and watched the show and laughed with her for an hour." She paused again.

Ziggy gave a little yip. Would this never end?

"And when the lights came up, she was gone." Aunty Em nodded and patted Moku's hand on the arm of the chair between them. "Vanished."

"Wow. That's amazing. You'll have to tell us more stories, Aunty. What about the nasty ghosts?"

"Well..."

"Okay, Dorothy, Scarecrow, Tin Man, and Cowardly Lion. It would be helpful if you could be down here ready to go, so we don't waste time." George looked red even from the second tier above the center aisle. "That's why we have a schedule posted for each rehearsal."

"Sorry, gotta go." Mahina hopped over the seat in front of her and finger-waved at Moku and the old lady. "Can't wait to hear more."

Ghosts, my ass. Mahina smiled as inspiration struck. She could already see her weekly sketchbook assignment for art class taking on its spectral shape.

CHAPTER 5

Aprox THE BIG SATURDAY REHEARSAL MARATHON, GEORGE knocked back his second Scotch rocks in the darkness of his screened-in *lanai*. The lights of Hilo stretched in an arc far below, outlining the water's dark edge. Crickets and coqui frogs whirred and pinged in the garden, while the liquor sent warmth in little rivulets through his body. His mind began to loosen. Cal was already asleep, disappointed in George's lack of ardor. Another thing to worry about.

This production could be a disaster. Dorothy was a bratty diva who refused to be directed. She had been the standout candidate during auditions, with those big eyes and long dark hair, the gorgeous voice, a starring role in last spring's Waiānuenue High musical. But even then he'd had a funny feeling about her. Larry and Fred had loved her, not to mention Phil, the imbedded board member. Probably friends with the mom, who seemed to know everyone in town. Iris had sold George his house as well—kind of a space cadet but she knew her real estate. Casting Mahina had been a mistake.

He felt it in his director's bones. And someone should get rid of that vicious puffball she carried around. If it hadn't crapped on his book, what had?

George drained his glass and got up for more.

At least the Cowardly Lion was fabulous, no worries there. Merle was an old community theater pro. The Scarecrow and the Tin Man were coming along nicely, and the Witch had the laugh down pat.

Oz was a surprise sensation. He had come out of nowhere, as if from the sky. During his five years in Hawai'i, George had learned not to ask too many questions about people's pasts. Griff was here now, and that was all he needed to know.

George shoved aside the horror of Dorothy for a moment. There was still hope for the chorus, a rag-tag group of regulars and wannabes—some with real talent. Emotion flared in his chest, like heartburn. His people. With a lot of hard work and discipline, they could at least make credible Munchkin townsfolk, Ozians and Winkies. But in eight weeks?

Returning to the *lanai* with his third drink, George thought again about a disturbing experience he'd had at the health food store the day before. It was silly but he just couldn't get over it. The checkout girl was new—large and doe-eyed and a bit slow. He'd only had a few items: a bag of shade-grown, water-processed coffee beans, two honey sticks, blackberry iced tea, and a salad from the deli bar.

As she laboriously scanned each item and weighed his salad, fumbling behind the counter for the forks—which should have been within easy reach up top, next to the chopsticks and napkins—she stopped to scrutinize him, wrinkling her eyes and thinking.

She's going to say she saw me in *Hello, Dolly*, George thought, pleased, though still annoyed at her for taking so long. He was hungry and wanted to eat his salad, which wasn't enough but would have to do if he didn't want to turn into a fat old queen. Cal might leave him if he developed too big a paunch.

Instead she leaned closer. "Do you qualify for the senior discount?"

George was speechless. He was only fifty. He looked forty-five tops. Everyone said so. Was she implying that he looked sixty? Sixty-five? Perhaps only fifty-five. They did start young with their discounts sometimes, these places, vying for customers. He felt deflated. Old. How dare she?

"Not yet." His voice choked. He gathered his purchases—no bag, please. On second thought, he wouldn't eat the salad here.

George took a big gulp of his scotch. Ridiculous to keep brooding about some half-witted fatty's faux pas. Although he really should write a letter to the store owner with a few sharp comments about customer service. Or he could go back in and pause, look at the offending cashier with squinched-up eyes, then ask if there was a chapter of Overeaters Anonymous in town. Or when the baby was due.

George grinned, then frowned when he realized it had been nearly a year since he last called his father. Trust a memory of humiliation and self-doubt to bring the old man to mind. Too late to call the east coast tonight. He'd have to wait until morning.

◡

GOING OVER THE DAY'S REHEARSAL PHOTOS—COURTESY OF HER boyfriend, Keola, who had dropped by the theater during the endless yellow-brick road rehearsal—Mahina cropped George out as often as possible. Why was he always up in her business? Move stage left, Dorothy. Turn and cheat out now, Dorothy. What did he think she was, a windup toy? She knew exactly who Dorothy was and what Dorothy would do. She didn't need an old man to tell her how to act like a girl.

And how dare he accuse Ziggy of pooping on his stupid book? Her dog was perfectly house-trained. What was his script doing on the floor, anyhow? Pig. Mahina would prove to George that Zig was born to be Toto. She'd get Moku to help train him. After the poop incident, he'd hung around cooing and petting the little dog for ages. Wait. Could he be BomBoy? No, definitely gay—a real *māhū*. They weren't violent, right?

Her cell phone mooed, and she texted back. Keola. She texted again. Cherise, best friend. Again. Jenny, sub-friend. Again. Keola. Zzzzzzzz, she thumb-typed. Enough was enough. She stared approvingly at a close-up shot of herself singing. She looked great. New profile pic. Click. Nothing from BomBoy tonight. She should block him.

Mahina closed her laptop and grabbed her sketchbook. She added more shading to the pencil drawing she'd started at the theater. Aunty Em's screaming face looked so real. Mahina hummed as she added floating shapes in the background. Perspective was so tricky. She wished she'd paid better attention when Harriet/Mrs. Furneaux had demonstrated foreshortening techniques last week, but if she looked too geeky, her crew might turn on her. Artistic excellence was not worth social death.

In spite of her name, which she loathed and planned to change as soon as she was eighteen and moved to New York to star in Broadway musicals, Mahina was not Hawaiian. She had been born on the Big Island, sure, but both her mother and her father were from California, of Latinx heritage. Not that she knew anything about it, since Iris had cut off ties with her own family, and her father didn't have one. Or so Iris said. The only nod to their culture was Mahina's *quinceanera* the year before, which had felt really weird, frankly, since she didn't even speak Spanish. She'd only agreed to it because Iris was so excited—and the dress was so fabulous. Iris had paid for Mahina and her friends to take salsa lessons and hired a mariachi band for the big party.

Thanks for getting yourself killed, Dad, thought Mahina. I'd have a normal name like Tiffany or Angelina if I'd been born in California. She thought of her childhood in Hilo, dancing hula, swimming, gymnastics, a short span at a charter school until she came home with *ukus*—Hawaiian for head lice. Apparently *ukus* were an epidemic in Hawai'i at least until middle school when kids stopped rolling around together like puppies. So Iris pulled Mahina out and homeschooled her until last year, when she had insisted on going to a real high school.

At fifteen, Mahina had hit Waiānuenue High by storm, and within the year was queen of her particular niche group of singer/actors, most of whom were marginally attractive misfits, in her opinion. She, on the other hand, was gorgeous, confident, and cutting. Her motto: Always strike first. Mahina wanted off the rock, and she would do what it took to make it happen. No Hilo U for her. It would be a theater scholarship at an East coast college or bust. Landing a leading role in a non-school production was just the beginning. Playing Dorothy would give her the ruby slippers to find her real home.

She had watched all the men at rehearsal today, trying to spot her stalker, but no one had seemed any creepier than anyone else. BomBoy's identity was still his secret. Since Ziggy loved just about everyone except George, he was no help. He'd actually jumped up and licked that nosy, totally bald board member who kept telling everyone his name was Phil. Sorry old guys, but naked scalp is gross. Oz was weird—and super old. She'd caught him looking at her once or twice. But everyone always looked at her. As her mother said, she radiated.

Mahina closed her sketchbook and set it on the nightstand. Time to brush her teeth and take care of her skin. Her nighttime routine took half an hour—totally worth it. She never slept in her makeup like some of the other girls she knew. Slobs. No wonder they had blackheads. When she tore off her pore strips, they still looked clean.

Mahina plucked a wet cleansing wipe from the packet on the bathroom counter and got started.

⌣

AFTER A DRUNKEN POST-REHEARSAL NIGHT OF FUMBLING PASsion, Evan the Tin Man woke up again to find Belinda the choreographer in his bed out in Orchidland—their second time together. He swung his feet onto the floorboards.

"Tell me again why we're keeping this a secret?" Belinda stretched and yawned.

"Because we don't want people poking their noses in our business." Evan launched himself to the closet and pulled on shorts.

"Who even cares?"

But he was outside on the porch already, lacing up his shoes for a run.

"I'll make coffee." Belinda's voice trailed after him as his footsteps crunched down the driveway.

Evan ran faster down the road, careful not to slip on the cinders or step in a pothole. He liked the seclusion of his neighborhood, but the roads were hell. He should sell the Camry and buy a pickup truck. Not to mention a couple of pit bulls.

Evan's nearest neighbors were classic Punatics, another local word he'd learned. On one side were an earth mother with sniveling kids, skinny horses and a racy libido, and on the other, a long-haired Vietnam vet with an eye patch and a Rottweiler he let roam free at night.

Evan had given up night runs.

Belinda was cool, but too clingy. He could tell she wanted a real relationship. All he wanted was sex. Quick sex. Preferably from behind. Evan supposed he might be bisexual, although he'd never discussed it with anyone. He was definitely more attracted to women, even if he thought about men while he was with them. That weird thing in the men's room had been an aberration. He'd been restless afterwards, sure, and decided to leave the Midwest, but not because of that.

Whoa. Evan's ankle twisted a little on a rock, but he recovered. He'd fallen once and spent half an hour picking little chunks of red cinder out of his leg with tweezers. Maybe he should start running in town instead, after work.

On the verge of turning thirty, Evan had transferred to the small Hilo branch of his large financial planning firm, and immediately the stock market had begun its spectacular dive. Now he felt nervous every day. He arrived at work early and left late, working his clients assiduously; they were mostly new *haole* immigrants, like George. The old money stayed with the local advisors. Evan had to be the best one there, because otherwise he'd be toast. Full disclosure? Keeping George happy was a big part of why he was in the play. He just hoped his efforts didn't backfire.

Evan pounded back up his driveway, the sweat pouring down. He stripped off and stood under the outside shower he'd installed. He'd bought the place in Orchidland for peanuts after the housing bubble burst and a rash of foreclosures swept across Puna district. He could probably double his money already—that is, if anyone was buying. At least he had electricity, which not all houses in the neighborhood could boast. Like everyone else, though, he had catchment water from rain funneled off his roof into a big covered tank, and he bought bottled water to drink. Belinda used it to brush her teeth, too. ("Imagine rubbing all that bacteria—even bugs!—into your mouth.") Evan wasn't as fussy.

There she stood in the doorway, holding a steaming cup of coffee. "Caffeine? Or bed?"

Evan grabbed a towel from the plastic bin next to the shower. "Water first, then both." He grinned. Why not be nice to the poor girl? He was an actor now, after all. And companionship beat solitude.

As he stepped into the house, Evan had a disturbing thought. Moving to Hawai'i hadn't changed his life at all so far, not in essentials. He was just doing the same things in a different setting, and getting the same results. Even the play—a new venture for him, since he hadn't done any acting since high school—had only landed him with another eager woman in his bed.

If "living in paradise" didn't make him happy, what would?

CHAPTER 6

HARRIET THE WICKED WITCH COULDN'T BELIEVE IT WAS AL-ready a week into September. She'd been back teaching at Waiānuenue High for a month already with the infernal "year-round" school calendar so many warm-weather states had adopted. Between her students and play rehearsals and the relentless humid heat—with no air-conditioning—she was exhausted. Her only salvation was swimming. In fact, she was on her way to Four Mile beach right now, anticipating the ecstatic chill as she submerged her steamy flesh in the spring-fed ocean water and struck out to swim laps along the shoreline until her whole body hummed with vitality.

At this Saturday afternoon's rehearsal, George had given them the countdown, as he always did: just six weeks to go before the play opened. "Remember," he warned, "I want you off-book by next weekend."

Was that her phone? The car swerved as Harriet rooted around in her handbag on the passenger seat.

"Mom."

"Luke?"

It should be illegal to drive and talk on these things, she thought, getting a firmer grip on the wheel with her left hand and clamping the phone to her right ear.

"I'm at the Hilo Airport." He paused. "Can you come pick me up, or should I take a taxi?"

Harriet pulled the car onto the narrow gravel shoulder of Kalaniana'ole Road, nearly hitting two pedestrians, who made obscene gestures at her. She ignored them and turned off the ignition. "You're here? In Hilo?"

"I can take a taxi, no problem."

"No, no, no." Harriet shook her head. "It's just such a surprise. How wonderful! What—"

Luke interrupted. "I'll explain when I see you."

"Are you okay?"

"Mom."

"Okay, then." Harriet took a deep breath. "I'll be there in ten minutes—maybe less."

Harriet executed a clumsy U-turn, yearning briefly for the blue water lapping against the black lava rocks only fifty yards away. But her maternal instinct had kicked into high gear. She tried not to drive recklessly in her haste to get to her son, who suddenly seemed in peril. The last she'd heard, he was living happily with his boyfriend in the Bay Area, working at an entry-level job in a large architectural firm. Successfully launched.

She stepped on the gas, tailgating a small pickup truck piled high with papayas.

Luke had seemed to take the dissolution of his parents' marriage in stride. They had parted amicably and remained cordial, as civilized people should. Everyone's parents were divorced these days, so now he was in the majority. Full stop.

Had something happened to Howard? Harriet's chest tightened and she took a slow deep breath. No. She simply had to stop speculating and get to the airport.

After waiting an interminable length of time for the left-turn signal onto Kanoelehua Avenue, double lanes finally opened up. Harriet screeched around the papaya truck, only to be stopped again by a rusty little hatchback cruising next to yet another truck, this one with a huge metal cooler strapped in back, for fish. The passenger and driver of the two cars were actually talking through their open windows, baseball caps shading their faces, their arms draped out over the doors.

Harriet honked. They ignored her. Damn Hawaiian time.

After what seemed like hours, but was in fact less than ten minutes, she turned left again onto the airport road and flew unimpeded to the pickup zone, which fronted the modest, low-lying buildings of Hilo International Airport. Palm trees waved above the covered walkways.

And there was Luke, standing next to the Agricultural Inspection station. She would have recognized him anywhere, at any distance, in any disguise. He lifted his hand, and she pulled over to the curb.

Before she could jump out of the car to embrace him, her son had tossed his bag in the back and climbed into the front passenger seat. His dark hair was disheveled and his eyes shadowed with fatigue. He leaned over and kissed her on the cheek.

"Let's wait till we get to the house." He buckled his seatbelt and gave her a half smile. "I'm really tired."

Waiting till they got to the house stretched into waiting till Luke had a shower and settled into what Harriet always thought of as his room, even though he had never lived with them in Hawai'i.

Finding the old plantation house in Hilo had been a selling point for Howard, who had agreed to give up his thriving renovation business in L.A. so Harriet could move back to the islands she loved and longed for. For nearly a year, Howard had worked happily as Harriet settled into her new teaching job. He opened up more space by knocking down walls and making small rooms into larger ones. He added light and increased airflow by installing windows in the solid wall on the *makai*, or ocean, side of the house. The large master bedroom now had a glimpse of Hilo Bay through the trees and rooftops that led down to the water. Harriet's studio, also on the top floor, on the *mauka*, or mountain, side, had a partial view of Mauna Kea on a clear day. She rarely used it now. The creative impulse seemed to have fled, along with Howard.

After he finished the Haili Street home project, Howard had taken a quick renovation job with his former partner back in L.A. Just one, he'd said, to replenish the coffers. But one had led to another, and then another, until they had faced the inescapable truth. While Harriet had found her home again in Hawai'i, Howard had not. With surprising grace and minimal recrimination, they parted ways and Howard moved back to the mainland.

Downstairs, the house was open, with living room, kitchen, and dining room combined. Harriet despised people who pretentiously called this arrangement a "great room." Who did they think they were, British aristocrats? Saxon lords in a mead hall? The best part was outside: a large *lanai* leading to the walled garden Harriet so loved. A team of huge, polite Tongans had built the six-foot lava-rock wall around the back yard in just three days.

She waited there now, on the deck of recycled plastic boards made to look like wood, sipping a glass of extra cold Sauvignon Blanc and staring into the green depths of the torch ginger that flourished against the dark wall, its blooms a hot red accent, even in the dusk.

Luke emerged at last, carrying the wine bottle and another glass for himself.

"Sit," she said, smiling.

"It's beautiful out here, Mom." He refilled her glass and poured his own. "What's that divine smell?"

"Night-blooming jasmine." The tiny white blossoms formed a ghostly veil over the rocks, their scent a sweet intoxication.

They sat and breathed, drinking their wine.

"Bruce threw me out."

"Oh, Luke."

"It wasn't like I didn't see it coming." He stood up and walked to the edge of the *lanai*, leaning against the railing.

"What about work?" Harriet was immediately sorry she'd said it. "Are you on leave?"

"I quit." He turned and looked her straight in the eye.

Harriet swallowed. "I see."

"So here I am." Luke laughed and lifted his wine glass to parody a toast.

⌣

Just down the hill, Desiree primped for her second date with Hunter, the Grey Goose martini man. He was a fast worker. On the first date he had taken her to the most expensive restaurant in town, decked out with colored glass chandeliers straight from Italy—even in the bathroom. A few diners had still worn shorts and slippers. It was Hilo, after all.

This time Hunter was going to surprise her. He'd said to dress casually, with shoes she could walk in.

"Ma, Nakai and Malia won't mind me, and I'm in charge." Now that Kolea had reached double digits, she was the designated babysitter when Desiree went out, with their elderly next-door neighbor as backup. Desiree did Mrs. Chen's shopping for her every few weeks, so they were square.

Desiree stuck her head out the door. Mrs. Chen was sitting in her canvas folding chair on the narrow balcony that ran along outside their doors. Her head flopped to one side, showing the balding spot on top of her head. A soft snore whiffled from her open mouth, and her glasses had slipped onto her lap.

"You can start the movie now, okay?" The children cheered. Desiree heard the percussive soundtrack of microwave popcorn as she dabbed on mascara and sprayed herself with patchouli.

"I have my cell phone, so call me if there's an emergency—but not every five minutes, yah?" Desiree hugged their squirmy bodies, avoiding sticky hands. "Mrs. Chen is sitting outside, okay?"

"Bye, Ma." They charged for the couch, shoving and grabbing for the ends. Malia ended up in the middle as usual, snuggled between her older siblings. She pulled a handful of red vines from the big discount bucket on the coffee table and started chewing.

The main feature music blared, and Desiree slipped out the door. She didn't want Hunter to see her crummy apartment and judge her, so they were meeting at the open-air bar on the corner. It had palm trees in pots, twinkle lights, and laid-back island reggae playing through speakers. She sat on a plastic chair and breathed deeply.

"Babe." It was Kama, with a beautiful young woman in tow. Desiree narrowed her eyes.

"Where the *keiki*?" Kama leaned in for a kiss. Desiree tried not to smell him. She didn't need that swooning feeling right now. "Makani wants to meet them." The young woman smirked, one hand on her hip.

Desiree stood up and leaned in to give the obligatory half-hug and cheek peck to Kama's girlfriend, resisting the urge to grab handfuls of her dark, luxuriant twenty-something hair and tear it out by the roots.

"They're at a sleepover tonight," she lied. "With school friends." No way was she giving this upstart a chance to think she was a bad mom, leaving her children home alone.

"So, you're out on the town, eh?" Kama gave her that smile. Makani shook back her hair. She had a plumeria blossom tucked behind her left ear, showing she was taken.

"Makani's aunty has a big place up Pa'auilo *mauka*—horses, cows, fruit trees. Real Hawaiian style." Kama looked at Desiree. "The *keiki* would love it. We can take them up tomorrow, yah? Meet the *'ohana*. Pound some poi."

Oh-ho, instant extended family now. That was rich. "You could have called ahead." Desiree lifted an eyebrow. "Some warning would be good. My number's still the same." She sat back down.

"Sorry, babe." Kama smiled his special smile again. "Living in the moment, yah?"

"Call me tomorrow, and we'll see how much homework they have left, okay?"

"Shoots." Kama leaned in for another hug and kiss.

Desiree held her body stiff.

"Great to see you—looking good." He gave her the once over, and Makani glared at him.

"Nice to meet you." Desiree gave her a finger wave. One set of kisses was enough.

Makani showed her teeth, then treated Desiree to a close-up view of her wiggling ass, with Kama's hand cupping it, as they strolled off toward the bayfront.

"Aren't you going to introduce me to your friends?" Hunter's hands grasped Desiree's shoulders from behind. He was twenty minutes late.

"Another time." Hunter's hands felt clammy. She stood up and turned, forcing him to let go.

"Time for our adventure." Hunter kissed her cheek, and she caught a whiff of aftershave with a chemical undertone. Oh, Kama.

Desiree gave him a big smile. "I'm ready." Shake it off, baby, she told herself. That road is closed.

"Chardonnay or Sauvignon Blanc? I've got Riesling, too, if you want something sweeter." Hunter half turned toward her from the wet bar.

"Riesling would be great." Desiree sat with her legs crossed on one of the sleek leather couches. Despite her expertise in cocktail innovation, she actually preferred those fruity wine coolers—the sweeter the better—but Riesling would do. She didn't want Hunter to think she wasn't classy.

The drive out to the coast had taken more than half an hour. Then Hunter had led her down a winding path through dense vegetation for a good quarter mile to reach his house. Desiree didn't relish the walk back up, especially after a few glasses of wine. He would probably ask her to spend the night. Hell no. She would play hard to get, raise the stakes. Plus, her kids were alone in the apartment.

Hunter put a delicate wine glass into her hand. Crystal. He'd poured himself a vodka tonic. Consistent. In Desiree's experience, vodka was a serious tipple. A colorless, get-drunk-without-much-flavor choice. Desiree's dates were usually beach-bum beer drinkers or hearty proud-to-be-American bourbon drinkers. Certainly not affected scotch drinkers. After her years of bartending, Desiree could tell the difference between Johnny Walker red and black by the color in the glass, even with ice. It was a gift. Maybe there was a contest somewhere she could enter, with a big cash prize. God knows she needed it. But all vodka looked the same: clear and deadly.

"Cheers."

They clinked glasses and drank. While the sweet, though under-chilled, wine smoothed out a few wrinkles in Desiree's mind, she still felt jumpy. Out of her depth. Seeing Kama hadn't helped.

"Do you want the tour?"

Hunter showed her through the house, which must have been five or six times the floor space of her cramped apartment, even though it was only two rooms. As they walked and gawked, Hunter attached price tags to his top-of-the-line decor. What a show-off. He called the big open plan area they had entered the "great room": kitchen, dining, and living room, a central fireplace—because it gets so cold in Hawai'i? Huge plate glass windows and sliding doors led to a wide *lanai* overlooking the ocean just down the hill. A covered hot tub smelled faintly of chlorine.

They stood, shoulders barely touching, still holding their drinks, and looked over the dark ocean. The breakers' white foam glowed faintly under the crescent moon. A wooden stairway led to a tiny beach below.

The second room held an enormous bed and a big-screen television, with more huge windows and doors leading onto the *lanai*. It also had an adjoining bathroom.

"Nice place."

Desiree thought of her two-bedroom apartment on Kapi'olani Street, one step up from low-income housing. She was proud she'd never gone on welfare, like some of the other single moms in her building. She worked for a living and paid her bills. Food stamps and free school meals for the kids were different.

"So, what do you do, Hunter?" She turned and smiled, bending her knees a bit so she didn't look down at him, since he was a good inch or two shorter.

"Well, I'm semi-retired now." He guided her back to the great room with a hand on the small of her back. "I had my own business in Vegas and sold out a few years ago. Came here to enjoy my golden years, like everyone else."

"Semi-retired?" Desiree leaned back on the couch, ready for a long story, but he was brief.

"I have my hand in a few local businesses, just for interest's sake." Hunter sat back and rested one ankle on the other knee. "I'd get bored just staring at my view now, wouldn't I?"

"Really?" Desiree drank her last swallow of wine, and he hastened to refill her glass. "I'd like to retire and stare at a view someday." She held out her half-full drink. "Could I get some ice with this?"

After dropping a few chunks of ice into her glass with silver tongs, Hunter took a hand-rolled joint out of a cigar box on the side table and lit it. "Here, try this."

Nothing subtle about this guy, she thought. Desiree took a deep drag and held it. Didn't often smoke pot these days—reminded her of early times with Kama. She closed her eyes and let the smoke ease back out, holding down an explosive cough. She took a swig of wine, almost gagging, then opened her eyes and smiled. Sexy and sassy, now, don't get lazy. She adjusted her neckline to reveal the curve of her breast.

"I can give you as much of this as you want." Hunter handed the joint back to her. "In fact, that's one of my business interests here in Hawai'i. Especially now the county's passed a resolution to make going after pot growers a low police priority."

"I thought that was just about personal use—not dealing."

"Who's to say what constitutes business or pleasure?" Hunter leaned back and toked deeply. "I have other less-protected interests, too, but you might not be interested in those."

"Try me." Desiree tried to shake off the sluggishness induced by the combined effects of alcohol and marijuana, realizing too late that she was wasted. Nice going, girl. Real smart.

Hunter's face hardened. "No gossiping to your friends about this, now."

"About what? Excuse me, mister, but I've been tending bar long enough to know how to keep my mouth shut."

"Let me show you something, then—not on the official tour."

⌣

After Luke's bombshell, he sloshed a bit more wine into his glass and lowered himself back into his chair. He and Harriet sat for a few moments in silence, sipping their drinks.

Through sheer force of habit, Harriet listened for any nearby coqui frog chirps. She still hunted the deafening little creatures with a headlamp and caught them in jars, which she put in the freezer for a humane death. She consolidated the frozen coqui nuggets in a baggy, which she passed along to a colleague for her chickens. Good protein shouldn't go to waste.

"Have you spoken to your father?"

"Dad." Luke laughed again, a grunt. "He's way too busy with his new life to worry about me."

"New life?" A strange pounding started in Harriet's stomach.

"You didn't know?" Luke emptied the bottle into their glasses. "I thought Dad would have told you."

"Told me what?" Now Harriet could feel her heart fluttering. Old lady palpitations.

"He's getting married again. To his new office assistant."

Bam!

Harriet closed her eyes. A long moment passed. "Well, how about that?"

"She's thirty-five years younger, blonde—and pregnant." Luke scooted closer and put his arm around her shoulders. "That's probably why he hasn't gotten up the guts to call you."

"I'm surprised." Harriet struggled to control the shaking in her voice. "But I guess it's what men of a certain age do, isn't it?"

"I never thought Dad would."

"You'll have a brother or sister."

They looked at each other and laughed, a little hysterically.

"God, Mom, I'm sorry."

"You know, Luke, it's okay. Really." Harriet downed the last of her wine. "I hope your father will be happy. He's a decent man. He deserves it."

And there's my plug for divorced mother of the year, she thought. Always speak positively of the other parent. She had to admit, though, it wasn't hard to do in Howard's case. She truly did not hate him, although she felt humiliated by this new development. He had become a cliché, and in so doing, had turned her into one as well. Harriet felt the seeds of resentment sprout in her heart. Had they been there all along, lying dormant?

She got up and started pulling little green shoots out of the rock wall. You had to be vigilant or the porous lava rocks became a weed garden overnight.

"Have you met her?" Her voice sounded steady. Good.

"Tiffany? No, I just found out last week, when I called to ask if I could move in with Dad for a while."

Ah. Harriet's stomach fell—it was getting quite a workout. Not first choice after all.

"I just thought it would be easier. Don't feel bad, Mom." Luke started to pull weeds, too. "I thought I could just move down the coast, change cities, find a new job. Start a new life."

"Did he say you couldn't move in?" Harriet's heart was pounding faster now, a cardiovascular workout. Heat spread through her body. *Et tu*, menopause?

"Not in so many words." Luke didn't look at her.

They weeded in silence for a few minutes, throwing the little plants onto the grass.

"Well, I'm glad you came, darling." She didn't add, even though I was second choice. "You can stay here as long as you like. Maybe you'll even find a job here."

Luke made a noncommittal sound.

"At least stay for opening night of *Wizard*—it's only another month or so. Well, six weeks, to be exact. You could help with the sets."

He shrugged. "We'll see. I do need to get on with my life."

"Of course, darling." Harriet thought about sheets and towels—good thing she'd just done the laundry.

"But I'll see what I can do while I'm here." He smiled like he really meant it.

Harriet wiped her hands briskly on the sides of her pants. "Let's go out for dinner."

"That place with Murano glass chandeliers?" He raised an eyebrow.

"Certainly not. We'll go to Luigi's. I have a craving for their ahi carpaccio." She smacked her lips in the cartoonish way that always made him laugh.

They linked arms and walked up the steps into the house.

⌣

OUT ON THE COAST, DESIREE FOLLOWED HUNTER ALONG A PATH for what seemed like miles. The light from the flashlight he'd given her jerked around like one of those horror movies shot with hand-held cameras. She felt dizzy and fed up. What was he going to do, rape her and stuff her body in a lava tube?

A long low building appeared, roughly constructed out of ply-wood sheets with a corrugated iron roof. There were no windows and the door had a heavy padlock on a chain.

"Should I be worried?"

"That depends." Hunter unchained the door and flipped a switch inside. Then he pulled Desiree in and closed the door be-hind her.

The light from the long fluorescent tubes lining the ceiling was blinding after the dark. Desiree rubbed her eyes and gazed around in wonder. So, this is what a meth lab looked like. Hunter was a drug lord. He was probably semi-retired from the mob in Las Vegas. Business interests, my ass.

Her mind raced. Why was he showing her this incriminating evidence when he barely knew her? Better be careful, go along with anything he wanted.

"Yes, it's a meth lab, and no, I don't run it." Hunter gave her a scary smile and walked down the passage between long tables covered with gas burners, big glass containers and tubing, cardboard boxes stacked against the walls. "I have a well-paid chemist who works regular busi-ness hours and then goes home to his wife and family. A Hilo U gradu-ate. He is fastidious because he doesn't want to blow himself up. And he's not a user. That's where you run into trouble."

"Wow." Desiree was careful not to touch anything. Fingerprints. "How did you get into the business?"

"Connections." Hunter turned to look at her. "I told you I was semi-retired—same line of work, new location."

Desiree's heart rate accelerated. The effects of the wine and the joint had vanished.

"Well, it's all very impressive, Hunter, but it makes me a little nervous, okay?" Desiree moved toward the door. "I'd like to go back to the house now."

"Sure, baby." He opened the door. "The explosions only happen while the drugs are cooking, so nothing to worry about. I wouldn't put you in danger."

Yeah right.

The walk back was quicker, but just as disorienting. No wonder he'd said to wear comfortable shoes. Desiree's new sandals from Cheap & Cheerful pinched her toes, even if the heel was low.

Back at the house, she refused another glass of wine, asking for water instead. The mood was broken.

"So, why do you think I showed you the lab?" Hunter leaned back and smirked at her.

Desiree shrugged. Because you're an egomaniacal asshole. She had that unwholesome right-down-to-her-bones exhaustion from coming down off a mixed high too early in the evening. She longed to be in her bed. Alone.

"I have a business proposition for you, Desiree." Hunter leaned closer. "I like working with women, and I've found single mothers are particularly motivated."

Her head snapped up, nerves jangling. Had she mentioned her kids? He smiled, his bright blue eyes like shards of broken glass.

"I'm not dealing drugs," she said.

"Of course not—you're hardly qualified, sweetheart."

Was that an insult? Desiree decided to ignore it. Hunter was really creeping her out.

"No, what I want from you is much simpler and easier. Not to mention ridiculously well paid." He laughed. "Now I've got your attention."

Desiree thought about her rent, the rising cost of electricity, her children's clothes, which they grew out of every couple of weeks, it seemed. She still made good tips, but the money wasn't nearly enough. Makani looked expensive, so Kama might not be upping his contribution any time soon.

After finishing his degree at Hilo U and dumping Desiree, he had also quit construction and gone into music full-time. Never mind that they had three kids together, and she had worked her ass off putting him through college. He wanted to return to his roots, he'd said. Apparently shacking up with a mainland *haole* was an outgrowth of imperialist oppression. Nothing personal. Bullshit. Now he sang his heart out at Uncle Roy's—or if he got lucky, a classier hotel on Kona side—earning peanuts unless some rich tourist gave him a big tip. Wasn't that a worse case of post-colonial exploitation than hanging out with her? (Back atcha, college.) But hey, at least he *had* a culture.

She pulled her mind back to Hunter's great room. "Well? Go on—not that I'll do it. I can't risk going to jail just to make a few extra bucks." She sat up straight.

"You haven't even heard what the job is yet. Or how much it pays." He paused again, the sadist.

Desiree hated to be manipulated. Count to ten, she thought, taking a slow sip of her now lukewarm water. Her head felt very clear.

"All you have to do is take a package from me once or twice each week and put it in the basement of the Palace Theater. Five hundred dollars cash when delivery is confirmed. I know you're in the play, so you can hang around the Palace legitimately. It won't look suspicious."

"I don't hang around in the basement. And how big is this package?" Desiree's heart was doing little flip-flops. Five hundred bucks! It was almost enough to pay her rent.

Hunter handed her a key. "This is for the door leading to the basement from backstage." The metal edges pressed into her palm. He explained where to deposit the package, then paused. "I'd also like a report on any, let's say, strange things happening at the theater. Keep your eyes and ears open."

Desiree nodded. Did Hunter know something about the "ghost's" pranks? Or the dog shit? You can still turn back, a small voice said in her ear. But she knew it was already too late. Hunter had chosen well. She had a lot to gain—and too much to lose.

"So, who picks up the package after I drop it off?"

Hunter just looked at her.

She didn't look away. "Oh, okay. If you told me you'd have to kill me, right?"

They laughed.

"You're all right, Desiree." Hunter stood up. "Time for me to take you home. Don't forget your first delivery." He handed her a brown paper parcel the size of a makeup case, and a small flip phone "for business communications only."

As her fingers grasped the package, her hand cupping its dense weight, Desiree felt a chill seep through her scalp and down her body. She was about to cross a boundary, and there would be no going back.

But all that money.

She slipped the package and phone into her handbag and tossed her hair back. Never let them see you sweat. She put an extra swing in her step through the door Hunter held open to the night.

CHAPTER 7

F RESH FROM A VIGOROUS SATURDAY MORNING SESSION WITH Cal—that issue dealt with, at least for the moment—George showered and thought about the morning rehearsal with the Munchkin chorus. He had to tread carefully there. The board listed community outreach as the number one priority for Palace productions, and this meant happy children, with happy parents. Friggin' Phil, his private name for the jolly baldy, had even shown up at auditions and looked through the information sheets all the cast hopefuls had filled out.

George released a loud sigh—a habit he was trying to break. His childhood had been punctuated by that same gusty, exasperated sound. Get over it, he told himself. After all, Phil had come through with the okay for the Wizard to play the organ. But still. The micromanagement. And the grin. George stifled another sigh.

With just five weeks left until opening night, it was getting harder and harder to keep his temper. He swallowed a Xanax and roared down the hill in his red Miata.

⌣

ACROSS TOWN, MAHINA HAD NOT YET LEFT FOR REHEARSAL.

"I can't find him," she yelled in the general direction of her mother.

Her face was hot and itchy from dried tears. She had already spent an hour outside that morning, searching the hibiscus hedge and ornamental shrubbery in the yard, walking up and down the wide, flat streets of their neighborhood, calling for Ziggy. Whoever had bribed the little dog with a forbidden chicken bone before the read-through must have come back and captured him this time. It was the only explanation. He'd slept on Mahina's bed as usual last night, but this morning he was gone. Had her stalker come into the house? A chill dampened Mahina's anger.

"Calm down, love. Ziggy will come back. He's probably asleep—or playing with another dog."

As if. Ziggy hated other dogs.

Iris bore down on Mahina with fresh aloe slices she'd cut off the spikey plant outside. "Your eyes will puff up if you carry on like this."

"Get that stuff away from me." Mahina flung herself down on the couch and sobbed. "You don't even care that some psycho is stalking me. He's probably torturing Ziggy right now. He'll send us a paw in the mail."

"I've already called the Humane Society. They have his chip number on record in case someone brings him in." Iris sipped her herbal tea. "We'll go down to the police station after rehearsal this morning to file a report. You need to center yourself and send out positive energy, sweetheart."

"Like that's going to do any good."

"You should try it." Iris closed her eyes. "I'm sending Ziggy a gentle message right now. Come join me." She reached for her daughter's hand, but Mahina snatched it away.

Sometimes her mother's New Age crap irritated the hell out of her. Crystals, energy, meditation, detoxing, centering—it was all so stupid and bogus. A DIY belief system for idiots.

Mahina intended to watch everyone very carefully at rehearsal, cast and hangers on alike. Some pervy father, boyfriend, or geeky techie drooling over her would be easy to spot. She was damned if they were going to get away with it. She slipped the Mace canister she'd ordered online into her bag. Ziggy's torturer was going to wish he'd never tried to mess with her.

"I'll drive myself, Mom." She would appear vulnerable and flush him out into the open.

"Are you sure that's a good idea?" Iris had an irritating concerned look with her eyebrows drawn in. "You need support right now."

"Stop smothering, Mom." Mahina stomped out the door and squealed off in her shiny Civic. Guys always offered to modify it for her. She would set the trap and see who fell in.

⌣

"Time to go, darlings!"

Nora hated to tear the children away from Saturday morning cartoons, but it was only for an hour or two, then they could go buy shave ice with three flavors for a dollar at Willy's by the Bay, and she could pick up some fruit and veg at the bustling Mamo farmer's market across from the bandstand.

"We'll record the rest, okay? You can watch when we get home."

The twins groaned and flung their bodies around.

"Shave ice afterward." Nora's voice was high and cheerful, almost at the cracking point.

They trudged down the steps to the carport like convicts reporting for laundry duty.

After ignoring the inevitable for as long as she could, Nora's dwindling bank balance had finally driven her to search through the newspaper want ads. Denial had always been her go-to coping mechanism, and opening the door to harsh reality made her queasy. Was she really prepared to work as a home health aide, gardener, housecleaner, childcare provider or telemarketer? Was she even qualified? Perhaps she should enroll in the auto mechanic training program at the community college. Underwater welding was an even more lucrative skill, although perhaps too dangerous for a mother of young children. As the only child of elderly parents, Nora was accustomed to solitude and self-reliance. Her parents had been bewildered by the divorce and gamely supportive, but she knew they couldn't afford to help her, and she didn't like to worry them.

Just after they'd moved to Hawai'i, Nora had calculated exactly how fast she could wind things up and leave for good if Clyde died—an event she had been fantasizing about for years. She'd figured seventy-two hours would do it.

But now, as they crossed the singing bridge over the Wailuku River, named for the sound the metal grating made under rubber tires, the bay sparkled, and the sun lit up the weathered old storefronts of downtown Hilo. And here we still are, Nora thought. We may be divorced, but with children it's still till death us do part.

Although she felt like even more of an outsider in her new home, Nora preferred Hilo to Waimea. Hilo was a real place. At the bottom, so was Waimea, but its base was so covered with shifting layers of transience and pretension that unless you were from an old local family, you'd have trouble locating the authentic beneath the kitschy *paniolo* tourist trappings.

Hilo had the hippie, back-to-nature Puna layer and the immigrant intellectual university and observatory layer, but the town's solid foundation was built on Asian families from the sugar plantation era, with their community service ethic and tight family groups. Nora was drawn to the eccentric charm of old Hilo with its crumbling architecture and overgrown gardens. She savored the thin walls of her 1940s plantation rental house, sunlight gleaming through cracks in its termite-eaten single-plank construction, and her neighbors' rusty, multi-colored roofs that stair-stepped up the street. Dozens of fighting cocks staked out on hillsides with their little corrugated iron lean-tos filled her with horrified delight, as did the scent of burning rubber and screaming engine when the teenager down the road tested his hot rod before the Saturday night drag races out by the airport.

Nora hated pretension and Clyde was full of it, sneering at Hilo and at local culture in general from his new cookie-cutter house in Waimea. While she might not feel much affinity to Hawai'i herself (and who could blame her, under the circumstances?), she could at least recognize that this didn't make her superior—or inferior, for that matter. Just out of place. Finding a way to live with integrity under these less-than-ideal conditions was the challenge. Unless she could find a way to escape instead.

Nora wedged her old Volvo station wagon into a small parking place right in front of the theater. Now they wouldn't be late. Clyde hated her car, too, which she'd insisted on shipping from Vancouver. One of his first purchases on arriving in Hawai'i was a big brand-new pickup truck with a king cab.

Nora gripped the steering wheel and visualized the sign. STOP.

⌣

BY THE TIME NORA ARRIVED AT THE PALACE, GEORGE'S XANAX was already wearing off. This morning at least two dozen children swarmed below stage as Larry and Belinda struggled to organize them. Their parents sat farther back in the cramped wooden row seats, or leaned against the low dividing wall at the cross aisle, talking. Theater was a good part childcare in this town. George frowned. Some parents just dropped their children off at the door every Saturday and left to do their shopping.

Larry clapped his hands. "Now Munchkins, I hope you've been practicing your songs. We'll sing 'Follow the Yellow Brick Road' first, and then Belinda will run you through the dance steps again. All eyes front."

George concentrated on deep breathing as the Munchkins sang their song over and over, their voices sweet and shrill. Glinda winked at him and grinned. Three of them were hers. Dorothy looked red-faced and almost ugly this morning. She caught him watching her and glared. When George directed a play he always thought of the cast by their characters' names. Their own were irrelevant—he wasn't trying to be their friend. His job was to whip the best performance possible out of them and, like Machiavelli, he believed it was better to be feared than loved.

"Okay, kids, come up on stage." Belinda started the children out with their little Munchkin dance. She actually looked like she was enjoying herself as they tripped and giggled and whirled each other around.

George sighed and opened his script—a new, clean one. The defiled book had been bagged for evidence, should they ever catch the perpetrator.

⌣

MAHINA WASN'T EVEN TRYING TO STAY IN CHARACTER. SHE stood in her place, as directed, but gave the brats singing to her no encouragement whatsoever. She gripped the basket holding stuffed Toto. Oh Ziggy!

What about the Tin Man, Evan? He was always hanging around. Thirtyish. Straight? Gay? She wasn't sure.

On the other hand, George himself was a definite suspect. He didn't like her, and he hated Zig. Was he trying to make her crack so she would leave the production, and he could replace her with some simpering ninny who would do whatever he wanted? Not a chance. She owned Dorothy.

Who was BomBoy?

"Hey, where's Ziggy?" Moku said as she walked offstage. He was working on the framework for Oz's curtain, tendrils of dark hair escaping from his messy bun. "I miss my little brah."

"He disappeared. I think someone took him from our house." To her horror, Mahina started to cry.

Moku sprang up and put his arms around her, and she stiffened, then laid her head on his shoulder and sobbed.

"What if he's dead?"

He patted her back. "Hey, he'll show up," Moku soothed. "My dog Popo used to run off all the time, humping all the bitches in the neighborhood. He'd be gone for weeks."

"Ziggy is fixed." Mahina straightened up and wiped her eyes.

Moku handed her a real cloth handkerchief from his back pocket, ironed and folded. "My mother embroiders them for me." He shrugged. "I drew the line at dressing like a girl all the time— just on special occasions—so she has to find other ways to girlie me up."

"Thanks." Mahina blew her nose. "I'll wash it and bring it back.

"No worries." Moku grinned. "I have choke at home. Ma loves to sew."

⌣

"ANY LUCK WITH THE JOB HUNTING?"

Nora looked up, and the motion sent several beads of sweat speeding down her neck into her modest cleavage, soaking into the already moist elastic band beneath her breasts.

Desiree tapped her long fingernails on the wooden seatback next to Nora. She seemed to be waiting for an answer.

"I've been looking at the want ads, but there's nothing promising." Nora put down the book she was reading—or rereading, rather, for the comfort of inhabiting a familiar world among old friends. She laid her hand over the open pages to mark her place. Desiree might not be a kindred spirit, but she was a savvy local—local *haole*, that is. "I've been at home with the twins since they were born. And my psychology degree doesn't qualify me for much."

"Hey, how about a psychic hotline?" Desiree clapped her hands. "I saw a TV ad saying you could earn 100 dollars per hour."

Nora widened her eyes and stifled a derisive snort. Desiree was trying to help. "I think that's different from what I studied."

"How hard could it be? Maybe I should apply. I read minds every day at the bar."

"Well, whatever I do, I'll have to put the twins in school again." Nora grimaced. "Homeschooling was always a temporary thing. They went to kindergarten and first grade in Vancouver before we moved." The gracious school buildings surrounded by tall fir trees hovered across Nora's vision like a mirage. For a moment she could almost feel the damp chill of the living woodland soil.

"They'll survive. You'd better get them in quick, though. School started a month ago already." Desiree's leg was bouncing. "Which one are you zoned for?"

"Poʻokela Elementary." Nora fanned herself. She'd driven past the school, a pleasant-looking, horseshoe-shaped wooden structure on a grassy hillside. Dozens of children played out in front, kicking balls and pushing each other. No pale redheads.

"For real? My kids just started there this year. Used to be at the big barn up the hill. Kama used his new girlfriend's aunty's address to transfer them. Says it's a better school, with more Hawaiian culture." Desiree seemed on edge, looking around, clutching her big handbag.

"Well, then at least Oliver and Miri will have some friends." Nora perked up. "The Munchkins all seem to have hit it off."

Desiree turned to check on the three wild-looking children of indeterminate sex Nora had pegged as hers at the read-through. The tallest one was talking to the twins, with big hand gestures. Miri and Oliver were smiling. "My kids' dad is local, so it's easier for them, being *hapa*." Desiree laughed. "Not for me, though. He's not around much, anyway, so thanks for nothing." Merle brushed past her, knocking her handbag. Desiree swore and clamped it down with her elbow.

Nora raised her eyebrows. "My kids' dad is up in Waimea. He's supposed to have them every weekend. Joint custody."

"Lucky! I never get a day off." Desiree rolled her head from side to side. She was always in motion. Would she start dancing next?

"Well, it doesn't actually happen, but I guess once a month or so is better than nothing." Nora folded a corner down and closed her book.

"Still, it's better than living in Kansas—yes, really—which is where I'd be if I hadn't fallen in bed with the cute local guy on my vacation twelve years ago." Desiree laughed and twisted her blonde hair up into a knot. Her skin was deeply tanned, with fine lines and creases from the sun. "I just do here what I did back home—wait tables and tend bar—but I get to hit the beach when I'm off instead of the pool hall. No complaints, except how freakin' expensive everything is. And the lack of decent men." Her voice rose in volume and pitch until heads turned.

Desiree rolled her eyes, then leaned in to whisper. Her handbag swung down and almost hit Nora in the face.

Nora recoiled at the other woman's breath, hot and moist against her ear.

"They're all fairies and no good bums, so watch out."

Desiree straightened up and winked, laughing. A small girl with creamy brown skin and sun-bleached curls attached herself to Desiree's leg.

"My youngest, Malia. Her father's over on Kona side mostly, playing hotel gigs." She shrugged and adjusted her bag. "Pays peanuts for child support. And now he's got this gorgeous girlfriend. Maybe it's the real thing. I obviously wasn't."

"I'm sorry." Nora grimaced, then blurted, "I just worry about the twins being picked on, but I know I can't protect them forever."

"New kids always get pushed around, but they'll toughen up. And they have each other." In a rare moment of stillness, Desiree met Nora's eyes. "You can't blame local people for being royally pissed at all the mainland *haoles* buying up land and living in big houses while they cram three or four generations into one small place. Their kids pick up on the anti-*haole* vibe." She poked Nora with her elbow and grinned. "You can't take it personally—even when it's a bloody nose."

"Well, that's comforting. I'll be sure to pass on those pearls of wisdom to Miri and Oliver when they come home with black eyes."

Nora paused. "Maybe that's why people scream at each other in my neighborhood. A lethal combination of ancestral rage and close quarters." She'd never heard anything like it—not yelling, but actual screaming. Screaming obscenities. She'd almost called the police the first time.

"Kama and I used to yell a lot, and it scared the kids shitless. We get along better now that he's gone." She winked at Nora. "But I miss the makeup sex."

This was the longest conversation Nora could remember having since she'd moved to Hilo. She blinked back tears.

"Break's over," George yelled. "Back on stage, Munchkins— you, too, Glinda. Dorothy."

As Desiree whirled and dashed up onstage, still clutching her handbag, Nora met Merle's gaze across the floor and they both grinned. What a show.

As she leaned back in her chair, holding her book loosely and watching the action onstage, Nora turned over the psychic hotline idea in her mind. She had always been able to think on her feet, and people told her she had a soothing voice. In Desiree's words, how hard could it be?

CHAPTER 8

After George had made them run the big welcoming scene five times, finally releasing Desiree with grudging praise, she loitered for a few minutes to watch Dorothy and the Munchkins finish up. She thought about the heavy package, which still weighed down her oversized handbag after nearly a week. She had chickened out at the evening rehearsals, shoving her bag under a table in the dressing room and piling a couple of old blankets on top to keep it safe. Hunter was getting impatient.

Now she needed to slip backstage and find the door to the basement. She paused, weighing the probability that anyone would see her. Most cast members avoided the cramped backstage area during rehearsals because they would be confined there for hours every night once the run started, like prisoners chained in the hold of a ship. They roamed the theater and talked noisily in the lobby—everything they wouldn't be able to do later.

Desiree pushed away her growing panic. She had mouths to feed. If she didn't do this, somebody else would. It wasn't like she was making or selling the drugs, just moving them from place to place. Mustn't think about getting caught. Plus, she had no choice now that Hunter had shown her the lab. No telling what he might do if she backed out.

She eased out of her seat and meandered to the side door, which was standing open. The narrow backstage entrance beckoned. It was a sign.

Desiree felt her way along the mirrored hallway which served as one of the changing rooms backstage at the Palace. She groped in her handbag for the flashlight she'd brought from home and turned it on to cut the gloom. The tiny light shone a pale white beam against the walls until at last, she saw a door. She tried the handle. Locked. But she was prepared. She wondered how Hunter had gotten his hands on a key.

The lock clicked, and the door creaked open. Desiree eased her way down the narrow steps to the rough cement floor. A pale light filtered from a narrow, dirt-crusted window at street level, revealing a weird metal structure at the entrance and some old wooden cabinets on the far wall. She shuffled farther into the basement, which smelled of burnt toast and old socks. She sneezed.

"Go all the way toward the front and look for a crack in the floor," he'd said.

There, that must be it. Desiree squinted at the floor illuminated by her flashlight. Was that a crack? She squatted down and pulled at the protruding edge. Damn. She'd chipped a nail.

"Hey, anybody down there?" It sounded like Fred, the stage manager.

She froze, and clicked off the flashlight. She heard footsteps on the stairs, then silence. Her heart thumped in her throat. She pinched her nose to stifle another sneeze.

"That's weird. Phil said they kept this door locked." Another creak and the door clicked shut.

Desiree crouched in the darkness, her skin clammy. That was close. Damn door better not be locked on the inside. She turned the flashlight back on and got out the flathead screwdriver she had also brought from home, on Hunter's instructions. She pried up the rough edge and felt beneath it, her skin crawling at the thought of what might be lurking there: centipedes and spiders, unspeakable slime. But all she felt was a dusty indentation, just about the size of her package.

She wedged the square paper package into the space and plopped the cement chunk back down. A perfect fit. Easiest money she'd ever earned.

Now to get back out undetected. Desiree was dying to know who would retrieve the package. Hunter had warned her not to snoop, but it might be someone she knew. Someone in *Wizard*. The corners of her mouth quirked into a smile as she tiptoed back up the steps and eased open the door. She felt a rush of pleasure. This new life of crime was exhilarating. Cloak and dagger doings in the dark! It was theater come to life.

～

MAHINA FUMED AS SHE BACKED HER CAR OUT OF THE TIGHT SPOT she'd found behind the theater. She'd discovered at an early age that anger was more satisfying than tears. Not to mention more dignified.

What a waste of time. Why was she even acting in this silly production, standing around with a bunch of rugrats on a Saturday morning when she could be making out with Keola or tanning on the beach with her friends. Was this the road to stardom?

She was no closer to finding Ziggy or his abductor. No one looked sinister at all, just stupid. Moku was pretty cool, though. He went to Kamehameha School, which was why she hadn't met him in the Hilo after-school performing arts group. Kam had its own well-funded theater program, all for Hawaiian kids. Iris had taught Mahina about the sad stages of post-contact history in the islands, when white people had arrived, stolen the land and taken over by force, spreading disease and doing their best to destroy Hawaiian culture and language. Mahina sniffed. She'd be off the rock as soon as the acceptance letter came from the mainland college of her choice. And she might never come back.

Her phone rang again, the irritating *Chorus Line* tune she'd set for her mother's calls. She ignored it, as she had all morning.

Mahina pulled into the Burger King drive-through and ordered a vanilla shake and large fries. She could throw up later.

Her mother was calling again. Mahina slammed her shake into the cup holder.

"What, Mom?"

"Why don't you ever answer your phone? I've called you six times already. Ziggy came home!"

Mahina stopped chewing, her mouth full of fries. "Whah?"

"He's okay, love, although there's something a little...different about him."

"Don't let him out of your sight, Mom. I'll be right there."

Mahina screeched out of the parking lot, fries spilling out onto the passenger seat.

◡

WHEN HE PARKED THE MIATA AT HOME AFTER REHEARSAL, George felt a terrible lassitude overtake him. He trudged straight to the screened-in *lanai* and flopped down on the wicker couch. He tried to concentrate on his breathing, the way his yoga teacher taught them at the studio. She was one of those fresh, lissome young women who come out to Hawai'i for a couple of years, get some tattoos, give too-long hugs and make tender, piercing eye contact, sprinkle their conversation with Hawaiian words, say "awesome" a lot, then break up with their local boyfriend, feel hurt because the community hasn't embraced their authenticity—and/or run out of money—and retreat to the mainland, making room for the next wave of seekers.

Five years into his retirement, George felt settled, and a bit bored. Maybe it had been a mistake to check out of the game too soon. Even with his Palace board responsibilities, his community theater involvement, and the thriving gay community in East Hawai'i, he felt adrift. Cal had become alternately more distant and more demanding, a sure sign the end was near. This filled George with a resigned panic. Although just the thought of Cal still evoked a melting tenderness in George's otherwise stony core, he was who he was. Not even the risk of losing love was enough incentive to "get help with his issues," as Cal so delicately put it. Plus, apart from a personality makeover, he'd probably have to start using Viagra soon, and then why even bother?

He heard Cal's little SUV crunch on the gravel driveway. He sighed and swung his legs over the edge of the couch. Wouldn't do to let Mr. Cheerful catch him napping or feeling morose.

George forced a smile and did a little tap dance on the acid-washed concrete floor of the *lanai*. A light, misty rain had started to fall outside without him even noticing. Hilo rain.

"I'm singin' in the rain, just singin' in the rain." George tapped his way to the doorway. He pictured Malcolm McDowell in *A Clockwork Orange*, gesturing with his enormous codpiece.

"Let's go over to the Hilton tonight," he said to Cal, who broke out in a big smile—an expression George hadn't seen for a while. "We'll stay two nights, soak up some sun, eat at decent restaurants, do some shopping. What do you say?"

"I'll call right now and change my shift." Cal whipped out his cell phone. He was an Emergency Room nurse, with plenty of favors to call in.

George wished his heart felt lighter.

⌣

"WHAT HAPPENED TO HIM?"

"Calm down, love, he's fine."

Mahina clutched Ziggy in her arms and stared at her mother in disbelief. "Fine? He's shaved and—and purple! What's wrong with you?" She buried her face in the remaining puff of hair on top of the little dog's head, which was indeed a bright shade of violet. The rest of his skinny, shivering body was shaved, but at least still the pale color he was born with.

"How many times do I have to tell you not to talk to strangers, Ziggers?" Mahina crooned. "Look at you. Even Pounce will laugh at you now."

Ziggy whimpered and licked Mahina's nose.

⌣

WHILE BOTH MAHINA AND HER MOTHER WERE RELIEVED TO have Ziggy home again, even in his altered state, the fact that someone had planned and executed a prank of this magnitude was alarming. Who would have done such a thing? And why to Ziggy? It had to have something to do with Mahina. And that was disturbing.

Both mother and daughter were spooked, but Iris tried not to show it. She spent extra time on her positive visualizations that evening, holding Mahina in a circle of white light. She had raised her daughter to be a strong woman without a victim complex. This meant she herself needed to remain calm and centered now, even though the incident had dredged up memories she had buried deep. Their startling images now bobbed along the surface of her mind, demanding attention and keeping her from sleep.

"We're taking Ziggy to the police station," Iris announced the next morning.

Mahina was still eating her Lucky Charms—Iris had lost that battle, decisively—picking out all the cereal first so she would have a pure layer of marshmallow pieces floating in the leftover milk.

"They'll laugh at him." Milk dripped down Mahina's chin.

Iris resisted the urge to wipe it off. She pointed at her own chin instead. Mahina rolled her eyes, then reached for a cloth napkin. Paper napkins and tissues destroyed Gaia's forests.

"It's our civic duty. What if there's a ring of dognappers shaving and dyeing little dogs all over town? This could be the breakthrough the police have been waiting for."

"Very funny, Mom." Mahina closed her eyes as she ladled in the last bite of marshmallow bits.

"Still, we're going, so get ready."

When Iris had reported Ziggy's disappearance a few days earlier, she could tell the grizzled desk sergeant was just barely holding back his laughter. He had implied she was wasting valuable police time with a matter best handled by animal control.

Now Iris felt vindicated. A crime had clearly been committed, and she wanted a case file opened.

Today, a different officer sat at the Kapiʻolani Street station's front desk. Younger. Better-looking. Hot, in fact. Iris fluffed her still-luxuriant hair and sucked in her stomach, glad she had remembered lipstick.

Mahina clomped along behind, holding Ziggy, who wore a scarf.

Moses Kapili, it turned out, was actually a Detective Inspector filling in while the desk sergeant smoked a cigarette out back. They were shorthanded, he said. Budget cuts. He was polite and sympathetic, shaking his head in sorrow as Mahina uncovered Ziggy's purple poof of shame.

"This is the first report we've had of this type of crime." He slid the form across the scarred wooden counter for Iris to sign. "We'll certainly be on the lookout for any similar incidents. Whoever did this is a sick individual."

By the time they left the station, mother and daughter were smiling. Mahina left Ziggy's head uncovered, ignoring the stares and laughter of uncouth passersby.

"We'll go straight to the salon, darling," said Iris. "Kalani will know exactly what to do."

CHAPTER 9

A T EVENING REHEARSAL THE FOLLOWING MONDAY—LESS than five weeks before opening night—Griff observed Dorothy through his peripheral vision, the way he'd learned to scan the jungle in 'Nam. She didn't seem to notice him. Good. It was best she didn't know until it was time for her to act, to take her place—

"Pay no attention to the man behind the curtain," he cried, pretending to struggle with a prop which hadn't been constructed yet. Griff never missed a cue.

George strode onto the stage, shaking his head.

"Not you, Oz. That was fine. You too, Lion. Good cowering." He raised his hands over his head. "But *you*, Scarecrow, and *you*, Dorothy. What are you doing?"

They looked at him.

"That's right. Nothing. You're doing nothing."

"What do you want us to do, George? You haven't given us our blocking for this scene yet." The Scarecrow patted Dorothy on the shoulder, and she slapped his hand away.

Griff quivered with suppressed rage. The voices said, How dare he touch her? The greys will eat him, fingers first. Griff closed his eyes, visualizing the great ship hovering over Hilo. No! No ship. He wouldn't let the voices guide him. They just wanted him to fail. He was listening for a clear external Voice. The Voice. That's where his true path lay.

"Do I have to give you everything?" George looked dark and mottled, like a toad in distress.

Griff pushed the voices down. His therapist in the psych ward had told him to focus on visual cues, to stay in the real world. But how could you tell what was real?

"Okay, let's start this scene again. From the top. Oz."

Griff snapped back to the present and boomed into his disconnected microphone, one of the few props actually ready. "I am Oz, the great and powerful. Who are you?"

"If you please, I am Dorothy, the small and meek. We've come to ask you—"

"Okay, okay, stop." George bounded back on stage. "Dorothy, you're scared. You're stuttering and trembling. And cheat out, don't turn your back on the audience. Try again."

Griff saw George's wide toad jaws opening and closing, his big purple throat sac swelling out like a hot air balloon. Mahina was a cat, a black cat, sleek and disdainful. She could puncture George with one sweep of her claws as he croaked and puffed. She turned away and licked her paw instead.

NORA WATCHED THE REST OF THE OZ SCENE, HER EYES GLUED to the Cowardly Lion cavorting onstage. The man was brilliant, and so full of *joie de vivre*, so unlike peevish, hypercritical Clyde. She had decided to give in to her harmless infatuation. Why fight it? She knew what her friend Alice in Waimea would say: "Throw caution to the wind!" She could hear Alice's posh British accent in her ear, "Carpe diem, sweetheart." Alice had been the one person in Waimea who wasn't surprised by Nora's flight to Hilo. "You're well shot of that wanker, love," she'd said, prompting Nora's eternal gratitude.

And now, here was a man who could make her laugh. And the way he moved. She rubbed her arms.

"Hey girlfriend." Desiree bumped shoulders and stood next to her, leaning against the wall. She seemed more relaxed today—a mercy. The children were all in the lobby playing Pokémon until their next scene.

"How d'ya like Hot Stuff up there?"

Nora blushed. "Who do you mean?"

"Oh, come on." Desiree nudged her again. "There's only one man up there who could possibly be called hot."

They laughed. George whipped his head around.

"Oops. The General is angry." Desiree attempted a whisper, but it carried. She gave a sharp salute to George's back, clicking her heels. Merle guffawed.

"You're terrible." Nora giggled. She was having more fun than she'd had in a long time.

Merle shook his finger at her, and she tossed her head.

"Watch out, sistah." Desiree raised her eyebrows. "He's a playah."

"Oh, I'm just enjoying the view, don't worry," said Nora. "No men for me, thanks very much."

"I wouldn't be so sure." Desiree did a little shuffle step. "Maybe it's time to follow the yellow brick road, yah?"

"Hey," Nora said. "Thanks, by the way. I called the psychic hotline number you gave me, and I've submitted my application. I should find out tomorrow if they want to do a phone interview."

"You go, girl!" Desiree lifted her hand for a high five. "Or should I say, Madame Nora?"

George turned again and glared as their laughter rang out.

As she blushed and clapped her hand over her mouth, half in jest, Nora was struck by the irony of her situation. How rich would it be if she, who had made such a misguided, disastrous decision in moving to Hawai'i to save her already-doomed marriage, only to be blindsided by fate and made to stay forever, like a modern Persephone in Hades (although Persephone at least got to go home for six months of the year)—if she, Nora, mistress of delusion, should then be hired to reveal the unknowable to others?

Priceless.

⌣

EVAN THE TIN MAN ALSO WATCHED MERLE, SNEAKING GLANCES even during their scenes together. He hoped he still looked that good in twenty years.

Things were spiraling downward with Belinda. It was hard to pretend any interest, and she could tell. He hoped she wasn't the hysterical, I'll do anything, just tell me what you want type. So painful. He would really have to let the ax fall soon. Gently.

As they started the scene again, he glanced offstage and saw the Witch walk up the center aisle with a gorgeous stranger.

"Need some oil, Tin Man?" George approached, his face stretched into an exaggerated look of concern.

"Sorry. Just spaced out there for a minute." Evan shook his head.

"Less than five weeks left, people. Stay focused." George stalked back to his chair.

Evan was tempted to slap an extra fee onto George's brokerage account for hardship pay. He sneaked another look. The beautiful young man sat in the box seats with the Witch, deep in conversation.

Toy boy? No, surely not.

The Witch pointed to the stage and Tall, Dark and Handsome looked straight at Evan and smiled.

Evan smiled back, then looked away, embarrassed.

He'd speak to Belinda tonight.

⌣

After rehearsal, Griff settled into the driver's seat of his old pickup and turned on the ignition.

The familiar music played, then the smooth voice said, "You're listening to *Shore to Shore a.m.* This is Buck Leary, your host. Let's take a caller from the Wild Card line. Hello? You're on *Shore to Shore.*"

Griff never got tired of hearing Buck's mellifluous voice. He admired the host's patience with every caller, no matter how inane. Buck could spin even the lamest conversation into an interesting topic, especially if the paranormal were involved, which it usually was on *Shore to Shore.*

"Hello, Buck. I just want to tell you how much I love your show. Listen to it every night. My wife says it's my religion, haw haw haw." The caller rambled on, the way they did, about how much it meant to talk to Buck, and, well, he had this theory he wondered if anyone else had ever thought of, and blah blah blah.

Griff let the words wash over him as he drove up Kanoelehua Highway to the Kea'au Bypass. He didn't know how Buck could stand listening to all those morons who called in. Most of them sounded like they hadn't finished sixth grade. Probably messed with goats.

Griff had a high opinion of goats. He raised them on his Puna spread, along with chickens and fruit trees. They loved climbing on the lava outcroppings and munching on the invasive strawberry guavas, or *waiwi*, as the locals called them. The alpha goat, Cookie, always trotted over so he could scratch between her horns, sniffing at his hand with her velvety nose and nibbling at his skin and clothing.

Along with food, he had catchment water, solar panels and a diesel-powered generator. He was self-sufficient and completely off the grid.

Griff had been camping out of season in the North Cascades National Park in Washington when fate had handed him his new identity. A chance meeting, conversation over a flickering fire, practically an invitation. In September, it was already so cold in the northwestern mountains that he woke up the morning of The Transaction, as he'd labeled it, with frost in his beard. Time to move on, and why look a gift horse in the mouth? Seeking both privacy and warmth, Griff paid cash for a twenty-acre parcel on the Big Island—cheap because of its location in a high-risk lava flow zone downslope of the very active Kīlauea volcano. He could disappear into the landscape without risking hypothermia. So far, no one had come looking for Griffin K. Peterson.

Griff thought about the night before the read-through, when he'd been given a name for the power he felt in the Palace—the night The Voice had spoken to him through Buck Leary. The aliens must have planted the Energy Center in Hilo after the second tsunami in 1960. Now Its force was growing stronger.

Shortly after he'd arrived on the Big Island, Griff had gone to see the movie *Contact* at the Palace. Entranced by the prophetic story flashing across the big screen, he felt a thrumming throughout his whole body, an energy that penetrated the soles of his rubber slippers, moved up his legs, and surged all the way down to his fingertips as they gripped the wooden armrests of his seat. Its heat radiated up to his scalp as the rays healed him from within.

These rays were unlike the harsh beams Griff sometimes felt bombarding him from above, the CIA lasers shot from satellites, trying to penetrate his brain. The Agency had found him through his cell phone once, back on the mainland. Afterward, he only bought prepaid disposable phones every now and then, making sure to crush and discard them far from his lair.

Now the comet was on his radar. Was it a power for good or evil? The Voice would speak again, through the radio or the website. He had to pay attention.

CHAPTER 10

Unaware of Griff's observation, Mahina remained preoccupied with Ziggy's abduction. Two days after her little dog's altered reappearance, she was no closer to a solution. Their hairdresser, Kalani, had worked his magic by shaving off the purple poof, and now Ziggy's fur was already growing out a bit. He seemed untraumatized by the experience.

Mahina's weekly voice lesson was in an hour. She had come home after school to do her stretching and warm-ups first. "Somewhere Over the Rainbow" had to be stunning—no holds barred. She wanted to blow George and all his criticisms away. Scooping? Flat? Thin and screechy? Ha! He was just trying to get to her, undermine her confidence. Impossible.

Mahina was secretly riddled with self-doubt, but she succeeded in hiding it pretty well, even from her mother. She worried that throwing up was affecting her voice. She just had to eat less. But life was so stressful, and vanilla shakes and fries were so soothing. Keola had jokingly pinched more than an inch of her belly fat the last time they were at the beach, so he obviously thought she was fat, too.

Deep breaths. Mahina bent down, stretching her arms out across the floor, legs spread in a wide triangle.

Being a girl sucked.

She took another deep breath, feeling the burn along the inside of her thighs. Keola was getting impatient, but she didn't want to have sex with him. He was cute, but not The One. Her first time had to be special. After that, the Keolas of the world might do for amusement. She would never let a man get the better of her. She was going to be the one in control. Always.

But now her mother was dating that policeman. She'd given him her telephone number right there at the station. For the report, of course, but one thing had led to another, hadn't it? Why now, Mahina wondered, when Iris had never had a boyfriend before? She couldn't remember any men hanging around. Ever.

She was probably worried about someone abusing me. Mahina lifted her leg over her head. As if I would fall for that.

She wasn't one of those girls with daddy issues.

A year ago, Mahina had googled her father's name—Carlos Guerrero. Hundreds of different references had popped up, although none of them referred to a fatal car crash before her birth. She'd given up clicking on the links after half an hour. It was a common name, apparently. She'd thought of writing to the lawyer who handled the trust to see if he knew anything about her father's family, but he would only tell her mother, who would smile and hug Mahina—and repeat the same canned story she'd heard all her life. Still, she'd copied the lawyer's return address from one of the large blue envelopes which arrived every three months. Just because.

Iris kept the papers in a locked file cabinet. Mahina had sneaked a look at one of the reports before her mother had whisked it away, though, and it had been disappointing. No secrets of her family history, just columns of numbers and abbreviated names of stocks, bonds, funds, etc. Financialize.

As for her mother's side of the family, Iris just said they were religious fanatics who had disapproved of her marriage to a non-Catholic and cut her off, so she had just let them go. Sometimes, she'd told Mahina, love requires sacrifice. Sometimes you have to release people who try to bring you down, even if they're your own flesh and blood. Gaia provides and protects. "You and I," she said to her daughter, making her most serious eye contact, "are enough family for each other."

Mahina concluded her session with child's pose, arms extended. The face-down stretch felt so contained and comforting. The muscles alongside her torso stretched as they pulled against her thighs, glutes, and lower back. Her feet were tucked in, safe and warm. She stayed in the pose for a long time, breathing, her forehead resting on the mat.

⌣

MAHINA WAS NOT THE ONLY PALACE THESPIAN CONFRONTING ghosts of the past.

At home in his Volcano workshop mid-week, Patrick picked up the rough, clunky mango bowl from the drying shelf and inspected it. Sides still an inch thick from the initial turning. Very little warping, no cracking. It was large—no need to attempt paper thinness. A quarter inch would be just fine. Safe. Still attractive.

It was time.

Cindy was sure he had a complex about the finishing stage. Okay, so he'd had a bad run, with those three botched jobs. The images came unbidden into his mind. The exquisite *koa* bowl he'd shaved just a bit too thin. The Norfolk pine platter with the hidden flaw right down the middle. And the last mango bowl he'd let dry for too long. Cindy's theory was that this unfinished bowl had become an obstacle. A flash flood of creative work and bliss would barrel down the dry streambed of his psyche if he could just finish it.

Bowls cracked. Big deal. Cats scratched. Dogs bit. Women nagged and felt unappreciated. Men withdrew and punished. It was the way of the world. What should he do, cry about it?

Patrick mounted the bowl on the lathe and set it spinning. He picked up the chisel and applied it to the middle of the bowl's interior, sliding it outward with a light touch. The sawdust flew in a thin spray, the rich, dry scent an incense offering to the gods.

Be merciful, he thought.

Half an inch now, too thick to stop. Patrick focused his mind on the wood spinning beneath the chisel, connected to him through his vibrating hands. He thrummed like a divining rod, feeling for the bowl, the curve of the wood, willing his hands not to press too hard or worse, unevenly. He bore down gently, peering through his protective goggles at the thinning wood, which spiraled endlessly, hypnotically. He was afraid to continue, afraid to stop.

He willed himself to be calm. To be there with the wood. Nearly there. Yes.

He pulled back and stopped the lathe. He took the bowl off the mount and inspected it on all sides. He noticed he was breathing hard, sweat dripping down his forehead and running around the edges of his goggles. He took them off and wiped his face with a gritty cloth.

The bowl was perfect. A bit of sanding, then waxing and oiling, and it would be done. Perhaps his best work ever. All his choices had led to this moment in this place, Patrick reflected, floating in a giddy, heightened state of consciousness. His life was validated.

He gazed at his creation, still in the rough, felt the graceful curve of the sides, the lovely hollowing of the interior, the evenness of the edges. The grain had come through in beautiful stripes that would gleam like sunlight when the bowl was polished.

So this was happiness. He set the bowl on the shelf as if it were made of glass, then sat down on the bench and put his head in his hands.

⌣

As Patrick set down his bowl, Desiree took another step across the line into her underworld career, feeling the thrill only risky behavior delivers.

Kama was happy to take his children for the evening. Turns out he and Makani were living in Hilo with another of her many aunties, this one in Puʻuʻeo, a once-gracious neighborhood located in the flood zone not far from Desiree's neighborhood, now fallen on hard times. In fact, the *keiki* could stay the night, and he'd drive them to school in the morning.

"Plenny ono grinds." Kama made a smacking sound over the phone. "Aunty stay cooking all the time."

"Enough with the pidgin, Kama." Desiree was annoyed. "You know I want the kids to speak proper English." Since their split, he had reverted completely to his local roots. She didn't buy his insistence that "Hawaiian Creole English is a language as rich and complex as any other." That was fancy college talk.

"Ho."

"Thanks for taking them." No need to antagonize him. It was good for the children to spend time with their father—better than leaving them alone in the apartment, anyhow. Plus, Makani should step up to the childcare plate now that she was dating a man with kids. She'd soon learn life with Kama wasn't all fun and romance.

Kama laughed. "You make sure he treat you right, now."

"Why, because you didn't?" Desiree snapped. No matter what la-di-da cultural excuses he gave for dumping her, she would never let him forget it was an asshole move.

"Shoots, girl. Right in da balls, yah?"

"It's a business dinner, anyhow."

"Ho! High flyah now. You starting up one bar or someting?" Kama's disbelief made Desiree bristle.

"You think I couldn't?" Oh stop, she told herself. "So, two-fifteen at the school, right? You won't forget?"

"I get 'em. No worries." Kama chuckled. "And when you get your *haole*-girl bar, you can hire me play music. I give you one good deal."

Desiree smiled as she hung up the phone.

She was puzzled by Hunter's dinner invitation. He didn't think they were dating, did he? She'd set him straight pronto if he tried anything. They were meeting tonight at the Thai restaurant near Kalakaua Park—no more colored glass chandeliers and overpriced fancy food.

It had been a while since Desiree really dated. She usually just met guys at the bar or the beach, had a few drinks, and took them to bed—or not, depending on her mood. She didn't get involved. It was easier that way with the kids. Every now and then she thought about Prince Charming—hey, even Hunter had her going for a couple of hours—but she didn't want to rely on a man. Not after Kama. Besides, men always wanted you to *be* something for them. Their mother, their maid, their mistress, their whatever—all of the above. No thanks.

She remembered a guy she'd dated briefly right after Kama left her. Until the night he mentioned he liked to see a woman on her hands and knees scrubbing the floor.

"Nice job with your first package, by the way."

Desiree couldn't tell if Hunter was paying her a compliment or being sarcastic. He poured her a glass of Chardonnay—it was one of those unlicensed restaurants that let you bring your own bottle. He obviously hadn't remembered her wine preference, and her face puckered at the sour taste. She'd stick to water.

They sat in the corner, Hunter's back to the wall. The lights were dim in an attempt at romantic ambiance. Not working.

"I trust the next one won't take as long, now you've got the hang of it. We have a lot of product to move."

The young female server approached their table, smiling. Hunter turned to her. "We'll have the spring rolls and green papaya salad to start, then the garlic shrimp and red pumpkin curry—medium—with sticky rice." He shut the menu and Desiree stared. The server hurried back to the kitchen.

"Is that all for you or did you just order for me, too?"

"Don't you like what I ordered?" Hunter's bottle-blue eyes glittered.

"That's not the point." Desiree wished she hadn't worn her push-up bra. He didn't deserve the view.

"Do you want me to call the waitress back?" Hunter showed his perfect white teeth, like an aggressive dog.

"Don't bother." Desiree fastened the next button up on her blouse. "I don't want to give the poor thing more work."

"All right then."

Asshole. Desiree took a deep breath. "By the way, when do I get paid?" She wasn't about to let it slide. This was business.

"I prefer not to conduct business where any watching eyes can see."

"Then why are we here? Plus, you didn't answer my question."

"We're establishing our public relationship. Makes it more natural to meet—in case anyone is watching." He paused. "We'll have a walk in the park after dinner, and I'll give you your payment and the next package." A candle on the glass-topped table cast flickers of orange light on his face. All he needed was a pitchfork, horns, and a barbed tail.

Desiree snorted. "You're a little old for me, don't you think?" Customers always told her how young she looked. A hot forty-year-old shouldn't have to settle for a creepy sixty-something.

"On the contrary, you're a little old for me." Hunter drained his glass. "I like my women young and fresh."

Desiree rolled her eyes. Just then, their server wove through the crowded restaurant with a loaded tray in her hands and set the steaming plates between them. Thank god. She'd only eaten a side salad on her break at the Aloha, and her stomach was growling.

Hunter didn't attempt small talk while they ate, just looked around the room as if registering faces for later use.

"So, where are your kids tonight, sweetheart?" He wiped his mouth and leaned back in his chair.

Desiree felt chilled in spite of the restaurant's steamy atmosphere. "With their father—and you can leave my kids out of it."

"I know where you live, you know." Hunter set his glass down on the table with a thunk. "Pretty soon you can afford to move to a nicer place."

Desiree felt a surge of anger in her chest. "We like our apartment—great neighbors."

"Of course you do." Hunter filled her already full wineglass to the brim. "Now, for the other part of your job, remember?" He grilled her about the theater, cast and crew, who else came to rehearsals, the odd sounds, the dog poop, petty thievery, Aunty Em's ghost stories.

Why was he so interested? The longer she knew Hunter, the weirder he got.

Back in the empty apartment an hour later, with a package of meth crystals and a big wad of cash, Desiree was struck by longing for her children. She envied Kama that he could provide something for them she couldn't. A family. She imagined laughing faces around a big table full of homemade food. Then, more realistically, Nakai spilling his milk and Kama yelling at him, Malia spitting out her poi and crying, Kolea throwing rice at her brother.

Still, a new happy family that didn't include her.

꒦

MAHINA WAS TRYING, REALLY SHE WAS. IT WAS JUST HARD AFTER all these years of being the two musketeers, the mother-daughter team. The sole focus of her mother's life. Now, suddenly, a third person had come between them.

"Does he have to be here *all* the time?" Mahina spat out the words, jerking her head at Moses Kapili, who sprawled on the couch in the TV room across the counter from the open-plan kitchen, watching a football game. He'd been there when she got back from her voice lesson. Football! In their house. All that testosterone and violence. Did Iris's goddess beliefs mean nothing now that she had a man?

"Shhh. He'll hear you." Her mother bustled around the kitchen getting dinner ready. Again. The Policeman seemed to eat with them every night. He did offer to help, but Iris always shooed him away, the way she did Mahina. She said working in the kitchen was her zen practice.

"Go talk to him. Get to know him." Iris gave her a gentle shove. "You'll like him."

"I'm sure he's wonderful, but my friends are wonderful, too, and I don't want them practically living in my house. What happened to Family Time?"

The TV volume was high enough that their conversation's subject probably could not hear this statement in full, rising as it did from a stage whisper to a near shout.

"Mahina." Iris made calming motions with her hands.

"Is it time?" A sudden silence fell as the TV switched off. The Policeman leaned against the granite counter, smiling his handsome smile.

Damn it. She could see her mother melting into it, as if Mahina weren't even there.

Iris smiled at Kapili and handed him a stack of plates and flatware. "Here, you can set the table."

That was her job. A line had been crossed.

"I just remembered. I'll have to grab dinner to go." Mahina's heart turned to stone. She shoveled wild rice, free-range chicken, and organic vegetables into a squat glass jar. Iris abhorred plastic—all those chemicals.

"What?" Iris stared at her with an "I know what you're doing" look of mingled annoyance and concern.

"We have an extra rehearsal tonight at the Palace." Mahina popped a purple potato into her mouth. Hot. "Stahs ih fah minahs."

"Be sure to park under a streetlight." Iris called out the front door as Mahina fired up the Honda. She sounded forlorn. Well tough.

There was no extra rehearsal.

Mahina parked the car in a half-deserted parking lot by the shops on Bayfront and ate her dinner with a pair of chopsticks she found in the center compartment under a jumble of makeup and tissue packs. She was starved. Iris's cooking had improved with the intrusion of Moses Kapili. Fewer lentils and weird, chewy mushrooms with antennae like space aliens. More meat. No loss without some gain.

Her phone rang. Keola again. She'd been ignoring his calls all night. Break up time was close, but it would be nice to have a boyfriend for opening night—photos, flowers and all that.

Iris always came through with a dozen red roses, but it wasn't the same from your mother.

She wrapped the chopsticks in a tissue, screwed the lid back on the jar, and placed both on the passenger seat. Now what?

She'd told her mother she was going to the theater, so that's what she'd do. Maybe she'd see the ghost.

Aunty Em had given everyone ghost fever. Now there were almost daily sightings of shadowy figures, plus weird noises and items gone missing. It had even happened to Mahina. The little box she'd left backstage with her specially tied Jolly Time hair bands and clips had disappeared, although she figured it was those thieving Munchkins, not a ghost. Then she'd seen Desiree go backstage the other day and come out again with cobwebs dangling from her hair. What was in the basement?

Mahina felt restless. She wanted to do something bad. Maybe break something. She strolled up Haili Street and then stopped.

As usual, the homeless people were camped out in the alley alongside the theater. That was a problem. It was crazy to do this alone, at night. She pulled her trusty cell phone out of her bra strap.

"Keola? Hey, are you busy?"

‿

TEN MINUTES LATER, HE SAUNTERED UP HAILI STREET, AND THEY entered the alley together. Keola threw *shakas* to the homeless guys leaning against the wall under a slight overhang.

"Babe." He tried to pull Mahina in for a kiss, but she stiff-armed him.

"Not here." She stared at the snickering onlookers. "Let's go."

She led him around the corner, out of sight. "Did you bring flashlights?"

Keola held out two tiny LED lights, the kind they sold at the hardware store checkout register.

Mahina made a disdainful sound but took one. He was definitely history. A real man would have a big maglite in his truck, ready for emergency adventures. She bet Moses Kapili had two or three. But then, he was a cop.

She found a window low to the ground and pulled on it, then pushed. Shit. It was stuck. She wiped her dirty hands on her jeans. Yuck.

"Let me." Keola kicked around the edges, then pushed. The window creaked open, just wide enough to squeeze through.

"You go first." Mahina motioned with the back of her hand.

Inside, the Palace basement was dark and dingy.

"Look for a stairway leading up to the theater." Mahina stayed close to Keola. Majorly creepy down here.

They stumbled around, shining their weak white beams on the dusty cement floor.

"I bet this is for the pipe organ." Keola trained his light on a large, horizontal metal cylinder the size of a dining room table.

"It feels warm." Mahina rested her hand on the flat surface. "Maybe it has to be turned on all the time."

"Waste of electricity."

"Didn't know you were a conservationist." Mahina gave Keola a playful shove.

"Yeah, you think I'm just a dumb surfah dude." His expression was hidden in the darkness.

Mahina looked at him. Maybe there was more to Keola than his pretty face and rock-hard abs.

"What exactly are you looking for?"

"Oh, nothing. Just bored. I've heard stories about tunnels, sabotage, ghosts. And there was the dog poop I told you about. But really, I just had to get away from Iris mooning over the Policeman. Gag me." Mahina made a rude gesture.

"There's a door over there." Keola rattled the knob, but it was locked. "I could pick this if I had a bobby pin."

Footsteps sounded overhead. The metal cylinder let out a "whoosh" into the wide tubing which rose through the ceiling, and the organ started to play.

"Oh my god." Mahina grabbed Keola. "We have to see if it's Oz. Come on." They swept their flashlights around until they found the steps leading to the backstage door. It stood open.

They crept up and peeked around the stage entrance until they could see the organ podium. A bright light shone down on whoever was playing, hidden behind the tall backboard. The music crashed through the theater. Mahina thought she recognized a movie soundtrack, sort of eerie and spacey.

Keola whispered, "Definitely not Bach's Toccata and Fugue in D flat minor. What, you think I'm ignorant? My sister's at Julliard on a piano scholarship."

Mahina elbowed him. The music stopped abruptly, and she recognized Griff as he hopped down from the podium, just as he'd done after he played the organ for the first time, and Fred had had a hissy fit. Now, he was heading straight for them.

They scrambled back down the stairs, knocking over a bucket of mops on the way to the open window. Keola boosted Mahina up and out, then followed as Griff pounded down the stairs.

Not daring to head back along the alley, they dashed across the gravel parking lot behind the theater. Keola gave Mahina a lift halfway up the chain-link fence and she pulled herself the rest of the way over, ripping her jeans. They jumped down and raced through the potholed alleyway to Waiānuenue Street.

Mahina bent over, panting, her heart racing.

"You're filthy." Keola wiped something off her nose.

"So are you." Mahina plucked at a cobweb in his hair and laughed.

They stood there, wheezing with laughter, on the street lit dimly with orange-colored sodium streetlights so as not to interfere with the telescopes on the summit of Mauna Kea.

"Well that was fun, babe, thanks for inviting me." Keola flashed his white teeth.

Mahina felt stirrings of interest. "Let's go swimming at Four Mile." Her belly tightened. It was a night for taking chances.

As they strolled down to Kamehameha Avenue to find their cars, neither one noticed the man who had followed them out of the Palace.

He stood under a streetlight, head covered by a baseball cap, his face a shadowed crater in the lurid orange glow.

PART TWO
OIL CAN

CHAPTER 11

FOR THE FIRST TWO WEEKS AFTER LUKE'S ARRIVAL, HARRIET alternated between worry and annoyance. He was despondent and moody, listless and restless by turn as he mooched around the house. He helped himself to everything in the fridge, leaving her short of ingredients for the meals she'd planned. Then he said he wasn't hungry when she offered him dinner. He also drank all the booze.

When she tried to engage him in conversation, he brushed her off.

"I don't want to talk about it, Mom." Then he took the car and disappeared for hours. It was like having a teenager in the house again.

Harriet had started walking to school and to rehearsals. Both were within a few blocks of her house, so it was no real hardship, even though carrying student work in a backpack felt a bit undignified, and made her neck muscles even stiffer. Frankly, walking had never been her preferred form of exercise, especially in this heat—she still swam several times a week down at Four Mile Beach—but she didn't want to argue with Luke and drive him away.

He did seem mildly interested in the play, now with only four weeks left to rehearse. And he'd agreed to come to the work party the following weekend, which would mark the three-week count-down to opening night.

The other night, she'd noticed that young Evan, the Tin Man, seemed pretty interested in her son, even if Luke pretended not to see it. A new romance, or even a fling, would help him get his mind off that wretched cad Bruce, who'd dumped him and ruined his life, at least in his opinion. She'd always thought Bruce a bit pompous, but she'd managed to hold her tongue throughout their relationship. No point in saying "I told you so" now, when Luke would just resent her for it. Evan seemed nice enough, and did it even matter? She'd thought he and Belinda were involved, but they didn't seem too friendly lately. These young people were so versatile.

Harriet couldn't stop thinking about Howard and his new bride. She had called to let him know Luke was with her—that was her excuse, anyhow, and a valid one. Luke might be grown up, but he was still their son. Soon now, Howard would have another child. She still couldn't wrap her head around this fact, which seemed incongruous and just plain wrong. He had sounded flustered to hear her voice, guilty and furtive, although perhaps she was reading that into his words and tone. Surely he must feel the awkwardness of the situation.

In the end, she had been merciful and told him she knew. "I hope you'll be very happy, Howard."

How many lies had she told in the interest of civility and family coherence? They were still a family, tied forever with the bonds of blood. But now he was tied to someone else, too. How did that work? Did it mean his new wife-to-be and unborn child were also part of her family? They were part of Luke's—that seemed clear.

Harriet headed into the kitchen to pour herself a gin and tonic. Mother's friend. She'd hidden the green Tanqueray bottle under the kitchen sink, behind the Pine Sol. Unless Luke suddenly went on a cleaning spree, it would be safe there.

⌣

Nora had just finished scrubbing a sticky pool of congealed passion-guava nectar off the kitchen floor when a horn honked outside.

Alice's visits from Waimea were an oasis of talking, laughter, and what seemed like real life in the midst of the alien social landscape of Hilo. Even with play rehearsals, her unlikely new career as a psychic, and the twins in their new school, Nora was still struck—far too often—with the urge to cry or scream.

She and Alice had immediately recognized each other as kindred spirits at an office party in Waimea, shortly after Nora and Clyde had moved to Hawai'i—aliens married to Americans and mothers of twins to boot. Alice was British. She'd met her husband, Gabe, on the beach in Australia while she was vacationing with friends and he was working in Sydney. Now Gabe worked at the same observatory Clyde had joined as a software engineer, lured by the unequaled views from the telescopes on Mauna Kea. Gabe was an astronomer, a real head-in-the-clouds kind of guy. Alice was plump and down-to-earth, anchoring him to the material world of home and children.

"He forgets to eat all day," she confided to Nora that first evening. "And then he's all bolshy and confused until I get some dinner into him. It's like having a third child."

This sounded attractive to Nora. Clyde was all too attentive, pointing out the chores Nora had failed to do while he was away at work, and criticizing her cooking.

With children the same ages and sexes, Alice's friendship was a gift Nora valued more and more as her already troubled marriage crumbled. Hawai'i was just too much temptation for Clyde. Far away from family and old friends, he saw a chance to reinvent himself, and Nora was baggage he was tired of carrying.

For her part, Nora felt like she had been granted early release from prison and slipped out of his grasp as quickly as possible before he changed his mind.

Eager to get out of Waimea, where tongues were wagging and single women were already sidling up to Clyde in the streets, Nora appealed to Alice to help her move to Hilo—a good-sized town, right on the water. She was still reeling in shock from the news that she couldn't just return to Vancouver and pick up her life again. But Clyde wanted joint custody, favored by the family court. Like it or not, she was stuck on the rock—a rock, she'd already learned during her short residence, which had been stolen from the Hawaiians by missionaries, sugar barons, and the U.S. government. No wonder she felt out of place and unwelcome. *Haoles* like her shouldn't be living there in the first place.

Let me go, she prayed furtively to the mountain, to the ocean, to the rattling palms.

On this sunny Hilo afternoon, the friends walked from Nora's rental house down the narrow, winding road to Honoli'i Beach, the children gliding ahead on their scooters. Nora and Alice ran to catch up from time to time, and called out warnings about cars.

The sun was still high and hot, and it was a relief to enter the shade of the forested gulch. The sun-dappled road was slippery with fallen leaves and rotting fruit.

"I have a crush." Nora grinned at Alice. "He's completely unsuitable, which is why I'm attracted to him."

"It's about bloody time! Tell me everything." Alice gave her a hug and plucked a plumeria blossom off a nearby tree. "Which ear do I put this behind again?"

They giggled.

Nora tried to find the words to explain Merle. "He's not my type—a total exhibitionist, really over the top. But he's refreshing and so sexy. I think I'd like roll around in bed with him and not think any rational thoughts for a while."

"Darling." Alice clapped her hands. "Exactly what you need."

They caught up to the children at the first bridge. All the twins had picked up sticky overripe breadfruit on the road and were throwing them like cannon balls onto the rocks below, where they splattered out their yellow innards. It was like a scene from Swiss Family Robinson.

"Brains!" Giles yelled, and Oliver roared his best zombie roar. Miri and Amelia wiped their sticky hands on the boys' shirts and ran away screaming.

The waterfall roared, too, spilling over the rock ledge on the other side of the bridge into a deep pool far below. Thick guava forest lined both sides of the gulch, with splashes of orange from African tulips. The river slid between its banks to the sea.

"It's good to see them so happy." Nora smiled, her tension starting to dissipate. "Since they started school last week they've been pretty glum. Their teacher seems kind, and the class sizes are small at Po'okela, but they look so lost—and so pale." She sighed. "Miri just told me a big mean girl who sits next to her has been stealing her pencils and poking her with them, then threatening to 'bus her up' if she tells. I've made an appointment with the teacher, but what I really want to do is 'bus *her* up'—the bully, not the teacher. Or maybe her parents." Nora sighed. "Too bad Desiree's kids aren't in the same class—she's Glinda the Good, and they're Munchkins. So at least Miri and Oliver have some allies at recess."

"I'm sorry, darling." Alice squeezed Nora's shoulders. "But I'm glad they have some friends. And Miri's a tough little cookie. She has twin power, too, remember."

They laughed. It was true. Giles and Amelia were also a single unit, like Oliver and Miri. Nora and Alice often joked about being the odd person out, repelled by the twin force field.

"By the way, someone new joined the homeschooling group this week." Alice gave Nora a sidelong glance. At Alice's urging, Nora had also joined the group during her residence in Waimea, although she had always felt out-of-step with the other mothers. Several of them had seemed positively gleeful at the news of her divorce and had immediately started setting Clyde up with their single friends. Nora's neck hairs tingled.

"Greta. She's Belgian. Enormously wealthy." Alice looked down at the waterfall's plunge.

"How lovely." Nora waited, feeling the rough concrete of the bridge wall under her hands.

"Well, the thing is..." Alice looked at her. "Greta is a recent divorcee. Her ex is some Euro-trash bounder who lived off her and then ran away with an even richer woman."

"Don't tell me." Nora slapped a mosquito. "She's Clyde's new girlfriend."

"Spot on." Alice paused. "And she mentioned your children."

Nora could already see it. Clyde and Greta setting up house together, wealthy beyond description. Greta homeschooling all of the children in between fabulous European trips—educational, of course. Skiing in the Alps, visiting museums and cathedrals. Then back to the quiet green hills of Waimea for horseback riding and lei-making.

Nora held up her hand. "She's horsey, isn't she? Let me guess—dressage?" No wonder her new psychic job was such a snap. She had powers.

"I'm afraid so." Alice grimaced.

"Wonderful." Now Nora could picture her, too. Tall and lean, with a slightly equine face. Confident, patronizing. The children in black velveteen riding helmets and jodhpurs, posting on sleek Thoroughbred horses around a green paddock.

"Sorry darling, there's more." Alice paused. "Greta said Clyde wants her to homeschool the twins, too, so they can 'come back home and live with him'—her words, or his, or whatever." Alice held up her hand. "But she laughed when she said it."

"Perfect timing." Nora clutched her head, only half in jest. "Miri's not the only one being picked on. Oliver got pushed down at recess yesterday and called a 'fuckin' *haole*.' And then Desiree's oldest girl, Kolea, told the mean kid to eat shit and die."

They burst out laughing and Nora wiped away tears.

"Intelligence-gathering, my dear. That's all." Alice put her arm around Nora's shoulders. "I just know you don't like to be taken by surprise."

"Well, she's welcome to Clyde. But there's a special circle in hell for women who try to take over other women's children." Nora's fists clenched so hard her fingernails dug into her palms.

Alice gave her a squeeze. "You're their wonderful, peerless mother, and they live with you. She can't have them."

Nora blotted her eyes with a crumpled tissue and blew her nose. "Why can't he just go on neglecting them? I should have known he'd come back in for the kill."

They looked at each other and began laughing again. Nora's chest loosened. What was the old saying? A sorrow shared is a sorrow halved.

"Mom." Oliver raced over, carrying a huge, lumpy breadfruit, already cracked on one side. "Come and watch this one."

They crossed the bridge to the rocky upstream side. Oliver pitched the round yellow globe over the wall. They huddled together and peered over the edge, watching the long, slow arc of its fall.

Splat. A fountain of yellow goo sprayed across the rocks below.

They cheered. "Yay! Best one ever." The children jumped up and down.

Nora hugged Oliver; he leaned against her for a moment, then wriggled away.

"Let's go down to the beach." The children glided down the hill on their scooters, yelling. Alice and Nora followed at a trot, their feet scuffing up the fallen leaves.

"The homeschooling group is eating her up, of course," Alice panted. "You know how impressed those California transplants are by wealth and sophistication—especially when it comes with an accent." She winked at Nora. "Personally, I think there's something off about her. I'm just not sure what. And it goes without saying, I hope the treacherous harlot rots in hell."

Nora heard a rumbling on the bridge behind them. "Car," she shouted down the hill. The children veered to the sides of the narrow road.

Ahead, the road flattened out and the view opened up. The crashing waves grew louder. When they reached the edge of the cliff, the ocean stretched out to meet the sky.

"Cheer up." Alice grinned. "Maybe she'll bugger off to Tahiti, or Clyde will bollix up the relationship too quickly for anything to happen. He does go through them, darling."

"I know. The children mention a new name just about every time they stay with him."

"Well then. I'll keep a watchful eye. Perhaps I'll lure Greta into my confidence and use her secrets against her."

Nora choked out a laugh. "And I can practice my psychic powers. Did I tell you about my new job?"

"You sly thing. Do tell."

They followed the children over the cliff's edge, down the steep dirt path through the trees to the rocky beach below.

CHAPTER 12

GEORGE WAS IN DENIAL, POISED AT THE EDGE OF A DROP OFF. How could this happen now?

His eighty-six-year-old long-widowed father's next-door neighbor had called that morning from Buffalo to say she had found the old man lying semiconscious in his kitchen. The paramedics said he must have slipped and wrenched his hip the night before. A miracle it wasn't broken. He was in the hospital in stable condition.

George, as the only child, knew he would have to sort things out. His father had Medicare, of course, but someone had to see to the house and organize nursing care when his father was discharged from the hospital. Someone meaning George. But there was no need to fly all the way back east, was there? Twelve hours one way. He was directing a play, for Christ's sake. Opening night was just a month away. The future of the Palace depended on him.

George had a wild thought. Maybe he could ask Cal to go in his place. No, things between them were shaky enough already. Besides, his father was physically incapacitated, not mentally, as far as he knew, and this was no time to spring a boyfriend on him. He might die of shock.

A long time had passed since George had seen George Sr. His had not been a happy childhood. His mother had died when he was a toddler, and his father hadn't known what to do with him. He'd alternated between ignoring George and whipping him with a belt when he was displeased—or drunk. George had never even considered discussing his attraction to other boys. He'd kept his head down, got straight A's and a scholarship to NYU, where he was finally able to become himself, at least moderately. He still majored in political science rather than theater, and then went to law school. He didn't go home for the holidays.

About twice a year George called the old man to check in, but their conversations never lasted more than five minutes or so. What was there to say? He had hoped his father would be proud that his son had become a successful lawyer, with his own personal injury practice. Instead, George Sr. muttered about ambulance chasing and insurance scams. George didn't mention he was also active in community theater and never missed a Broadway show. He had not dared to participate in the drama society at his high school, just watched with longing.

The time between phone calls had lengthened since his move to Hawai'i.

And now, right in the middle of a production, he was expected to drop everything and go running home to help his abusive father.

"Well, cheer up, darlin'." Cal came up behind George, slumped in a chair, and started to rub his shoulders. "The old fart may oblige you by getting pneumonia and dying. Once they're lying in a hospital bed, it's just a slow slide down to the end."

George snorted. "He would never do anything that convenient. You have no idea." He grunted with pleasure at Cal's touch.

Cal's parents in California were progressive and accepting, of course. Cal had come out to them as a teenager, and they'd been completely supportive. They treated George like a son-in-law. He still wondered what Cal saw in him, apart from the money. Cal made a pretty decent salary himself, even at the dysfunctional, money-hemorrhaging East Hawai'i Medical Center. Perhaps he was the Beast to Cal's Beauty: both challenge and rescue mission. He wondered how long Cal would wait around for the transformation George was sure would never come.

"You know, you don't have to go." Cal kissed the top of his head. "Social services will take care of things if you're unavailable. Does he have any money?"

"I'm not privy to that information." George sighed. A long gusty sigh. His father's sigh. "And I've already decided. I can't possibly go. They'll just have to cope with him themselves."

"Well then." Cal gave his shoulders one last squeeze. "Let me know if I can help."

IT WAS EASIER TO GET OLIVER AND MIRI TO GO TO THE THEATER now that they'd made friends with Desiree's kids and some of the other Munchkins, a few of whom also attended Po'okela Elementary.

Nora just couldn't stay away. All the rules she'd lived by seemed irrelevant now—holding back, not seeming too eager. Who cared? This was a new world. Fortunately, plenty of other hangers on liked to come and watch rehearsals, too, some of them not even in the cast or crew.

Free publicity, said George. Word of mouth buzz.

Tonight she recognized the jolly, shiny-headed man she and the twins had met at their first visit to the Palace. Phil. She had seen him at the auditions, too. When she'd thanked him for encouraging her to try out, he'd winked at her and tousled Miri and Oliver's hair, which they hated. Since then, he appeared every now and then to chat with George about Palace business. George always looked gloomy these days.

"Enjoying our performance?"

Nora had drifted into a delicious daydream, which now vanished in a poof. She flushed: the curse of the redhead.

Merle leaned against the low wall above the first section of seats and looked at her. "You're really beautiful. Sorry I keep staring at you, but you must be used to it."

Even while Nora registered the corniness of his pickup line, his voice melted over her like hot fudge over vanilla ice cream. She shivered.

"Do you mind my asking if you're married?"

"Not anymore." She held up her ringless hands and laughed.

"That's hard to believe. What man in his right mind would ever let you go?"

Nora choked on a giggle. A vision of Clyde's disapproving face hovered between them. "How about you?" She needed to be sure. No other woman role for her, even in a fling.

"Oh no, not for years. Still good friends with the ex, though. No children." He moved closer. "How old do you think I am?"

Nora laughed in pure enjoyment. "Mid-forties?" Why not flatter him?

"I'm fifty-three years old." He smiled triumphantly and ran his hand through his luxuriant, wavy, too-dark hair. "Not so bad for an old man, yes? But you—you couldn't be a day over thirty."

"Thirty-five, actually." She felt every year of it, the clock ticking, wrinkles appearing, especially in this sun-struck climate. Practically middle-aged.

"So young, so lovely."

She wished he'd stop talking and touch her. They were standing so close together she could feel his body heat.

"I want to take you out for coffee."

"I'd like that." But how? Maybe Belinda would babysit. She was so good with children. Or even Desiree. They could take turns looking after each other's kids. She needed to take the next step toward making friends other than Alice if she was going to survive in this town, even if they weren't kindred spirits. Nora saved the thought of what "coffee" might mean for later, when she could be alone with her torrid fantasies. Perhaps she could earn some money writing bodice-rippers as well.

"Places," Fred yodeled.

Merle gave her one last look and bounded back onstage.

She felt eyes on her and turned to see Phil grinning with all his big white teeth. The better to eat you with, my dear. He waved, and she waved back, reluctantly, her private joy sullied.

GEORGE HAD ANNOUNCED THAT THE VERY NEXT NIGHT, SATURDAY, would be devoted to perfecting "Lions and Tigers and Bears," and also the unfamiliar "Jitterbug" scene. Since it wasn't in the movie, Nora had never seen it. But everyone said "Jitterbug" was going to be a show-stopper—one way or another. Only one month until opening night.

Now, onstage, Merle flung his head back, sniffing the air in terror.

Nora gazed at him, not caring who saw.

Belinda demonstrated the steps to the Lion, Scarecrow, Tin Man, and Dorothy—again. Better this time. Some of the flying monkeys were also onstage, flapping around. The twins were absent, whisked away to Waimea that morning by their suddenly attentive father.

Nora felt tears start behind her eyes and held her breath to stop them. Self-pity was so tiresome. Besides, it was good for children to be close to both their parents.

George strode onstage and barked out orders, then motioned to Larry, who sat down at the keyboard and began to play.

The Witch and the young man, who turned out to be her visiting son, were onstage, too, measuring. Earlier, Evan the Tin Man had gotten pretty chummy with the son; Belinda kept having to call him back to work on his jitterbugging. Her usual cheerfulness showed signs of strain.

While the principals took a break, Belinda worked with the Flying Monkeys onstage. Their dancing was wild and passionate—not exactly in step, but infectiously fun.

A fierce pain stabbed Nora at the sight of the monkeys flinging themselves about. Oliver and Miri loved the flapping best. Kids always want to fly.

"Look at me, miss," Kolea, Desiree's eldest girl, shouted to Belinda, whom the children all adored. Kolea had real talent—and looks, her hair a mass of sun-streaked curls, her eyes a vivid blue against golden skin. Classic *hapa* beauty, as Nora was beginning to recognize. No wonder white supremacists didn't want racial mixing. The result was gorgeous.

"Fabulous job, monkeys." Belinda beamed at the children as they leaped and waved their arms. "I'm so proud of you."

"Hello beautiful," a voice murmured a few inches from the back of Nora's neck. Hot breath sent tingles through her body, which drove away all thought of sorrow.

⌣

"Ouch." Back onstage after the break, Evan grabbed his shoulder. "Something just hit me."

A rock lay a few feet away. Merle, Patrick and Mahina stood, transfixed, the "Lions and Tigers and Bears" scene at a halt.

"Not funny, Munchkins." George glowered into the wings. "Who threw the rock?"

Fred stuck his head out from backstage. "There's no one back here, actually." He walked out. "And I can't find Elmira Gulch's bicycle in the storeroom. Did someone take it?"

"You heard the man," George boomed. "Did someone ride off with the Witch's bike?"

"Who dares to take the bicycle of the Wicked Witch of the West?" Harriet snarled, glaring around the theater.

Merle guffawed.

Harriet had noted the growing attraction between Nora and Merle. They stood just a little too close together and laughed continuously. Why was Nora even at the theater tonight, if not to gawp at him? Fueled by her attention, Merle's signature exuberance had reached a manic pitch. Nora sat in the seats just below stage, enraptured, her ever-present twins absent for a change.

Harriet felt as though she'd stumbled onto the set of *A Midsummer Night's Dream*, except Shakespeare in the Park had been in July. Still, she had to admire Merle's unflagging talent and appetite for seduction. He must be around her age, and she had zero interest left in sex or romance. That part of her life seemed to be over, and good riddance. Just nature's cruel way of compelling you to reproduce.

"I suppose it was the ghost again." George did not look amused.

Scattered laughter and murmuring arose from the seats, where those not onstage sprawled or stood in clusters. The Flying Monkeys had camped out in the lobby, their shrill voices a distant cacophony.

George shrugged, and Fred went back to resume his search.

"Okay, people, let's run the scene again."

Mahina had smiled at Harriet this evening—a first. The girl actually had some artistic talent when she let up on the social maneuvering long enough to put brush to paper in Beginning Drawing and Painting class. This week Harriet had given her an A on her self-portrait, which showed attention to line and value, as well as brush strokes and shading. It was a haunting likeness—in spite of the anime eyes. One step at a time. Mahina was keeping up with her weekly sketches, too, always a source of grumbling among students. Harriet reminded them the idea for their final project would come from their sketchbooks, so they'd better stop flapping their jaws and get busy with their pencils.

From a nearby row of seats, Luke looked at Harriet with pleading eyes. Aunty Em had him trapped.

"Aunty was just telling me about the ghost." He bounced out of his seat as Harriet approached.

Thanks, son, she thought, careful not to sit down, even though her feet and legs ached—another delight of aging.

"There are several ghosts, you know. Poor souls lost in the tsunami." The old woman continued her tale, skewering Harriet with a keen eye. She seemed not to notice or care that her original audience had vanished. "When I was a girl, they used to sit with me in the balcony, dripping wet, every time I came to the theater. The nice one was a little girl about my age. But the nasty ones were a teenage boy and an older woman." She gave a throaty chuckle. "The boy pulled my hair and knocked things over. He nearly set fire to the projection booth once."

"My goodness." Harriet glanced around for a polite exit.

"But the old woman was the worst." Aunty Em's voice lowered to a hiss. "She used to grip my shoulders with hands that felt like talons." She made a little lunge at Harriet with claw hands and Harriet rocked backward, nearly losing her balance. "And then she would whisper into my ear that she was watching me, waiting to take me to the basement, where I would meet my doom. 'Soon, very soon,' she always said. I think she hated that I was alive and could leave the theater, while she was dead and trapped here forever."

Aunty Em threw up her hands in triumph. "And I'm still here."

"My goodness," Harriet said again. "So you think the teenage boy ghost is our prankster?"

"Oh yes." Aunty Em nodded vigorously. "But there was a fourth ghost I never saw, a man, who I heard was the worst of all. They say he killed people. In the basement."

"You don't say." Harriet ignored the shiver that passed through her. Must be a cool breeze wafting through the muggy air trapped in the big dome. She didn't believe in ghosts.

⌣

AT THE OLD TIME TAVERN, WHERE SOME OF THE CAST AND CREW had converged for drinks after rehearsal, a band started to play. Old guys with banjos.

Nora loved bluegrass.

Aunty Em had squeezed in to sit at the small table where Merle and Nora had retreated from the crush at the bar. Now, the old lady was knocking back Wild Turkey shots like nobody's business. Couldn't she see the sexual tension shimmering in the dim light? Nora shifted on her seat in annoyance.

Then Merle opened his mouth, and a flood of information gushed forth.

Nora tried to listen, but the band was so loud and Merle's voice so mellifluous she only heard a wall of pleasant, variegated sound.

Every now and then a word or phrase penetrated the roar until finally she sensed the torrent of words abating.

Merle was moving house. Some problem with the landlord. During his monologue, his eyes had locked onto Nora's as if she were the only person in the room.

She had stared right back, making interested noises, wishing he would shut up and touch her—all over.

Aunty Em let out a great belch and giggled. "Excuse me, dears, but when you're my age liquor creates quite a stir."

Nora sipped her watery Cosmopolitan—in retrospect, a poor choice at this beer and shots establishment.

Evan and Luke laughed at the bar with Desiree. Patrick chatted to the band members across the room.

Baseball-capped Fred was in close conversation with frizzy-haired Larry, an anxious look on his face, arms gesticulating. He was always worried about something. Probably George again—or the ghost, of course.

"Just this evening I felt a presence." Aunty Em signaled for another drink. "And I think it was the old man ghost I've never seen before." She gave an exaggerated shiver. "It was a different energy. Not eerie like the old woman ghost, or naughty like the boy ghost. And certainly not friendly, like the little girl ghost."

She had their attention. "No, this was a cold, powerful force. Evil and dangerous. It held me in my seat, like a weight on my chest, just toying with me. And then it was gone." She threw back the rest of her drink and picked up the replacement.

"Maybe we should try to communicate with it." Merle sat up in his chair. "I know a medium we could work with. Find out what this spirit wants—and the others, too."

"I don't think you want to find out what this spirit wants." Aunty Em shook her head. "All of us dead. Or worse."

"I'd like to attend a séance." Nora leaned forward. "I'm fascinated by the idea of ghosts." She grinned, dropping her voice to a spooky groan. "Who knows what lies beyond the grave?"

The band started up again, a bouncy number. Nora stood up. Enough talk.

"If you'll excuse us," she said to Aunty Em, and then to Merle. "May I have this dance?"

She held out her hand, and he took it, raised it to his lips, and drew her in close. They moved out to the dance floor, their bodies pressed together. Nora's mind hummed in a wordless trance of desire.

CHAPTER 13

ONE WEEK LATER—JUST THREE WEEKS BEFORE OPENING night—George's father started making trouble at the hospital in Buffalo. He wanted to go home.

"You think you can just put me away and take all my money!" was his usual greeting when the nurses put George through for his daily phone call. Sometimes he just asked them for an update and skipped the abuse.

"Now Mr. Hitchman, you should be nice to your son," George heard a nurse chide. She was probably checking his father's catheter bag. "He's calling all the way from Hawai'i and this is how you treat him?"

"It's just rehab, Dad, nothing permanent," George reassured the old man. "The doctor said you'll need nursing care and physical therapy before you can take care of yourself. Then you can go home." He had talked to his lawyer about getting power of attorney. It would be tricky. His father, however incapacitated physically, was still sharp mentally, not to mention verbally. George took a moment to envy his friends dealing with parents in the throes of dementia. His father would probably be a lot more pleasant if he lost his mind. At least he might forget he hated his son.

Cal would be better at this, thought George. He would charm and manipulate the medical staff. Maybe even charm and manipulate George's father. But probably not. George had never seen his father really take to anyone. He wondered, not for the first time, about his parents' marriage. How had the dour, irascible man he knew ever wooed a lovely young bride?

The phone line was still open. His father had probably dropped the receiver on the bed. George could hear the TV blaring. It sounded like an old Jeopardy rerun. George's memory drew up an image of his father at about the age George was now, his face rapt as host Alex Trebek uncovered the next square: "Famous red square shakable drawing toy."

"What is an Etch-a-Sketch." George's father had clenched his teeth in a fierce grin. "Morons. This show is for idiots."

"Dad," George began, but there was no reply. He could hear clapping and laughter on the TV. Then the line went dead.

꙳

"DAD SAID HE HAD A SURPRISE."

Nora glanced at Oliver in the rearview mirror. Clyde had demanded the children again this weekend, even though she had relayed George's decree that all cast members—including the Munchkin/Monkeys—must attend every rehearsal for the three weeks remaining until opening night. Nora wondered if she would have put up a fight if she weren't dying to be alone with Merle. She also had piles of research to do before she checked back in to the psychic hotline on Monday. Nine-to-noon five days a week. The work was nerve-wracking, but she was starting to get a feel for it. She'd realized her clients came in two flavors: lonely and fearful or angry and bent on revenge.

"Maybe it's a pony." Miri bounced in her seat.

"Well that would be a great surprise." Nora forced a tone of cheer. She was becoming skilled at insincerity. The other part of her brain sang a siren song. No matter how hard she tried to focus on the present, images of lips and flesh pressing together flashed in her mind and swirled down through her nerve endings.

The graceful old station wagon swooped around the lower curve of the gulch along the Hāmākua Coast highway and started climbing. Nora pulled into the right lane to let a souped-up lowrider pass her. The driver threw her a *shaka*, and she waved back, feeling a warm little glow of belonging. She was learning the customs of this place.

"Can we listen to Eric Clapton?"

"Sure, sweetie." Nora slipped the old cassette into the tape deck and the distinctive chords of "Cocaine" thumped out.

The twins started to sing along.

Nora told herself it was okay because the song was about the dangers of drug addiction—something she had pointed out to the children several times, just to make sure they understood.

She turned right to Ōʻōkala after the last gulch ("Number three," she and the twins always shouted) and pulled into the post office parking lot, the halfway meeting point between households. Abandoned and now overgrown sugar cane fields waved and rustled in the ocean breeze. Clyde's big truck was already there. Nora saw with a plunge of her stomach that he was not alone.

A tall, reed-thin woman with short, angular blonde hair stood next to the car with two blond children about the twins' age next to her. Clyde leaned against the gleaming hood, then straightened up and waved as Nora parked, and Miri and Oliver jumped out. Something was different about Clyde. The shape of his head. His gently receding hairline was slicked back, and—no, surely not! His longish hair was pulled into a tiny ponytail at the nape of his neck. As if this weren't enough, a groomed stubble darkened his face.

The twins hugged their father, then turned to the other children, who were obviously their friends.

Nora stiffened her spine and walked forward, smiling.

"Nora, this is my friend, Greta. Greta, Nora."

Nora moved to give Greta the half-hug and air/cheek kiss customary in Hawai'i, but Greta had already held out her hand, arm stiff, for a European handshake.

They shook hands and smiled.

Greta's eyes were hidden behind huge mirrored sunglasses, her hand bony and strong.

"Nice to meet you, Greta. Are these your—?"

"Come and meet Nora, children." Her voice cut in, husky and guttural.

Nora shook their small hands, smiling into their bright blue eyes. They looked like an advertisement for the Aryan Nation.

"Hans and Karen. They are excited to spend the weekend with their friends." Greta wore a short green linen dress with leather sandals, her long legs shapely and tanned.

Nora felt frumpy in her shorts, tank top, and rubber slippers, hair pulled into a ponytail. (Much thicker than Clyde's pathetic tuft.) She tried to stay out of the sun since her pale redhead skin freckled and burned.

"Greta's children are in that great homeschooling group now with Alice and Gabe's kids. They all miss Oliver and Miri." Clyde paused. "I'm not sure about that school they're in down in Hilo. Maybe we should reconsider."

Nora's temper flared. The entire time they had lived together in Waimea, Clyde had berated her about homeschooling instead of putting the twins in a private school they couldn't afford. He had called the group a joke. She took a deep breath. "Poʻokela is a wonderful little school. If we're going to live in Hawaiʻi, the kids need to learn about the culture and be part of the community."

"Calm down, Nora. No need to get defensive." Clyde held up his hands and smiled. "Just making a suggestion. Greta might even be willing to help out."

Greta just smiled, her large sunglasses giving her the look of a predatory insect.

"How kind." Nora's jaw hurt, and she unclenched her teeth. No point in rising to the bait. "So, what's this surprise the children have been talking about?" May as well get it over with.

"We're going riding this afternoon. Greta has horses."

"Daddy, can I ride a horse? Really?" Miri jumped up and down.

Nora kept a big smile on her face through sheer force of will. "How lovely. What a treat for the children."

"We can bring them to your house on Sunday afternoon," Clyde said, a note of triumph in his voice. "We're going to take all the children to a movie and have lunch somewhere in town. Any recommendations?"

Nora could only afford Bub's Drive-In or the Farmer's Market herself. "Café Rialto is always nice." She did not want Greta anywhere near her house. Invasion! STOP.

"Well, I'd best be off." Nora hugged the twins.

Oliver stiffened, then squirmed away in front of his friend, but Miri gave her a big kiss.

"Lovely to meet you." She smiled at Greta. So many smiles.

Greta smiled back and took Clyde's arm, her other arm wrapped around Miri's shoulders.

As Nora started the Volvo, trying not to gun the engine in despairing fury, she thought about a caller from earlier in the week. One of the angry, vengeful types convinced her husband was cheating on her. Nora had told her she saw green and gold, which signified money, so the betrayal might be a different kind. Always a safe bet. Who didn't have money problems? Also, there might be a money trail for an affair.

Brilliant job, Nora, she congratulated herself now. It had been her most successful psychic consultation to date. Steering with one hand as she pulled out, she rubbed under her cheekbones with the other to ease the tightness in her jaw.

And, she thought, bonus points for giving conformist, social-climbing Clyde a fit when he found out his ex-wife was working as a psychic. Even better, if he knew she was about to jump into bed with Merle the top of his head might just pop right off. He'd always been possessive, snarling at her if she so much as smiled at another man.

She laughed out loud and leaned into the steep downward curve of the first gulch. Merle, the Palace ghosts, her new career as a soothsayer—all in all, a perfect antidote for her mousy, dutiful past.

⌣

BACK IN HILO, HARRIET HAD AN APPOINTMENT OF A DIFFERENT kind.

She walked into Café Rialto, assaulted by the noise, but invigorated by all the humanity gathered in one place. Here she was, out on a Friday night for dinner with Luke and Evan, whose romance had taken off at full gallop. Da boyz. Her students were rubbing off on her.

Harriet had found a friend or two among the teachers at her school, as well as some bright, talented students. She'd always had natural authority, plus she remembered her own public school days on Oʻahu. She made short work of the unruly students who tried to wreak havoc in her classes—like Mahina, who she'd won over first by giving genuine praise for her painting, and second, clinching the deal, by putting her in charge of cleanup. Mahina loved to order her peers around, and with at least half the class vying for her approval, Harriet's classroom sparkled. This had gained her some respect from the old guard of teachers, some of whom saw her as another mainland *haole*, even though she'd grown up in the islands. Most of them were descended from Big Island plantation families, so she was an invader from Oʻahu as well as from California.

Harriet thought about the irony of this. Because she was white, any person of color looked more at home here than she did, even if they were just visiting. She felt, but did not look—would never look—like a native. Just the other day a grocery store checkout clerk had asked if she was enjoying her vacation.

Oh boo-hoo, she told herself. Poor privileged *haole* settler. She had been born and raised in Hawaiʻi, and no place else would ever feel like home, so there it was. She couldn't roll back time and right the injustices of the past, give the Hawaiian kingdom back to the people, erase her own family's long residence and land ownership in the islands—however reprehensible it all was. She should probably feel guiltier than she did, but Harriet had never been given to self-blame. Besides, teaching at the high school must count as public service, surely. A kind of atonement for her undeniable privilege.

A wall of windows faced the bay, and the ceiling formed a high dome over the broad expanse of black-and-white parquet floor crowded with tables, each with a single rose and a battery-operated candle. Potted palms stood in the corners, and lava-scape photos splashed color on the walls. The convivial buzz, punctuated by laughter and clinking plates and glasses, made her feel part of something larger, drawn into a communal gathering place.

Luke and Evan waved at her from a table next to the window.

Harriet pointed at them to the smiling hostess and made her way through the throng of chattering dinner guests.

As they both stood and leaned in for hugs and kisses, Harriet felt a warm surge of maternal pride in their glowing good looks and obvious happiness. Young love.

"We've been hauling lumber around all day," said Luke. "And huge cans of paint."

Harriet clapped her hands together. "The work day for the sets is this Sunday already—I'd nearly forgotten with all my school duties getting in the way. I'm up to my eyeballs in color wheels and algebraic equations. Can it really be only three weeks until we open?" She stretched her face into Munch's *The Scream*. "Thanks again for taking over for me, by the way."

"Your brilliant design." Luke smiled. "I'm just overseeing the grunt work. Easy."

"I've never worked on sets before," said Evan. "I'm not very artistic."

"Believe me, most of it isn't the least bit artistic." Luke waved his hand. "It's basic carpentry and wall painting. A child could do it."

Harriet grimaced. "Which is a good thing, since there will be no shortage of children."

They ate their seared ahi and drank a decent bottle of Sauvignon Blanc.

"I always know what to order for you, Ma." Luke smiled at her.

"The old lush." Harriet raised her glass.

Talk twisted and turned between the play and work and the theater. Evan's rock incident and the missing bicycle were much discussed. The latter had shown up again, painted bright red. Even more disturbing, Harriet's broom had also vanished, then reappeared in her classroom at Waiānuenue High, dangling from the ceiling. Mahina had sworn it wasn't her doing, but Harriet was skeptical. Who else could it have been?

They'd all noticed other oddities—hoots, creaks, and moans from below and above, doors slamming. To be expected in an old building, they agreed. Half the cast and crew were convinced the place was haunted. Aunty Em had indoctrinated them all. Even Harriet was sure she'd seen someone, not a stagehand, lurking in the basement shadows during her trapdoor scene.

"Not that I think it was a ghost, necessarily. Maybe the homeless folks have found a way in out of the weather. Wouldn't blame them." She shrugged.

"And I still think the rock was a Munchkin's doing, as well as the dog poop a few weeks ago." Evan laughed. "Some of those kids are out of control."

"Just full of unbridled energy, my dear," Harriet chided. "In need of good role models. Perhaps you two should volunteer to be Big Brothers. Help set them on the right path."

They looked at her, aghast.

Luke added, "Fred gave me an earful about some of the other props going missing, just small things, like the Lion's medal, the Scarecrow's straw, Toto's basket. Easily replaced. Of course, he's hysterical about it." They laughed, thinking of Fred's catastrophic propensities.

"And then there's Belinda's story." Harriet raised her eyebrows. "True, do you think? Or a bid for attention?"

Belinda had arrived late for rehearsal the night after Evan's rock-throwing incident, claiming someone had flattened her car's tires and written, "Boo!" on the windscreen with shaving cream.

Evan shifted in his seat and looked away.

"Yeah, seems strange." Luke scratched his head. "Don't ghosts stay in one place? How would it know where she lived?"

"Oh ha ha." Harriet winked. "Just like my broom miraculously showing up at school. If that wasn't Mahina, I'll eat my hat—if it doesn't disappear first."

They chuckled.

Evan leaned back in his chair. "On a related note, have either of you noticed anyone acting weird?"

Luke paused, his next bite hovering in the air. "Define weird. This is a theater production."

"Maybe Fred is playing the pranks himself—a case of theatrical Munchausen by proxy?" Harriet offered. "Or Griff. He's certainly an enigma."

"My money's on that bald board member, Phil," said Luke. "He's way too cheery and flamboyant. Must be hiding a criminal nature."

Evan leaned forward. "I think Desiree is up to something. Maybe not the pranks, but something."

"Glinda the Good?" Harriet drained her glass and widened her eyes. "Do tell."

"I've seen her going in and out of the basement door, and she looks worried."

"Hmmm. How odd." Harriet tapped her finger on the table. "She doesn't have a trapdoor scene. In fact, her part is quite small. So why is she there so often? I see her at all the evening rehearsals as well as Saturdays."

"Oh, come on, you two," Luke scoffed. "You know how people like to hang around the Palace. It's not like there's anything else to do at night in Hilo." They both looked at him and started to speak. He held up his hand. "No offense, but take my prime suspect, the ever-present, always-grinning Phil. He obviously has no life. Why shouldn't Desiree be there, too?"

"Doesn't she work as a bartender? We've seen her at the Aloha."

"Maybe she's meeting someone. A married lover?" Evan snickered.

"In the basement? Eew." Luke puckered up his face.

"The one with a lover is Nora, the redhead in the chorus. Merle has swooped down on her like a bird of prey." Harriet picked up her glass. "Don't tell me you haven't noticed."

"The gorgeous older guy with the bad dye job?" Luke leaned forward, and Evan shot him a dark look.

"He's a bit of a chancer." Harriet took a sip. "Calls himself a spiritual landscape designer. During last year's production of *Hello, Dolly*, he tried to talk us all into 'investing' money in some dubious 'gifting circle.' Some people actually fell for it and lost their stake."

"Poor Nora." Luke took a drink of his wine.

Harriet chuckled. "Perhaps not. Merle might be exactly what she needs right now."

"How do you know, Mom?"

"Not from first-hand experience, thank you, dear."

"Oh yeah?" Luke leaned closer. "Come on, spill."

"Just a colleague who had a fling with him a few years back, after he gave her garden a spiritual overhaul—it does look rather nice, by the way. She said he's harmless fun until he starts asking for money." Harriet dabbed at her mouth with her napkin. "Since Nora has just taken some sort of phone hotline job to supplement her child support payment I doubt he'll get much out of her."

They passed on dessert, even though the crème brûlée with 'ōhelo berries looked enticing. Harriet kissed them both good-bye—da boyz—and they ushered her into her car, waving as they walked down the street.

Harriet felt unsettled. What was bothering her? Desiree? Nora and Merle? Was she worried or envious or just getting old? Maybe it was time to join the Red Hat Society and start wearing huge chunky jewelry and bright flowy clothes. She could embrace her age and espouse a complete disregard for decorum. Take up plein air painting—in the nude. If Howard could be so disappointingly predictable in late mid-life, so could she.

She shook her head and started the engine.

CHAPTER 14

IRIS CAME UP BEHIND MOSES KAPILI AS HE POKED STEAKS ON the barbeque grill and put her arms around him, leaning her head against his back.

"Whoa. Hey, that feels nice." He flipped the steaks over with an expert motion. "Nearly done, here. Anything else I can do to help?" A flame shot up and he doused it with beer.

This was all so new to Iris, this man energy. Not to mention the huge slabs of meat. She had shut herself off from even the thought of romance for so many years, intent on creating a safe, female bubble to inhabit with her daughter. But now, with Mahina pulling away from her, growing more independent every day and having relationships of her own, Iris had begun to feel her own need. Being with a man, with Moses, was dizzying, but she was open to it. Maybe one bad choice didn't have to define her life after all.

Mahina was out with Keola. She'd been so secretive lately, Iris was never sure what she was doing. Come to think of it, when had she last consulted their horoscopes? She used to keep such careful track of the stars and planets that affected them, but it had been weeks now, even months, since the astral plane had even crossed her mind.

Well, too bad, Iris thought. I love my daughter, and it's also my turn. I'm not doing anything wrong by having a healthy relationship with a good man. In fact, I'm setting a fine example and filling our home with positive energy.

Moses was forty, only five years older than Iris, and had grown up on O'ahu. Every few months he flew over to visit his big extended family, and they all roared off in trucks to fish, drink beer, and talk story at their favorite campsite.

This was an alien concept to Iris, and she felt conflicted when he talked about it. Was she jealous or threatened because he was so close to his family? Or was she just sad she hadn't been able to provide that experience for her daughter? How could she when she'd never had it herself?

Moses was a veteran of the first Gulf War, but he didn't like to talk about it. He'd spent ten years on the mainland, married, and divorced—no children—and then missed Hawai'i too much to stay away any longer. She wondered how a handsome, kind, successful man like him had managed to avoid getting tied down again, or at least reproducing, given the guppy-like tendency of so many women she knew who just popped out babies with whichever man they happened to be seeing.

Iris considered it in poor taste to have children with more than one partner. This judgmental attitude was out of step with her inclusive, New Age beliefs, and she kept it to herself. But she was surprised by how many mature women did it, as though a couple had to have children together to legitimize and solidify their relationship. Iris felt just the opposite. She would never have another child. Even with the money, it had been hard and lonely raising Mahina by herself. Despite her best efforts, the girl had grown up with a chip on her shoulder about men—fathers in particular. It was probably too late for any other man to fill even a fraction of the void left by her absent father, or to help Mahina see that not all men would disappear when you needed them most.

Iris laughed at herself. So much for her intention to have an evening focused solely on her own desires; she seemed incapable of it. The pathways in her brain were entrenched. Her thoughts ran through them as effortlessly as water through an irrigation system, feeding the same instincts and impulses that had consumed her for the seventeen years since she had first discovered she was pregnant with Mahina. At least Ziggy's strange adventure had not been repeated, and Iris's worries had subsided. No secrets from her past were going to surface. Her daughter was safe.

It was time for some groundbreaking. New channels, new roads, new ideas to nourish. She would have to get back into a regular meditation practice—starting tomorrow morning.

Iris and Moses sat outside at the mosaic-topped table she had found at a Puna estate sale. The wide *lanai* opened to the dark expanse of lawn bordered by hibiscus hedges. Candles flickered and soft music floated through the French doors from the living room.

"So, what's new downtown?" Iris leaned across the table. She loved to hear Moses's tales about his colleagues, the strange crimes people committed, the odd characters who came into the station, and the stories they told. She knew it must be routine and sordid in many ways, but he always found the unusual, amusing, or touching parts in every story. He was a student of human nature and eccentricity. An old soul.

"Well, actually, things are getting serious." Moses paused to chew his steak, wiping his mouth with a napkin.

Good looks and table manners too. Iris knew it shouldn't matter, but it did. She could observe that thought and not judge it.

"There's a pretty active meth operation in Hilo." He took a drink of wine and then filled both of their glasses from the bottle of pinot noir he'd brought because he knew it was her favorite.

Iris sipped her smooth, rich wine and looked into the dark green depths of the garden. The air was slightly cool, but balmy, velvety with moisture. She felt it nourishing her skin.

"How terrible." The idea of drugs and danger seemed incongruous in this setting. Iris gloried briefly in the lovely, sheltered life she had created here on the island, a life where she controlled her own narrative.

"We've had our eyes on several local guys for a while, but there's definitely someone higher up the chain calling the shots." Moses ate a bite of green salad. "We think he's fairly new in town, maybe a couple of years. Definitely the marks of organized crime. Our usual guys aren't professionals. He is."

"How can you tell?" Iris felt a chill as a breeze wafted in. She might have to slip on a cardigan. Just a thin layer.

"Mainly the volume and spread. Things have really picked up. And there's definitely a drop point in the old downtown area, which is unusual. We're not sure where. The drug trade usually stays out in Puna." An owl screeched, and the ghostly white bird floated overhead and disappeared over the hedge. "The new police chief is dragging his feet on letting me put together a real task force. Says we don't have the money, and there isn't enough evidence to justify one."

Iris was struck by a sudden irrational fear. She'd been letting Mahina go to the Palace at night by herself. The girl was sixteen, after all, and had her own car, thanks to the trust fund. Iris had been trying to let her daughter grow up, loosen the apron strings, stand back and trust the universe. But Mahina was her life. What if she stumbled onto something at the theater she wasn't supposed to see? Iris gave her head a little shake and closed her eyes tight.

Then she opened them. She would not succumb to fear. She would be positive, radiating light from the light within her. Mahina was perfectly safe. And now Iris had someone else in her life, too. She had put her past away. She had created her surprisingly successful career.

Iris enjoyed the real estate business: the clients, the houses, all that possibility. She loved to imagine the lives people could create in each empty structure just waiting to become a home, full of energy, sound, and color. Iris prided herself on her ability to match people with houses that would bring them happiness.

She had done it for herself and Mahina. She had created a good life, a happy life, in this house. Nothing, and no one, was going to take it away from them. But this didn't mean no additions were possible.

"Are you all right?" Moses had stopped talking and was looking at her with concern.

She smiled at him across the table, then reached out her hand. He took it and squeezed.

⌣

RELATIONSHIPS WERE ALSO IN THE FOREFRONT OF PATRICK'S mind. Something was definitely going on with Cindy, he thought, busy in his Volcano workshop the next morning. What he'd put down to bad moods and relationship doldrums had morphed into an almost complete withdrawal. He tightened the screw to hold a *koa* blank in place. A little distance was healthy, but this was more extreme.

Patrick turned on the lathe and squinted through cloudy safety goggles to guide his hand on the chisel. Must remember to clean them. He hated to admit it, but Cindy had been right about the flood of creativity. He'd been turning bowls like crazy since his success with the mango. He felt invincible.

She had started staying out late "with the girls." What girls? In the two years they'd been together, Cindy had never been one to hang around with women friends. She'd moved in with him, and they'd been more or less inseparable. Which had been a problem, Patrick admitted. In fact, he'd tried out for the play partly just to get some time to himself.

He pressed harder on the chisel as the rough bowl began to take shape. The familiar smell of fresh sawdust wasn't soothing today.

Cindy had also been ignoring his amorous advances. When he sang love songs in the shower and then lay naked on the bed in the late afternoon, she always used to join him. It was their unspoken signal. But now she just stayed in the other room until he felt chilled and had to pull on his clothes. He'd even picked wild ginger—her favorite—and presented her with a bouquet. She'd just pecked his cheek and put the delicate blossoms in a jar of water on the kitchen table, where they quickly wilted and turned brown.

This was serious. At thirty-eight, she wasn't old enough to be menopausal, was she? Patrick made a mental note to google it. Come to think of it, how long had it been since they had made love? Two weeks? Three? They used to do it at least two or three times a week, if not more. Cindy had always been so responsive.

Patrick stopped the lathe. What was going on? He realized his own perversity. He'd been bored with her, irritated by what he'd labeled her controlling behavior—and now he missed it.

If she were a man and a woman friend were telling me this, he thought, unscrewing the rough-hewn bowl and setting it on the drying shelf, I'd think it was an affair.

Was Cindy having an affair? Was she about to leave him?

Patrick wasn't sure how he felt about that.

On one hand, if Cindy left him, maybe it would give him the jolt he needed to get on with the next stage of his life, whatever that might turn out to be. Go back to school? Write a book? Become a better man? On the other, did his ambivalence prove something vital in him was missing? If he were a whole person, wouldn't he feel the drive to hang on when a relationship became less pleasure and more work, instead of just shrugging his shoulders and waving goodbye?

Patrick looked at the clock on his workshop wall. Time to stop brooding about his character flaws and practice his songs for this afternoon's rehearsal with the orchestra. He found himself looking forward to rehearsals more and more. The companionship and humor of the theater group buoyed him up. Even George's autocratic grumpiness masked a deep vein of caring—or at least they all joked that it did. He had chosen them, and they were worthy. Wasn't every relationship a matter of interpretation? The shenanigans, as Patrick always thought of them, just added an extra fillip of excitement, like last weekend's rock-throwing episode. The vandalized bicycle was more annoying, but still easily remedied.

Why was it the farther down the mountain he drove, the lighter his spirits became, and conversely, the higher he ascended on the way home, the heavier his mood weighed? Was it Cindy? His not-as-exciting-as-he'd-hoped-it-would-be "real life"?

He closed the door of his workshop—Cindy always called it his studio—and walked along the path toward the house. She had gone out to see a client this morning. Was it really a client? Patrick shook his head, trying to dislodge his suspicions. But her car was back in the driveway now. He quickened his step.

⌣

TONIGHT WAS GOING TO BE THE NIGHT. NORA COULD TELL Merle would leave it up to her—lady's choice—and she was ready. Boy, was she ready. She was grateful for this infatuation—and always careful to call it that so she didn't get silly about it. Her feelings for Merle helped calm the panic that had overtaken her when she drove away from the twins, leaving them with Clyde and Greta and their quasi-stepsiblings. She could not afford to let paranoid fantasies of losing the children take over. Fantasies of sex were much healthier, and the real thing would be better still.

She would spend a few hours on the "teach yourself to be a psychic" website she'd found, and then get ready for the big Saturday afternoon rehearsal with the orchestra. And what followed. You're a free woman, Nora told herself. Shake off the foreboding. This is good.

After their first date the weekend before—if you could call drinks with the cast a date—Merle had said he wanted to cook for her. Their plan was to spend the evening at his house tonight, after rehearsal—even though, he warned her, everything was in boxes pending his move. He was waiting to pack up the kitchen last. She could use his bathroom to "freshen up." He actually used the term, which Nora found amusing.

Merle often used quaint words and phrases, which reminded her of their age difference. He also sounded like a self-help audio book sometimes—with paranormal overtones. But who cared? Certainly not her, not now. Come to think of it, what was wrong with making affirmations and believing in astral traveling and reincarnation anyhow? Nothing. Where had her fatalism and overdeveloped sense of irony gotten her? Nowhere she wanted to be, that was for sure. Meeting Merle—and getting this job—were signs. This was her chance to shake off her western rationalist mindset and embrace New Age positive thinking and mysticism. She may not be a real psychic, not yet, but she would try to stop thinking so much and believe in possibilities instead. She would roll around in suggestibility. What could it hurt? She wasn't on the mainland anymore.

Nora reclined on her bed, laptop closed beside her. She pushed aside images of Clyde, Greta, and the children and let her mind slip sideways into a graphic fantasy about dinner at Merle's and what would follow—or precede. This would be her first sexual encounter since she left Clyde. But she wouldn't think about him. Sex in their relationship had been another miry area of competition and guilt and putting her to the test. That was all over now. This was going to be so much better. She lay there in the sultry morning air, imagining.

~

GEORGE'S FATHER HAD FINALLY AGREED TO SPEND A WEEK IN the rehabilitation center, a special wing of the assisted living complex near his home. After that he'd be on his own until the next accident.

"You did your best," Cal comforted him. "That's all you can do. I see this constantly with my patients and their families. Old men are the worst. They think they're indestructible even though evidence to the contrary is shoved right up under their noses."

George sighed and rolled his head back and forth. Between phone calls back east and rehearsals at the Palace, his neck was holding a lot of tension.

Cal moved over to massage it with his strong professional fingers.

God, he'd almost forgotten. The orchestra was coming to the Palace at three p.m. today. They could only afford one music rehearsal before the nightly marathons during Hell Week, and today was the day.

"Now may not be the best time to bring this up," Cal said.

George's neck went rigid as he dragged his attention back to the present. What now, for god's sake?

"Lydia said her temperature was up a degree this morning."

"What?" George was baffled. He pulled away and rubbed at his neck in irritation. "Who is Lydia? And why should I care about her temperature?"

"I should have known you weren't listening." Cal frowned, his hands dropping to his sides.

George remembered all the long talks they'd been having—or, to be more accurate, the monologues Cal had been delivering every night as they lay in bed and George's mind raced between Buffalo and Hilo until he was so exhausted he fell asleep. Cal's voice had been so soothing he'd listened to the sound of it, not paying attention to the sense. Every now and then he'd grunted assent to keep the words flowing. What had Cal been saying?

"I just don't know anymore, George." Cal shook his head. "Can't you even listen to me when it's something important? I thought you'd agreed."

"I was under duress, damn it." George moved toward him, but Cal held up his hand. "Okay. Tell me now—please. I'm listening."

Cal turned his back, his arms folded together.

"Who is Lydia?" George put his hand on Cal's shoulder and turned him around.

"She's going to have our baby." Cal's eyes filled with tears and he smiled, his lips trembling.

⌣

KICKING OFF HIS WORK SHOES ON THE MAT OUTSIDE, PATRICK opened the door to the house and walked in. "Cindy?"

A muffled sound came from the living room.

Cindy sat in the rocking chair by the window, gazing out into the garden. She held a mug and hiccupped.

"Hey, what's going on?" Patrick walked over, shocked by her puffy, tear-streaked face.

She shook her head.

"Come on, what happened?" He knelt down and took the mug out of her hand. Oof. It smelled like silage, a whiff of his youth in Eastern Washington, abandoned these many years. Youngest of five strapping boys on the wheat farm, the black sheep who'd gone astray. Now his older brothers were entrepreneurs with thriving vineyards, wholesome wives, and sturdy children, the pride of their grandparents. They liked to tease Patrick about his "alternative lifestyle" when he came back for family reunions—less and less frequently.

Cindy put her face in her hands and sobbed. Patrick took out a handkerchief and gave it to her. She blew her nose and wiped her eyes. They were swollen to red slits.

He waited, counting to ten.

"I'm so sorry, Patrick." She looked at him and burst into tears again. "It's my hormones."

"Your hormones?" He rocked on his haunches, feeling the strain in his thighs. He'd have to start going to yoga classes again.

"I'm leaving you." Cindy hiccupped.

"What?" Patrick stopped rocking and stared at her. He hadn't actually thought she would do it. It was just a theory, a fantasy. He felt queasy.

"Mac and I—well. I didn't mean to. It just happened." Cindy sniffed and blew her nose again.

Mac. Yellow blobs swam in Patrick's vision.

"And I'm pregnant. Please try to be happy for me." She turned her suddenly smiling, shining face on Patrick, who sat back on the floor with a thump. A thick greenish fluid slopped over onto the floor, and he set down the mug.

"Careful! Those are my Chinese pregnancy herbs," Cindy snapped. "I traded a massage for them."

"Is it mine?" Patrick's heart pounded in his ears.

"No, Patrick, the baby is not yours." Her voice rose in a crescendo. "You know how I know? Because we haven't had sex for three months, that's why."

"No!" Patrick exclaimed. Then, "It's been that long?" He was dumbfounded. That couldn't be right. He'd thought three weeks tops. But maybe his memory was going the same way as his body.

"You're not interested in me anymore, not for a long time. And Mac is. I've tried and tried with you, and you just don't care. Mac loves me." Cindy sounded triumphant, her teary eyes glittering. She threw the handkerchief down on the floor and stood up. Did her stomach already look round?

"Okay, easy does it." Patrick struggled to his feet, knocking over the mug. More green sludge spread across the floor and seeped into the edges of the Turkish carpet.

"Jesus, Patrick!" Cindy shrieked.

"I'm sorry, Cindy. I'm in shock. Mac?" Anger started to bubble in his gut. "I can't believe you would do this to me." He shook his head, struggling to control his surging emotions. "Do you love him?"

"He's the father of my child." Cindy wrapped her arms around her belly. "I just came over to say goodbye. I thought I owed you that. I'm moving in with him."

Patrick noticed a couple of bulging duffel bags near the entry-way. They both belonged to him.

"I'll clear out the rest of my stuff as soon as I can." Cindy moved to pick up the bags, but Patrick got to them first.

"I'll carry those." She shouldn't do any heavy lifting.

Patrick felt hollow and disoriented. Should he protest? Beg her to stay and let him help raise the child? Was he really as uncaring as she implied? He must be if he'd driven her into the arms of that poser. Had she just been a warm body in bed to him, an occasional home-cooked meal—casual companionship? If so, maybe he deserved to live alone. But then he wouldn't feel this miserable, would he?

"Goodbye Patrick." Cindy hugged him and kissed his cheek.

He held her until she pulled away.

Patrick fit the bags into her car and closed the hatchback, stepping away as she reversed and turned. He watched the car roll down the driveway, its red taillights glowing in accusation.

CHAPTER 15

THREE WEEKS BEFORE OPENING NIGHT, DESIREE PONDERED A new dilemma. What should she do with all the money? This was not a problem she'd ever faced before.

Hunter paid her five hundred dollars in cash for each delivery, and the pace had picked up to three or four packages a week now. After the first set of hundred-dollar bills, Desiree had asked for fifties, which were less conspicuous, although still a little rich for her blood. Twenties were more her style, but the bulk would be unmanageable. She now had six grand stuffed under the bras and thongs in her underwear drawer. So much cash didn't feel safe in the tiny apartment.

Her first impulse was to spend it. Fly to Oahu and hit the boutiques at Ala Moana Shopping Center. But Desiree was clear about why she was taking such a tremendous risk. She wanted more for her children than she could afford on her bartending salary plus tips. Too bad her knowledge of money management was a big fat zip.

The obvious first step was to start paying for everything—rent, food, utilities—in cash, so her legitimate earnings could go into a bank account. Maybe even investments. How did you do that? Desiree was not risk-averse—obviously—but she had seen how fast you could blow your wad on bad stocks. She still remembered the dot.com crash in 2000. Grown men crying into their drinks, moaning that if only they'd sold the week before they'd be million-aires. But they hadn't. Of course. Because they were dumb greedy schmucks. Like most people, including her.

No, she would be smart. She would use this money to turn her life around and lift her children out of the gutter. *She* would be their fairy godmother. Evan was a financial planner, and he must be good if George trusted him. Maybe she could pick up some free advice during rehearsals.

Desiree bent over the counter in the bathroom and stared into the cloudy mirror, carefully brushing on mascara. God! She was turning into a hag. Look at those dark circles under her eyes and the way the flesh pouched up a little at the bottom of her cheeks, like it was sliding off her face and didn't quite know where to go.

Hunter had finally dropped the dating pretense. It was a re-lief not to make conversation over dinner while her blood pres-sure spiked. Now they just met several times a week to exchange packets of drugs or money. Hunter changed the venue each time: Wailoa Park, with its arched bridges and spreading trees, the break-wall jutting out into Hilo Bay, wide enough to walk on, the big cem-etery off Ponahawai Street with manicured grass and flowers at ev-ery grave—even once in the musty nonfiction stacks at the Public Library. Weird.

Desiree's three children were crammed on the couch watching TV in the tiny living room. Cars screeched past on the narrow road below.

"Get off your butts, we have to go sing now. The orchestra is coming—it'll be cool." She tried to sound enthusiastic.

"Can we stay home and watch TV, pleeeeeease? It's a Power Rangers marathon, Mom." They didn't even turn their heads in her direction.

"Nope, it's time to go." Desiree grabbed the remote out of Nakai's hand and turned off the TV, ignoring their shrieks of outrage.

"Ice cream after rehearsal if you're out the door in 5, 4, 3, 2..."

The children scrambled for the door and spilled out onto the narrow balcony.

Time to make another delivery. Desiree took her handbag down from the high shelf in the closet where she always kept it now.

Follow the yellow brick road, she thought, and closed the door behind her.

⌣

EVEN WARMING UP, DESIREE COULD TELL THIS ORCHESTRA WAS A huge cut above the high school groups she'd performed with so many years before. Her blood stirred to see the musicians lift their instruments out of velvet-lined cases and deftly fit them together, to hear the toots and wails and drum beats, the swoop of bow on strings, to feel the camaraderie between the musicians, as well as their laser-like focus, as they set up their music stands and spread out their scores. This was going to be a real, professional show. Bigger than anything she'd been a part of before.

"They get paid. That's why we only have them once before Hell Week," Fred had explained to her when she asked. Larry had a cadre of seasoned musicians he called on for Palace productions. This rehearsal was just to give the cast a feeling for what it would be like to sing with the orchestra, now that they knew the music, as well as a meet and greet between cast and musicians. "We can barely afford this, between you and me." Fred added. "We really need some more donations to cover their costs for the run. And we have only three weeks left till we open." He grimaced and bustled off.

Paid performers. Desiree felt lucky to do it for free. In her world, pay was for tasks you wouldn't choose to do otherwise.

BACKSTAGE, MAHINA HEARD A SOUND THAT MADE HER NECK hairs stand up. Someone was singing her song. And singing it really well, the notes high and pure. She followed the sound up the back staircase to the catwalk and stuck her head into a little alcove she'd never seen before, high above stage. Good thing she wasn't afraid of heights.

Moku's long hair was stuffed into a striped Rasta hat today as he rummaged through the dusty props and old set pieces piled against the walls. He was just belting out the refrain, "Somewhere over the rainbow," when he saw Mahina and stopped short. "Hey, don't get your panties in a wad. Bruddah Iz sang this song, too. Dudes can sing soprano—even huge dudes." He spread out his hands and laughed. "What can I say? I'm a natural."

Mahina laughed, her temper flare fizzling. Moku was different from any of the other teenagers she knew. He didn't seem to care what people thought of him. "What are you doing up here?"

"Scavenging for materials. Amazing what you can find up here from old productions. All covered in rat shit, but who's complaining?" Moku handed her a two by four. "Make yourself useful, girl-friend—got a show to put on."

Ziggy bounded up the stairs behind her and trotted over to the corner of the alcove, sniffing. He started to bark, a series of sharp yips.

"Hey tiny brah, what's the matter?" Moku picked up the quivering little body and looked down. "Hmmm. Cigarette butts. They still stink. Maybe the ghost smokes Camels."

"You'd better tell George." Mahina didn't want to think about Ziggy's probable abductor being here, so close. "He'll pitch another fit, this time about burning the place down." She started down the stairs, carrying the splintery piece of wood. Talk about a creep fest. What next?

"Okay, we're starting. Everyone on stage," George bellowed from below.

⌣

AFTER THEY FINISHED SINGING AND THE MUSICIANS WERE PACKing up their gear, Desiree made her way through the hallway backstage. The children were playing with other Munchkins in the lobby, so if she was quick, they wouldn't come looking for her. She slipped through the basement door—unlocked—and closed it behind her, padding down the steps. She didn't even turn on her flashlight, although she held it in her hand like a club.

As she reached the basement floor, someone grabbed her arm and she stifled a scream, lashing out with the flashlight.

A light shone in her eyes.

"Why are you here?"

She pointed her own beam at the voice.

It was Griff. His eyes fixed hers with a wild glare. Was he Hunter's pickup man?

"Let go of me." Desiree shook him off.

Griff turned and held his hands to the warmth of the big metal organ blower. "You shouldn't be here. You aren't supposed to be down here."

"Who made you boss of the basement, mister?" Desiree's heart rate was slowing, but she was still on high alert.

"It's the other one they want."

"What are you talking about?" Desiree stared at him. "Who are 'they'?"

Griff shook his head. "You shouldn't be here." He climbed up the stairs.

Oh good grief, thought Desiree. What a kook. She was shaken up, unsure of what to do. Maybe the drop spot was compromised now. This was getting crazy. If Griff was poking around he could find the meth—and point to her. She couldn't risk it. She would have to tell Hunter, and he would probably blame her, think she had been careless. But she hadn't. No one else had seen her. Had they?

Desiree stood in the darkness, fingering the packet in her purse.

◡

GRIFF HAD TROUBLE KEEPING THE VOICES DOWN ON THE DRIVE home. They were getting louder, whispering, jabbering, accusing. He didn't want to hear what they were saying. They were wrong. The last time he'd listened to them, back on the mainland, he'd ended up in the psych ward. He'd been lucky it was overcrowded and they'd had to discharge him. That was right before he'd gone up north, before he'd found his new identity.

He hit the side of his head but it didn't help. *Pakalolo* tamped the voices down. He grew his own supply of top-grade weed, as did so many Big Island residents, although some of them, at least, had medical marijuana licenses. He'd roll a fat one when he got home.

⌣

MERLE LIVED IN AN OLD PLANTATION HOUSE VERY LIKE NORA'S, but even more dilapidated and with no view. She followed him home after rehearsal, keeping his rusty little car in sight as he raced through the narrow streets. He hadn't exaggerated. The house was bare and full of boxes. When she'd asked where he was moving, he'd been vague. A scarred wooden table and two chairs sat on the cracked kitchen linoleum, and a large mattress covered with sheets and a blanket lay on the floorboards of the small bedroom, nearly filling it. Nora's heart rate quickened as she peered around the corner and saw the makeshift bed.

In the kitchen, Merle was stirring a big pot on the stove. Shirtless.

"I hope you don't mind something simple," he said. Saimin?"

"Sounds just right." Nora looked out the window into the darkness of palm fronds. "I'm not very hungry." She felt shivery and tingly, like she might need to sit down and put her head between her knees.

"I feel sorry for your ex." Merle threw a chopped onion into the pot. "He must be grieving for what he's lost."

Nora gave a short laugh. "I can assure you he's not. He's got a rich girlfriend and affects a sparse ponytail with accompanying male-model stubble."

"Don't be so certain." Merle turned to look at her. "Sometimes people can't even admit to themselves when they've made a terrible mistake, but it doesn't mean they're not suffering."

"Right now, I think he's more interested in trying to take the children away from me. He wants to win." Nora felt tears well up in her eyes. Damn it. She wasn't supposed to be thinking about this. Couldn't she even let herself be seduced without bringing her children into it? "Never mind. Forget I said that."

"It's okay. You have to feel what you feel. It's not good-bad-right-or-wrong." Merle chopped up one of those rubbery fishcakes Nora had seen in the grocery store. He threw in the chunks—lurid pink on the outside, pasty white on the inside. What were they actually made of? But if eating fishcake was part of embracing the moment, she would do it with gusto.

Nora walked across the room and laid her hand on Merle's back. She could feel him quiver.

"Don't stop." He didn't turn around. "It feels so good to be touched. It's been a long time."

"For me, too." Nora rubbed her palms against his warm skin, feeling awkward but thrilled. Her hands trembled.

"You can tell me anything, you know." Merle turned around. "I'm a spiritual guide."

"I'm enjoying our focus on the physical right now." Nora smiled up at him.

"Spirituality *is* physical." Merle drew her in and kissed her. It was electrifying, like the song from *Grease*.

He reached behind him and turned off the burner.

"Won't dinner be ruined?" Nora pushed back her hair and tried not to gasp for breath.

"I haven't put the noodles in yet." He smiled. "It will be fine. And so will you, I promise."

"I'm counting on it." She took his hand.

CHAPTER 16

WHEN PATRICK ARRIVED HOME FROM THE ORCHESTRA RE-
hearsal, it was late afternoon in shady Volcano, and the
house was dark. He reached for one of his home-brewed IPAs and
noticed he was down to the last dozen bottles. If he didn't place an
order with the brewing supply store soon, he'd have to buy beer for
the first time in years.

Everything was slipping.

Patrick sat on the porch swing, taking an occasional refreshing
pull from the bottle as he gazed into the semi-darkness of the ʻōhiʻa
and hāpuʻu forest. A breeze rustled the leaves and brought up a
fresh, green earthy scent. He wondered why both sound and scent
seemed to intensify at night. A science major would know.

Solitude pooled around him, reflecting its silvery light. He felt
he might drown in it.

Did he only want what he couldn't have? Was he that sort of person?

He had to take action before the emptiness engulfed him. What
was he doing with his life?

Substitute teaching was a thankless, soul-crushing task, a matter of cunning and endurance that Patrick had become pretty good at over the years. In the beginning he had relied on candy and videos. Let's face it, he still did. But now he actually tried to do some teaching. He had developed relationships with some of the faculty, like Harriet, who left lesson plans and materials for him when they were out for workshops, and he had an occasional day where he felt he really connected with the students. Engaging their attention and getting them to think was gratifying. Exhilarating, even.

He had thought many times about going back to school to get his teaching credential, but it just seemed like such a slog. Besides, it was far too much like a career he might have chosen if he hadn't left home in the first place. Subbing was temporary—no commitment, no settling down. His prospects still hovered out there in a bright haze of possibility.

But why not sign up for some education classes? Just do it instead of thinking about it? He'd heard certification only took one year. Hilo U was cheap by comparison with other colleges, and he was a Hawai'i resident, after all. Single. Childless—at least for now. If he hated it he could quit. With Cindy gone, he had no one to please or displease but himself. What else was he going to do in a year anyhow?

Patrick thoughts zoomed back to Cindy's pregnancy. He was forty-five years old. He liked children. Did he truly want the baby to be his? He was sure she was wrong about the last time they had sex. He thought about this for a few minutes, drinking beer and swinging, smelling the air. This could be his last chance at fatherhood. Could he really stand back and let a bounder like Mac raise what might be his child? How could he be this old and still not feel old enough to have children? Was it because he was the youngest child in his own family, still teased by older siblings? Or was he just another aging hippie-wannabe unable to take responsibility for his own life, let alone another's? This felt uncomfortably close to the truth.

On the other hand, he did own his own home. Lucky he'd bought it back when Big Island real estate was cheap, and he'd still had enough of his grandmother's bequest for a hefty down payment. Three bedrooms, two bathrooms: big enough for a family. He had his bowl-turning. He had regular employment as a sub, which made him a semi-decent living. He wasn't doing too badly. But somehow he didn't feel like a real adult. What was he doing, living with a series of women who always left him for someone more stable or prosperous or at least more enthusiastic?

The bottle was empty. Patrick rose from the swing and walked down the short gravel path to his workshop. Some of his bowls were nearly dry enough to finish. He had to keep an eye on them. Maybe he'd do some more turning tomorrow, get a few pieces finished for the Volcano Sunday Market next weekend.

When he switched on the light, his eyes went directly to the shelf where he'd placed his perfect mango bowl: his magnum opus. He had just finished oiling and waxing it a few days earlier, and it was ready to go. He'd decided to enter it in the annual East Hawai'i Woodworkers' Contest coming up the same weekend *The Wizard of Oz* opened.

Something wasn't right. Patrick blinked his eyes and looked around the room, searching. His eyes came back to rest on the shelf. It couldn't be true, but it was.

The bowl was gone.

⌣

GRIFF WAS SOOTHED BY THE BIG REEFER HE SMOKED AS SOON AS he reached his house. He sat at the computer, watching as images flashed by. He had opened a Facebook page shortly after he'd rigged his internet connection—no profile picture, all settings strictly private. It was part of his surveillance system. He felt safer keeping an eye on those both near and far.

But George had insisted that everyone in the production join the *Wizard* Facebook group to simplify communications. He also urged them to promote the show on their own pages. Griff had reluctantly "friended" George, who added him to the group. Now his newsfeed was full of chatter from every member of the cast and crew, all of whom seemed to spend twenty-four hours a day posting random thoughts, photos, and links.

This was good. He was still hidden. No one paid him any attention, and he never posted anything. He just observed.

Ping. A private message? How was that even possible?

Smoke and curtains won't hide you forever.

BomBoy? He'd never seen the name before. No profile picture, just a faceless head and shoulder outline, identical to his own.

The voices in his head reared up, throwing off the calming blanket of smoke he'd inhaled to quiet them.

Ping.

I know what you did.

The voices said, The CIA has found you again. You knew they would.

Griff stared at the screen, paralyzed.

You're worried, aren't you? You probably have lots of secrets. Which one, you're asking yourself? What does he know?

Griff's heart pounded fast. He had just read an online article about cyber-bullying. Was this what they were talking about?

I knew the real Griffin Peterson, and you're not him.

Ba-boom, ba-boom, ba-boom. Griff felt dizzy.

How does he know? Well might you ask.

Griff saw the flickering campfire cast its light and shadow on the other vet's face that fateful night, his dog tags gleaming. Had it been too easy?

He hit reply. The voices were shouting now. Griff had a hard time typing with his whole body shaking. He'd have to give himself a shot of horse tranquillizer, his drug of last resort.

Who are you?

You'll find out soon. BomBoy logged off.

Griff stumbled to the cupboard and rummaged for his drug stash. He'd found information online about cheap ways to medicate himself, some of the best tips from his special veterans' site. Most of the drugs were available at the local feed store. He lay down on the saggy couch and plunged the needle into his thigh. Oblivion followed.

⌣

CAL WASN'T SPEAKING TO GEORGE. ONCE A HAVEN, THE SECLUDed house perched high above Hilo had become a cage.

George had to admit yelling at Cal about the baby idea probably hadn't been wise. But good God. It wasn't the kind of thing you just sprang on someone. And it certainly wasn't a topic to discuss late at night when the other person might be preoccupied or dozing off.

George was flabbergasted. He had never even considered having a child. For one thing, he was gay. In the old days that meant if you didn't try to pass as straight and marry some poor deluded woman whose life you proceeded to make miserable, you didn't have children. For another, he'd had an unhappy childhood with a father who was neglectful at best, abusive at worst. Why would he want to inflict that kind of conditioning on another helpless kid?

George didn't believe people could overcome their upbringing—not really. The best you could do was try to limit the damage by not getting into situations where you were likely to perpetuate the suffering visited upon you. For him, this meant not having children.

He could understand why Cal wanted a baby. He'd had a blissful childhood with loving, affirming parents who, as far as George could tell, had done everything right. Everything except prepare Cal for people like George, that is. He'd gone straight for trouble like a moth to the flame.

George knew he was happier because of Cal, and probably a better person, too. But he also knew Cal was probably unhappier, and perhaps a worse person, because of him. George didn't allow himself to see chilling truths like this very often. Why torture yourself? Why wallow in regret and self-loathing any more than you had to? Cal was a grownup. He could make his own decisions.

But perhaps it was time to cut him loose, let him go find a partner who had the capacity for joy and love and giving that George simply did not, and would never have. Cal was absurdly loyal and clung to the belief that if he just tried hard enough, George would surrender to his ministrations. Like the Grinch, his heart would grow three sizes and his whole life would turn around.

George knew better. Even Oz couldn't give him a bigger heart.

He eased the door shut behind him as he entered the house. He could hear the TV playing in the other room. It sounded like one of those sad but uplifting movies where a luminously good person dies of cancer. This was going to be bad.

George squared his shoulders and walked through the doorway.

⌣

AFTER HER CHILDREN WERE IN BED, DESIREE CALLED HUNTER on the phone he'd given her. She'd texted him from rehearsal, but he hadn't replied.

"What?"

"Hunter." Desiree paced the length of her tiny kitchen.

"Don't ever text me incriminating information again, you stupid bitch." His voice was flat.

Desiree felt the menace coming through the airwaves. She started to explain, and he cut her off.

"No excuses. Here's how it's going to be. You'll meet me tomorrow morning at nine sharp at Boiling Pots, and we'll go for a little walk. I'll give you your new instructions then."

He hung up before Desiree could protest. She threw down the phone. Fucking bastard. No one called her the b-word. No one ordered her around. Did he think she was his slave? What was he going to do if she didn't show up, kill her?

Desiree knelt down and picked up the pieces of the cheap burner phone. She clicked the battery into its slot and slid the plastic back into place. She pressed the button, and the screen lit up. Her heart rate slowed down a little. She couldn't afford to be stupid now. Stupider than she'd already been, that is.

She sat cross-legged on the sticky linoleum floor and rested her head on her arms, feeling the stretch in her back and inner thighs. She'd always been flexible. Maybe she could train to be a yoga instructor, like Patrick always joked about doing after a few beers at the Aloha. Give up bartending and turn over a new leaf. Become wholesome—like Nora, who'd actually been married to the father of her children and got regular child support because he had a well-paid, professional job. Nora would never be so skint she got suckered into working as a meth mule. Desiree felt herself teetering on the sharp edge of decent society. The murky criminal underworld gaped beneath, ready to swallow her up.

Oh, cry me a river. She lifted her head. First, she had to deal with Hunter. He thought he had the upper hand, but he didn't. Oh no. She hadn't grown up poor, tough, and sassy for nothing. Her hometown in Kansas's claim to fame was having the biggest ball of twine in the world. She'd like to roll it right over Hunter and crush him flat. He thought she was a patsy, some loser hippie chick grooving for peace and love in Hawai'i. He was going to find out how wrong he was. But only when the time was right.

Desiree rose to her feet in one fluid motion. Not bad for a woman of forty. She'd have to leave the children at home in the morning. Later on they were all going to the theater workday out in Hawaiian Paradise Park to help paint the sets. Hunter had better not want much of her time. She planned to keep well away from steep cliffs and rock pools. One push and she could be trapped under a boulder by the river's strong current and never seen again. She'd leave a note for the children to tell them where she was and who she was with, just in case.

Suck on that, Hunter.

As she brushed her teeth, Desiree thought of Kama. Even though he had a hot young girlfriend she could tell he still felt something for her. She may not be his cultural soul mate, but they still had chemistry. Should she try to seduce him again? She stripped off her clothes and threw them in the direction of the laundry basket, stretching and yawning.

As she lay down in bed, pulling just the sheet over her naked body, Hunter's shadow blotted out Kama's smiling face and Desiree shivered in spite of the heat.

CHAPTER 17

Sunday morning, Griff arrived early for the workday at Larry's house in HPP (aka Hawaiian Paradise Park). Fred, who was set builder in addition to being stage manager and assistant director, didn't have room at his place out in Keaukaha, or so he'd said. Since Larry was a wood-working enthusiast and had lots of tools—and space—here they were.

This was the way community theater worked: from each according to his ability, or more often, availability.

Griff saw with approval that Larry had a table saw and heavy vice grips in his workshop, open to the carport, which also served, Hawaiian style, as a party extension *lanai*. At rehearsal yesterday, Fred had said he, Larry, Harriet's son, and the Tin Man had done a lot of prep work on the wood already.

Griff still felt groggy from the previous night's dose of horse tranquillizer, but the voices were at a low hum. BomBoy could say whatever he wanted. Griff wasn't going to run this time. He had the Energy Center to protect, and the girl, too—although from what exactly he still didn't know. The Voice had spoken, and he had listened. It was the real Voice, and It would speak again.

Griff set his food offering of bananas on the table set up in the shade. Cookie and the other goats had stuck their heads through the hog-wire fence and bleated at him as he waded into the thick grove of banana palms and hacked down the ripe yellow bunch with his machete. He'd hand-fed each goat a banana, which they gobbled down peel and all, jostling and butting each other for position. Cookie ate two bananas, because she was the boss.

Griff sat down to wait.

⌣

"MAHINA."

Mahina groaned and rolled over onto her stomach. The light hurt her eyes. Shouldn't have drunk that lemon-flavored vodka last night with Keola.

Iris opened the door. "Third warning—we need to leave for the workday in fifteen minutes."

God, am I a child? Must get a lock. Mahina threw the covers off and sat up, glaring at her mother.

"Keola's going to pick me up. We're going to the beach after."

Iris stood for a moment and tapped her fingernail against her tea cup, a habit Mahina found infuriating. "Well, thanks for letting me know in time for me to plan my own day."

"I just did." Mahina flopped back down, turning her back on her mother.

⌣

Iris turned and walked back to the kitchen. A mother's defense: retreat to the fortress. She poured herself another cup of green tea, her third, not a good idea, even if it was organic and caffeine-free. She had to discourage compulsive behavior in herself so she didn't encourage it in her daughter. Mahina was so highly strung, so driven. She must get it from her father. Iris took a couple of long cleansing breaths to banish the memories, which were becoming louder and more demanding. If she ignored them, they would go away.

"Is the Policeman coming?" Mahina had started making herself morning coffee in a French press. She bought the beans herself and ground them in Iris's spice grinder, rendering it useless for anything else. She poured herself a cup of the sludgy liquid, and Iris bit her tongue as Mahina added a generous dollop of the artificial hazelnut creamer she also bought and kept in the fridge. Caffeine and sugary toxins in the morning weren't going to help her daughter's energy body. The only sweetener Iris kept in the house was organic *lehua* blossom honey from a local beekeeper.

"He might. I hope so." Iris held back her irritation. "And his name is Moses."

"How did he get such a weird name?" Mahina put her cup in the microwave. "Was his family super religious or something? I mean he's Hawaiian, isn't he?"

"I've never been rude enough to ask." Iris reached for the teapot, then retracted her hand. "I like his name. I like him."

"Relax, Ma." Mahina stirred her syrupy coffee. "My name doesn't reflect my heritage either. Maybe I'm being sympathetic."

Iris was speechless. Mahina flounced back down the hall to her bathroom, coffee slopping out of the cup and spattering onto the floor.

～

PATRICK RARELY WENT TO THE NINE A.M. SUNDAY YOGA CLASS IN Volcano. He preferred to sleep in. To be honest, he hadn't gone to any yoga classes for several months. But this morning he had woken up early after a restless, agitated night, a slow burning in his stomach. He had to calm down before he did something stupid. Some deep breathing and stretching would be just the thing. After all, this was the new Patrick, the changing his life Patrick, the setting himself on the right track Patrick, and if he could take care of his body and his mind at the same time, so much the better. Plus, maybe he'd have a bright idea while he was trying not to think.

Patrick kicked his rubber slippers into the heap of discarded footgear on the woodsy building's doorstep, then carried his rolled-up mat, a bag with his block, strap, and towel, and a bottle of water (reusable, of course) across the threshold of the home studio his neighbor, Prema, had set up. It was a larger version of his own pre-fab workshop, and very different in interior finishing detail, especially the golden mandalas hanging on opposite walls and Buddha statue in the corner.

After nodding hello, he crossed the polished bamboo floor to his favorite spot in the left rear corner of the room. He lay on his mat, his senses subdued by subtle incense and soft, eerie sitar music as he concentrated on the quality of his breath—*prana*—in and out, letting the outside world fade away as he moved to the interior life of the body.

Patrick's relaxed spine stiffened as a familiar voice intruded into his meditation. He kept his eyes closed and lay supine, arms in a T, palms upward, focusing hard on keeping his breaths long and even.

"Hi Patrick." Mac and Cindy stood over him, beaming, as though delighted to see him. Perhaps they were. How better to measure their own happiness than to contrast it against his loss? Showdown at Yoga Central.

"Hey." He lifted a hand in greeting, but did not sit up. Pre-yoga-class protocol supported him. Not that they would know. Cindy had never practiced yoga in the nearly two years they'd been together. She preferred Tai Chi. It had been a point of mild contention. He'd never seen Mac at the studio either.

Patrick concentrated on his breath. In through the nose, expanding the ribs and filling the spine. Then out through the nose, lips closed, feeling heat against the back of his throat, kind of like a gargle—*ujjayi* breath—making a conscious effort to release the last vestiges of air from the corners of his lungs until he could feel his pelvic floor curling slightly at the edge of the exhale. Maybe he could train to be a male yoga instructor, as he'd joked with Desiree at the bar. Was it allowed? They always seemed to be female.

"I didn't think you were practicing yoga anymore." Cindy had set up her mat right next to his. Mac was on her other side. "Mac and I have been coming for a couple of months now."

Considering that Cindy had only moved out a few days ago, Patrick found this an aggressive statement.

Fortunately, Prema sounded the gong and invited them to sit and bring their thumbs to their feeling hearts and join her in chanting three overlapping "Oms" at their own pace, to acknowledge the connectedness of all being.

"As you chant, tapping into the divine light within you, release the outside world and its distractions, and think of your intention for today's work."

As Patrick sat in lotus position (ouch, make that half-lotus), thumbs to chest, and let his "Oms" echo sonorously across the room, his bright idea arrived. He had come to class wanting to put the breakup, jealousy, longing, and suspicion out of his mind, and move on with his life.

But now his entire being was filled with a powerful new intention: I need to get my bowl back. Now.

꒰

BACK IN TOWN, HARRIET HAD ALREADY BEEN UP FOR HOURS. She'd always been a morning person, but as she grew older she woke earlier and earlier, often before dawn. Sometimes it felt as if she hadn't slept at all. Once her eyes opened, she knew it was no good. That was all she was going to get. Better to get up immediately than to lie in bed thinking dark thoughts.

Her black cat, Salome, who had come with her from California, stalked stiff-legged through the six-inch opening Harriet always left in the sliding door between the *lanai* and the kitchen and meowed for her breakfast. Harriet scooped a portion of kibble into the bowl and the cat dug in, lying flat on her stomach with the dish wedged between her paws.

Harriet watched Salome fondly. She supposed she had become one of those women who think of pets as their children, or perhaps grandchildren in her case. And why not?

Luke had stayed over at Evan's again last night. Why did she even think he might not? She was happy for him. Nothing like a new love affair to cure the hurt of the old. She would see da boyz at the workday in five hours. Between now and then she could do a little gardening, practice her lines. She could even tackle the ever-present pile of student work she carried back and forth between home and classroom: pointillist still lifes and story problems this week. She could swear they reproduced overnight.

Or, revolutionary thought, she could climb the stairs to her studio and splash some paint around, stop feeling cramped and stymied.

Harriet sighed. Love. She kept thinking about it. Love was all around. Luke was in love. Merle and Nora were in love. Her ex-husband was in love.

That must be it. Harriet had always been good at putting things out of her mind. Lord knows she had dealt with the divorce efficiently. She'd known forcing the move to Hawai'i was a risk and, sure enough, even though he'd tried to adapt for her sake, Howard had chafed at small-town life and a culture he found alien. Without their circle of old friends and familiar pastimes to sustain—and distract—them, Harriet and Howard found they had grown so far apart there seemed no way to fill the vast amount of time and silence that now pooled between them.

While she missed being part of a couple, with all its attendant privileges and social approval, the thought of living out her days in L.A. was intolerable. Harriet was home now, and there was no going back. She was content with her choice and could live with its consequences.

But this new development. Howard's new life, his new love—his new family, for Christ's sake—was wearing on her. Even doing mental equations didn't drive it away. It seemed an indictment, somehow, of Harriet herself. Perhaps it was just the comparison. Men and women in late middle age with such different and unequal options available to them. She hadn't thought Howard was the kind to try to relive his youth, to deny aging. But then again, who in his or her right mind wouldn't, if given the chance? Why simply accept gradual decline followed by death?

Harriet thought she had made peace with the inevitability of aging. She tried to love her body as it grew older, heavier, droopier, wrinklier, as new aches and stiffening joints manifested themselves. She realized she should probably reframe the process in more positive terms. But none of it seemed positive. Her life force was waning. Her body was starting to betray her. Maybe she should take up yoga, like everyone else. But the thought of sitting on a thin mat on a hard floor wearing stretchy clothes and trying to twist her thickening self into a pretzel, surrounded by a room full of lithe, flexible young creatures, horrified her.

Salome gathered her plump body and jumped into Harriet's lap with a chirp of exertion. She licked her paw and began to wash her face, purring like a small diesel engine.

Harriet took a drink of coffee and pulled her school box closer. She may not have love but she had work, which was better. Let Howard start his life over. The very thought made her tired. She had Salome for warmth and affection. If she never had sex again, what did it matter? Been there, done that.

She thought about the Wicked Witch of the West. She didn't have a man. Didn't need or want one. In fact, she would blast a man to cinders as soon as look at him.

Harriet thought of the future. She would have to hear about Howard's new wife and baby for years to come, maybe even see pictures. Would she be polite and positive? She always had been. A proper upbringing was hard to overcome.

But it was fun to think about inflicting terror and scorching the earth.

Harriet threw her head back and let loose with a full Wicked Witch cackle. Salome sprang off her lap, leaving claw marks in her flesh.

⌣

DESIREE'S ANGER HAD WANED BY THE TIME SHE PICKED HER WAY down the narrow, rocky path to Boiling Pots: a stretch of the Wailuku River on Hilo's north side with waterfalls, large rock pools, and treacherous currents that frothed and bubbled, especially after a heavy rainfall. Because of the name, tourists always expected hot springs and were surprised by the icy cold water, if they dared dip in their toes.

She winced as her ankle twisted and she nearly fell to one side. People always had accidents here—the rescue helicopter circled and then descended, coming back up with a bulky parcel dangling from a long rope. Fortunately the hospital was close by. People who drowned often washed over Rainbow Falls and then resurfaced out in Hilo Bay, days or even weeks later.

Hunter hadn't said exactly where he'd be, so Desiree picked her way along the shore until she was out of view of the overlook, where tourists in brand-new resort wear lined up with their cameras. She scanned the tangled guava forest bordering the river on both sides. It opened out upstream into a pool beneath a gushing waterfall. No way was she crossing those slippery rocks. She thought of calling Hunter's name, but he would probably go apeshit. His fucking secrecy was ridiculous. Did he really think he was being watched? In Hilo?

A hand gripped her arm and Desiree stifled a shriek. She jerked away.

"You're late." Hunter stepped out from behind a big boulder.

"Jesus. It takes a while to walk along this path without killing yourself. I'm not a Girl Scout." Desiree glared at him.

"I told you to get decent footwear." Hunter had on hiking boots that made him look like a tourist.

Desiree wore rubber slippers like a local. "Stop telling me what to do." She looked at his boots in disdain.

Hunter frowned. "You'd better shut up and get used to it, baby. This is my business, and you're an incompetent amateur."

"Yeah yeah yeah." Desiree stood with her hands on her hips. "I'm here and I don't have all day, so let's get to it." She could tell

Hunter wanted to hit her and braced herself for a feint, followed up by a kick to the groin.

"Two things. Think you can handle that?"

Desiree cocked her head and narrowed her eyes.

"First, the drop spot is compromised, so since you screwed it up, you get to take two packages directly to the buyer now."

"What? I didn't screw up anything. And I'm not going to some drug dealer's house."

"Second, I'm not happy about this person who saw you down there."

"Griff?" Desiree wished the name back into her mouth, but it was too late. "He's a loony-bird, Hunter—totally bonkers. One of those whacked-out Vietnam vets. No one listens to a word he says, and he doesn't say much, anyhow."

"Still, he may be a problem—your problem." He handed her another package and a slip of paper with an address written on it. "Memorize this and destroy it. I'll be in touch with the time."

"This is way on the other side of town."

Hunter moved closer.

Desiree wished she were on the uphill side, not next to the water, which rushed past at an alarming rate.

"Do you want out? Fine. But remember, I know where you live and where your children go to school." He grabbed her upper arms and squeezed, giving her a little shake.

Desiree closed her eyes. "No, I don't want out. I want a thousand dollars." Her voice shook in spite of herself.

"Oh-ho. You don't get a raise for incompetence in this game. You're lucky I don't dock your pay." He let go and Desiree rocked backward, catching herself. He laughed, then stared at her, fury glittering out of his fake blue eyes. "Get it right this time." He strode up the path and disappeared around a corner.

Desiree waited for a minute until her body stopped shaking, then turned and spat on the ground.

⌣

OUT IN ORCHIDLAND, EVAN WAS FEELING AN EMOTION BOTH equal and opposite to Desiree's. He was in love for the first time in his life. At least, that's how it felt. He had seen the Wicked Witch's son across a crowded room and bam. Cupid's arrow had skewered him to the wall. All his previous doubt and struggle and shame were obliterated. He hardly even felt bisexual anymore. Maybe that had been a crutch on the way to discovery of his deepest, truest feelings.

I'm gay, Evan thought. He stretched his legs and pumped his arms as he ran along the bumpy road, holding steady when he skidded on loose cinders. I have a boyfriend. We have sex. And it's the most wonderful, mind-blowing sex I've ever had. Better even than my fantasies.

Still, he was glad his parents lived back in the Midwest, so he could put off telling them about Luke. Maybe forever. He didn't have to take it all on right now. He could just enjoy himself and get used to being out in such a supportive place. Evan sprinted along a straight stretch of road. Luke was lucky he had such open-minded parents. Harriet was great. Evan's parents had never even been enthusiastic about his girlfriends, so he didn't have much hope for their feelings about a boyfriend.

Evan rounded the turn and trotted up his driveway. Luke wasn't a runner or an early riser, but that was okay. Evan was still working on him. He stood under the outside shower and let the lukewarm water wash over him, draining away in the gravel under his feet. His whole body felt alive. The blood thrummed through his veins, carrying nutrients and oxygen, removing waste, replenishing his cells, each one radiant with energy.

As he reached for a towel, Evan realized he was experiencing a moment of pure happiness. Luxuriating in the rough, sun-dried cloth against his wet skin, he remembered Luke mentioning job applications.

Evan's bubble started to deflate. He was making up a whole scenario that didn't exist. In a few weeks, Luke would go back to his real life on the mainland and Evan would just be a memory.

Unless he did something to change it.

⤳

PATRICK KNEW WHAT HE WAS DOING WAS CRAZY, BUT HE RODE the current of his intention. He stood up, rolled up his mat, and walked out of the yoga studio without a word of explanation to anyone. Prema was murmuring to a new student and looked at him in alarm, but he waved and kept going, right out the door. He was afraid for a moment that Cindy would come running after him, thinking he was upset and wanting to show how caring she was, but she didn't.

He slung the mat's carrying strap across his chest, shoved his bag into his bike basket, and pedaled off in the direction of Mac's enormous designer house. They would be busy for an hour and a half, which gave him enough time to toss the joint. He just hoped he could get in.

It couldn't be a coincidence. He'd discovered his bowl missing the first time he'd checked—less than twenty-four hours after Cindy's departure.

He and Cindy had looked after Mac's pet box turtle and plants during one of his vacations to a lavish resort in an impoverished country, so Patrick knew where the extra key was hidden. He had a strong feeling Mac was involved in the theft. Go ahead, call it jealous paranoia. Maybe it was.

Still, he trusted his intuition. Actually, now that he thought about it, the bowl was more likely to be in Mac's studio, which would have a different lock. Maybe he'd find an open window. He had to hope, and he had to try. This might be his only chance.

Patrick hid his bike behind the garden shed and walked over to Mac's studio, which was surrounded by trees and shrubbery, creating a little cottage in the woods effect. He grasped the door handle but it was unyielding. He looked under the flowerpots on either side of the door. No spare key.

Patrick struggled to get to the window through the dense bank of hydrangeas growing against the outside wall. Twigs snagged on his T-shirt and poked into his tender flesh. The shade was three-quarters drawn, but he peered through the narrow panel of glass beneath it, the window shut tight against his prying fingers, and waited for his eyes to adjust to the gloom.

Inside, the studio was swathed in dusk. The other windows were completely covered. Patrick never drew the blinds in his workshop. This was Volcano. You were lucky to get enough daylight to work without turning on your blazing fluorescent overheads.

Mac clearly had something to hide. The lathe was covered with a sheet of canvas, and the floor looked clean. No drifts of sawdust. Unnatural. This did not look like a working concern. What was going on?

From this slice of window, Patrick could see two of the interior walls, each covered with shelving. The wall opposite the window held row after row of finished, polished bowls. Dozens of them. Was his among them? He squinted but they were too far away to identify. On the wall closer to him, the shelves held crude, misshapen starter bowls. Even in the dim light their terrible flaws were clear to his expert eye. Bowls with one side too thin to finish, the other twice as thick. Bowls that had already cracked in the drying process. It was woodworking carnage. An idea started to take shape, turning in his mind. He pressed a little harder, getting closer to the edge.

But how? Why? And how then did you explain the finished bowls? Bowls of fine craftsmanship? Patrick drummed his fingers against the rough wooden siding. He had stumbled into an aesthetic conundrum bordering on the criminal. Was Mac a talentless thief posing as a bowl turner extraordinaire? Had he targeted Cindy just to get to Patrick? Where was Patrick's bowl? And who were Mac's other victims?

Wait a minute. A fragment of something familiar caught his eye. Patrick craned his neck and peered as far to the right as he could.

And there it was—his flawless, breathtaking mango bowl—tucked into the corner, sitting on a large piece of bubble wrap next to a cardboard box. The bastard was about to ship it out.

Patrick felt an unaccustomed feeling rising up inside him, worse than a bad case of indigestion. Could it be? Yes, it was. Rage. He felt violated, appropriated, swindled, and impostered. Mac was not going to get away with this. Not his bowl and not his baby either. He froze for a moment at this unexpected offering from his subconscious. He turned his new resolve over in his mind, feeling for cracks, but it felt solid. He meant it. He would get the truth out of Cindy even if he had to pay for a DNA test. But first he would steal back his bowl.

The sound of a car crunching up the gravel drive jerked Patrick out of his trance. Heart pounding, he plunged back through the shrubbery, ripping several holes in his shirt, grabbed his bike, and pedaled down the other side of the circular drive as fast as his feet could pump. Thank god for the thick *'ōhi'a* and *hāpu'u* sheltering him from sight. His mind surged with every beat of his heart, every rotation of his feet. The rescue would have to be bold and swift. Tonight!

Tomorrow was Monday, and Mac would undoubtedly have a Fed Ex shipment ready for pickup.

⌣

IT WAS A SHORT DRIVE BACK TO NORA'S HOUSE THROUGH THE narrow winding roads leading from Merle's makeshift neighborhood. Houses with iffy-looking additions, *'ohana* houses built in crowded back yards, tents erected as carports, rusting cars set on concrete blocks. It was a maze, not to mention a building inspector's nightmare. But the place made Nora's neighborhood look respectable and middle class by comparison. Hers had houses, lawns, and gardens all distinct from one another.

As she drove, Nora basked in the afterglow of amazingly fantastic sex, and even more than that, in the deep sense of wellbeing that results from someone taking care of you, paying attention to you, listening to you. She had always been snapped up by men who expected her to perform those functions for them. She was not supposed to have needs herself. But she did. Oh yes.

She smiled as she pulled into her comparatively civilized carport, its roof her bedroom floor.

Nora rummaged through her fridge and cupboards for potluck food, humming. Cheddar, the humble workhorse of cheese, with crackers and apples. A Pacific Northwestern offering in the tropics. She loaded her small cooler, then sat down with her laptop and logged on to the "Teach yourself to be a psychic" site to prepare for work the next morning.

Nora was surprised her job had turned out to be more rewarding than terrifying. Most people just wanted to talk. If she listened carefully, they told her everything she needed to know. In the midst of her own alienation, she found her troubled clients a source of companionship. She understood their loneliness, their desire to be heard and accepted. The pay wouldn't amount to much, but it would keep her out of debt and even provide a few small luxuries.

Nora had always been a good improviser and she had a flexible relationship with the truth. Her psychology training and natural listening skills should take care of the rest. Hopefully. She scanned the fallback questions the site suggested, from the innocuous, "Why are you calling today?" to the bizarre, "A strange spirit is breaking through now. Could it be a bird?"

Loss comes in many forms, each with its own grief and longing to assuage. She remembered a quote from classic horror writer, H.P. Lovecraft: "The oldest emotion known to mankind is fear, and the strongest fear is fear of the unknown." Welcome to life, thought Nora. So much of our behavior is a variation on trying to understand, control, or avoid the unknown. If she could bring solace to a few people, wasn't that a good thing? Did it matter that she was a fake?

Merle had wanted to come home with her this morning, but she had to set boundaries. It would be so easy to fall into another full-time relationship, especially with an adoring, sexy man, but Nora valued her hard-won freedom. Besides, lovely as he was, Merle was a constant talker. Before, during and after their lovemaking, he had expounded on his spiritual landscape design practice.

"Nature seeks harmony," he said. "The earth talks. Plants and trees talk. You just have to listen." He told her stories about clients whose lives had turned around completely once their gardens were in alignment with their own spiritual energy and that of their houses. Love, success, miraculous cures from fatal diseases flowed freely when spiritual harmony prevailed. "Let me read your landscape," he urged.

But Nora wasn't so sure. Sex was one thing, spiritual evaluation quite another.

Merle travelled all over the island to see clients, a number of them in Waimea. "Neurotic rich women love me." He winked at her. "But I never get romantically involved with clients."

Nora thought of asking Merle if he knew Greta, but decided against it. For now. That evening, Greta and Clyde would land their superior armada on Nora's shores to return the twins.

She picked up her phone and pressed Alice's number. Time for reconnaissance. Nora needed intelligence, and ammunition, if she hoped to repel the impending invasion.

PART THREE
PUT 'EM UP

CHAPTER 18

D ESIREE WAS AMONG THE FIRST TO ARRIVE AT LARRY'S HOUSE after Griff, plopping bags of store-brand tortilla chips and chocolate chip cookies on the food table. Kolea, Nakai, and Malia scattered to the corners of the property. Although still shaky from her altercation with Hunter, Desiree's instincts had rejected flight. She was ready to fight.

Desiree saw Mahina's mother and waved. The woman sometimes came and watched rehearsals. Pathetic. That's what happens with an only child—not a problem Desiree would ever have. She was standing with a good-looking local guy who must be her boyfriend. Mahina always called him the Policeman, her voice dripping with scorn. Iris, that was the mother's name. Desiree's bartending instincts kicked in, and she crossed the gravelly yard.

"It's so nice of you to come and help." Desiree looked up slantwise at Iris's companion and smiled. "We're always short of strong men." Then she reached out to hug and kiss Iris, who felt a bit stiff, just to show she wasn't trying to move in on her man or anything.

Some women were so sensitive about their territory. "Where's that daughter of yours?"

"Goddess only knows." Iris shrugged. "Just wait until yours are her age. Better yet, enjoy them while they're still young and sweet and like your company."

Desiree laughed. "I don't see them liking my company much, do you?" They were nowhere to be seen.

"I'm Moses Kapili," said the Policeman, holding out his hand to shake.

Desiree gave him a hug instead. Mmm. He felt and smelled almost as yummy as Kama. She must have a special chemistry with local men.

"Nice to meet you, officer." Desiree clapped her hand over her mouth. "Oops. You're obviously off-duty, but Mahina told us her mother was dating a policeman."

"I guess news travels fast." Kapili smiled.

God he was hot.

He wrapped his arm around Iris's shoulders and pulled her close. Her jaw looked tense.

"Well, I feel much safer myself." Desiree could feel an idea start to form.

⌣

GEORGE HATED THEATER WORKDAYS, BUT AS DIRECTOR HE NOT only had to show up, he had to really put on his game face, especially when he needed to inspire the troops to greater effort as he would have to do today. His fellow board member, frigging' Phil, had called this morning with killing news about the Palace finances. It wasn't enough to harass George at rehearsals, yapping when he was trying to concentrate on directing. Oh no. Now he had to crush George's spirit.

News from the personal front wasn't much better. Cal had ostentatiously moved to the spare room, and George didn't know what to do next. He'd chickened out on telling Cal to move on. He didn't want him to leave. But a baby? How could it be anything but a disaster?

He hated driving his Miata on these terrible Puna roads. If he and Cal were getting along, he'd have asked to switch cars today and driven Cal's SUV instead. He inched along, easing over each little bump and pit. The undercarriage scraped at one point, and he cursed loudly. Shortly after, an old Jeep roared past him, spraying gravel against his pristine paint job. George felt faint with rage.

At last he pulled into Larry's driveway and parked under a shady spreading tree he hoped wasn't shedding anything sticky. Retrieving a small cooler from the passenger side, George took a deep breath. He smiled. Then he walked toward the house, trying to put a spring in his step. He wished he could stay behind the curtain and project a large intimidating face to the crowd, accompanied by thunderclaps.

George heard another car pull in and turned. Some idiot was parking a truck way too close to the Miata. Now the door was opening—Aaaaaaagh. No, just missed. But now that damned little dog playing Toto jumped out and lifted his leg against the tire. This just couldn't be happening. He heard a plop, and sure enough, a squashy, rotten-looking blob had spattered its innards all over the Miata's beautiful candy apple red hood. He should wash it off immediately and move to a safer location. Or better yet, just drive back home.

"Howzit, George?" Dorothy smiled at him. She looked even snarkier than usual.

"Hey brah." This from a tall dark surfer dude. George refrained from checking him out. Obviously not one of the guys. "Nice car."

"Thanks."

The surfer dude gave him a chin lift and a *shaka*.

Toto growled at George, and he visualized himself punting the little dog like a football, the fluffy body tracing a long arc into the trees. His foot twitched.

⌣

DESIREE HAD SPLINTERS IN HER HANDS FROM HANDLING THE rough wood of the sets, and her old work jeans were spattered with all the colors of the rainbow. She squatted on the tarp covering the gravel and aimed a can of red spray paint at the first set of rubber Winkie galoshes.

"My, my, a multi-talented woman."

Desiree almost dropped the can, catching herself as she rocked backwards. Damned if she was going to fall on her ass in front of Hunter.

"What the hell are you doing here?" She struggled to her feet, legs stiff after hours of bending and crouching.

"I'm hurt. Don't you want to include me in your social life?" Hunter smiled, his eyes covered by dark glasses. He looked like a phony mobster. "I thought it would be nice to meet your theater friends. And your children. They're here, right?"

Desiree held herself back. She wanted to spray him in the eyes till he went blind. She wanted to grab his throat and squeeze until he stopped breathing. At the very least, she wanted to kick him in the balls and then stomp on his head when he fell down, whimpering, curled up like a baby.

Just then Kolea ran up, her curly hair flying. "Mom, Nakai's in a fight." She grabbed Desiree's hand and pulled her to the other side of the yard. A larger Munchkin had Nakai pinned on the ground and was hitting him.

Desiree grabbed his arms and pulled him off. "What's going on here?" She looked from the sullen, paint-streaked bully down to her son, still on the ground.

"He said you were a skank." Nakai mumbled the words into the ground.

Desiree turned to the other boy, who was looking down and to the side. "Who are your parents? Are they here?"

He shook his head.

"Have some respect for your elders, you little punk." She let go of him with a push. "And stay the hell away from my kid."

She pulled her son to his feet and hugged him. He started to cry. "Are you hurt?"

He shook his head.

"Don't do that again, Nakai." Desiree crouched down and looked hard into his dirty face. "You don't have to protect me. I'm supposed to protect you. Okay? Sticks and stones, right? That kid's an asshole."

"Anything I can do?" Hunter had materialized at her side and was smiling down at them.

"Yeah," Desiree spat. "You can get the fuck out of here and stop stalking me before I call the police."

"Oh I wouldn't do that, sweetheart." Hunter's voice went flat.

"Everything okay over here?" It was Moses Kapili, the Policeman, holding a paintbrush. He raised his eyebrows and looked at Desiree.

Fuck. Much as she'd like to bust Hunter's operation wide open, she couldn't. She was part of it. "We're fine." She straightened up.

Nakai ran off.

"Hunter, here, was just leaving."

"Oh, I can stay a while longer." He put one arm around Desiree and held the other out to Kapili. "Hunter Craddock. Is it time to eat yet? I brought some *poke* from the fish market. Not that previously frozen garbage they sell you at the grocery store."

⌣

IRIS STOOD IN THE SHADE. SHE SAW MOSES ACROSS THE YARD, talking to Desiree and a man she didn't recognize. Probably a boyfriend. Desiree's son stumbled away, looking filthy and upset. Desiree's aura was a murky orange-red. She needed to calm down.

As the man and Desiree walked toward the carport/*lanai*, Fred snapped a picture of them. "That's a good one—raw emotion."

Desiree glared at him.

"I'll get these up on Facebook tonight—*Wizard* Workday album." Fred hustled off to take more pictures.

Iris reached behind her and picked up a deviled egg. She was starving, but it wasn't officially time to eat yet. She turned away to pop it in her mouth, trying to chew discreetly.

"I see you, potluck abuser," Moses said in a low voice, right behind her.

She choked and laughed.

"Have you seen that guy with Desiree around before? At the theater?" His voice sounded casual. Too casual?

"Why are you so interested?" Iris caught herself. She sounded jealous. Was she slipping back into a scarcity mindset after embracing the concept of abundance for so long?

"Just curious. She doesn't seem too happy he's here. Cop instincts, I guess." Moses popped a goat cheese-topped cracker into his mouth.

Fred saw their full mouths and wagged his finger.

They giggled.

"I think Desiree can look after herself." Iris felt prim. The good girl censuring the bad girl. Worse and worse. This relationship was bringing all sorts of negativity to the surface—attachment issues, possessiveness. Not to mention other powerful, unresolved feelings. It was ugly. She had been foolish to think she could keep her past safely locked away, that a solid wall protected her present life from its toxic leakage. She reached up to clutch the crystal pendant she wore around her neck, rubbing its faceted surface.

"You're right." Moses gave her a smile that made her knees quiver. She pushed away her inconvenient introspection and released the crystal. "Hey, I'm off duty," he said. "Let's go paint something."

They linked arms and walked over to the set, which gleamed like a beached sea monster in the sun.

⌣

HARRIET SAT IN THE SHADE AND WATCHED THE COMPANY SLAP paint on the newly constructed sets, noting who was drawn to which. She prided herself on the cleverness of her design. Hers and Luke's, that is. He'd actually had some good ideas—when he bothered to put his mind to it.

The Kansas farm was drab and brown, but Munchkinland on the other side sported all the colors of the rainbow. Oz was full of brilliant green spires, but turn it around, and the witch's castle and spooky woods loomed dark, jagged and twisted.

Mahina's mother was sure frisky these days, with that handsome boyfriend in tow, she thought. Good for her. They headed directly to Munchkinland—of course. No dark shadows there. Not yet.

"There's a bright and a sunny side of life," sang Harriet. "There's a dark and a troubled side, too, but if you do do do do do do dooooo, the sunny side you also may view."

She was tired from supervising the set construction. Lots of enthusiasm from Fred, Larry, and the crew but not much expertise, except for Griff, who had handled the skill-saw with precision and grace. He cut most of the difficult pieces himself and then attached the hinges so that parts actually lined up and moved easily, as they were meant to. Couldn't have done it without him. He was a strange one. But she was strange, too, and bent on becoming stranger still.

"Keep on the sunny side, always on the sunny side, keep on the sunny side of life." Harriet picked up a paintbrush as she sang and dipped it in a bucket of black paint. She had work to do on her castle. "It will help you every day, it will brighten all the way, if you keep on the sunny side of life."

"Hey mom." Luke and Evan stood side by side, dark and light, grinning.

"Hey yourself, lazybones." Harriet tilted her head. "You two need to get messy. Here." She handed them each a paintbrush. "Take your pick—flowers, emeralds, or blighted trees."

"We were hoping it was time to eat already." Evan flicked some yellow paint at Luke.

"Dude." Luke dipped his brush in a red can and held it up.

"Boys." Harriet used her schoolteacher voice. "Not in front of the children."

Luke lowered his brush, then made a lightning-swift strike to Evan's jeans.

"Enough!" Harriet's voice carried and everyone turned to look.

"Jeez, Mom, okay okay." Luke set down his brush. "Just having a little fun." He stomped off toward the food table.

Harriet turned her back and slapped black paint on the castle wall.

Evan lingered. "Sorry, Harriet."

"Oh go on. Don't mind witchy me." She smiled at him. Such a nice young man. "Too many noisy Munchkins and too much sun. Can't wait to get in the water and swim later."

"Maybe we'll come with you." Evan seemed eager to ingratiate himself.

"Sure, if you can keep up." Harriet stood back to eye her handiwork. Very sinister.

Evan wandered off, and a short man Harriet didn't know walked up to look at the castle.

"Are you the witch?" He smiled appraisingly, his eyes hidden behind dark glasses.

"How could you tell?" Harriet's gaze flicked over him. She'd seen him hanging around Desiree. He looked like an extra in one of those cheesy mobster movies. She must have picked him up at that bar where she worked. Oh listen to yourself, Harriet, she thought. No wonder Howard left you and took up with a young floozy. Much more fun than sour old you. Now you can live alone in your castle and terrorize children. And why not? Harriet felt a loosening deep inside.

She turned and knocked her brush hand against her other arm, sending a shower of black paint drops over Desiree's boyfriend, still standing too close to her.

"Oops." Harriet smiled. "Hope those are your work clothes."

He swore, looking down at his tan chinos and white polo shirt, now spattered in black.

Harriet pressed the brush into his hand. "Here. There's still some touching up to do on this one. Go to it."

Walking away, she cackled under her breath.

⌣

PATRICK ARRIVED LATE FOR THE WORKDAY. HE HAD TO WEDGE his old Mazda into the bushes bordering the narrow dirt road and walk down the car-lined driveway to the house.

His mind was in turmoil. After he pedaled home from his abortive attempt to recover his missing, now confirmed stolen, bowl, he had gone straight to his workshop to check for other missing bowls, just in case, but everything seemed to be in place. He'd pulled the blinds and locked the door, then locked his house, although since Cindy still had her key, that was pointless. Was she in on it? The mother of his child? If it *was* his child.

Patrick struggled to wrap his head around the multiple layers of betrayal. It was a new world now, the end of innocence. His girlfriend didn't think he was up to fatherhood and was prepared to lie about it. Master bowl turners were frauds and thieves, Volcano Village was a crime scene, his secluded woodland home was violated, unsafe. He'd have to get a Doberman. And win Cindy back.

Another thought wiggled up from his subconscious. Maybe she felt he'd betrayed her, hadn't appreciated or supported her enough, and she'd left him to save herself and their child from a life of disappointment. If so, had she taken his bowl as an act of revenge or as a cry for help? Maybe this was the ultimate test of his manhood.

Halfway up the driveway, Patrick realized he hadn't brought anything for the potluck. Shit. He always brought a big dish of his special homemade vegetarian lasagna to theater functions. He'd completely forgotten. People would notice. He felt dizzy. Should he just turn around and go home? No, that would be worse. He stumbled over a rock and nearly fell.

"Hey." Belinda was right behind him, also a late arrival. She grinned. "That was a good Scarecrow move, Patrick. Keep it." She caught up, and they walked in step. She smelled good, like gardenias, but sharper.

"There you are." Harriet brandished a black paintbrush, then said in her Wicked Witch's voice, "Where's the lasagna, Scarecrow?" She let out a long cackle. Jeez, she was taking method acting too far.

He did a little shuffle and wobbled, Scarecrow-like, throwing out his arms. "Do your worst, witch."

They all laughed a little more than was warranted. Maybe he wasn't the only person on edge.

He headed straight for the coolers to get a beer and almost collided with Desiree.

"Still drowning your sorrows?" She patted his shoulder.

He'd poured out his heart to Desiree after beers and shots at the Aloha the other day—and then had to stagger down to the river bank near the singing bridge and sleep it off under a tree before he could drive home.

"I'm going to beg Cindy to come back to me," he said, uncapping an IPA with his teeth.

"That's the spirit." Desiree clinked her beer bottle with his and they both drank deeply.

⌣

EVAN MOVED ASIDE FOR PATRICK, WHO DOVE FOR THE BEER cooler a second time. Was everyone but him having a bad day? Evan had always been focused but even-tempered, self-contained yet responsive to others. He had learned as a child to manage his own behavior in order to get what he wanted, which was mostly to do well but not so well he attracted undue attention. He was confused by Luke's sudden shifts in temper. Luke was mercurial—that was the word.

Evan's favorite section in the *Reader's Digest,* which arrived every month when he was growing up, was "It pays to enrich your word power." He had learned so many interesting words there and felt smarter afterwards, immediately using them in conversation or in his English assignments—with mixed results. Math always came easily to him, but English was tough. Especially writing essays. Mercurial would be a "word power" entry for sure. Maybe he should get a subscription to *Reader's Digest*. Did it still exist? He had also liked "Drama in real life," but not the medical pieces ("I am John's pancreas"). Those were just weird. It was best not to know too much about what lay beneath the surface. Better just to let it work there in the dark by itself.

"You don't have to suck up to my mother, you know." Luke startled Evan out of his reverie. He leaned against the carport strut, drinking a beer, his dark hair flecked with yellow paint like a punk dye job. "It's actually kind of irritating."

"Well, excuse me for having manners." Evan opened the cooler and got his own beer. "That's what it's called where I'm from." He refrained from adding that where he came from, Luke's behavior would be labeled "spoiled brat" and cured in the teenage years, not tolerated into the late twenties. He couldn't afford to become the scolding partner, parent to Luke's child. Is that what was happening? Evan closed his eyes briefly and took a long pull from his beer bottle. He had to stop reading women's magazines in the dentist's waiting room. Next he'd be filling out those quizzes about sex appeal.

"There are lots of strong women in my family." Evan moved a little closer. "My mother and her sisters, and then my sisters, too, and my girl cousins. I learned early on to say 'Yes, ma'am' and then go and do what I wanted anyway."

This got a grunt out of Luke, which may have been part laugh. Evan was encouraged.

"My older cousin Hal couldn't take it. He had to sass all the time." Evan pulled up a chair. "I watched him get the strap, get sent to his room—every punishment in the book—and I thought, what's the point? Just give them what they want: respect and the appearance of obedience. And that's your pass to freedom."

"Thanks for that inspiring story, Oprah." Luke finished off his beer, then grinned at Evan.

Whoop, thought Evan, from freezing to boiling in seconds.

"I feel like painting the yellow-brick road now, don't you?"

"Either that or the poppy field, sure." Evan felt the familiar sense of satisfaction he always got from bringing a volatile situation under control. This ability had helped him survive as a financial advisor in a dismal economy. You had to be part therapist, and all that meant was that you didn't get sucked into other people's emotions. When people acted out, you nudged them back to the center, away from those scary, dangerous edges that dropped away into nothingness. You remained calm.

As if to illustrate this thought, Evan caught a glimpse of George laboring on the sets, reminding him that he needed to confirm the date of their next portfolio review. But not today. He'd call tomorrow from the office.

Evan and Luke walked past Mahina and Griff working together on the balloon. Odd combination, Evan thought. He couldn't remember Griff talking to anyone, really, and especially not the young prima donna. Her little dog lay curled up in a tiny patch of shade cast by the ladder upon which his mistress stood.

Evan shrugged and walked on, following his heart.

CHAPTER 19

GEORGE WAS HOT AND DIZZY. SHOULD'VE WORN A HAT. HE could feel his scalp burning and tightening. The itching would come next. He longed to go home and drape a cold wet cloth over his head.

Oh great. There was that useless Scarecrow and the inane choreographer, just arriving when the work was almost finished. They'd probably been screwing all morning—he'd seen them get all touchy-feely at the "Jitterbug" rehearsal. And over by the food, that red-haired minx in the chorus was canoodling with the Cowardly Lion. Did they think no one noticed them making goo-goo eyes at every rehearsal? Get a room already. Not to mention the lovebirds, Tin Man and the Witch's son, having a little tiff right now, then making up. Love was all around.

If Cal could listen to my interior monologue, George thought, he'd know there was no hope. I'm a very angry person.

"Lunch time, everyone," Larry sang out. "You've earned a break. Come and get it."

People dropped their paintbrushes and hammers and rushed for the carport.

George groaned as he stood up. Something in his back had gone into spasm. He would make his announcement after everyone had some food in their stomachs, then maybe they wouldn't want to kill the messenger.

He loaded his partitioned *lūʻau* plate with all the local delicacies Cal would shake his head over: potato mac salad, kalbi, teri chicken, bright orange Jell-O-sorbet squares, white rice doused with shoyu, *lilikoi* bars. If Cal left him, he'd probably just eat his way to oblivion—obesity, heart attack, stroke. Maybe he'd start smoking again. He already drank too much.

The children pushed and laughed and yelled, chasing each other around, food sliding off their plates. Didn't their parents even try to teach them manners? This "let your children express themselves freely" method of childrearing was just an excuse for total abdication of parental authority. A weak attempt to elevate laziness and lack of responsibility to the moral high ground. George didn't buy it. If he had a child—well. Never mind.

Before filling his plate a second time, George stood and banged a serving spoon against an empty saucepan.

"Thanks for coming today, everyone. Good work." He looked around at the happy faces of his cast and crew, the sunburned, bulging cheeks, the animated conversations. He frowned and raised his voice. "If I could have your attention for a moment, I have an important announcement to make."

There wasn't exactly a hush, but at least a reduction in noise, so George pressed on. "You know the Palace already operates on a shoestring budget." Mouth dry, he took a swig of diet soda. Disgusting. "Well, the shoestring just became a couple of threads last week when one of our largest annual donors, the Miyamoto

Foundation, pulled out. With the current financial crisis, their shrinking dividend income can no longer support the performing arts in our community."

The group gave a collective groan.

"The board is facing an impossible situation. Unless more funds are secured, it looks like the Palace may have to close down again at the end of the year."

A cacophony of protest broke out.

George waited, then raised his hand. "So. We need to sell as many tickets to *Wizard* as we can, and we each need to solicit donations. Hit up anyone and everyone you know. We need the Palace to stay alive. If you have ideas for fundraising or possible big donors, let me know, and I'll take them to the board, or talk to them yourself, if you'd rather. And if you have any experience in grant writing, we need you." George paused. "This grand old theater is the heart of the arts community in Hilo, folks. We need the Palace, and now the Palace needs us. Let's get busy. We can do this!"

He sat down and drained the soda can. The lukewarm liquid tasted exactly like what it was—artificially sweetened chemicals. He rose halfway out of his chair to find a real soda, or better yet, a beer.

Fred plopped down beside him. "Well now I'm having heart palpitations."

"Join the club, Fred." George propelled himself to standing.

The stage manager lit up a cigarette.

"Losing the cancer sticks would help," George snapped.

An unfamiliar man approached and held out his hand. What now, for god's sake? George smiled reflexively. The man's silver hair was sprayed in place, but his clothes and Ferragamo loafers were speckled with black set paint. How careless. George held up his hands. "Better not. Greasy." He hated touching people.

"Hunter Craddock. Friend of Desiree's."

"Thanks for helping out, Hunter. Looks like you sacrificed a nice outfit to the cause today." Fred had abandoned his seat to join the conversation. He took a deep drag on his cigarette and turned to blow smoke over his shoulder—into the wind, as it turned out, which flung it back into their faces.

"So, George." Hunter turned a shoulder against Fred. "I may have a donor for you. A real civic-minded do-gooder looking to spend some money in the arts."

"Well then, Hunter." George felt a genuine smile stretch across his sunburned face. "You may be my new best friend."

The flash exploded as Fred snapped a photo of them. "One for the memory book." He hustled off.

George blinked as blinding white blobs swam around in his eyes, but he didn't stop smiling.

~

NORA SAT AND PICKED AT HER PLATE. AFTER LOBBING HIS BOMB-shell at them, George had moved to the food table and started schmoozing with Desiree's friend, to whom Nora had taken an instant dislike. Was it the pitch of his voice, or his body language, or some other intangible element? She found such questions fascinating.

She'd chatted briefly to Mahina's mom in the food line. The woman had been so sympathetic during her house rental search that Nora had poured out her whole sad divorce story, which now made small talk over the sushi platter feel awkward. Fortunately Merle was deep in conversation with Fred. She'd told him she'd talk to him later about her phone call with Alice.

A shadow fell across her plate.

"You look glum." Harriet towered over her, smiling, a streak of black paint on her cheek. "Where are your delightful twins?"

"They're with their father." Nora looked up, feeling suddenly tremulous. STOP. She hardly knew Harriet. It wouldn't do to break down. She always felt the older woman was watching her in amusement. Well, let her chuckle. She thought of Mr. Bennett's comment in *Pride and Prejudice* after the family's reputation had been dragged through the mud by youngest daughter Lydia's shameless behavior: "For what do we exist but to make sport for our neighbors and to laugh at them in our turn?"

Harriet sat down next to her. "Well, my ex-husband is about to marry a woman younger than our son and start a new family with her." She smiled at Nora and cocked an eyebrow. "It just keeps getting better and better."

"Mine wants to start a new family, too—with his wealthy new girlfriend, her kids, and my kids—and take it to Australia, cutting me out of the picture altogether." Nora couldn't believe she'd blurted out her dark secret to a virtual stranger, but she felt better. Harriet had an undeniable power.

"Well, I doubt he'll be able to do that unless you agree to it, which you won't, right?" Harriet looked closely at Nora. "The family court isn't going to take kindly to one parent whisking the children out of the country. Why Australia, by the way?"

"Apparently he's had a job offer from an observatory in Sydney. You know how the astronomy people make the rounds to all the big telescopes? Here, Arizona, Chile, Australia, etc." Nora wiped her eyes. "He and Greta, the girlfriend, have piles of money between them and can probably hire a team of lawyers and investigators to make me look like an unfit mother."

"Nothing like facing the worst-case scenario, eh?" Harriet crossed her arms. "I'm sure you have some ammunition, and you *are* the mother. That still counts for a lot."

"I can't believe I told you all that." Nora laughed, shaking her head.

"My secret powers." Harriet grinned. "No one can withstand them." She stood up. "Come on, throw that food away before you hurt yourself. You need some 'paint it black' therapy. Never fails." Her deep voice carried.

Merle's head swiveled around. Nora smiled and waved.

"You and Merle seem very friendly." Harriet gave Nora a paintbrush and a can of paint, steering her in the direction of a partially painted castle wall.

Nora blushed.

"He's a talented man, but perhaps not husband material."

Now Nora felt annoyed. "That's exactly why I like him."

"Fair enough. But while I'm being intrusive, I'll just say I wouldn't want to see you hurt or disappointed."

"Too late, Harriet, but thanks just the same."

"I meant again."

Nora slapped black paint onto the rough plywood. "What do you have against Merle? He's been nothing but kind to me." She felt a surge of power. Maybe it was the paint.

"I'm sure he's very kind." Harriet paused. "Never mind. I'm being a nosy old bag. Sorry."

"Thank you, though." Nora turned and looked into Harriet's eyes. "It's helped me, talking to you. Somehow Clyde can still make me feel powerless and victimized. It's loathsome. Makes me hate myself and everyone and everything."

"That's a lot of hating." Harriet smiled. "But I know what you mean." She dipped her brush in the can. "Let's paint."

⤳

It seemed fitting to Mahina that she, Dorothy, and that weirdo Griff, Oz, were painting their getaway balloon together

—even though technically it didn't turn out to be her getaway balloon after all, since that pea-brained Toto had to run off at the last minute. Mahina wondered if she personally would jump out of the basket to rescue Ziggy and decided she probably wouldn't. Zig would find a new owner and do just fine. She, on the other hand, needed to get the hell out of there.

Mahina didn't believe in waiting for ruby slippers. They were just a way for people to manipulate you. That sneaky Glinda could have told Dorothy about their powers right from the start, and then there would have been no story at all. But no, she had to put Dorothy to the test, had to use the girl to get rid of her arch rival, the Wicked Witch of the West. People only thought of themselves.

The balloon was huge and had rainbow stripes. Mahina kept having to climb down and move her ladder so she could finish the whole top red arc. She'd already finished the yellow and orange. Farther along, Griff was painting the bottom in green, blue, and purple stripes. He was a restful person to work with because he didn't try to boss you around like most men did. In fact, he didn't really talk at all. Maybe her father would have been like that, a quiet but reassuring presence. Most people just talked and talked and talked. Didn't they realize how boring they were?

"You missed a spot."

Mahina jumped, and nearly dropped her brush. The ladder wobbled. She turned and glared down at Keola's laughing face. Ziggy gave a warning bark.

"Hey, chill out Mahi-mahi. It's just a rainbow." Keola broke into "Somewhere over the you-know-what." He actually had a pretty nice voice. Not as good as hers, though, or Moku's. No training. Moku couldn't come today, he'd said yesterday. His family was performing at a *lūʻau* Kona side. Making good money, too.

"Jeez, Ke, you're such a jerk. Shut up already." She dipped her brush in the bucket perched on top of her stepladder and resumed painting. "Some of us are busy here."

"Okay, just wondered if you wanted a break. I just finished the farmhouse. All that brown and grey made me thirsty."

Mahina knew he was referring to the vodka he had stashed in the car. Maybe it would help her mood. Then again, drinking it last night may have created the mood to begin with. She was tired of being angry. Why was everyone so stupid and irritating?

"Well, now that you mention it." She smiled, deciding to be sweet. Even easy-going Keola wouldn't stick with her forever if she kept being such a bitch. She climbed down the ladder, bringing the red paint with her. Nearly done.

She smiled at Griff, and he smiled back. He had a nice face. Funny how you didn't really notice him, like he was sort of a blank. "I'll be back," she said, not really meaning it, her father fantasies forgotten.

Keola carried Aloha Maid guava drinks in one hand and plastic cups filled with ice in the other. They walked down the curving driveway to the truck, Ziggy trotting behind. She'd no doubt hear from Iris later about her early departure, how she was shirking her responsibility to the production and yadda yadda yadda.

Mahina felt the sharp warmth of the alcohol as she took the first gulp of her sweet, icy drink. The loud voices and clatter of the workday had decreased in volume, buffered by trees and vines.

"Better?" Keola put his arm around her, and she leaned against him.

"I heard something weird earlier," she said, remembering. "Desiree—you know, Glinda—and her boyfriend were fighting. He said something about making the drop tonight. It sounded like he was threatening her." Something clicked in Mahina's mind. Could he be BomBoy? She'd blocked her stalker on Facebook after Ziggy's abduction, but maybe she should unblock him, see what happened next.

"She's a tough *wahine*." Keola poured another drink. "I wouldn't try to mess with her."

"I wonder if it's drugs. The Policeman is always going on about ice this and meth that." Mahina held out her cup for more. "Maybe Desiree's into that. The boyfriend looks pervy."

"You should tell Kapili." Keola looked at her.

"What? No way." Mahina shook her head.

"He's a good guy. Why do you hate him so much?"

Mahina didn't answer. She was starting to feel dazed and blurry. No more ladders today. She needed a nap.

"Let's go to the beach, Ke."

"Okay by me."

They climbed into the truck, leaving their empty cups stacked on the roof of George's Miata, and rolled away down the shady driveway.

⌣

GRIFF WATCHED MAHINA WALK AWAY. HE KNEW SHE WOULDN'T be back. There was so much he wanted to tell her, so much she needed to know. But the time wasn't right. They had worked together in near silence. He had sensed the girl's tension at first, then felt it drain away, leaving her relaxed and happy, given over to the creative task. Passing buckets and brushes, moving without words, they had painted as a team, the sharp scent and glistening flow of paint over wood revealing the color, the connection of hand and brush bringing the thing into being, like music. It made Griff feel things he hadn't felt for years, since before the voices started talking to him.

He was tired now. He felt his sixty-five years after hours of labor in the sun. It was time to go home and check in at the website. He picked up two of the buckets and turned to walk back to the workshop.

"I don't believe we've met."

It was the weasel, pointing his sharp face forward. He made Griff uneasy, just as weasels had when he was a boy in Idaho. You never knew what they might do, and they were vicious. A weasel had snuck into the chicken coop on the farm Griff grew up on and killed all the hens one night, just bit their throats and left them to bleed out. Didn't even eat them. Weasels were cruel and wasteful.

"Hunter Craddock, friend of Desiree's, your good witch." The weasel held out his hand, but Griff held onto the buckets and nodded slightly. "And you are?"

Griff saw a gleam enter the weasel's eyes. Even without speaking, he had given something away, something precious. He could feel a buzzing in his head, the alert system blaring.

"Ah." The weasel pointed at him and gave a little laugh. "You must be the one who scared Desiree in the theater basement. Griff." He paused, tilting his head to one side. Griff tensed, waiting to see the weasel's teeth. "So, what was that all about?"

Griff's mind was racing now. What was this—thing? Part of the threat. All his fibers shouted it, and the voices shouted with them.

"Why were you down there?"

Griff didn't answer. He could sense the weasel's tension, as though readying itself to strike. He gripped the paint buckets. A surge of energy shot through his body and he moved forward with it, shouldering past the weasel, who dropped back.

"Whoa, buddy. Touchy subject, eh?"

Griff didn't look behind him, although his back tingled and snapped.

He passed Desiree, who looked at him in alarm. She was unimportant, a goat, appealing, willful, capable of damage, but ultimately harmless. He needed to get online. Go to the source. The Energy Center had entered him. He had felt It earlier with Mahina, how he was able to channel Its beams to calm her down. Now, It was moving him, directing him. He was a vessel.

⌣

PATRICK SAT HUNCHED OVER HIS PLATE, SHOVELING POTATO MAC salad into his mouth on autopilot as his mind circled around Mac's studio, reaching in vain for his beautiful mango bowl. He imagined Cindy lying on one of Mac's carved Balinese chaise lounges, drinking her pregnancy herbs and hating him—or still loving him.

"Hungry?" Belinda sat down in the plastic chair next to him and smiled, taking a bite of coleslaw from her otherwise empty plate. "Eew." She wrinkled her nose.

"Sweet and soggy?" Patrick gestured with his fork. He should pull out of this funk. Here was a lovely young woman trying to engage him in conversation.

"Do you ever go to the Friday night swing dancing at Black Cat Coffee?" Belinda flushed, then stabbed again at her squishy coleslaw.

Whoa, that was abrupt, he thought. "I live in Volcano, so not really." Patrick took another bite and chewed. Time to rally. "But it sounds fun. I like dancing." He smiled, trying to mean it. "I also like their coffee and bagels. And their cats."

"Well, we should go sometime. When the play is over and we have Friday nights free again, that is. I mean, you don't have to have a partner, but it's okay if you do—come with someone."

Patrick could feel her eagerness and tried not to recoil. How could he be kind but not encourage any romantic energy between them?

"Do you like to ride bikes?" There, he was making an effort.

"I *do.*" Belinda gave Patrick a big smile with lots of teeth. Someone must have told her it was dazzling—her best feature. What a sweetheart. She was so young.

"I haven't ridden for a while, but I brought my bike with me from Oklahoma. Just need to pump up the tires and I'm all set." She gave a little bounce in her seat.

"You should bring it up to Volcano. There are some great rides." Patrick infused his voice with enthusiasm. "Although I guess it might have to wait till after the run."

"I guess so." Belinda paused. "How about lunch sometime?"

"Sure, although I really only come down to Hilo for rehearsals or when I'm subbing." This is a ridiculous complication, he thought, but on the other hand, the poor girl needs friends.

"Okay, well—nice to see you." Belinda's cheerful bubble had deflated. She stood up and headed for the trash can.

"You know, I probably can do lunch," Patrick called after her. "Sometimes I just teach in the morning or afternoon."

Belinda turned and flashed her toothy smile at him again. "Well, okay then. Give me a call!"

"Great." Patrick turned back to his plate but found it empty. Oh Cindy, he thought.

⌣

"Ready to go, sweetheart?"

Merle's easy endearment poured a soothing balm on Nora's turbulent heart. She looked at her watch. She didn't expect Clyde and Greta to arrive for a few more hours, but it would be wise to hurry home and be ready. Anger was beginning to take over from fear, and that was an improvement.

Merle put his hand on her lower back and she felt a wave of sensation zing through her. She thought of Harriet's veiled warning and wondered what the older woman knew. Did she want to find out? Not really. Should she? Probably. All right, yes, she should, although it could just be vicious, small-town gossip.

Painting the castle had been therapeutic. All those dark, twisting, sinister vines, the grey, jagged rocks, the towering black spires. It must be some kind of externalization thing, transferring the interior darkness to the exterior, bringing it to the surface, embellishing and then leaving it to dry. Right there in the open. Then moving away.

"Would you like me to come over?" Merle looked at her, his eyes playful.

Nora hesitated. Clyde had always been possessive. Seeing Merle with his recently divorced wife might throw him off balance. But what was Greta's weakness? There must be a chink in that elegant armor, and she had to find it. Fast. Merle might be an ally, or even a catalyst.

Merle persisted. "You're teasing me with that floppy hat. I want to rip it off and get my hands in your glorious hair."

Nora laughed, warmth washing through her body. Why not abandon caution and throw herself into sensual oblivion? "Well, in that case..."

"I'll follow you home."

Hollow yet giddy, Nora put the Volvo in gear and headed down the bumpy road.

CHAPTER 20

NORA HAD JUST SLID OUT OF MERLE'S SLIPPERY EMBRACE UNder the shower and climbed out of the claw-footed tub when she heard Clyde's truck pull up outside. Shit. He was an hour early. She grabbed a towel and ran to her bedroom in a crouch, leaving wet footprints on the old wooden floorboards. Pulling on a sleeveless rayon dress she found draped over a chair, she pattered back to the bathroom and opened the shower curtain.

"Back for more, sweetheart?" Merle's head looked small with his luxuriant hair slicked down, grey roots showing, his grin oversized. The steam billowed out.

"They're here," Nora hissed. "Clyde and Greta and the kids. Get dressed right now and stay out of sight. Please." The decision sprang fully formed from her mouth, but she trusted it. The less Clyde knew about her the better. Especially now, when lawyers might be involved. She ran a comb through her wet hair. "I mean it." He gave her a mock salute and turned off the water.

Thank god she'd had Merle park his car on the road. She just hoped no one would need to use the toilet.

Nora opened the front door and paused for a moment before she walked down the steps. Calm and graceful, she told herself, smiling. Grace Kelly—with red hair and freckles.

The house was the typical plantation-style post-and-pier, raised off the ground, with storage space underneath. Many Hilo-dwellers closed in this area to make extra rooms, or even a separate apartment, but that hadn't happened to Nora's rental. She and the children perched above empty space, like a treehouse with no tree.

Clyde and Greta were climbing out of their seats, and the four children were already running around on the front lawn, blocked from the road by an unruly hibiscus hedge.

"We're flying, Mom!" Miri zoomed past, arms outstretched. "We're birds migrating south for the winter."

Oliver held his arms out and hopped, opening and closing his mouth. "I can eat while I fly," he said. "I never have to come down."

Greta's children seemed hesitant, Nora noticed, with a mean little sense of triumph. They looked awkward and self-conscious, as though giving way to flights of fancy was new to them. They kept looking over at their mother, who stood with her arm linked in Clyde's.

Nora took her time reaching the bottom of the stairs, and walked over to Clyde and Greta. "Looks like they had a good time." Happy happy happy, she thought, feeling the reluctant lift in her cheeks.

"It was lovely," said Greta. "The children get along so well together. So nice for Hans and Oliver each to have another boy, and for Karen and Miri to be girls." Her smile was a challenge.

Nora kept smiling, too, her teeth clenched.

"Listen Nora," said Clyde. "We're thinking of taking the kids to Oahu next weekend, to the zoo and the water park and all that. We went to the Hilo zoo today and it was pathetic. They need to see what a real one looks like." He and Greta shared a superior little smile.

"They have, remember?" Nora's anger boiled to the surface. Perhaps there was just too much of it to suppress anymore. After all these years, it had finally achieved critical mass. "We practically lived at the zoo in Vancouver every summer until you moved us to Hawai'i—not to mention the aquarium in Stanley Park." How dare Clyde confront her in front of Greta? "Plus, they'd miss *Wizard* rehearsal again, and opening night is in three weeks. Can't you wait until the show is over?" She crossed her arms. "It's important they follow through with this. You should support them."

"I hardly see them, Nora." Clyde was getting that look on his face. "They're supposed to be with me on weekends, remember? I don't know why you got them involved in this play since you know the custody agreement."

"That's funny," said Nora, "you were totally on board when I mentioned the auditions in the first place." Reminding Clyde of a promise he'd conveniently forgotten was an unspoken taboo in their relationship, but she couldn't help herself. She almost added that until recently he hadn't bothered to observe the agreement himself. "Are you saying you want them to quit the play? After all this time?" Nora kept her voice calm.

Greta was quiet.

Bet she put him up to it, Nora thought. And she's *smirking*. I mustn't say anything about Australia. Not now.

"Don't they know their parts already? And don't they have rehearsals during the week? Why are weekends so important?" Clyde made an impatient gesture, which also nudged Greta away.

Oliver zoomed between his parents, flapping his arms. "We're flying monkeys!"

Damn, thought Nora. He probably heard us and is trying to intervene. Oliver was the more sensitive twin, always trying to keep the peace.

Miri and Karen flapped behind Oliver. "Eee, eee, eee, eee."

"Surrender Dorothy," shouted Oliver.

Hans flapped off to the side, arms a little crooked.

"You really want to take this away from them, after all they've been through?" Zing. Nora saw her cheap shot hit its mark.

Clyde glowered at her. "Don't be hysterical, Nora. This is about my time with the children. I *am* their father."

"Of course you are," Nora soothed, ignoring the insult. "It's just a couple of weeks, and it means a lot to the children. There should be a way we can work it out."

Clyde shrugged. "We can just take them during the school week then, if weekends are so important. It's not like they're learning anything much except Hawaiian folklore at Po'okela, anyhow."

Nora was dumbstruck.

"We'll talk in a few days," he said.

Greta moved closer and smiled at Nora. "A trip to Oahu will be very educational. My children love to travel to the other islands."

"Oh, and Australia, too?" The words were out of her mouth before she even knew it. Wow. No wonder so many people—Clyde, for example—crashed through life shooting their mouths off and ignoring the destruction. Letting loose was thrilling! "When were you planning to talk to me about that, Clyde? Speaking of our custody agreement."

"Who told you that?" Clyde was purple, sputtering with outrage.

Nora opened her mouth to speak.

"Well, hello there." Merle appeared at the top of the stairs, wet curly hair sticking out all over. A towel was tucked in at his waist, and the formidable muscles of his bare chest and arms gleamed in the sunlight. He grinned, sending out warm beams of goodwill, like Jesus on the mountaintop. "I'm Nora's friend, Merle."

Nora had a close-up view of Clyde's absolute consternation before his man-of-the-world mask slid into place.

Greta, on the other hand, looked like someone had handed her a present wrapped with a big sparkly bow. "Merle." Greta's voice was a husky purr. "I was going to call you for another spiritual reading, and now here you are. The herb garden I had Ricardo plant gives off such vital energy, and the fan palms you recommended last time channel it right into the house." A wide carnivorous smile covered her face below the mirrored glasses.

"Greta. What wonderful news." Merle opened his arms wide. "I'll be up in Waimea again this week."

Nora acted on split-second instinct. "Why don't you two come up for a drink?"

"Delighted." Greta pulled off her sunglasses and moved toward the stairs. Even though she only had eyes for Merle, Nora saw as she passed that they were dilated, the pupils big as saucers. Interesting.

"Greta," Clyde barked.

Nora remembered that tone. How pleasant not to have it aimed at her.

"I have work to do at home. Come."

But Greta had already reached Merle. She turned and said, "What a pity," then gave Merle a lingering hug, her whole body pressed against his.

Nora could almost hear Clyde's teeth grinding.

"Call me," Merle said, as Greta put her sunglasses back on and glided down the stairs, nodding at Nora.

"Bye, then." Nora waved as the truck pulled out of the driveway, tires squealing.

＞

By the time Desiree finally gave Hunter the slip and herded her kids to the car, her nerves were jangling. He was hob-nobbing with George of all people. Fuck. She wasn't built to handle this kind of stress. She took a deep breath. Priorities, Desiree. What was most urgent? The threat to her children? He wouldn't, would he? Just trying to scare her.

No, the scariest thing facing her was making the drop tonight. What if the cops were watching this guy's place and caught her in their net? Hunter told her the dealer would give her a thousand bucks if she showed up with both packages.

It was never easy finding street parking on Kapi'olani and Desiree's apartment building didn't have enough room in its tiny lot for all the tenants. She finally found a small spot barely big enough for a motorcycle and seesawed her rusty old Honda into it.

Maybe the kids would be better off with Kama and his dancer. The thought flashed into Desiree's mind like a billboard. But that was ridiculous. Ever since the split, their father had gone through girlfriends like potato chips. Cultural differences my ass. He'd just wanted to screw around and kids shouldn't live with that. Sure she'd had guys over to spend the night, who hadn't? She was human. She had needs. But she always pushed them out the door early and she'd never let them touch the children. Now this thing with Hunter was getting out of hand. What if he kidnapped them? Or what if something happened to her and they were left alone?

Desiree slumped back in the recliner, kids crowded onto the couch watching cartoons. She pressed Kama's number on her phone and listened to it ring. His voicemail greeting bugged the shit out of her, but she waited through the 'ukulele strumming until his "Ho brah!" finally came.

"Kama, it's me." How much should she tell him? "I need to talk to you about the kids, see if they could stay with you for a while. Maybe. Call me." There, she'd made the first move.

Her heart thumped, and her head felt hollow. She wasn't one of those unfit mothers who abandoned their children for a life of crime. Was she? Would she end up on one of those reality shows she loved to hate? She could see it now—*Mothers Behind Bars*. She could hear her own lame excuses: I just needed a little more cash to make ends meet. I just wanted a better life for my children. Fuck. She got up to shower and change. How did you dress for your first meeting with a meth dealer? She pulled on jeans and a black T-shirt.

"I have to go out for a little while, you guys. I'll be back soon, and you'd better be ready for bed, okay?" She kissed the tops of their heads.

They were eating a bag of cheese puffs, eyes glued to the TV screen. She should make them eat more vegetables. Nakai had dark circles under his eyes. Did he feel the responsibility of being the "man of the house"? Malia, sitting in the middle, leaned on her older sister and sucked her orange-crusted thumb. Had some of her curls morphed into dreadlocks? They all needed haircuts, another of Desiree's skills. Maybe tomorrow. Kolea's arm circled Malia. What was she wearing? A tight halter top on her flat chest that said "Wild Child" and tiny shorts below, leaving a wide expanse of brown midriff in between. Had she bought that outfit for her ten-year-old daughter? Holy shit. Desiree was not given to introspection, but this new danger had stripped away her defenses. What kind of a mother was she?

She straightened up. Get a grip, she told herself. Stop whining and do your job.

She hadn't destroyed the piece of paper with the address on it—are you fucking kidding? Her memory was shot. These days she couldn't even keep more than three drink orders in her head at the same time. Squinting at Hunter's scrawl in the meager glow of the stairway light, she climbed into her car and seesawed back out into the street, knocking into both the car in front and the one behind her. That's what bumpers were for.

Driving at night in Hilo was a stark reminder that you lived on a rock in the middle of the ocean—so dark, with those half-assed orange streetlights, and hardly anyone out. Especially on a Sunday. She passed Kenji's Pancake House and headed out to Keaukaha.

The moon was full. Its pale light cast the landscape into eerie monochrome, like one of those old movies. At least she could see, although that meant she could also be seen.

Her headlights lit up a tsunami evacuation zone sign, and she slowed down to read the name on the street sign next to it. It was her turn. She wound her way along, passing one broken-down house after another, paint peeling, roofs rusted out, cars up on blocks, laundry hanging in carports, old refrigerators sinking into the ground, yards overgrown with vines. The jungle reclaiming the land.

At the end of the dead-end street a house squatted, nearly invisible in the darkness. Jesus. Did someone actually live in this dump? She pulled over and parked, waiting a moment before she opened the door and climbed out. A dog barked. Then another. And another. A whole pack of dogs. Motherfuckers. Desiree stood close to the car, ready to jump back in if they attacked her. She could hear the clang of chains. Hopefully they weren't as rusty as the roof of the house.

As she drew closer, a blinding light flashed in her eyes. Must be on a sensor, she told herself. Don't panic.

"Stop right there," a voice rasped out of the darkness.

Desiree held up her hands, like he'd said, "Stick 'em up."

"You must be the friend I've heard about."

All she could see was the white spotlight. She tried not to look at it directly, but yellow blobs were already playing bumper cars across her vision. "That's me."

The light went out as suddenly as it had come on, and Desiree was blind.

"Come inside."

She walked toward the house, trying not to stumble. The dogs growled and lunged against their chains.

"Shut up," yelled the voice.

They lay down.

The door creaked on its hinges. Inside, the house was dark. Desiree felt the cold clamminess of panic.

"Could we have some lights, please?" Her voice sounded tough, not even a quaver. Her eyes were adjusting.

The shadowy figure bent to turn on a light.

A lava lamp—how seventies.

The figure turned. His entire head was covered with one of those rubber clown masks. Really? She choked back a laugh. "What's with the mask? I already know where you live."

"So, what have you got, pretty lady?" His voice sounded like he was trying to disguise it. Did she know him? Desiree pulled back her shoulders and lifted her chin.

"Wait a minute, buddy." She stared at the smirking mask. "I want to see the money first." As if the asshole couldn't pull a gun on her and take the drugs, then feed her to his dogs. Her legs felt like they had the jitterbug spell on them, but she stood rock solid.

"Relax. I know the deal." He walked into a back room.

Must have a safe or something, she thought. Deep breaths.

He returned with a small package of bills, which he counted out for her, one thousand dollars in fifties.

"Okay." Desiree pulled out the packages and shoved them at him with one hand, holding the other out for the cash. After a moment's hesitation he gave it to her. She stuffed the folded bills into her bag and turned to go.

"Why in such a hurry?" He motioned toward the living room. "Come sit down. Tell me all about your big musical at the Palace. Who do you play? Dorothy?" He laughed. "Are you friends with the Wizard?"

The windows were covered with dingy curtains, and the lava lamp cast a weird purple light on the fast-food wrappers and beer cans strewn over the couch and floor. Gross. "None of your business," Desiree retorted. "If you're so interested in the play, why didn't you try out yourself?"

"Jeez, lady." He did a mock recoil. "Just trying to be friendly. I'm a big supporter of the arts." He moved closer. "Why don't you stay and sample the goods? Hunter's cook is the best on the island."

"I don't do drugs. Especially not with masked men. And I'm going home now." She stared at his piggy eyes, barely visible through the mask's eyeholes. "Hunter won't be happy to hear you've been hassling me."

"Hassling you?" He shrugged. "Matter of interpretation. And Hunter didn't sound too happy with you when we last talked." The clown face sneered back at her. "Come to think of it, I'm not either. The Palace was a great drop spot, with all those underground passages leading between buildings. I barely had to come above ground."

Desiree's surprise must have showed.

"What? Didn't know about the great Hilo underground?" He laughed. It was an ugly sound. "They built the first tunnels back in the old days, for bomb shelters. From there, people improvised. And now, because you screwed it up, I have to wait for a dumb-ass bitch to come to my door, probably leading the cops to me."

Two words flipped a dangerous switch in Desiree, and he had just said one of them. She started toward him, then stopped, glaring at him in contempt. Her legs were still trembling, but now with rage.

"Feisty, just how I like them. Come on, baby." He held out his arms.

"You're disgusting," Desiree spat. She hoisted her handbag higher and put a hand inside, groping for her mace.

"Ah-ah-ah, little lady." He stepped toward her. "Don't be doing anything foolish."

Desiree backed away. That mask was really starting to freak her out. "Just so you know, asshole, I told someone where I was going tonight—in case anything happened." He stopped moving. "That's right. It all comes back to you." She felt for the doorknob. Greasy. She wrenched it open and half-ran down the rocky driveway to her car as the dogs barked and lunged at her back.

His growling laugh followed her. "Until next time," he called.

Next time I'm bringing the flame-thrower, she thought. You're toast, asshole. She gunned the engine and peeled out.

Yet what Clownface had said about the great Hilo underground had sparked her curiosity. What other places besides the Palace might have hidden passages? She thought of the basement at the Aloha Bar and Grill. It had a door she'd never opened, assuming it led to a closet full of old mops, just as she'd also assumed about that door in the Palace basement. Maybe she'd been wrong about both. It was time to do some investigating.

⌣

PATRICK REALIZED HE HAD LEFT A TRAIL OF EVIDENCE FOR THE crime he planned to commit, even though it wasn't a crime to take back your own property, he reminded his internal critic. The internet history of the how-to videos he'd watched on lock-picking, the testimony of the hardware store clerk about the tools he'd bought, including a doorknob to practice on. His first attempt took an hour, his second half an hour. He'd have to hope Mac was as sound a sleeper as Cindy. His method wasn't exactly noiseless. And he'd have to remember not to swear.

Patrick dressed in black and stashed his tools in a fanny pack. He would ride his bike. The bowl would fit in the basket Cindy had always laughed at, calling him an old granny. Had she meant it affectionately? His bowl had to still be there. He had to get it back. When he had accomplished this first goal he would turn to the second, more difficult task of winning Cindy back. Then he would man up to the third, most challenging endeavor of all. Becoming a father. If it was his baby.

At two a.m., Patrick pedaled up the road with his bike light switched off. He reached Mac's driveway and peered through the dense vegetation. No lights. He pushed the bike up the gravel drive as quietly as he could, cringing at every crunch. He left it leaning against a tree at the fork of the turning circle nearest the studio, poised for a quick getaway.

The house loomed large on the other side, a matte outline against the starry sky. The moon had already set, and the air was cool and fragrant in the darkness.

Patrick tiptoed up to the studio door and switched on his adjustable-beam headlamp—another hardware store purchase. He pulled on a pair of thin gloves, fished out his improvised lock-picks and set to work. A dog next door started to bark and Patrick swore under his breath, trying to concentrate. After what seemed like hours, the lock still had not sprung. Sweat poured down his face and he rubbed his stinging eyes.

Okay, he thought, one more try at the discreet approach before I get out the chisel and pliers. He checked his watch. Two-forty-five a.m. Almost the hour of deepest sleep. He took a long breath and remembered his straightened bobby pins. Maybe a lighter touch would work. Sure enough, after just a few minutes of wiggling, he heard a sound that filled him with joy. The lock clicked. He turned the knob and the door opened like an invitation.

The thin beam of light from his headlamp swept across the floor in front of him, pinpointing the corner where he'd seen the bowl. It wasn't there. Patrick's breath was ragged and his heart thumped in his throat. Calm down and think, he told himself. Mac probably packaged it up tonight to get ready for tomorrow's delivery. The beam crept around the room until it rested on the workbench. A sturdy cardboard box sat there, all taped up.

Patrick turned to his lock-picks again and found a narrow blade to cut through the tape. He pulled the bubble wrap aside and there it was, gleaming in the sharp white light: his perfect bowl, with a yellow invoice nestled inside. USD 2500. The address was in Tokyo. Damn.

He tenderly lifted the bowl and set it to one side. Taking one of the misshapen starter bowls off the shelf and laying the invoice inside it, he covered it snugly in bubble wrap and re-taped the box. Take that, Mac.

As he headed for the door, bowl tucked under his arm, his foot caught on something.

Crash. A cascade of wood clattered onto the floor. The dog next door started up again, its barks sharp and urgent. Clutching his precious bowl to his chest, Patrick switched off his headlamp and fumbled his way to the door, pressing in the lock button before closing it behind him. A light flashed on upstairs in the house. The dog barked louder and faster as it caught his scent.

Patrick abandoned caution and pounded down the gravel drive, each step an explosion of sound. He shoved the bowl into the bike basket, already lined with his yoga towel, and pedaled for home, lungs bursting.

When he pulled into his own driveway he bent over and wheezed, then straightened up, grinning.

He shook both his fists in the air, his mouth open to the night sky in a silent shout of triumph.

CHAPTER 21

"**W**ELCOME TO THE HELL BEFORE HELL WEEK," BOOMED George.

Laughter verging on hysteria burst out in isolated pockets. A full week of supercharged rehearsals had passed since the workday, and now cast and crew were back at it after a Sunday off. The humid early October heat was stifling, even at six o'clock at night, and George could feel his troupe's fatigue and irritability.

"Just two weeks until we open. We have to step up the intensity now. I want fine-tuning, not still learning." He paused to let them think about their deficiencies. "And by the way, don't forget we'll need volunteers with trucks to move the sets over to the theater next weekend, right Fred? Larry?"

A few hands lifted from the seats where the cast sprawled, fanning themselves. George noted them down. Only the Munchkins were on their feet, scampering around in the aisles and out into the lobby.

"Okay, this will be brutal, but I promise you it will be worth it." George injected an extra dose of energy and positivity into his voice. "We're really close, and the added rehearsals will bring us where we need to be to really knock 'em dead on opening night. Everyone needs to focus—and practice at home, too. I want you living in Oz 24/7."

Scattered laughter.

"This week we'll do two work runs of each act. Tonight we're going to run Act One, so pay attention to your cues. Remember your blocking. When you're offstage, write notes for yourself. You better believe I will be. We'll need an hour or so for notes before we go home. Act Two tomorrow night."

Merle roared from the second row and everyone laughed and clapped.

George found himself smiling too, in spite of his persistent gloom. If they didn't pull this thing together the Palace would sink. It probably would anyway. He could hear his father's derisive voice in his mind, a daily occurrence since the accident. Was his fight for the Palace a fight against his father? A fight for his own values, for the identity his father had never acknowledged? Enough. He couldn't afford this DIY psychoanalysis right now.

At their portfolio review last week, Evan had assured George that while his personal finances were holding fairly steady, in spite of the plunging economy, he would be ill-advised to take on the Palace expenses. Maybe for this show, if necessary, but that was it. Since mild-mannered Evan rarely spoke so forcefully, George gave up the idea, half-hoping the new donor Desiree's friend had mentioned would still give the Palace a life-saving cash injection. If he materialized. George had left several voicemails at the number on Hunter Craddock's card, but the jerk hadn't called back. Probably just a big talker. George would get happy when he saw the money, and not before. Meanwhile, he would lash his cast into the best performance of their lives, even if it killed him.

Oh yes, he had almost forgotten. "Enid is bringing the costumes tonight, so when you have a break, go try yours on and arrange with her to make any adjustments. If you need accessories, make sure you get them this week, and start practicing putting on your makeup. Belinda has volunteered to help, so see her if you don't have any or don't know how to use it." George paused. "And Phil has offered to help with hair. Apparently he's had training." A few guffaws. "Yes, he's bald. Hahaha."

He moved to the side. "Okay, places. Techies, make sure the props are there."

Fred had fitted new bolts with padlocks to try to secure the theater. He and George both took boxes of the most portable props home with them between rehearsals. The police had deemed the vandalism and petty theft a nuisance rather than a more serious crime, and suggested the theater hire a security guard. The players were on their own.

George sat down in the front row with his clipboard.

Fred appeared next to him with the marked-up script. "Here goes, eh?"

George grunted. "Why don't you go take care of things backstage, Fred? If they don't know their lines by now, let them squirm. No more mollycoddling."

"Sink or swim, eh?" Fred raised his eyebrows and shrugged, then hurried off, switching hats from assistant director back to stage manager.

Out of the corner of his eye, George saw an unfamiliar shape walk through the door from the alley. He turned to get a better look. It was Hunter Craddock. George beamed and motioned for the man to sit next to him.

"Thought I'd take you up on your offer to sit in on rehearsal." Craddock shook George's outstretched hand and lowered himself into a seat with one armrest broken off. "I can already see why you need funding. This place is a dump."

George bristled but tamped down his annoyance. He wiped his hand surreptitiously on his pant leg. Craddock's grasp had been clammy. "We prefer to think of the Palace as a grand dame who's fallen on hard times. 'Distressed elegance' is our catchphrase."

Hunter laughed. "I'll include that in my report to my very generous friend." He crossed an ankle over a knee. "I'll need a tour, of course—top to bottom. And a building inspector's report."

George met Hunter's electric blue gaze. "Of course. We'll set it up. And invite your friend to come along. I'd love to meet him—or her—in person, and so would the president of our board." George badly wanted to believe the donor existed, but there was something sideways about this guy. Those eyes. "And now, if you'll excuse me, we need to get started."

George motioned to Larry at the keyboard. "From the top."

‿

DESIREE SLUMPED IN A SEAT BELOW THE CROSS AISLE, STILL shaken by Hunter's appearance earlier. He hadn't stayed long, and she'd been able to hide in the wings until he said his goodbyes to a fawning George and strutted back down the alley. What was that scumbag up to?

She didn't go on until after the tornado. The *keiki* wranglers kept the Munchkins corralled in Actors' Alley, safely closed to the road with a tall iron gate, so she didn't have to keep track of her kids. Desiree closed her eyes and rubbed her temples. Kama hadn't called back. Fat lot of good he was. She was on her own. Her anger had worn off and now she just felt trapped and afraid. And stupid stupid stupid.

During her lunch shift at the Aloha, one of the pretty young servers had bounced up to the bar and slapped down a folded paper with "GLINDA THE GOOD" scrawled on top.

"This must be for you." She smirked and flounced off.

"Wait, where—" Desiree sputtered, but the server was already across the room, taking orders from a table full of men.

Desiree unfolded the paper and turned her back to the bar. Inside, the handwriting was dark and spiky: "I know what you're doing in the basement."

She grabbed the sink, her legs wobbly. She closed her eyes and breathed in through her nose, then out again, slowly. Mustn't lose it in front of the customers.

"Hey, are you okay?" One of her regulars tapped his glass on the bar.

Desiree turned around, beaming. "Just a fan letter. Did you know I'm in the Palace musical? I'm doing a star turn as Glinda, in *The Wizard of Oz*. Don't miss it!"

She was still feeling shaky and paranoid when Hunter gave her another package that afternoon. She didn't tell him about the note.

Fucker had made her leave work to meet him at Boiling Pots again. Laughed when she told him about the clown mask and the threatening asshole behind it. Told her to suck it up, and of course hadn't said a word about showing up at the theater. She had to end this somehow. But in the meantime she had another drop to make tonight, back at the dealer's house. She shuddered. Maybe she should get a gun. No. Not with the kids around. She'd have to make do with her mace, and maybe a knife.

Before Hunter interrupted her shift, Desiree had used her break at the Aloha to settle her nerves—and investigate her hunch about the restaurant basement. There were two doors and she tried them both. One was the utility closet she had expected, with mops and buckets and big custodial brooms. The other was locked.

She pulled a bobby pin out of her hair and straightened it. There were advantages to a juvenile delinquent past. She closed her eyes and felt for the magic place. Hot *damn*. The lock clicked and the knob turned. Move over, Nancy Drew.

Stale air wafted through the doorway. She stepped into a murky passageway, lit only a few yards by the basement fluorescents. Should have brought a flashlight. She squinted down the tunnel but could see nothing. Steps clattered down the stairs and she leaped back in and shut the door, leaving it unlocked.

"Glinda," Fred called to her now. "Places."

God, she was really losing it. Dorothy and Toto were almost done with the flying house scene. How had she not noticed? Crime was taking its toll on her. And someone was watching.

"Are you a good witch, or a bad witch?" she muttered as she hurried backstage and into the wings.

⌣

A FEW ROWS DOWN FROM DESIREE, PATRICK WATCHED THE AC-tion from a seat just below stage. Though still riding high from the previous night's caper, lack of sleep was catching up. He yawned and stretched, trying to keep his eyes open. Letting that poodle play Toto was a mistake. He was always running offstage, and Moku had to catch the little dog and toss him back on again. Stuffed would be so much better. But Mahina was stubborn. Interesting to see George stymied. He was usually such a tyrant.

"Toto, I've got a feeling we're not in Kansas anymore." The girl had grown into her part, putting forth a naïve, goodhearted

Dorothy. She was still a spoiled princess, but what pretty sixteen-year-old wasn't? Cindy's baby might be a girl. They could be in plays together. He could see her now, an adorable *hapa-haole* child with sticking out braids.

The Munchkins tittered as Desiree approached. She looked pissed off, not at all like a good witch. Patrick leaned forward.

"Where are the feet, goddammit?" George gestured at the empty space.

Moku hustled over and shoved the mannequin legs under the house, ruby slippers gleaming under the lights.

Patrick leaned back again. His attention drifted between the play, his imaginary child, and his stolen-but-now-recovered bowl. He imagined Mac's face when his irate Japanese customer called to complain. Should he confront Mac himself? And if so, how?

"Only bad witches are ugly." Glinda looked as bad as they came. What was with her?

Soon Mahina was singing "The wind began to switch," and all the Munchkins joined in the chorus, beefed up by the adults singing offstage. It sounded surprisingly good. Patrick felt a surge of excitement. This show might be great. And he had a starring role.

The smoke cloud appeared, and Mahina started to cough.

"Who killed my sister?" Harriet hunched toward her, and Desiree intervened. She looked like she could kick the Wicked Witch's ass and enjoy every second.

"Glinda, get in character. Enough with the mood." George had noticed, too.

In a startling transformation, Glinda's face turned radiant, happy, beaming with goodness. The woman could act, after all.

"Okay," George cut in. "Let's do that ruby slipper exchange again. Too slow."

Patrick sighed. It was going to be a long night.

"I'll get you, my pretty, and your little dog, too." The Witch shook her broom at Mahina. "Ha ha ha ha ha—ha ha ha ha ha!"

Whew, thought Patrick. Lots of female hostility playing itself out up there. As much as he shrank from conflict, there was no way around it this time. He would confront Mac. And Cindy. She had to have been in on the bowl theft, and he needed to find out why if he wanted a future with her and his possible child. The Scarecrow wasn't just passive and floppy. He was strong.

He moved into the wings to await his cue.

᠈

GRIFF SAT IN THE THEATER BALCONY, FEELING THE HARMONIC waves. The vibrations had sped up and jangled when the weasel intruded, moving from harmony to cacophony. Now that he was gone the energy had realigned, although a throbbing undercurrent remained.

Griff didn't go onstage again until much later. Dorothy hadn't even met the Cowardly Lion yet. Before rehearsal he'd heard an update on the radio: the comet was flying closer and would be nearest to earth on opening night. He expected the attack on the Energy Center then, but the weasel showing up tonight triggered the alarms. Maybe it would happen sooner. BomBoy hadn't posted anything since his threats about Griff's identity, and Griff was still on high alert. He needed to hear The Voice again. Soon.

Ah. The poppy field at last. Time to make his descent. But his sixth sense was tingling. Something was about to happen. Was Mahina in danger? Had the weasel set something in motion? Why had Desiree been in the basement? Was she part of the threat? Griff knew there were clues all around him. Everything was present that would be manifested. But the truth was hidden. How would he know what to do? The Voice must speak.

Crash. Screams rose from a cloud of dust right below stage. Griff hurried down the stairs. It was too soon for the comet. What had attacked the theater?

"Okay, okay, people, stay calm." George shouldered his way through the crowd. "Is anyone hurt?"

Dust hung in the humid air. A chorus of coughing. "What happened?"

Aunty Em, her face streaked with dirt, pointed at a large chunk of plaster. "It must have fallen from the ceiling. Just missed me!"

Griff looked up, but it was impossible to see through the murk if there was a corresponding hole in the high-domed roof.

"It's the ghost. I could feel him, the evil man. He's coming for me." The old woman started to wail and disappeared into a wave of comforting arms.

"But why? How could that just happen?" Patrick asked. "And if it did, does that mean the whole ceiling is compromised? Is it about to collapse?"

More screams, and people started stampeding for the doors.

Griff stood still. He knew it was a sign.

And then The Voice spoke, through Evan, the Tin Man. Griff had never paid much attention to him. "This is sabotage. All the thefts, the vandalism. And now this. Someone is trying to stop the show."

"Hear, hear! What? Oh please," said Merle, Patrick and Harriet in chorus.

George looked unconvinced.

The Voice spoke again, through Mahina. "His name is BomBoy."

CHAPTER 22

EVAN STAYED BEHIND AFTER THE ABORTED REHEARSAL TO help put away the props. Poor Enid. Only a handful of cast members had tried on their costumes before the sky had fallen. He helped her carry the boxes back to her van. Obviously the theater was not secure enough to leave valuables, especially after tonight's incident.

She reached up and patted his cheek with her manicured hand. "Thank you, love. So thoughtful."

Everyone had questioned Mahina and exclaimed over Ziggy's abduction and BomBoy's Facebook posts. Why didn't you tell us? was the general refrain, most emphatically from George. The police took their time coming.

BomBoy. What a corny name.

Patrick and Griff had climbed up the narrow stairway backstage and figured out the chunk of plaster could have been thrown from a high catwalk that ran the length of the theater, from backstage all the way to the projection booth at the rear. Holes for the lights opened to the house along the way—big enough for projectiles to fly through. Disturbing to think someone had been lurking up there, watching them. Even more disturbing that he (Evan assumed it was a man) had been violent, although maybe he'd been aiming to miss. Aunty Em had been six feet away, at least. Being old didn't mean she wasn't a drama queen. Getting the cast back on board might be tough, and who knows what the police report would say.

Luke was in a mood again. Evan wasn't sure if he was even coming over tonight. Maybe he'd gone back to Harriet's place. This roller-coaster ride was wearing him down. The women in Evan's past had never had this kind of power over him. Probably because he hadn't loved them. But what was love? Surely this was just lust. Pure physical desire. But no, he also felt a deep tenderness for Luke. He cared about his lover's wellbeing, wanted to hear his inmost thoughts. This was all new.

But it also sucked.

"Hey." Belinda smiled as he nearly bumped into her. "How's it going? I mean, apart from the saboteur and all."

George's voice carried through the theater as he talked to the two uniforms who had responded to the call. He motioned up to the ceiling by the lights and made a sweeping movement, tracing the arc of the projectile.

"Great." Evan grinned, trying to look carefree. "How about you?"

"Fine. A little worried about the show. Especially now. But, you know." She paused, smoothing back her curly hair. "How are things with Luke?"

"Great," Evan lied. He searched for words. He'd never actually apologized to Belinda. "Look, I'm really sorry for how things turned out—you know—"

"Don't worry about it." Belinda's laugh sounded forced. "I have this history. The men I'm attracted to. So I wasn't surprised. Not your fault."

"Really?" Evan stared. "I'm not the first—gay man you've dated?" He started to laugh. "I'm sorry, but what a bummer."

"Yeah." Belinda laughed again, a looser sound. "Sucks to be me."

"But you're great! You're so bright and pretty and talented and fun—"

"I think Patrick might like me." Belinda looked at Evan hopefully.

"Patrick's a great guy—a little old for you?" He thought, My god, I'm becoming Belinda's gay best friend. Next she'll ask me for fashion tips.

They picked up either end of a folding table and shuffled it offstage, leaning it against the wall in Actor's Alley. Evan listened as Belinda prattled on about her conversation with Patrick at the workday and their plans to have lunch, to go dancing and biking. How she could tell he was lonely. His girlfriend had just dumped him, and he was probably going through some kind of mid-life crisis. But wait, did she want to be his transitional person—or worse, his trophy girlfriend to prove he wasn't old yet? What was she getting into?

"Slow down there, missy." Evan held up his hand. "Just have lunch with the guy and see what happens from there."

"You're right," Belinda wailed. "I always over-think everything. I'm such a disaster."

Evan shook his head. "Stop it, now. Go home and have a nice cool shower. Eat some ice cream. You'll feel better."

"Thanks, Evan. You're a real friend." Belinda gazed at him with glowing eyes.

Evan thought, Okay, I can do this. Maybe I owe it to her. "That's my girl." He winked and pointed his finger at her.

Belinda giggled and gave him a finger wave. "'Night."

"'Night."

A pause, then she said, "Call me later?"

Evan groaned noiselessly as he walked down the alley to the street.

⌣

GRIFF STAYED AT THE PALACE AFTER EVERYONE ELSE HAD GONE home. The Voice had spoken, but what was he supposed to do? He pushed down the other voices in his mind. Their chatter had become deafening during BomBoy's attack and its aftermath. He needed to be alone so he could hear and feel the Energy Center without distraction. Was BomBoy still there in the building? No matter. He wasn't afraid. Fear had burned out of his system forever when he crawled through the tunnels of Vietnam to lay explosives. He climbed up to the organ console and turned on the switches, waiting as the instrument hummed to life.

He played the opening notes from 2001: A Space Odyssey, followed by the two climactic chords. The music vibrated up his arms, all through his body and beyond, filling the theater. Can you hear me? He paused, the sound echoing away. The darkness pulsed in silence. He played the next sequence, then stopped and waited again. Nothing.

Griff played the whole theme, giving himself over to the music. His mother had taught him the piano as a boy and he had messed around on the church organ in their small Idaho town. But this magnificent instrument was his destiny. It was better than any drug he'd ever tried. The old organ filled the entire womb-like space of the theater with gorgeous sound, ringing out from the pipe chambers high on each side wall, powered by the warm glow of the Energy Center in the basement. This was the music of the spheres. The answers were here. He had to give voice to the organ so the Power could communicate Its wishes, desires and commands. He whirled through the vibrations, unwinding like a spindle of fuse through the tunnels, spiraling higher and higher until the white light engulfed him.

⌣

MAHINA LISTENED, PERCHED IN THE PROJECTION BOOTH AT THE very top of the house. No one ever thought to look there, so it was her favorite hiding place. At least it used to be. How creepy to think that BomBoy had been climbing around in her aerie, watching her, watching all of them, and then striking. Everyone was so mad at her, like it was her fault she had a stalker. She shivered. He could still be here, hiding in the shadows. The police were hanging around outside, though. He'd probably crawled back into whatever hole he came out of.

She stiffened. The officers would tell Moses Kapili her story about BomBoy, and he would tell her mother about tonight's "attack." Iris had downplayed any connection between the Facebook stalker and Ziggy's abduction, but this latest prank might tip the balance. All she didn't need right now was Iris laying down the law.

The huge sound of the organ filled the theater: her own private concert.

Mahina yawned and slumped down in the controller's chair. The music sounded familiar, kind of spacey and ominous, like the night she and Keola had snuck into the basement. The sound was so loud it felt almost like the vibrating hotel bed her mother had let her try on vacation to Disneyland when she was a kid. She hadn't been able to sleep the whole rest of the night, just knowing that buzzing energy lurked in the mattress beneath her.

Mahina put her feet up on the console, and suddenly the stage lights flashed on. Whoops. Griff stopped playing and the echoing sound died away. Busted.

"Who's up there?" His voice was harsh.

Mahina stepped out of the booth. "It's just me. I was listening to your music and I hit a lever or something. I don't know how to turn it off again."

Griff switched on a flashlight and climbed the long flights of stairs between the rows of seats to the booth near the theater ceiling. He dealt swiftly and expertly with the control panel, and the stage plunged back into darkness.

"You shouldn't be here." He closed the door and locked it. "It's dangerous. You could fall, or break the equipment."

"I know." Mahina scuffed her foot. "I hear that a lot. But I'm tired of being where I should be all the time. And why are you here? Why is it okay for you, but not for me?"

Griff turned and pattered back down the stairs.

"Where did you learn to play the organ?" Mahina called after him, feeling her way in the dark. "You're really good."

"I taught myself."

"Could you teach me?" Mahina was surprised to hear the words come out of her mouth. She didn't like to ask for anything, especially from men.

Griff stopped and turned around. The flashlight cast his features into weird shadow. "Tell me more about BomBoy."

ᴗ

MOSES WAS LATE FOR DINNER, BUT THAT WASN'T UNUSUAL. IRIS remembered all the movies she'd seen where cops' marriages fell apart because of their long and unpredictable hours on the job. A job that always had to come first. But Kapili's dedication to his work, his obvious integrity and character, were a large part of his attraction for Iris. Especially given her past experience, which had blazed back into the present that same afternoon.

Iris was still reeling from the letter she'd received. It wasn't the worst possible news, but close. She'd known this would happen at some point, but assumed it would be much later, long after Mahina had grown up and become an independent adult. But later had become now. And now she didn't know what to do, except to wait for her opponent's next move.

Wait, and focus on other, more positive things, like Moses. Iris pulled her mind back to the present. She wondered why no suitable term had evolved for mature, romantic but non-marital relationships except for partner, which sounded so sterile and businesslike. Lover was too overtly sexual and man or woman-friend seemed contrived. But boyfriend and girlfriend were such juvenile terms. Moses was no boy, and she was not a girl, although she still felt like one sometimes. Maybe one's inner person never really grew up. Or perhaps she just had a case of arrested development, due to early relationship trauma.

As strongly as she was attracted to Moses, was it really safe to let him into her life so completely? Especially now that the truth could come out any day. What would he think of her? Also, the violence of his profession could throw off her balance and serenity if she didn't keep it at a distance, particularly while she was so vulnerable.

But Moses had such a warm, life-giving aura, and he seemed to love her for herself—the self he knew, anyway. He didn't see her as weird or damaged. At least not yet. Perhaps he had come into her life to remind her that stereotypes were false, that the path to happiness and peace might look different from what she had imagined. Perhaps Moses would accept her even if he knew the worst. She had to be open. Especially now, when exposure could come at any moment.

Would Mahina hate her mother if she learned the truth? Make that *when*. Iris thought of all the lessons and rehearsals she had sat through over the years: piano, voice, dance, plays, recitals, concerts. She had gone to a few rehearsals of *Wizard* early on, but it had felt awkward since Mahina could drive herself, and she had no real purpose for being there. She would wait and see the finished product on opening night and embrace the natural progression of life. Her little girl had grown up. Perhaps it was time she found out the real story of her birth.

Car wheels crunched into the gravel turning circle in front of the house. The oven was preheated, so Iris just popped in the pizza she'd bought from Hilo Naturals on the way home. A salad from the deli bar chilled in the refrigerator.

She'd been out the whole day driving a client all over greater Hilo to look at houses and properties he probably had no intention of buying. A mainland window shopper. Iris sighed. Still, sometimes people surprised her. After days of vacillation, one couple she had been about to push off a cliff out in Paradise Park had actually stepped up and bought a large house—and the adjoining lot. Maybe this joker—correction, this lovely human being—would come through as well. That was the business.

"Mmmmm! You smell so good." Moses buried his face in her neck.

Iris giggled. Mahina wouldn't be home from rehearsal for hours and the pizza needed thirty minutes to cook. "Come with me." She took his hand and led him back to the bedroom.

Later, they sat out on the *lanai* in spite of the tiny insects drawn to the warmth of their skin. A light breeze wafted across the wide lawn, flickering the candles. Pizza and salad had never tasted so delicious. They ate in silence, then looked at each other and laughed. Whatever happened next, this moment was purely good. Iris breathed in and felt gratitude permeate her being.

"I've had a breakthrough in the drug case." Moses wiped his mouth and leaned back in his chair. "You might not like to hear it, though."

"What do you mean?" Iris was suddenly vigilant. Was Mahina on meth? Surely she would have seen the warning signs.

"Don't worry, Mom, Mahina's not a user. I'd be able to tell." Moses gave her his crooked smile. "But the good witch in her play might be involved. Her boyfriend is a very shady character."

Iris hadn't paid much attention to the short, dapper man trailing around after Desiree at the workday.

"We had an alert a couple years ago when this person bought land and built a house out in Hawaiian Beaches. Hunter Craddock is one of his aliases, so when he introduced himself last Sunday, bingo." Moses drained his beer, but waved away Iris's offer of another. "Never forget a name, although it took me a couple of hours to make the connection." He lifted an eyebrow. "He's a known associate of a mob boss in Vegas. They never got Craddock on anything, but he had lots of suspicious connections. Especially drugs. We've kept tabs on him in a general way, although our department doesn't have the resources to do much. But now, coincidence?"

"You think Desiree is a drug dealer?" Iris was amazed. Sure, Desiree was a little on the edge, a middle-aged woman working as a bartender. But she had three young children. She was the good witch. Then again, she looked like a renter, probably a cheap apartment, not even a house—and that was an uncertain lifestyle. There but for the trust fund go I, she thought.

"I have no reason to believe Desiree is involved, but it *is* suspicious that Hunter Craddock is hanging around the theater. He was talking to your director about a big donor for the Palace, too. I listened in." Moses winked. "Mob money is my guess. Anyhow, I shouldn't really be telling you this, but I know you're discreet. And I know you want to look out for Mahina."

"But how? Is she in danger?" Iris rose to clear their plates. She needed to do something with her hands. She could feel her aura turning a smudgy brownish red.

"He may be using the Palace for his business. Before the tsunamis hit Hilo there were some underground passages between buildings in old downtown. Most have either collapsed or been blocked off for decades. But we've found a few that are still open, and they all lead to the theater."

"And you think there's a meth lab down there?"

"No, no, no." Moses laughed. "At least it's unlikely. Ventilation would be a big problem, not to mention flooding. But I think Craddock may be moving the goods down there." He leaned back in his chair and sighed. "Between the budget cuts and the new police chief, it's hard to get enough resources to investigate. The chief is more interested in money-makers like speeding tickets and expired safety checks. Half the force is out on the roads doling out fines to harmless citizens while the real bad guys operate unchecked."

Iris sat down with another full glass of pinot noir.

"Don't worry, sweetheart. I'm going to keep an eye on Desiree, see if she leads me anywhere." Moses got up and kissed her cheek. "In fact, sorry to run, but that's where I have to go right now. Rehearsal should be over soon." His phone rang mid-sentence and he picked it up.

"You're at the Palace?" He listened, his body tense. "How long ago? And you're only calling me now? Just two of you? I'm on my way." He looked at Iris and paused. "There's been an incident at the theater—it looks like a malicious prank. Don't worry. No one was hurt, but the rehearsal was cut short. The uniforms are over there investigating." He hugged her tight. "Mahina should be home soon. She's fine." He hurried to his car.

Iris watched his taillights roll down the driveway as she punched in Mahina's number and listened to it ring. Her daughter's voicemail greeting chirped, "Not heee-eeere. Leave a message."

"Where are you? Call me *now*." Iris disconnected and clutched the phone to her heart.

The engine roared as Moses pulled out onto the road and accelerated away.

CHAPTER 23

Desiree grabbed her kids and rushed out of the theater with everyone else, straight to her car parked on Haili Street. No way was she staying to get crushed when the whole theater fell in on itself. Besides, she had a job to do, and she had to get her kids home before she did it.

Desiree hustled her chattering offspring up the stairs and into the apartment.

"That rock was almost as big as you, Malia." Nakai gripped his little sister's shoulders. "It went *blam* and left a big hole in the floor." Malia's face crumpled and she started to wail. She'd been asleep backstage during all the excitement.

"Liar! Mom, Nakai's trying to scare Malia." Kolea grabbed Desiree's arm. "She'll have bad dreams and kick me all night."

"Okay, okay." Desiree ruffled Nakai's hair. "Don't scare your little sister. I have to go out for a while, so I want everyone ready for bed before I leave." She ignored their cries of protest and peeled Malia off her leg. She carried the little girl into the bathroom and set her on the toilet. "You can skip brushing your teeth, just for tonight." She tucked her into the bed she shared with Kolea and kissed her soft cheek. Malia's breath grew even and her cheeks and lips pooched out. Asleep.

"You guys can watch TV for half an hour, then bed, okay?" They'd probably just make a bag of popcorn and start a movie the minute she was out the door. She'd find them slumped in a pile on the couch when she got back, fast asleep. Sometimes she just covered them with a blanket. They were getting too heavy to carry to their beds. Desiree didn't have internet, or even a computer, so at least they couldn't go to gaming sites and get stalked by pedophiles.

⤳

THE DEALER'S PLACE WAS JUST AS DARK AND SINISTER AS BEFORE. She stood at the door and rang the bell while the dogs slavered and barked, clanging their chains, but no light came on and the door didn't open. Desiree tried the knob. Locked.

Great, she thought. Well, I'm not hanging around here, that's for sure. She hurried back through the darkness to her car, then stopped. She bent down, picked up a handful of rocks and threw them at the dogs, who quit barking long enough to yelp, then started up again in an even greater frenzy.

"Take that, you monsters." Desiree climbed into her car and slammed the door. She would have liked to hit that clown-faced dealer with some rocks—or a baseball bat. Hunter too. Making her drive all the way out here for nothing. Then two comments clicked together in her brain. Hunter's request to look out for anything strange going on at the Palace and Clownface's remark about the great Hilo underground. Was the dealer the ghost? It would explain why he wasn't here. Too busy throwing rocks. But why would he sabotage the play? Desiree gunned the engine. She wasn't waiting around to ask.

Just after she turned left onto the main road along the beaches, a car pulled up close behind her and flashed a blinding blue beacon of light with a single "bloop" of siren. Desiree kept driving. There must be some mistake. The light kept flashing and the "bloop" sounded again, twice. The car stayed right on her tail, so she pulled over. Her heart had left her chest and was pounding up in the top left corner of the car. Calm down, she told herself. You probably have a burned-out taillight or something.

Then she remembered the brown paper package nestled at the bottom of her purse. There was no time to hide it. And nowhere to hide it even if she had time. No. This had to be a coincidence. She would sweet-talk the cop the way she used to back in Kansas when she got pulled over. Those long flat roads stretching straight over the horizon were meant for speed, and she'd never gotten a ticket, not even the time she and everyone in the car with her were drunk. Ah, to be young again. But she still had some juice. Desiree fluffed her hair and turned a bright smile to the window, ready to perform.

A cop shone a flashlight on her face. She squinted, still smiling, and rolled down her window.

"Desiree, isn't it?" He lowered the light so she could see his face. It was Mahina's mother's boyfriend, the Policeman. "We need to ask you some questions back at the station." He wasn't smiling.

"What's this about?" She wasn't going to give up so easily. "Was I speeding? I'm really sorry if I was, Officer—Kapili? It was so nice of you to help out at the workday last weekend. Mahina is such a talented girl. It's going to be a great show." She kept the smile pasted on her face.

"We need you to step out of the car, now, Desiree. Leave your handbag where it is."

This was bad. Desiree climbed out of her seat and followed him back to the patrol car, feet crunching on the gravel. What if someone saw her and reported back to Clownface or Hunter?

"My officer will drive your car to the station." Kapili was impassive, holding the back door open for her.

"But my kids are home alone." Desiree thought of Malia in her bed and Nakai and Kolea's warm, vulnerable bodies curled up together on the couch. She had put them in danger, their own mother.

"We'll send someone over if there's no one you can call."

This late at night, Kama was either drinking beer and talking story in someone's carport, or screwing his girlfriend. Mrs. Chen next door was stone deaf and went to bed early. She'd never hear the phone. Desiree thought of Nora. She was a decent, kind person who would help out in an emergency, but she could hardly leave her own sleeping children at home by themselves. Besides, how would Desiree explain her predicament? No, it would have to be Kama.

Desiree fell silent on the drive, barely registering the lights of the town on one side and the deep darkness of the ocean on the other. This couldn't be happening. But it was.

⌣

EVER SINCE THE BLOW-UP WITH CAL, GEORGE'S DRIVE HOME UP long, winding Kaiwiki road had changed in character. In the past he could hardly wait to get there. He had relished the curve-hugging speed of the little Miata, his body one with the car as the night rushed past. But now the engine lagged. He never even shifted out of second gear.

The house was dark. Cal must be working a night shift. In the past he would have known, but George was no longer privy to his partner's schedule.

He was more shaken by the incident at the Palace than he cared to admit. The police had promised a regular patrol. He snorted. He'd fire off a soothing email to the cast tonight—he had to make sure they all came back tomorrow. After all, a saboteur wasn't nearly as bad as a collapsing building.

The show must go on.

George pulled into the empty garage and hit the button on his rearview mirror to close the automatic door behind him. His phone rang. He twisted in his seat and struggled to pull it out of his back pocket. No time to check the caller ID.

"Hello?" George listened. "What?"

The hand not holding the phone went to his head. The voice just kept going on and on, then ended on a questioning note.

"Thank you for calling."

George sat in the dark for a few minutes. His father was dead. *Dead.* If he opened the car door, he would have to start dealing with the reality he had just been served—at the worst possible time. His life was in crisis: Cal about to leave him, the theater under attack, the still ragged play about to open. And now this. It was too much.

George leaned forward and hit his head on the steering wheel, then again, harder. He stopped. His throbbing head rested against the firm, textured leather.

"Okay," he said aloud. "Okay."

He opened the door and angled his body out and up, every joint stiff and protesting, as though he had suddenly become an old man.

"You're not really in a position to bargain." Moses Kapili stared across the scarred wooden table at Desiree.

They sat in a small room at the Kapiʻolani police station—so close to her apartment, but so far away. She had tipped over the edge.

"But he'll kill me. He'll hurt my children!" Desiree's face was streaked with tears. A heap of wadded up Kleenex lay on the table next to the box. Did everyone cry during interrogation? So fucking humiliating. She was terrified, although whether more of the police and the threat of fines and jail time or of Hunter, the dealer, and their shadowy organization she wasn't sure. But Kapili was right. She didn't have much choice. Fuck all, in fact.

"We can take your children into protective custody until this is over." His face looked kind. "Or we can work with their father to keep them safe if he wants to maintain a more normal schedule for them."

Kama had sounded bright and chirpy on the phone. He said he'd go right over to the apartment and stay there with the children. Makani's big family could absorb them for a while. Desiree slumped down in her chair and rubbed her eyes. She must look like a raccoon, but she didn't care. Her pride was in shreds.

Kapili paged through a file. "He has no history of violence—that's good. And from here on out, from what you've told us, we're on Hunter Craddock 24/7."

"How about the dealer?"

"We followed you to his house the other day, so it wasn't hard to find you tonight." Kapili leaned forward and forced Desiree to meet his eyes. "Look. This is your chance to redeem yourself. We're talking no fine, no jail time—not even a suspended sentence. You can walk away clean."

"If I survive." Desiree hunched over and rubbed her face in her hands. Tears and snot. Gross. She reached for another tissue. God she was exhausted. There seemed no way out except to say yes. If she didn't, she would go to jail for a long time. Her children would be grown up by the time she got out—if some psychotic inmate didn't kill her first. The choice was simple: risk death or worse at the hands of Hunter and/or Clownface with exoneration if she survived, or rot in jail for years.

Desiree had never had trouble with risk, which was her whole problem. Well, let it be the solution, too.

She sat up straight. "Okay. I'll do it."

"Good. Let's just go over the plan again."

They leaned on the table and talked. Kapili pointed to a blown-up street map and wrote on a tablet. Desiree nodded and occasionally asked a question. Finally, they were done.

"God I'm tired." She rested her head on the table. "I could just go to sleep right here."

"Sorry, accommodations are full tonight." Kapili stood up. "Okay, we're good to go. I'll be in touch with the final plan. You have my number if you need it." He moved toward the door. "We should be ready to move on opening night."

"I'll be there." Desiree pushed her chair back. "I'll be the one in the poofy white dress and tiara." She stood up, too, stretched her arms over her head and yawned. "Can I go home now?"

CHAPTER 24

HARRIET WAS SURPRISED TO SEE LUKE slouch out of her guest room the next morning, rubbing his eyes. He hadn't slept at her place for weeks. After the "incident" last night, she had decided to take sick leave. A mental health day was in order. Patrick was subbing for her. He had jumped at the opportunity. No nerve problems there.

"You'll never believe what happened last night." Harriet handed Luke a cup of coffee and poured another for herself. His eyes widened as she described the falling chunk of plaster, the hysteria, the aftermath. "Although I slipped out early. I think Evan stayed behind to help sort things out." She looked at Luke, and he shrugged. "Poor George was just beside himself. You can imagine."

They chuckled.

"I can't wait to hear more, Ma, but I have an appointment." He gulped his coffee and set down her favorite Wonder Woman mug. "I'll explain later. How about lunch at Siam Palace?"

Luke was drinking a Singha beer a few hours later when Harriet slid into the cracked vinyl seat across from him in the booth. The table top felt sticky. Pictures of the Thai royal family covered the wall, and wailing atonal music wafted through wall-mounted speakers. A family of tourists sat in a corner booth in the otherwise deserted restaurant.

Harriet didn't comment on the lunchtime beer—Luke was a grown up. In fact, perhaps she'd have one herself. It wasn't like anyone from school was going to see her. They were all slaving away in their un-air-conditioned classrooms, just as she would be tomorrow.

"I'll have one of those, too," she told the smiling waiter. "And the red pumpkin curry lunch special, please. Medium."

"Same for me, and another beer. Thanks." Luke leaned back in the booth. "Guess what?"

Harriet quirked her eyebrow.

"I have a job offer."

She sat forward. "You do?"

"Don't act so shocked, Mom. I am a qualified architect, even if that big San Francisco firm had me working as a draftsman."

"But where? When?"

"And how?" He smiled. "It's here, as a matter of fact. Up the Hāmākua coast, near Hakalau. Some multimillionaire wants a fancy house with all kinds of indigenous woods and green technology. Right up my alley. Evan put him on to me; he manages the guy's money."

"Wow. That's wonderful, son." This meant Luke would stay, at least for a time. Would he continue to live with her? Did she want him to? Would he move in with Evan? Get a place of his own?

"Evan asked me to move in with him." Luke finished his first beer and poured the second into his glass. "But I'm not ready for that."

Ah, thought Harriet. This explains the sudden need for distance. Too soon. "You're welcome to stay on with me for as long as you'd like."

She smiled at the waiter as he set steaming bowls of sticky rice and curry on the table. She scooped rice onto her plate and covered it with fragrant sauce and chunks of chicken and vegetables, feeling a sudden, urgent hunger.

"Thanks, Mom." Luke took a bite of curry and groaned in appreciation as he chewed. "But I've actually been offered a house-sitting job, too, quite near the property this guy wants to build on. One of his buddies wants a caretaker for a few months, which might be all I need. Nice to get out into the countryside—and live in luxury, with a great oceanfront view." He smiled. "Looks like your boy has landed on his feet."

"It does seem perfect. Like it was meant to be." Harriet hated being trite, but all her wit seemed to have fled. This was good news. She was happy, wasn't she? Of course she was.

They ate in silence for a while, the hot, spicy food working its magic.

"I always think I'll take home the leftovers, but then there aren't any." Harriet sighed and rubbed her ample stomach. No one to stay slim for anymore. She must have put on ten pounds since the divorce, even with all the swimming. Muscle, she thought. And it's not healthy to be thin. Studies have shown. Etc.

"So I'll be moving up the coast this week, but I'll still help with the show. And it's not like I'm dumping Evan or anything. I just need my own space. He's a little overeager—first boyfriend and all."

Harriet refrained from commenting on his relationship. "Speaking of the show, we've had another upheaval. I got an update from Fred after you left this morning. George's father died and he's debating whether or not he has to fly to the East Coast to deal with it. Apparently there was no love lost, but still. We have tonight off, and then Fred will run rehearsals if George leaves."

Harriet filled him in on the investigation, with the consensus that foul play and not structural instability was at fault. "Although," she added, "I always feel the Palace is only standing because all the termites are holding hands."

"Wow." Luke upended his beer. "And I thought nothing ever happened in Hilo. This sounds downright sinister. Do they think it's kids playing pranks, or something worse? Are you sure you're safe?"

"Half the cast thinks it's the ghost—the sinister old man, not the little girl or the teenaged prankster, or even the evil old woman. Of course." They rolled their eyes together, recalling the earful they'd both had from Aunty Em. "Merle wants to have a séance, and Fred is countering with appeals for an exorcism. Who knew he was a devout Catholic?" Harriet sighed. "But the show must go on."

Luke gave a wry smile and stood up, throwing his napkin on the table. "Well, I'd better get started. Lots of research to do."

"Luke, I'm so proud of you." Harriet stood up, too. She tucked a wad of bills into the check folder. Great food, low prices, and the satisfaction of supporting a local family business. "I'm glad you'll be around a little longer. I'll try not to cling."

Luke put his arm around her, and they walked out of the restaurant into the blazing afternoon heat.

ONLY A FEW MILES AWAY, NORA SNUGGLED DEEPER INTO MERLE'S arms as they lay in her bed, slippery with post-coital sweat. Even with all the jalousies cranked open and the ceiling fan turned on high, the heat was stifling. The fan wobbled and clicked over the bed, its blades spinning in a blur. Nora hoped whatever held it to the ceiling wasn't as rusted as the other fittings around the house. She could see the headlines: "Couple Killed in Ceiling Fan Tragedy: Rush on Hilo Hardware Stores."

Merle tightened his grip and kissed the top of her head. "This just feels so right."

He had dropped by after Nora's morning shift on the psychic hotline, and she had welcomed the distraction from self-analysis.

"Mmm-hmmm." Nora tried to luxuriate in the moment, but the tiny electronic voice of her laptop sensed a break in her attention and began to call. With her concentration shot to pieces by worry over the children, this last week on the job had been rocky. She needed to focus, to read and practice. For that, she had to be alone. Besides, she was hot now. And she had to pick up the children from school in an hour.

She had called Alice after the Clyde-Greta-Merle incident. So much to work with! When Alice told her their next homeschool get-together met at Greta's house that week, Nora suggested she snoop around: medicine cabinet, Greta's underwear drawer, anywhere she might hide illicit substances. Alice was thrilled. "No stone—or thong—left unturned, darling."

Now Nora wanted to enlist Merle's help, even if Greta was his client. She needed ammunition, especially after the incident at the Palace last night. Could they make a case for reckless child endangerment? STOP.

Nora wriggled away and sat up, pushing back her sweaty, tangled hair with both hands.

"That was wonderful." She smiled down at Merle. "I feel like a sex goddess. And now I have to get back to work." She frowned. "Yesterday I predicted a new baby for a menopausal woman and a strong, passionate man for a lonely lesbian. And this morning when I suggested a caller's dead father was asking for forgiveness, he told me the man was sitting right beside him. Then he demanded his money back." She laughed. "I don't know what's wrong with me. I did so well at first, and now I'm all over the place. If I don't become a better psychic quick, they'll fire me."

"You have the power, Nora." Merle rubbed her back. "I can feel it. But maybe you're thinking too much and getting in your own way." He started to kiss her neck. "That hibiscus hedge isn't helping either—totally stops the ocean's energy from pouring through your front windows." He held up his hand. "I know, the landlord won't let you cut it down. But don't be afraid to pause and let your own energy possess you. Insights will come if you invite them."

"Thanks, Merle." Nora hopped out of bed. "I'll do that." It was sweet that he believed in her—or even just said so to keep her in bed with him. With Clyde it had been all about him, all the time.

"Spend some time communing with your *jaboticaba* tree out back," he called after her. "It exudes gallons of wisdom and courage."

Ten minutes later she had showered and dressed, but Merle was still in bed. She poked her head through the doorway. He was propped up on her pillows, doing the sudoku in a pool of hot light from the bedside lamp. Reading glasses perched on his nose and his forehead furrowed in concentration.

"Ahem."

Merle looked up and smiled his heart-stopping smile. Nora's heart kept on beating. None of her problems were Merle's fault. In fact, he and the play were the only good things in her life right now. Except the twins, of course, although they were also at the center of her greatest fears and potential loss. But that was just the way things were. Once you had children, you were a hostage to fate.

"Before you go," she said with meaning, "I wanted to ask you a delicate question."

"Anything for you." He lowered the puzzle page.

"I know Greta is your client, and I don't want you to do anything you feel uncomfortable about—"

"But you'd like me to investigate for you?" Merle grinned. "Find out her intentions and maybe even sabotage her relationship with your ex?"

"Why, yes." Nora grinned back. "Although I was trying to be more discreet in my wording."

"I see no conflict at all." Merle winked. "Behaving in a destructive way wouldn't be good for Greta, so my interference is in her interests, too. Can't let her misspend all that new herbal vitality."

"Splendid." Nora clapped her hands. "And now you need to leave, so I can get some work done." She tilted her head to the side and made a silly sad face.

"But this is so companionable. I won't make a sound, I promise." Merle set down the newspaper. "And I could make dinner later for you and the kids."

Nora shook her head. "This house is too small, and the walls are too thin. I can hear a mosquito rubbing its legs together two rooms over. Besides, don't you have clients waiting? And don't you have to move out of your house this week?"

Merle shook his head. "No one scheduled for today." He got up and stretched. Nora admired his heavily muscled body—as had Greta. Merle had worked on the docks as a young man and hadn't let himself run to fat in middle age. But now as a landscape designer, he didn't seem to do any actual physical work. He didn't even drive a truck, just rattled around in his battered old Corolla.

"I just feel the energies and ask where they want to go," he'd told her. "My wealthy spiritual clientele appreciates my lack of attachment to material objects."

Merle found his boxer shorts on the floor and pulled them on. "We get along really well, don't we?" He looked at her for confirmation. "I do whatever you ask, right?"

"Sure." Nora wondered where this was going. "You're wonderful and I adore you."

"So I was thinking I should move in with you. Cook for you, help you with the twins. Release the energy in your tangled-up backyard." Merle beamed at her, still bare-chested. "Your ex knows about me now, so that's not a problem."

Nora was speechless. She liked things just the way they were. She felt a fierce need for Merle to leave. Right now. Did he think she could support him? That he would be her wife?

"Well." She struggled to mask her horror. "It's sweet of you, but now is not a good time, Merle. I was married to Clyde my whole adult life until less than a year ago, and now I have this mess with him wanting to take the kids to Australia." Her anger mounted. "I'm insane with worry. I can't possibly even think about you moving in."

"No, of course not. I know it's too soon." Merle pulled on his T-shirt and shorts. "I just hope you'll be open to a new relationship. Not every man is like Clyde." He left the bed unmade and walked toward the doorway. Nora moved out of the way. "But not every man you meet will want a ready-made family either. I love your children. I'll help you take care of them."

Nora's consternation morphed into rage. Ready-made family indeed. Who was she, June Cleaver from *Leave it to Beaver*, looking for another man of the house? Did he expect her to be grateful he was willing to take her on, with all her baggage? And why this sudden assault on her privacy? Did his new rental fall through, or was he just trying to save money?

Nora took a deep breath and forced a smile, pushing her anger down into the mental box she'd constructed for it many years before. She closed the lid. She thought of an old college friend who'd gone into management. He'd told her his standard reply to employee requests was, "No, but I'll think about it." Then he added, "But I never do."

Nora said, "No, but I'll think about it." She paused. "And thanks for your help with Greta."

Merle looked confused. "Okay." He rallied, smiled, and moved in his lazy lope to gather her in his arms. She let him hold her, but something inside felt sharp and flinty. She turned her face when he tried to kiss her, so his lips landed on her cheek.

"See you at rehearsal." Nora closed the front door behind him and felt a savage sense of relief as he walked down the steps to his car. She couldn't bear to watch him climb through the passenger's side and over the gearshift again, since the driver's door lock was frozen shut and he couldn't be bothered to fix it. She shook herself all over like a wet dog. Was this the beginning of the end, already? Why couldn't things ever stay simple?

Because people want and want and want more. And you're not in Kansas anymore, dearie, she told herself. Taking people at their word is a luxury you can no longer afford.

Maybe it was time to talk to Harriet.

⌣

MAHINA WAS SURPRISED IRIS HADN'T TOTALLY LOST IT OVER THE Palace "attack," especially since the police seemed to think BomBoy might be a suspect. In fact, her mother had seemed preoccupied, her usual laser focus on Mahina's wellbeing diverted to something else. Something more important. Which was great— but disturbing. Nothing had ever been more important to Iris than her daughter.

Yesterday Mahina had seen another lawyer's envelope sticking out of the kitchen counter mail heap. Later it was gone, no doubt filed away in Iris's locked cabinet. But this one was different from the others, smaller, and it hadn't been three months yet since the last report arrived. Mahina always spotted the signature blue-grey envelopes, engraved with the lawyer's logo and return address. This was too much of a coincidence. Something must be happening with the mysterious trust that had Iris worried. Maybe the money had run out.

Although Mahina didn't pay much attention to the news, it was hard to miss all the grownup talk about the housing bubble that had popped, causing the mortgage crisis, which brought on the financial meltdown and on and on and on, just like the song about the old woman who swallowed a fly. Especially when your mother was in real estate.

That afternoon, Iris had texted Mahina saying she would be home late. She was out scouting properties in Puna with some other realtors from her office—mostly foreclosures going up for auction soon.

Mahina rummaged around in her mother's desk. Where would she hide the key to the filing cabinet? If Iris had attached it to the big jangly ring on her purse lanyard, Mahina would be out of luck, unless she could jimmy the lock. But she had a feeling. She lifted paperweights and dumped out a little ceramic bowl holding paperclips, coins, buttons, and safety pins, searching for likely hiding places.

A large heart locket with Mahina's picture appliqued on the front hung from the neck of the stained-glass desk lamp, a leftover from Iris's crafty stage when Mahina was a child. The crude results of those nonstop art projects still littered the otherwise tasteful house. She remembered the flowered corduroy jumper she'd worn every day for months, screaming when Iris tried to wash it. In the crinkly, faded photo, her cheeks were plump, and she was missing one front tooth. So attractive. Mahina pried the locket open with her thumbnail, and a small key fell onto the desk blotter. Score.

Her hands shook as she turned the key in the lock. She pawed through the bulging legal folder in the second drawer down. Sure enough, there was the small envelope tucked among the big ones, slit neatly along the top by her mother's carved wooden letter opener. She drew it out and sat down at Iris's desk.

Two sheets of paper were folded inside. The first was a brief note from the lawyer, informing Iris that the owner of her trust had died and his heirs had some questions. They would like to speak to her in person, if possible, and could she please reply immediately. Mahina read the note over several times. Owner? Heirs? Her father was dead and had no family. Or so Iris said.

The room tilted, and she closed her eyes.

A long moment later, she turned the lawyer's letter over like the page of a book and read the second letter, only a few paragraphs long. But long enough to break her whole world into tiny, unrecognizable pieces.

Heart pounding as though she'd just run her fastest mile yet in P.E. class, Mahina took out her cellphone and photographed both letters, then folded them carefully back into the envelope and slotted it into the folder, more or less where she'd taken it out. She closed the drawer, turned the key, placed it back in the locket, and snapped the heart shut. Her innocent gap-toothed smile dangled before her, saying, "I told you so."

No one is trustworthy, not even your mother.

CHAPTER 25

A FTER A FULL DAY OF SUBBING FOR HARRIET, PATRICK WAS exhausted, yet invigorated—and glad to have a night off from rehearsal, even if he felt a bit guilty since the reasons were death and sabotage.

He could do this teaching thing. He had a rapport with the kids, and they needed more decent male teachers. Especially the boys. Low pay and an increasing load of blame had turned teaching into women's work. That and the mommy track hours and vacations. There were a disproportionate number of women in education—through no fault of their own, of course. And this led to resentment and misogyny.

Patrick had never shared this theory with anyone, for obvious reasons. But if his child turned out to be a boy, he would need strong male role models. Including his own father, of course.

When he reached the turnoff for Volcano Village, instead of heading home, grabbing a beer and putting his feet up in front of the television, Patrick drove to Prema's yoga studio for the 5:30 restorative class. He had some loose clothes and his mat in the trunk.

He could change in the adjoining bathroom. This would feel good, get his *chakras* aligned and his blood flowing. His *bandhas* definitely needed activating.

He emerged from the bathroom and saw Cindy and Mac enter the studio. They saw him and waved, but didn't come over. He was torn between enjoying a wicked glow of wellbeing about the switch he'd pulled and agonizing over how to engineer a conversation where he could learn the truth about Cindy's real feelings for him—and whose baby she was carrying.

Mac and Cindy set up their mats on the opposite side of the room. She definitely looked stout.

Today Prema was playing whale songs. Patrick lay on his back and absorbed the sound, trying to empty his mind and become one with the pod. How nice to be a whale: no possessions, no sexual jealousy, plenty of krill for everyone, and a real community spirit. Until the naval sonar made your head explode, that is, and you ended up beaching yourself just to end the pain.

Patrick flinched. No, that wasn't it at all. Try again.

"We're going to do a lot of hip openers and twists today." Prema smiled beatifically. "So good for us as we get older."

Patrick looked around the room. Sure enough, everyone was over forty—except Cindy, and she was only a couple of years shy. Didn't any young people live in Volcano? Probably too expensive now with the economy tanking.

"Cindy, you be careful, okay?" Prema walked over and touched Cindy's shoulder as she sat in lotus position, her belly jutting out like the Buddha statue at the front of the room. "I'll help you with some modifications. Don't do anything that hurts."

Cindy smiled up at her, basking in the attention. Patrick felt simultaneous stabs of longing and resentment. Not good. Empty the mind. We are all one: me, Cindy, the baby, Mac. But he just felt more irritated and alienated. Well then, just observe the part of you that isn't quiet and accept where you are and what is, his yoga voice told him. Focus on the breath moving in and out of the body, your connection to the present moment.

After holding pigeon pose for five minutes on each side, Patrick's hips were screaming. They didn't feel like opening today.

Prema kept hovering over Cindy, with Mac at attention. Why couldn't he mind his own business?

Finally, they came out of their final twist and set up for a ten-minute *savasana*.

Patrick lay there, submerged with the whales. His steamy breath shot through the blowhole on top of his head, and the water rippled along every inch of his skin as he swam along with his pod.

Then the music changed. He felt disoriented, pulled out of a dream. Where did the whales go? He had been wallowing in the ocean deeps, and now where was he?

A man began to chant in a pleasant baritone. He sounded familiar somehow, like—like Garrison Keillor.

Patrick felt his body go rigid. He tried to soften, breathing into his distress, but it was no use. At any moment, the chanter could break into the powder milk biscuit theme song from *A Prairie Home Companion*, with fiddles and banjos. He tried not to pant and fidget, consciously relaxing his jaw and his eyes.

The gong sounded. Thank god.

After they finished chanting three overlapping oms and the mantra for peace, Patrick sat on the floor and rolled up his mat. Yogi Garrison Keillor had stopped singing, and he felt better. Baby steps.

"Hey Patrick."

He looked up into Cindy's face. Her sleek black hair swung in curves just below her chin, her hand resting on the slight swell of her belly.

"Hey."

"I just wanted to tell you that I need to come back over to pick up a few more of my things. I can stop by when you're not there, so I don't bother you." She tilted her head to one side and smiled in the way he had found adorable when they first met. And still did.

"I'd rather you came when I'm there." Patrick felt the peace leave his body as it tensed for battle and further heartbreak.

"Suit yourself. How about right now? Mac and I can follow you back."

Patrick stood up, mat clenched under his arm, and looked down at her.

Mac was talking to Prema across the room. They were standing very close together, Mac leaning his stocky frame into the curve of space nearest to Prema's sylph-like body.

Patrick felt a surge of sympathy for Cindy. "Okay, that works."

"Great." She smiled, crinkling her eyes. "See you in a few minutes, then."

Patrick thought about the bowl he had hidden away and his mind started to work. Then, like the Grinch, he had a wonderful, awful idea.

⌣

MAC AND CINDY LINGERED AT THE YOGA STUDIO, SO PATRICK was able to race home and set up his tableau in the living room before they arrived. He placed the accusatory mango bowl in the center of his coffee table.

"Come in, come in." Patrick infused his voice with cheer.

Cindy looked tired, dark circles under her eyes.

Mac bounced through the door, carrying an armload of reusable grocery bags. "Yoga gives me so much energy." He grinned. "Should have been doing it for years. Who knew?"

"I'll just go back and grab my stuff." Cindy tucked the bags under one arm and put the other hand on her back as she walked down the hall to the bedroom.

After she left, Patrick had stuffed all her remaining things into a chest and shut the drawers tight. It sat there, a memory bomb waiting to go off.

"Would you like a beer, Mac? Come through to the living room." Patrick kept his tone casual, even though he wanted to ram his fist down Mac's throat.

He pretended not to notice Mac stare at the bowl, then look away. Yeah buddy, whatcha gonna say now? Patrick hid a smile and uncapped his last two bottles of IPA. He'd taken them out of the fridge when he got home so he wouldn't have to leave Mac alone with the bowl. He didn't trust him not to just grab it and run.

"Have a seat." He motioned to a squashy easy chair on one side of the coffee table and handed Mac a bottle. Patrick sat on the couch opposite, with the bowl right between them. He leaned back and took a sip. "Nothing like a home-brewed cold one after an hour and a half of virtuous exercise and meditation. Ahhh."

Mac took a long pull, then choked. He coughed and sputtered, trying to sit forward, but the easy chair had him in its grip. "Bitter," he croaked, looking at Patrick's self-designed label: Volcano Village IPA. Probably a lager drinker. Another sign of weak character.

"How do you like my piece?" Patrick motioned at the gleaming, multi-colored mango bowl, which curved gracefully in front of them. Its golden streaks glimmered in the lamplight. "I have a buyer in Japan, actually, but before I send it off, I'm going to enter it in the East Hawai'i Woodworkers' Contest. I think it's a winner. I've never sold anything for so much money before. Feels like the big time." He smiled at Mac and raised his bottle again. "Here's to us artisans. To reaping the fruits of our honest labor."

Mac looked sick, still coughing from his first gulp. He raised his bottle a miniscule amount and then took a tiny sip, sinking deeper into the cushioning folds of the chair.

"How's your turning these days, Mac?" Patrick raised his eyebrows and smiled.

"Oh great, great. Selling a lot." Mac struggled forward. "I think I'll go check on Cindy."

"Oh stay, stay. She's fine. You know women. She won't want you trying to help her—you'll do it all wrong." Patrick was enjoying himself. He rested an ankle over a knee. "My hips feel nice and open. Prema really knows how to work us up, eh?"

Mac didn't look so bouncy anymore, Patrick thought. Where had all that energy gone? Now he just looked tired, and he couldn't blame it on pregnancy.

"Drinking again?" Cindy set down five or six bulging bags. "Tsk, tsk."

"I was just telling Mac about my big break." Patrick lifted the mango bowl so she could see it. "Some Japanese collector is paying me twenty-five hundred dollars—American—for this beauty. Can you imagine?"

Cindy looked pale. She put one hand on the wall beside her.

"Well, I think we're done here." Mac wrestled his way out of the easy chair and picked up the bags.

"It was great to see you, Mac. Come by again sometime." Patrick held out his hand to Cindy. "Could I have a word before you go?" His heart thumped oddly in his throat.

Cindy nodded to Mac, and he shrugged before edging his way out the front door with the bulky Bag n Buy totes. Patrick closed it behind him.

"I know what you're going to say and I'm sorry, okay?" Cindy's voice was fast and high-pitched. "I was hurt and angry, and Mac was desperate for a sale. So I told him you'd given it to me, and I was giving it to him." She sat down heavily on the couch, burying her face in her hands. "And now you're both angry. I'm apologizing to you, and I'll apologize to Mac." She looked up with an expression Patrick had never seen on her face before. Was it fear? "Are you going to press charges?"

Patrick held up his hands in surrender. "Heavens no. I've got my bowl back. End of story." He moved over and sat close to her. "End of that story, anyhow." He put his arm around her. "It doesn't matter." He rested his head against hers, and she leaned on him. "I was a stupid, insensitive clod and I deserved to lose you—and my bowl."

She squeaked out a protest, and he went on in a rush. "But I do remember having sex a lot more recently than you said and I have to know, Cindy. Is the baby mine?"

She pulled back and looked at him, her face streaked with tears. "This isn't a matter of ownership, Patrick. This is a real human being we're talking about. Mac wants to be a father. It was partly why he and Crystal split up. She didn't want a child, and I didn't think you wanted one either."

"We never talked about it." Patrick sat back, flabbergasted.

"My point, exactly." Cindy started to stand up, but he caught her arm.

"Don't go." He paused, searching for the right words. "Losing you has made me think a lot about myself and how selfish I've been. Also about what I want in life." He gripped her hands. "I want you, Cindy. And our child. And I'm determined to be a good father and provider."

Cindy stared into his eyes, not returning the pressure but not pulling her hands away either.

"You haven't answered my question." He stared back, feeling a slight tremor in her fingers.

She dropped her gaze and withdrew her hands. "I can't answer, Patrick, because I don't know." She stood up and turned to face him. "Mac is fine with that."

"I'm fine with it, too," Patrick blurted, and realized it was true. A wave of warm feeling flooded through him.

He followed her to the door.

"Will you at least think about it? Coming back to me?"

Cindy paused, her hand on the doorknob. "Mac wants to marry me."

Patrick felt dizzy. "Well, so do I. I want to marry you too."

Cindy smiled. "My goodness. Who'd have thought little old me would have not one but two marriage proposals in such rapid succession." She kissed him on the cheek and opened the door. "I'll think about it."

"Will you come to opening night, at least?" Patrick touched her wrist. "I'll have a comp ticket at the box office for you."

Cindy smiled. "Of course." And then she was gone.

◡

GEORGE'S FATHER WAS DEAD. HE HAD TO KEEP REMINDING HIM-self. Funny how the living could be avoided, but the dead could not. He pushed aside guilt and regret. Would he go back and change his decision now if he could? Go and visit his still-living father?

A flurry of phone calls filled in the details. His father's neighbor—the one who'd found him when he wrenched his hip—had found him this time, too. She decided to check after the newspapers had piled up on the front porch for three days and the phone had rung unanswered. He'd only been home from the rehab center for a few days, and had refused the home health care service George had arranged. The hospital representative told him the autopsy had revealed a ruptured brain aneurysm. George Senior had just dropped in his tracks en route from kitchen to living room, his TV dinner dumped face down onto the old shag carpet where it congealed and hardened. A missing patch revealed where the Salisbury steak and mushroom gravy had refused to let go. The neighbor had a morbid attraction to detail—George cut her off before she could describe anything worse.

"I'm not going." He announced this to Cal, whose innate kindness required that he set aside his complete withdrawal—momentarily—to comfort George. "There's no reason for me to be there in person. I can make all the arrangements over the phone or even by email. And they can put a torch to the house for all I care."

Another flurry of phone calls. George opted for cremation, no funeral. He put an obituary in his father's local newspaper, hired a cleaning service, listed the house with a realtor, who agreed, for a higher percentage fee, to hold an estate sale and then dispose of whatever remained in the house. The lawyer signed off on everything, and George was surprised to discover he was the sole beneficiary of his father's estate, the value of which was still in question pending probate. Lucky if I get a dime after the creditors finish, he thought.

It was all remarkably quick—done in four days. He'd been sleepwalking through evening rehearsals that week. Everyone tiptoed around his feelings, and worrywart Fred reminded him five times a night that he'd be happy to step up and direct so George could "take care of family business."

George snarled back that he was just fine, even though, surprisingly, he wasn't.

After rehearsal that night, he watched late-night TV in his sleek black leather recliner. His father's ashes were already sealed in an urn in Buffalo. George tried to remember a time when he'd felt close to his father, when he had felt loved or protected. There must have been moments. Nothing came to mind. He remembered the single bed in his old room, hard and narrow, like a prison cot. He imagined the room stripped, as it must have been for decades now, no posters left on the walls, no old school paraphernalia in the closet. Bare, as though no one had ever lived in it.

He picked up a bulky express mail envelope the realtor had sent. An earlier email said she'd found something in his father's desk he might want to keep. What? Deathbed confessions? Pornography? He snorted and unfolded the paper, which enclosed a stiff little bundle.

Inside was a small collection of old black-and-white photos. George found his hands were trembling. He sat back in his chair and took a drink of his whiskey.

He pulled out the first photo. His parents on their wedding day. Father thinner, more hair, neat suit, big smile. Mother radiant in white.

Next photo: mother holding baby—himself. George. On the back, his father's writing: George, Jr., three days old. He was swaddled, wearing a little cap.

Next photo: the three of them, father's arms around mother, her arms around George. His face showed in this one, with big eyes and fat cheeks. No writing on the back.

Next photo: smiling father holding George, who looked quite a bit bigger. Same big eyes and fat cheeks, but more personality. On the back: George Sr. and George Jr., eighteen months old.

That was all.

He knew his mother had died before he was two years old. A drunk had run a stoplight as she was driving back from the grocery store. She had left George with a neighbor. His father was at the insurance office where he worked as a claims adjuster.

The neighbor had been hired to babysit George permanently after that. She had done her best, he was sure. She had fed, clothed, and helped him with his homework. But you couldn't buy love, and he hadn't been a lovable child. Grumpy, with a temper. He remembered his father looking at him sometimes as though he couldn't believe he was there. As though if he stared hard enough George would disappear.

George fingered the old matte photos, the paper sturdy and thick after all those years. He wondered if his father had ever taken them out and looked at them. The photos were pristine. He slid them back into the envelope, one by one, and set the envelope on the side table.

He thought of Cal's longing for a baby, his desire to create a family. With George. But how did you take that kind of risk? Not just for yourself but for an innocent child?

Cal was out, either working a late shift or with friends or maybe even a new lover. He had been sympathetic. He was a kind, decent person, after all. But instead of the tragedy resetting their relationship, as George had hoped it would—like a cold boot—Cal announced that he was looking for a new place and would move out soon. He was sorry about the timing, but it was what he needed to do for himself. The packing boxes stacked against the wall in the spare room were concrete evidence.

George had never felt so alone.

What would it be like to have a child? Would love teach him how to be a father? Or was he so crippled and stunted that he would inflict harm rather than good? Then Cal would leave him anyway, with even more pain and mess and regret. It was probably too late, anyhow. The damage to their relationship was done.

George finished his drink and got up to pour another.

GRIFF ALSO HAD A LOT ON HIS MIND. THE COMET WAS FLYING closer and closer to earth. It might be visible soon. More and more websites had picked up the story that the comet was really a time capsule sent by a past, space-travelling civilization to enlighten future generations of humans about their real potential, lost these millennia. Griff already felt enlightened. His body tingled as though bombarded by tiny energy particles. Maybe he was one of the chosen, and They were preparing him.

Earlier that day, The Voice had spoken—through his computer this time.

Great deeds await underground. A private comment from AdVisor on the super-encrypted website. The screen shimmered.

I am ready. Griff waited. The Voice had never engaged him in dialogue before.

A guide will approach you soon. Griff stared at the screen. He had waited so long for answers.

How will I know him?

He will speak with power and truth.

Griff wanted to ask, "And then what?" He finally typed, *Okay.*

With only George's physical body present at rehearsals, his mind swimming miles away, Fred was taking on more directorial authority. A spaniel, racing from one point to another, whining.

People kept talking about the ghost, about being attacked. A flock of mynah birds chattering and fluttering, smearing a mess of feathers and seedy excrement over the stage.

Every night after rehearsal he played the organ, sometimes for hours. Often Mahina stayed to listen. He had shown her the Energy Center, although he wasn't sure she understood.

She'd said, "Isn't that just the power thingy for the organ?" She was a cat, by turns indifferent, playful, imperious, cruel. You couldn't force a cat to do anything. It would always do exactly what it wanted and nothing else.

Griff opened the backstage door and walked down the steps, shining his flashlight. The Energy Center hummed. He laid his hand on It and felt the reassuring heat. The dusty recesses of the basement stretched into the darkness, to the old wooden cabinet against the wall with its rusty padlock. Grit dropped on his head from the low beams above, the air musty and close. It felt safe, like a cave. Maybe he'd bring a sleeping bag and a few supplies and just bunk down here for the duration, nestled close to the Source. He'd slept in far dirtier, buggier spots in 'Nam. The Palace basement was a four-star hotel by comparison. He could break off that padlock and store his gear in the cabinet.

He heard a sound: rustling, then tapping and creaking. He switched off the flashlight, trusting his other senses to kick in. The sound seemed to come from behind the door, which was bolted shut from the other side. He had thought about forcing it, or installing a bolt on the Palace side for security. In the end, he'd let it be. A portal to the unknown. Had BomBoy used it?

Now the door creaked open.

Griff tensed.

A beam of light gleamed through the crack, then widened, curved, and landed on him. He stayed in place. Could this be his Guide? So soon?

"Well, what have we here?" The Guide approached, his feet shuffling. His voice was low and raspy.

"I have been waiting for you." Griff turned his flashlight on. He saw a man with a rubber clown mask covering his head. An unlikely looking Guide, but who was he to say?

"Have you now?" The Guide came closer. "Are you Griff?"

"You know me." Griff felt a flood of emotion, like a warm river washing through him. Finally, a connection. A sure sign he was in the right place, at the right time. His waiting had come to an end.

"Of course I do." The Guide laid his hand on Griff's shoulder. "We have much to discuss."

CHAPTER 26

O N Friday night, the East Hawai'i Community Players sat onstage in a circle of folding chairs for the séance. Five days had passed since the "incident." Only one week remained until opening night.

It felt like an eerie replay of the first read-through. Nora gave a voluptuous shiver. What a lot had happened in two months.

After rehearsal George had wished them luck, albeit sardonically, and gone home.

Fred had also left, but not before expressing his disapproval. "As a person of faith I am deeply concerned by this satanic ritual. I only hope you don't call down the wrath of the Almighty—or the Palace board."

"We're all people of faith," Merle said. "We just happen to express it differently."

Fred made a choking noise, then tried to slam the alleyway door on his way out, only to have it bounce back open again, ruining the effect and eliciting some snickers from the circle.

Merle's friend Valerie, the medium, had swept through the open door looking just like Mrs Which from *A Wrinkle in Time,* which Nora was reading aloud to the twins. She wore a long gown with gauzy sleeves, and her silver hair hung in a thick plait down her back. In an incongruous literary twist, she carried a big bag with handles, like Mary Poppins.

Merle and Evan shuffled a table to the middle of the stage and, Poppins-like, Valerie pulled an astonishing number of candles and other objects out of her bag. She issued instructions in a high, flute-like voice, which carried through the theater.

Good for the hard-of-hearing spirits, Nora thought. She seemed unable to enter into the earnest state most of the others exhibited. Chronic irony syndrome. She stifled a giggle. The scene—and her reaction—reminded her of the long, quiet church services she had sat through, giddy with boredom, as a child of devout parents in Vancouver, during which any absurdity could send her into a paroxysm of laughter. The words of a hymn ("Who is he in yonder stall" was deadly), the hair grease of a pompous speaker, or most fatal, catching the eye of another bored child. With this in mind, Nora avoided eye contact with the others.

Clyde and Greta had taken the twins to Oʻahu that morning, in spite of her protests at yet another absence from school. She had called Alice for a good venting session, and learned that her intrepid friend had copied the names on Greta's prescription bottles. An internet search would reveal more. On the positive side, at least now Nora could attend the séance, which she hoped wouldn't be too obviously contrived—like her psychic predictions on the phone. Just this morning she had assured a young man his girlfriend wasn't cheating *and* that he was up for promotion at work. Maybe his higher confidence level would make both of these hopeful statements true. He had sounded so desperate.

"Lights," Evan called, and Griff, stationed in the booth at the top of the house, shut them down. Darkness fell like a curtain.

Valerie struck a match, the sulfur a sharp odor (like the fires of hell?), and began to light the candles clustered in the center of the table. "Everyone join hands and close your eyes," she instructed in her ethereal voice.

Nora looked around under her lashes. Merle's warm hand grasped hers on one side, and Aunty Em's birdlike claw dug into the other. Evan, Belinda, Harriet, Patrick, Desiree, Moku, Larry, Mahina, her mother, Iris, and a few other chorus members all had their eyes squeezed shut.

Griff had not joined the circle.

"We welcome you, spirits," called Valerie. "We have come together tonight to invite you to speak to us."

A gust of wind from the alley flickered through the candles and snuffed out one or two.

"I feel your presence." Valerie's voice dropped in pitch. "Speak to us, spirit."

Silence pulsed through the darkness around them. A stray hair tickled Nora's face, but she didn't dare pull one of her hands away at this crucial juncture.

Valerie lowered her head, as if in concentration, then lifted her face to the candlelight and began to speak, her voice high and childish. "I miss my friend, Keiko. She doesn't sit with me at the movies anymore, and I've been lonely for so long."

Aunty Em gasped. "It's her, the little girl ghost." She squeezed Nora's hand so tight Nora had to stifle a yelp. "She's speaking to me. I'm Keiko."

"Is that you, Keiko?" Valerie's childish voice asked. "Don't you like me anymore? Why won't you sit with me?"

"Answer her." Merle leaned in.

"I do like you, I do. But only children sit way up in the balcony," Aunty Em called. "I'm too old now." She added, "You were always sweet and nice, not like your friend the older boy. Is he here, too?"

Valerie's voice changed, deeper and sneering. "I'm always here, you old bat."

Aunty Em cried out.

"All you idiots making fools of yourselves night after night." Valerie paused, her eyes staring sightlessly at the candles. "I've been watching." She laughed, a sort of teenage giggle-cackle. "Not so much hair to pull now, is there, old lady?"

"Did you throw the rock, young man?" Merle spoke, his voice resonant.

"That's for me to know and you to find out." More high-pitched giggling, then Valerie slumped forward.

Aunty Em had pulled her hands away and grasped the sparse braids wrapped around her head. Merle and Nora reached up and slipped their hands into hers again, restoring the circle.

Well this is interesting, Nora thought. Nothing so far that Merle couldn't have told Valerie ahead of time. Apparently he'd moved into the medium's backyard ʻohana house, which Nora had yet to visit since he always came to her place. Still, it was a good show.

At the head of the circle, Valerie shook her head, and her body twitched. The candles flickered again, without any perceptible breeze. She lifted her head, her eyes alert once again.

"What other spirits are with us here tonight?" she called in her regular fluting tones. "We invite you to make your presence known."

The circle murmured assent.

"Speak to us, spirit." Valerie's voice rose to a higher, more urgent level. "Tell us what you want."

Nora moved a little closer to Merle.

A voice boomed out, but not through the medium. A jolt ran through Nora, and she trembled. The voice seemed to issue from all four corners of the theater, high up. A man's voice.

"How kind of you to invite me to speak in my own home," the voice echoed.

Aunty Em gave a little shriek. "It's him! The evil man."

"Shhhh," several people around the circle hissed.

"Who are you, spirit?" Valerie lifted her face, her eyes still closed. "You must be very powerful to speak without a medium."

"Sorry to circumvent your plans, lady," the voice sneered, "but I have no need of your assistance."

The sound system, thought Nora, her heart racing. Someone has hacked into it. The ghost!

She squeezed Merle's hand, and he squeezed back.

"What do you want, spirit?" Valerie persisted.

"*What* I want is justice." The voice paused. "But you haven't asked *who* I am, and that will surprise you." His words reverberated through the theater.

Even Valerie kept quiet, waiting.

"My name—" the voice paused again, "is Griffin K. Peterson."

A collective gasp rose from the circle.

"Is this a joke, Griff?" Merle called up to the projection booth.

"Shut up, you coward," the voice thundered. "You're a disgrace as a man, not just as a lion."

Merle shook his head and swore under his breath.

"Can it, Merle," Larry snapped.

"Let the circle be quiet," fluted Valerie. "Let the spirit speak."

"Now I've got your attention. You think you know me, but you don't." The voice paused, and they all waited. "In fact, the man you know as Griffin K. Peterson is not who he says he is."

Another gasp.

"Ai-ai-ai-ai," murmured Aunty Em.

Nora squeezed her gnarled fingers, half in sympathy, half in irritation.

"The man you know as Griff is, in fact, my murderer." The voice broke off with a shriek and echoing cries came from the stage.

Aunty Em clutched Nora, and Nora held on tight.

Valerie's voice rose high over the cacophony. "Can you tell us more, spirit?"

"What more is there to say?" The voice shouted. "Seize him! Bring my killer to justice."

A gust of wind from the alley extinguished the rest of the candles, and screams broke out as darkness enveloped the stage.

Nora held the sobbing Aunty Em and made shushing sounds, perhaps more to soothe herself than the old woman, who she was certain was thoroughly enjoying the drama.

And then there was light.

Griff stumbled out of the booth near the ceiling and fell partway down the steps.

Cast and crew dropped hands and half of them stampeded offstage toward him.

Valerie sat with her head lowered, hands in her lap, as spent as if she'd provided a voice for the spirit herself.

Merle stood tall on the stage. "It was obviously Griff speaking the whole time." His voice carried. "A cry for help or a bid for attention."

"I wouldn't be so sure," Valerie replied. "A murdered spirit has the psychic power to seek out its killer."

"And since when did Griff ever want attention?" Patrick added.

"Well, I hate to be skeptical." Evan stood up. "But it sounded an awful lot like the P.A. system to me."

Nora nodded and eased Aunty Em back into her own seat. "That shriek? It could have been feedback." She avoided eye contact with Merle.

People started to murmur.

Halfway up the house seats, Griff sat with his head in his hands, rocking back and forth.

Mahina crouched at his feet, gripping his knee, her mother clutching at her other hand. She pulled it away. Others clustered on the stairs and leaned in.

"We should take him to the hospital right away." Larry headed toward the door. "I'll drive, but I'll need some volunteers to ride along. He could get violent."

Harriet, Patrick, and Mahina's mother chimed in their assent. They helped walk Griff down the stairs to the wide aisle that led to the alley. He was slumped over, resting his weight on their shoulders, his feet dragging. He muttered something in a low voice and shook his head like a dog with ear mites.

"He probably hears voices," Desiree whispered to Nora, who felt a stab of sympathy. You never knew what other people were going through.

As the halting procession neared the door, Griff gave a sudden twist away from his supporters and launched himself into the alley. Shouts of alarm filled the theater as people rushed after him. Others pulled out their cellphones to call—who? The police? The ambulance?

"Just let him go," shouted Mahina. "You're such haters, all of you. Griff is not a murderer." She burst into tears and jerked away as Iris tried to embrace her. "Leave me alone, Mom."

Valerie the medium loaded up her candles, then wafted offstage and out the door in a gauzy gust of wind.

"What a shit show," Desiree said to Nora. "I'm going home." She tossed her head and walked out the door.

"Well, who knew Fred was tapped into the wrath of the Almighty?" Merle had not joined the surge into the alley. He put his arm around Nora's shoulders. "Let me take you home."

Nora slipped out of his embrace. "I'm awfully tired, actually. I'm going to go straight to sleep."

"Let me know if you change your mind." He smiled. "I'll be over in a flash to take care of you."

"Thanks, Merle." Nora's smile didn't reach her eyes. She turned and followed Desiree out the door.

⌣

GRIFF WEAVED AND DODGED THROUGH THE DARK, ORANGE-TINTed streets of Hilo, putting distance between himself and his pursuers. Every shadow set off blaring alarms. He ducked and struck out, spinning away. The voices shouted in his mind, drowning out what the therapist had told him was his own true voice. Griff had never been sure what she meant, and if it was there now he couldn't hear a peep.

Instinct kept him moving, and he circled around to where he'd parked the truck—in a different place every time, just to be safe. He always checked to be sure no one saw him and could follow him home. No one knew where he lived. He just had to pick up his getaway bag, then he could disappear again. Should have kept it in the truck, but street kids broke into vehicles at night. He couldn't risk losing everything.

The truck's engine coughed, then caught. Griff pounded his head on the steering wheel, trying to quiet the voices' evil chant:

They're going to kill you now. They're waiting for you at the house, the CIA has agents in the alley right behind you. There's no escape, you'll pay for what you did. Grab the girl and trade her for your life.

He rummaged in the glove compartment for his tin box. Only two pills left. He swallowed them dry, and put the truck in reverse.

"Tonight on *Shore to Shore a.m.* we're talking to special guest, Willard Whips, an expert in the science of—" the radio blasted static for a moment, then Buck Leary's smooth baritone returned. "—so, call in now with your questions about this amazing phenomenon."

Music faded in: "Fear the Reaper," one of Buck's go-to filler songs. Griff gripped the steering wheel, relaxing only when Buck's voice came back on.

"Okay, first caller, from all the way in Hawai'i. You're on *Shore to Shore.*"

"Well, Buck," drawled a familiar voice. "I'm calling about psychic justice tonight and I have a question for Willard Whips."

"What's your name, son?" Whips's voice was an old man's, high and crackly.

"Just call me BB."

Griff's neck hair prickled and the voices grew louder. What was going on here? How could BomBoy enter the radio waves just after invading the theater?

"My question regards an experience I had tonight. I think some of your listeners, or at least one of them, might know what I'm referring to."

Griff swerved and nearly hit an oncoming car, which honked a long angry blare.

"Can you tell us about it, BB?" The static crackled.

"I'll just say the spirit of a murdered man tracked down and identified his killer—and accused him in front of more than a dozen witnesses."

"That's unusual," said Whips. "In my experience spirits tend to haunt their murderers privately. This sounds like a bold one."

"And no one did anything. They felt sorry for this maniac. They think he's a harmless crazy." BB's voice rose and his sardonic tone fell away. "But I know better. He killed my brother, and I'm going to bring him to justice."

Griff's heart faltered. Brother?

"Now BB," Buck Leary cut in. "You know we don't advocate vigilante justice here on *Shore to Shore,* so why don't you let us know where this happened and who your suspect is. Then the police can investigate and see if the facts match up." He paused. "Wouldn't you agree, Willard? Sometimes spirits make false accusations out of spite. We can't just act on them without verification."

"Oh yes," the expert agreed. "I personally have investigated several false testimonies. Just because someone is dead doesn't mean they're telling the truth. The spirit world is full of mystery."

"Are you calling my brother a liar?" BB's voice turned flat and mean.

"Oh no, no, of course not."

"Because then you'd be my enemy, too, and you wouldn't like that."

Static roared on the airwaves again. Buck's voice returned. "It's time for a commercial break, and then we'll be right back with another caller on *Shore to Shore a.m.* Thanks for listening, folks."

Sweat trickled down Griff's forehead. His hands on the wheel were slippery. He concentrated on the road, illuminated just a few feet in front of his headlights. His heart pounded fast and his head throbbed along with the shouting voices. Ten miles to his turnoff.

Images flashed through his mind. The flickering shadows and orange glow cast on the other vet's face, nearly hidden by scraggly hair and whiskers, as he sat by the campfire on the shores of Lake Diablo in the North Cascades National Park all those years ago, the night before he died and Griff's fugitive life had ended in rebirth. The Transaction. He hadn't mentioned a brother, even though he'd been a talker. The guy had rattled on and on about explosives. They'd both spent time in the tunnels of Vietnam. The difference was, the other vet seemed to relish the memory of blowing gooks to pieces. Griff just wanted to forget. He slapped the side of his head and groaned.

Twenty minutes later the truck lurched and bumped up Griff's long driveway, pocked with untended potholes and lava outcroppings to discourage unwanted guests, meaning everyone. The house was not visible from the red cinder road, which, being in deep Puna, was only minimally maintained by the county. He stumbled out of the cab, the voices still raging. He would have to rest before he'd be fit to travel.

Griff went straight for his medicine shelf. Only half a dose of horse tranquillizer left. How had he let his supplies get so low? He was slipping. That's why this security breach had happened. He had relaxed his vigilance and missed something. And They had gotten through, at the theater and now on the radio. There was no refuge.

He jabbed the syringe into his hip and numbness washed over his mind and body. This time, though, with the reduced dose, he didn't lose consciousness. The voices finally muted, Griff sat down at his computer and opened his browser. Perhaps for the last time, since the internet was certainly responsible for his discovery. But how?

He logged in to the secret website for veterans, and entered the chat room. Almost immediately, AdVisor sent him a private message.

Chimera, do not abandon your mission. It was not The Voice this time.

Too dangerous. Griff's fingers trembled, his mind cloudy.

You were chosen for a reason. Stay the course.

Compromised. Griff's leg started to twitch, and his body shook as though he had a fever.

Say it was a prank. Apologize.

This unexpectedly pointed, practical instruction sent a ping through Griff's drugged mind. He shook his head. Thought was not possible.

Not me.

You need damage control to save the mission. AdVisor had dropped his signature lofty, prophetic style.

Unconsciousness drifted closer, like a shadow. Griff forced himself to concentrate. The pinging in his mind pushed a thought to the surface: AdVisor might be the enemy. But BomBoy was the enemy. AdVisor was his ally. Wasn't he? He had sent the Guide.

Need to go. Not safe. Griff shook his head. The voices were gaining strength again. He found another pill in the cupboard and gulped it down. His throat felt like sandpaper.

Be strong, Chimera. The survival of humanity is at stake.

Griff hesitated. He felt the pull of the Energy Center. It was real. AdVisor couldn't manipulate that, could he?

The sudden urge for sleep was irresistible.

Out, he typed. He shut down his computer before AdVisor could reply again.

He fell onto the couch, and merciful darkness covered him like a blanket.

～

GEORGE HAD GONE TO SLEEP IN TURMOIL. COME ON, PEOPLE, A séance? But he woke up Saturday morning with clarity. He was back now. Every cell of his body pulsed with urgency. Enough time wasted.

"We want different things, George, different lives, really." Cal's lack of passion had been even worse than his previous tears and pleading. "There's no point going on the way we are. It's too painful." His words echoed in George's mind as the shower tingled against his skin.

As he pulled on his clothes, a car crunched into the driveway. Cal's SUV.

He ran barefoot into the hallway and flung open the front door. Cal had reversed within a few feet of the garage door and was pulling a dolly out of the hatchback.

George's surging life force drained out of his body and he grasped the doorframe for support.

"I found a place." Cal's voice was unnaturally bright, even for him. "It's moving day." His smile didn't hold.

Really? George sagged. Was he supposed to play along?

Cal pressed the remote to open the garage door, and then handed it to George. "I don't want to forget, so I'll just give this to you now."

"You might need it later—if you forget something." George didn't raise his hand to take the plastic object, which now seemed imbued with symbolic meaning.

"I'll just put it on the counter, then." Cal patted his shoulder and George's eyes burned.

He sat on the couch and listened to the boxes smacking onto the dolly. Its wheels squeaked as they rolled in and out between the house and the garage. His cell phone kept ringing, but he ignored it. Finally, he straightened up and walked to the spare room where Cal was stacking another load.

Cal stopped and pushed his hair back from his forehead. "I'm sorry you have to see this, George, but I work tonight and—"

George tried to smile. "It's okay. At least let me help you."

Together they worked in silence to carry Cal's boxes to the car. The remaining furniture belonged to George, along with the house. They'd been together for three years.

"Cal, I've been doing a lot of thinking—"

Cal held up his hand, his eyes shut tight. "I can't do this right now, George. I'm sorry, but I can't."

"Okay." George lifted the last box off the dolly and wedged it into the front passenger seat of the car.

They stood there for a moment, then both started to talk at once.

"Maybe in a week or two—"

"I really hope we can—"

Although he knew he should probably keep quiet, George had to speak. "I don't want to be like my father, Cal. I realize I'm on that same path, and I want to get off. I want to change. I don't want to be a bitter, lonely old man with a few old photos in my desk drawer."

Cal was silent for a long moment. "Your photos are all on Facebook, George—hundreds of them." He climbed into the driver's seat and started the engine. The window slid down.

"I'll call you next week, okay?" The window started to slide back up, then stopped. "And I'll come to opening night. Wouldn't miss it."

Cal's half-smile just about stopped George's heart in his chest. Something twisted deep inside him. A heart attack would shoot down his arm, though, wouldn't it? He smiled back, as tears pushed behind his eyes.

The car reversed and turned down Kaiwiki road, then disappeared behind a line of trees around the curve.

His Miata sat next to a big empty space in the garage. The front door of the house stood open. If he were lucky, a tornado would descend and sweep it all away, lift him up to the sky, and carry him into an alternate reality, where Cal was the good witch who would finally tell him how to get back home.

PART FOUR
BEAUTIFUL WICKEDNESS

CHAPTER 27

Excitement buzzed through the Palace like an electric current, tingling and perilous. Tonight was the final dress-tech rehearsal. And tomorrow was opening night.

Cast and crew had been stunned into silence by Griff's unapologetic reappearance at rehearsal the Monday after his breakdown. He went about his business as though nothing had happened, ignoring demands to explain his part in the séance, whether as a fake spirit's voice or a real spirit's murderer. Stymied by his indifference, competing theories abounded and the gossip mill spun stories that floated and glistened like Glinda's bubbles.

In the end, George told everyone to shut up and leave Griff alone. He saw no need to contact the authorities, since the police had already been given ample evidence of the Palace prankster's work and didn't seem overly concerned. This was nothing new. "And, damn it, the show is about to open, people. Focus."

Hell Week had been grueling, with George fully reengaged and filled with an urgency bordering on mania. Rumors flew that his boyfriend had moved out, but no one dared mention it, much less offer sympathy.

No more sabotage had occurred since the "incident," and no more accusing voices rang out from the ceiling. Glinda the Good's tiara went missing, then turned up again the next night, an incident written off to pesky Munchkins. Sheer hard work and imagination filled the theater with energy and hope, erasing doubts and fears— at least temporarily. The orchestra reappeared, as if by magic. During rehearsals, Moku dashed up and down between the sound-board and the lighting booth until George bellowed, "Choose one or the other or get backstage where you belong."

"Just preparing for my multi-faceted career in theater arts, boss." Moku held his hands up in surrender and disappeared backstage.

Now, already made up and in costume, Desiree sat in the first row above the landing, trying to center herself. Her hands were shaking. This time tomorrow night—no! Fuck that. Glinda. That's what she would think about. The good witch. God, how she need-ed a Glinda in her life. Where were her fucking ruby slippers? Nowhere, that's where.

Below stage, multicolored lights blinked on the soundboard, tended by the legendary Luana, who worked all the Palace shows. The orchestra was tuning up. The discord usually sounded beau-tiful to Desiree, with its promise of soaring harmony to come, but tonight it made her want to scream.

Larry sat at the keyboard facing the stage, the musicians ar-ranged in a semi-circle facing him. One woman had an oboe, a flute, and a saxophone lying in cases at her feet. A musical badass.

George yelled up at the lighting booth and walked onstage, pointing at the side lights. He'd been a holy terror for days now. They were all exhausted from staying at the theater till midnight every night. George really knew how to put the hell in Hell Week.

Belinda demonstrated a dance sequence to the Tin Man on the floor next to the drum set. He tried it, and she showed him again.

Larry ran the orchestra through a couple of ragged transitions, breaking off with a blare of horns and crash of drums.

Supervised by Fred, the stagehands pounded nails into a floppy set piece and set out props for the opening scene on the farm in Kansas.

A truck drove down the narrow alley outside the open side door, releasing a pungent cloud of diesel fumes. Desiree's stomach churned.

The theater darkened until only the alcove lights glowed. Red and blue lights beamed from the left, pink and green from the right, orange and pink from the middle. Dust motes danced through their heat, drifting to the ceiling. George nodded approval, thumbs up.

Desiree leaned back in her seat and looked at the geometric patterns high on the domed ceiling overhead, which glowed in the reflected light. Chandelier platforms hung down, empty, from circular cross-hatched insets. They'd have to do a lot of fundraising before the Palace sported chandeliers again. Probably prohibited anyhow. Too hazardous, like the tall metal slides and wobbling merry-go-rounds of her childhood. Killjoy safety police. Didn't they know life was fatal? She strained her eyes to find the openings looking out from the catwalk that ran just below the ceiling. Someone could be up there watching right now. That bastard, Clownface.

She had been back to his house to make her drops several times in the ten days since her arrest. Kapili wanted it to look like business as usual.

Hunter didn't seem suspicious, although the locations he arranged to pass her the drugs were more and more remote. The last time, she'd had to hike through the ironwood trees at King's Landing. Sometimes she thought he was just messing with her, the psychopath. When she'd asked why he had come to the theater that night—suspiciously, the night of both the "incident" and her arrest—he had just laughed and said not to worry her pretty little head. Coincidence?

Desiree's children were staying in Puʻuʻeo at Makani's aunty's house. The police cruised by several times a day, and there was an undercover officer at the school. They had begged to stay in the play, so Makani's beefy next-door cousins provided an escort to rehearsals. Desiree was grateful.

This was her first experience of what it felt like to be part of a big extended Hawaiian family, since Kama's relatives all lived on Kauaʻi. The *ʻohana* took care of its own.

"Places," Fred shouted.

Desiree stood up, shaking out her dress.

Kama and Makani had dropped the kids off at the theater earlier, after taking them to the dollar movies and filling them with candy and popcorn. They had a gig at Uncle Roy's on Banyan Drive that night, but said they'd be back later to pick up the *keiki*. Makani was fully kitted out in tourist hula gear: grass skirt, coconut bikini top, *haku* lei and false eyelashes. Stunning. Kama looked sharp in a bright aloha shirt, his curly hair bushing out.

"Thanks, yah?" Desiree hugged and kissed them both.

"Shoots." Kama held her a little too long. "You okay? You can still tell the popo to shove it, yah?"

"I'm fine." Desiree had given Kama a sanitized version of the story. She didn't want him to think too badly of her.

Even Makani looked at her with concern instead of contempt. "They're good kids. We'll keep them safe." She glanced at Kama. "My cousin Denello thinks you're hot."

Kama shot Makani a dirty look, then shrugged. "Hey, he's got good taste, yah?"

"Thanks." Desiree laughed, straightening her shoulders, and lifting her chin. Denello, eh? She flipped back her hair.

The movie snacks had worn off, and the children were starting to whine. Desiree wrestled them into their Munchkin outfits. The costume designer, Enid, was in the hallway tacking down one of the Tin Man's panels, which kept popping off. One of the professional moms—as Desiree always thought of the immaculately dressed and coifed women who shepherded their glossy, happy children through dozens of extra-curricular activities, culminating in their acceptance to Ivy League universities—had brought a big platter of home-made sushi and musubi for backstage snacks. Nakai, Kolea, and Malia homed in and ate double-fisted. Grains of rice clung to their cheeks.

"Could someone please do their makeup?" Desiree could see the disapproval on the bevy of mothers' faces as they tended to their own Munchkins. "Thanks, you're lifesavers. I still have to do my own." She pointed at her face and grimaced, then hurried along the narrow passage past the basement door and along the curtain to the larger dressing room on the opposite side. She knew the good mothers would help her children. It was part of their code. Let them despise her.

After the finishing touches, she slipped out of the dressing room and sat in the house, trying to breathe.

Now she'd better go down and get her face mic taped on. Tomorrow night she'd be wearing two packs—one courtesy of the Hilo vice squad. Good thing her dress was so poofy.

She could hear Moses Kapili's voice in her head, going over the plan. She had already put step one in motion, asking Hunter to come to opening night and telling him to pick up his comp ticket at the box office. He was practically a Palace Friend now, she'd said, with his talk of bringing in a big donor.

"Glinda." George had spotted her. "Get backstage." That bald board member grinned at her from across the theater. Phil. She hadn't noticed anyone taking him up on his offer to do their hair. Creepy fucker.

"Yes dahling," Desiree trilled in her best Glinda voice. She fluttered down the steps and out the side door to Actors' Alley. There were her children, all Munchkined up, their makeup thick and bright.

"You look wonderful." She squeezed their arms and beamed. "How do I look?"

"You're all sparkly." Her youngest, Malia, gazed up at her mother, while Kolea and Nakai pranced over to join Nora's twins, giggling in excitement.

"That's because I'm a good witch, and good witches are always sparkly."

"Are bad witches always ugly?" Malia pointed at Harriet, visible through the doorway to the mirrored hallway next to the alley. She was made up as Elmira Gulch for the first act, pinning her pillbox hat into place. Her false nose jutted out in an evil curve.

"Mostly." Desiree patted her head and smiled at Harriet, who picked up the green greasepaint tube and shook it at them with a scary grin.

Malia hid behind Desiree, holding on to the gauzy folds of her dress. "She scares me, Mommy."

"She's not real, cupcake. It's Harriet, the nice teacher lady."

Harriet cackled. "Realer all the time, my pretty."

"I like being a Flying Monkey better than a Munchkin." Malia scuffed her foot.

"Just wait, sweet-cheeks. You get to sing your Munchkin song. It's your favorite, remember?"

"But Munchkins can't fly." Malia widened her eyes and flapped her arms, as though if she tried hard enough, she would rise into the air.

"Desiree, you're the last one." Fred waved the mic pack and motioned to her to follow.

"Gotta go, cupcake." Desiree air-kissed Malia's head and trotted over to the soundboard stationed below stage on the far right. Having wires strapped to her body—even the benign ones for the play—made her feel like the patsy in a mob movie.

But she wasn't a patsy. That's not how this story was going to end.

Desiree held up her arms and nodded at Moku, who was fiddling with the controls under Luana's watchful eye. Lights flashed up and down like colored waterfalls.

"Wire me up, buddy."

⌣

FINALLY, NEAR THE END OF DRESS REHEARSAL, HARRIET SLID down through the trap door, moaning and wailing, "I'm melting—melting!" The smoothest time ever, not like all the times her cape got stuck. But what was this? The two teenaged stagehands who caught her had the basement blazing like a chandelier. They were playing cards.

"The basement has to be dark when the trap door opens," Harriet scolded. "We can't have a shaft of light rising from the floor."

"Okay, okay." They piled up the cards and clicked off their headlamps, then switched off the humming fluorescent light, plunging the basement into darkness.

"Not now, you idiots." Harriet groped for the wall switch. "Before." Glaring light filled the dusty room. "Do you want me to fall and break my hip?"

Harriet's mother had contracted pneumonia and died in the hospital after breaking her hip. She was ninety-three, but still.

Harriet took her calcium twice a day, plus all the swimming. Maybe she should also join the gym. After the run.

Harriet brushed off the dirt. Why couldn't those kids clean the place up? She turned to climb the stairs to the backstage door. She had no intention of staying in the basement any longer than she had to, and it wasn't long before her curtain call. After the witch melts, events move to their conclusion at a rapid pace.

There was a door in the wall. She'd never paid any attention to it before, but tonight it was open. Just a little. Two inches, maybe. Harriet walked over and opened it wider. A draft of cold, damp air moved across her face from the blackness inside.

"Hand me a flashlight." She shone it into the darkness. A curving concrete tunnel stretched away underground. "My god! Do you see this? And I thought this was a broom closet."

"The police checked it out after the rock fell." One of the stagehands shook her head and her perky ponytail bobbed. "They said the tunnel was blocked."

"Are they quite sure?" Harriet closed the door. "This may be where the saboteur is getting in." She glared at them. "Did one of you open this door?"

They shook their heads and backed away. "No, not us."

"Well, we should tell George or Fred about this. Don't forget." Harriet had no faith in her own memory these days. The image of the door could easily slip right out of her mind on her way up the stairs to the stage.

"Okay aunty." The girls looked properly intimidated.

Harriet always felt like a teacher. It was her default mode, especially when she was around children. Luke accused her of hectoring him too.

"You're needed upstairs for the finale, so get moving." Why did young people dawdle so?

⌣

EVAN LOVED THE CLIMACTIC SCENE WITH THE WIZARD, WAITING
with delight until Griff delivered his famous line: "Pay no attention
to that man behind the curtain." It gave him a thrill every time.
Evan's back itched. He was sweating in his metal-plated costume
under the hot stage lights.

The Wizard gave the Scarecrow his diploma and the Cowardly
Lion his medal, then turned to the Tin Man.

"As for you, my galvanized friend, you want a heart! You don't
know how lucky you are not to have one. Hearts will never be practical until they can be made unbreakable." Oz shook his head. One
of his eyebrows was hanging loose.

"But I still want one." Evan thought of Luke's reaction when
he'd asked him to move in. He still felt a little sick and hollow.
Maybe he'd talk to Belinda about it after rehearsal. She was becoming such a comfort.

⌣

WHEN HARRIET EMERGED FROM THE BASEMENT, SHE HAD TO
jostle through the throng of cast members already gathered backstage to rehearse the curtain call. The *keiki* wranglers were shushing
the Munchkins corralled in Actors' Alley, stage right. Harriet headed
for the larger dressing room, stage left, where Nora leaned against
the wall in her short green Ozian dress and dancing headgear.

Everyone was more or less silent, practicing for opening
night. Onstage, the Cowardly Lion said, "Oh, oh—shucks, folks,
I'm speechless."

Harriet and Nora exchanged a smile. Nora motioned with her
head to the alley doorway. "This isn't a good time," she whispered,

close to Harriet's ear, "but I've wondered what you meant when you warned me about Merle."

"Ah." Harriet scratched under her hat, which she'd already put back on after the melting scene. She felt like she was forgetting something. Never mind. "I regret saying anything to you. Nothing worse than an old busybody."

Fred's brow furrowed at them and he put a finger to his pursed lips. Harriet jutted out her chin extension.

She and Nora walked down the steps into the gravel parking lot behind the theater. The homeless folks sitting under the overhang glanced over, then resumed munching on stale theater popcorn.

"Well, I'd like to know." Nora stood with a hand on her hip.

Harriet thought how lovely she was, how young. She knew Nora didn't realize it, probably thought she was old already. How little the young knew, to think they were old in their thirties. Or even forties. Harriet smiled. It was tragic. By the time you figured it out you really were old, or at least middle-aged. She thought of how she'd feel when she was eighty. Why, she was still a spring chicken. Better seize the day.

"Well, I'll give it to you straight." Harriet gathered her thoughts. "Merle has a reputation as a gigolo of sorts. I mean, as much as you can really be a gigolo in Hilo." She paused. "There are also reports that he likes to have more than one fish on the line." She raised an eyebrow.

"I see." Nora crossed her arms over her chest. "Can you give me any specifics, or is this just rumor?"

"Well, I know one woman personally, Robin, a colleague at Waiānuenue High who got involved with Merle about a year ago after he'd done a spiritual reading of her garden. He moved in with her and cooked divinely but never did any yard work, despite his profession. He also dodged any financial contribution, always waiting for some payout that never came." Harriet adjusted her cape. "She came home early one day and found him in her bed with another woman, who was just as surprised as Robin. Apparently Merle had told her he lived alone."

"Well." Nora gave Harriet a tight smile. "That does seem conclusive."

"I'm sorry, my dear." Harriet shrugged and grimaced.

"I had a bad feeling when he wanted to move in with me right after—" Nora's voice broke off. She looked up. "And then when he started living in Valerie the medium's refurbished garden shed. But wow." Nora shook her head. "Thanks for your candor."

"Well, we women have to stick together." Harriet patted Nora's arm. "Cheer up. You've had a good time so far, haven't you? No real harm done?" She gave Nora a devilish smile. "Robin gives us all piles of avocados and lemons from the trees Merle advised her to plant 'to infuse her energy body with richness and zest.' Definitely a win. She also said Merle was fabulous in bed. She quite missed the sex after she kicked him out."

Nora started to laugh and couldn't stop. She wiped away tears.

Fred waved his arms in the alley doorway and motioned for them to come back.

"Well, there is that." Nora grinned.

Harriet held up one finger, listening. The music had changed. "That's our cue." She hitched up her skirt and they broke into a run, still giggling.

CHAPTER 28

DESIREE STOOD ON THE CATWALK OVER THE STAGE, HOLDING her wand. Her glittering dress billowed over the railing. She wondered what would have happened by this time tomorrow night. Would she be dead or free or something in between? Wounded? Captive? Strapped down somewhere waiting to be tortured? She shook the images out of her head.

She watched the balloon scene below. When Oz left without her, Dorothy looked like she was really crying as she clutched Toto to her heart so tight he nipped at her ear. You go, girl, Desiree thought. Mahina was shaping up into a decent actor.

Griff scrambled out of the basket after the stagehands cranked it up to the platform. They shoved Glinda's bubble into place over the balloon basket, and Moku blew her a kiss. He had a hibiscus flower behind his ear tonight, on the available side. What a sweetheart. She blew a kiss back, then stepped in and descended, wand upheld, to give Dorothy the good news: the ruby slippers would take her home. It was hot under the lights, and the armpits of Desiree's white gown were starting to yellow. Would her wires short out and shock her tomorrow?

Desiree amped up her beatific smile. If they did, she wouldn't show a thing.

⌣

FORTUNATELY, GRIFF DIDN'T HAVE MUCH OF A COSTUME CHANGE to become Professor Marvel again for the last scene. He pulled on a tunic, stuck on a curling mustache, and patted down a floppy eyebrow. He would need more adhesive for the run.

After the séance and the shocking conversation on *Shore to Shore a.m.*, he'd had to buy more of his emergency meds from another vet he knew who had a regular supplier in the ER. He'd also stocked up on horse tranquillizer, wearing different disguises at two local feed stores so as not to raise suspicion.

Griff trusted no one now, not that he ever really had. AdVisor and BomBoy could be the same person. Hell, his masked guide—"Just call me X, it's safer that way"—could be the same person. Or they could all be who they claimed to be, and the voice at the theater could be someone else. One or all of them could be the dead vet's brother, bent on revenge. His internal voices clamored nonstop. The CIA had him surrounded with agents and the greys were going to eat him, arms first, then legs, then... He popped another pill. All his enemies were waiting to strike, but he could outwit and outrun them as he had before.

He upped his *pakalolo* intake and relocated his getaway bag to a plastic bin stuffed into a lava tube on his property. Not safe to leave it in the house, even though he'd swept the place for bugs and cameras again. He'd had to smash and then bury his small collection of dishes when they triggered his detector instinct. He bought paper plates and bowls, which he burned after using.

When he wasn't at the theater rehearsing or playing the organ, Griff spent hours digging up rocks on his land and stacking them into a huge pile for the goats to climb on. He found more lava tubes, some of which emitted steam and whiffs of sulfur. They hummed at him, an extension of the Energy Center. He communed with the goats as he scratched between their horns. They butted each other and munched on guavas. He'd hate to leave them, especially Cookie, but they had everything they needed to survive, with the drip-controlled rainwater tank—an old cast iron bathtub with a pipe hooked up to his catchment system—and twenty acres of tangled vegetation to browse. They could easily jump the five-foot hog wire fence if they wanted out.

X had warned him about Desiree. She was part of the enemy force. Griff was supposed to watch her and report back to X after rehearsal tonight. The door in the basement led to a safe place where his Guide would be waiting. Griff carried a knife in his pocket now, ready to strike if X turned on him. Who or what Desiree was remained to be seen.

When he'd started to ask questions the first time they met, X had just held up his hand. "All in good time, my dear fellow." He'd patted Griff on the shoulder.

Griff didn't like to be touched. X was hard to read behind the clown mask, but Griff could sense his tension. The man smelled of rubber and bleach. Toxic.

Griff had always worked through instinct. Even now he had no plan, but he was ready. The only imperative was to save the Energy Center, even if it meant putting his own life and freedom in danger. Mahina also needed protection. The comet had almost arrived, and the forces of darkness were strong.

Griff thought of the warm humming cylinder in the basement and yearned to run down and prostrate himself on top of It, absorbing Its heat, energy and power. No, there wasn't time. He adjusted his turban and glided into the wings.

⌣

MAHINA HUNG HER COSTUMES TOGETHER ON THE RACK, WITH her Kansas shoes and ruby slippers lined up underneath. She shut her makeup case after wiping her face so clean it gleamed. Her childhood may have turned into a black hole, but that made meticulous makeup removal even more important. No blackheads for her.

"Hey, you were great out there, Dorothy." Desiree's face was still smeared with thick, lurid makeup, her false eyelashes fluttering. She grabbed a wad of paper towels and started to rub at her cheek.

Mahina turned away. Gross. "Thanks. You, too." She headed out of the dressing room with Ziggy at her heels, and almost ran into the Witch. If she cackled, Mahina was going to scream. So over it. She felt like she could explode any second from the pressure of her volatile knowledge. Should she confront her mother and demand the truth? Should she call the lawyer? Should she write a letter directly to the "heirs"?

Everyone else seemed to be onstage or milling around below. Mahina had overheard Harriet tell George about the open door in the basement, and she felt a sudden urge to investigate. Exploring the underworld might get her mind off Iris's betrayal. The door had to be BomBoy's way in—and out. Or one of them. She drifted past the remnants of cast and crew backstage. Then she slipped through the door and pattered down the steps to the basement. She switched on the light and moved farther in.

Harriet was right. The door in the side wall was open.

Mahina picked up Ziggy and held him in the crook of one arm. Then she opened the door wider. Damn it, no flashlight. She held up her cell phone, but the greenish illumination was too pale.

Ziggy whimpered and struggled. Dank, stale air and darkness lay before her, and the hint of a curving wall. Mahina stifled a cough that was half gag. She didn't like enclosed spaces. The sound echoed, mocking her, and she shut the door, trying not to run as she hurried back up the basement stairs.

⌣

DESIREE HUNG UP HER GLINDA DRESS AND CLOSED HER MAKEUP case as far as it would go with all the lipstick and greasepaint tubes crammed into it. She'd picked up the whole kit at the thrift store for a dollar, and most of it was still usable.

Kama and Makani had showed up more or less on time to collect the kids. Kolea and Malia swarmed around Makani and petted her long, wavy hair. Nakai stayed close to his father and watched him with big eyes. Suck it up, Desiree told herself. No time to feel sorry for yourself—you're no Dorothy. You have to finish this thing, and then you can be a real mother again.

Desiree had overheard two stagehands talking about the open door in the basement, which confirmed her suspicions. Just like the restaurant. That was how the dealer got in to pick up the packages she left, and probably to play tricks on the theater group. All those petty thefts and then the "attack," as people called it now. Had he also been the "ghost" who accused Griff of murder? She wouldn't put it past the asshole. The voice had sounded familiar now that she thought about it.

Desiree decided to take a peek downstairs before she left. With her hand outstretched to grasp the handle, the door to the basement almost knocked her flat as Mahina burst through.

"Whoa there, little sis."

Ziggy gave a yip and leaped out of Mahina's arms.

"Gotta go. See you tomorrow night." Mahina hurried after her dog.

"See you." Desiree looked down the dark steps for a long moment. Then she closed the door and walked away. She could take a hint from the universe.

⌣

WHEN HARRIET PULLED INTO HER CARPORT SHE FELT AN ADDED buzz on top of the dress rehearsal high. The house glowed with light. Luke must be here. He'd been pulling away from Evan ever since his job offer and had stopped coming to the theater. He'd already moved into the house he was caretaking up the coast, so she hardly saw him anymore.

Her beautiful green bottle of Tanqueray sat half-empty on the kitchen counter. It had been nearly full when she last had a drink. The door under the sink was ajar. Was Luke okay? Maybe he'd lost everything and was moving back in.

"Hello?" Harriet called into the living room. "Luke?"

Someone had left the kitchen screen door wide open. Harriet suppressed her irritation. The house would be full of insects by now, drawn to the light. Why couldn't men close doors? She shut the cupboard and poured herself a generous dollop of gin on the rocks, then popped in a big green olive and added a dash of tonic water. No limes, alas. When she moved to slide the screen door shut, she saw a shadowy form sitting on her *lanai*.

"Luke, is that you?"

A familiar person turned around and held up his glass. "Cheers, Harriet. It's me." He took a drink. "Surprise."

Harriet took a step backward. "Howard? What on earth?"

"You haven't changed the locks." Her ex-husband stood up, swaying. "I'm afraid I've made a dent in your gin bottle—I remembered your old hiding place."

"What are you doing here?" Harriet stood her ground. "I mean, I'm delighted to see you, of course, but you could have called first." She looked around. "Is Luke with you?"

"He doesn't know I'm here. No one does." Howard rubbed his face. "I just drove to the airport and got on the first plane to Hawai'i. I have no luggage."

"Well, you always used to say all you needed to travel was a credit card." Harriet walked out onto the deck and pecked Howard on the cheek. He put his arms around her and drew her close.

"Now, what's all this?" She laughed and pushed him away. "Where's your lovely young fiancée? Or is she your wife now? Does she know you're here?"

"Tiffany." Howard sat back down on the deck chair. "No. She probably hasn't even noticed I'm gone. Her mother and sister and the sister's toddler arrived from Idaho and moved in with us. There to 'help' with the baby, who hasn't even been born yet." He tossed back his gin and plonked the glass down on the little teak table. "There's no fool like an old fool. Go ahead, laugh your head off, Harriet. I deserve it."

Harriet sat down next to him. "Well, I did wonder, but it's not my business anymore, is it?" She took a ladylike sip of her drink. She thought, but did not say, how hard is it to use a condom, you idiot? Readily available at drug stores near you.

"God." Howard pulled at his sparse hair. "I don't know why I came here. I'm sorry. I just had to get away." He looked at her, his eyes forlorn. "And I missed you."

"Well, I miss you, too, of course," Harriet said briskly. "Thirty years of marriage leave their mark."

He looked away and she relented. "You're always welcome in my home, Howard. We're family. You can sleep in the spare room. Luke doesn't need it anymore."

"I don't expect anything." He folded his hands. "I just wanted to see you and Luke."

Harriet sat up straight. "You'll be here for opening night tomorrow." She turned to him and grinned. "I'm one hell of a Wicked Witch of the West, you know."

"Oh, I'm sure you are." Howard smiled for the first time, his face creasing up in familiar lines.

Harriet's heart fluttered a little. And why not? Life-long relationships were complicated and went through many stages. This new one might be more interesting than she'd thought.

CHAPTER 29

OPENING NIGHT HAD ARRIVED. NORA FELT LIGHT AND INSUB-
stantial. No more lugging makeup case and accessories back
and forth for the three of them. Everything was at the theater now
for the run, waiting backstage with their names on it.

But she couldn't stop thinking about the call she'd received
about half an hour into her shift on the psychic hotline that morning.

She had answered as usual. "My name is Nora. To whom am I
speaking?"

"Let's just say I'm a friend." It was a man. An older man, by the
gruff sound of his voice.

"Well then, *friend.*" Nora paused. This was weird. "How may I
help you today?"

"You might ask how I can help you, *Nora.*" The mimicking em-
phasis on her name had an ugly tone, which, as a professional, she
ignored.

"Well, we all need help sometimes."

"Don't you worry your children are in danger, Nora?"

Nora's heart started thumping hard, and her head felt light. "What did you just say?"

"You heard me." The caller paused.

Nora cut into the silence. "Whether or not I even have children is no business of yours, *friend*, and whatever danger you're threatening is in your own pathetic, sick mind." The jungle drums were beating.

"I mean you and your children no harm, little lady. Quite the contrary." The voice sounded amused. "That theater group may not seem dangerous, but think about it. Ghosts, crazy people, drug dealers—oops. I'm not supposed to talk about that, but really. Is this a wholesome atmosphere for your young ones?"

"I don't know who you are or who you think I am." Nora gritted her teeth. "Or what theater group you're talking about. But since you called the psychic hotline, let me go ahead and give you a reading." She collected herself. "I see you rotting in a jail cell, where psycho stalkers like you belong. And if you call me again, or make any move toward my children, you will find out just how unwholesome *I* can be."

Nora clicked off and closed her laptop, shaking. First, she called the school office to check on the twins. Then she opened her laptop again and wrote a report to the hotline administrator, recommending the caller be blocked from future contact. If he hadn't mentioned the theater, it would have seemed more like a random sicko call. She'd already had one or two of those from male callers, asking what she was wearing and describing their erections. Why men thought women got excited by hearing about their engorged penises she would never know. Perhaps she was alone in her indifference to this crude form of courtship—or, more accurately, verbal assault. But this had been personal. The man had mentioned her children, *and* the theater group. Ghosts and crazies, sure. But drug dealers? Had his voice sounded familiar? Maybe she should call the police. She hesitated, considering how Clyde could use this against her in a custody fight. She picked up her phone.

Now, hours later, she still couldn't shake her feeling of dread.

Miri and Oliver danced down the steps from the house, singing, "Ding dong, the witch is dead."

Nora thought of Greta. Dead would be convenient, but neutralized would do. For now. She was just a placeholder, after all. There would always be another girlfriend waiting in the wings. Maybe Alice had found some more ammunition she could use, or even Merle.

Clyde had backed off about the children's rehearsals and hadn't even made a fuss about the vandalism, which of course Nora had downplayed. Probably because he was too busy plotting to whisk them off to Australia with Greta.

After what Harriet had told her last night, her already cooling feelings for Merle were nearly frozen. Still, he could help her with Greta. She couldn't afford to alienate him. Yet.

Nora sighed. All this scheming was making her crazy. Maybe she should call the psychic hotline for a reading herself.

"Come on Mom, we'll be late," Oliver called. The twins were already strapped in the car. "Dad's going to meet us at the theater before the play, and Hans and Karen and Greta are coming to watch us."

"Well, how nice." Nora fired up the Volvo and backed out of the driveway. "Alice, Giles, and Amelia are coming tonight as well. You'll have so many fans."

She and Alice had plans, although they weren't as clearly worked out as Nora had hoped. They'd have to improvise. She drove up the narrow road past rust-tinged, corrugated iron roofs of alternating colors. Palm trees waved their fronds in the wind, and lurid green yards gleamed. It was surreal.

A big rainbow-colored balloon hovered in her mind's eye, waiting to carry them away.

◡

"OKAY, CIRCLE TIME."

Circles had always made George uncomfortable, but in a town like Hilo you couldn't avoid them. Especially in theater. Circles and blessings. New business or home? A blessing in a circle.

But tonight, he felt a tightening in his chest as the cast and crew gathered onstage. There wasn't room backstage, and the house wouldn't open for another half hour. I must be getting sentimental in my old age, he thought.

A Munchkin reached up a small sticky hand, and he high-fived it.

George scanned his cast, amazed by their transformation in the space of a couple of months from an odd group of people—many of them strangers—to a family. Dysfunctional, plagued by petty jealousies and squabbles, ruled by a tyrannical father, but a family. His family. The principals looked good, he thought, fresh and raring to go in their Kansas gear. Dorothy had a sort of hectic flush—probably just too much rouge, or braids too tight. Toto growled when he saw George looking. The three farmhands lounged around, already with their Oz characters in mind—the shuffling, bashful Cowardly Lion, the loose-limbed, awkward Scarecrow, the stiff, morose Tin Man. Professor Marvel looked like a complete charlatan. Good. George congratulated himself again on his casting of the witches. They were perfect. The Wicked Witch (now dressed as Elmira Gulch) had added an extra wart or two on her long, hooked nose and looked like evil incarnate in a hat and bun, lips tight above an elongated chin. Glinda the Good was ethereal, her smile dazzling, even if she looked a little bulgy around the middle. Probably too many backstage snacks.

Fred corralled the rest of the Munchkins and the adult chorus (in Munchkin townsfolk garb), and they shuffled and jostled downstage until everyone was included. George felt a warm glow in his solar plexus. Was it heartburn? Or could it be love?

"You've all worked hard, and you've powered through some scary times."

Nervous laughter. One or two people sneaked glances up at the ceiling.

"Now it's time to have fun." George looked around the circle. "You know your parts. Relax and *be* them now. The audience will believe in you and be swept into the dream. You're that good."

He saw the caustic glance Harriet exchanged with Patrick, who tried to suppress a nervous convulsion of laughter when George caught his eye. They must be wondering the same thing I am: Who is this director?

"I want to give special thanks to Fred for his yeoman's labor, and to all of you for your support and extra hard work, and for hanging in there when things got tough. Whoever the ghost is, he's not going to win this one. We are." George paused as the cast cheered. "Whatever happens, however much money comes in, we can be proud of what we've accomplished here, together. Somehow, the Palace will live on."

More cheers and huzzahs, whistles and stomping. Gaudily costumed and made-up characters beamed at each other.

"So, in closing." George grabbed the hands of the people next to him: Fred, who was blinking back tears, and Merle, who gave a long sexy growl. "Go out there and knock 'em dead, folks. You're wonderful. And this is going to be a fabulous show."

❥

IRIS SAT WITH MOSES IN THE FRONT ROW JUST ABOVE THE MAIN cross aisle. Best seats in the house. As the lights dimmed and the orchestra struck up the overture, Iris felt tears pricking her eyes. She'd been so emotional lately—not surprising, since so much was at stake. Mahina had been unusually distant and aggressive ever since the lawyer's letter arrived, but her mood had to be a coincidence. Probably just the stress of Hell Week and opening night nerves.

Iris had checked and double-checked: the envelope seemed untouched, the file drawer still locked, the key safe in its hiding place. How could Mahina know? Plus, the daughter she had lived with for sixteen years would have started yelling the minute she discovered the pack of lies she'd been told, not withdrawn into herself and lashed out in occasional surprise attacks. Iris knew she had to talk to Mahina soon. Her daughter would be even angrier if she found out the truth from another source—and that was just a matter of time, judging from the letter. Iris wanted to cling to the last good old days of mother-daughter solidarity for as long as she could, but that golden period already seemed to have ended.

Moses put his arm along the back of her seat and squeezed her shoulder. She knew something was up with his drug investigation, but he couldn't tell her about it. He'd warned her he would probably have to miss at least part of the show. His team was shorthanded, since earlier that evening a meth lab had exploded out in Royal Gardens, a subdivision deep in Puna. The chief had ordered Moses to send most of his officers to investigate and canvass the neighborhood. Moses was upset, but nice enough to consider her feelings. His presence in the theater proved his commitment to her.

Iris felt a brief pang of guilt. She had only held him in the light for a few seconds during her morning meditation before turning the full force of her concentration to Mahina, and then to her own imperiled essence.

The people in the row behind them were connected to a couple of the Munchkins: Oliver and Miri, Nora's twins. Must be homeschooling friends from Waimea. Iris had heard them talking before the show started. One woman had a British accent and another a more guttural one. Dutch? German?

Iris had chatted briefly with Nora at the workday for the first time since she handed over the keys to Nora's rental. She'd seemed embarrassed, eager to get away. People so often regretted spontaneous confidences, another reason why Iris guarded her own secrets so carefully. On top of Nora's other challenges, the poor woman had the worst possible complexion for this climate with that red hair and fair skin. She was burning even with a broadbrimmed hat on—and those freckles. The twins had her coloring, too, poor things. Thinking of Nora's situation now, Iris thanked the universe for her own good fortune, for as long as it had lasted. A hostile, land-grabbing, living ex-husband was certainly worse than a fictitious dead one. At least she'd been able to live where she wanted, and she'd never had to share Mahina.

"Stop kicking your sister."

Iris heard sounds of struggle behind her, and smiled. She also hadn't had to negotiate sibling rivalry. Occasionally she regretted not having more children, for letting her life be hijacked by one early disaster. But having another child at her age would be a little ridiculous, and Mahina would be embarrassed. That is, if she didn't cut Iris off completely when the truth came out. Perhaps she was perimenopausal already, and these thoughts were just the slow ticking of her failing biological clock.

There she was! Iris reached up and clenched Moses's hand resting on her shoulder as Mahina came onstage, calling, "Toto! Toto?" Then she relaxed and let the story sweep her away.

⌣

MERLE DASHED THROUGH THE DRESSING ROOM DOORWAY AND embraced Nora, who was darkening her eyebrows in front of the long, brightly lit mirror. She gritted her teeth and smiled. "Must finish my face."

"I have news." He leaned down and whispered, "You'll be pleased to hear Greta is responding well to my spiritual guidance. Rosemary can work miracles."

"You don't say." Nora blotted her bright red lipstick, watching his reflection in the mirror. Desiree and Harriet were lined up at the counter, touching up their hair and makeup, pretending not to listen.

"I'll have her off the Xanax and Oxycontin soon." He paused. "That's confidential, of course."

"Of course." Nora lifted her reinforced brows in feigned astonishment. "And how about the move to Australia? Still flexing her stepmother muscles?"

"The fan palms and I are working on it." A smile twitched at Merle's lips. "She did make a few choice comments about your ex."

"Ha. That hasn't taken long." Nora turned and treated Merle to a genuine smile.

"Places," Fred hissed into the dressing room.

Merle bounded back out, headed for the narrow passage behind the curtain to the other side of the stage.

Desiree looked at Nora. "What hasn't taken long?" She dabbed more mascara onto her fake lashes.

Nora blushed. "Merle is helping me with a domestic issue."

Desiree laughed and peered down her dress. She reached in to adjust something. "I'm sure he is, honey."

Harriet pulled off a wart, added more adhesive and pressed it back on. "Damned thing."

Belinda stuck her head in the doorway. "You all look smashing." She flashed them a toothy smile and disappeared.

"My ex-husband is in the audience tonight. Have to look my best, don't I?" Harriet raised her bristling fake eyebrows. "Showed up unexpectedly and spent the night—in the spare room."

"Whoo-hoo." Desiree held up a hand to high-five Harriet, who just looked at her. "They always come back for more, don't they?"

"My ex-husband is here, too," said Nora. "With his new girlfriend and her children. One big happy family."

"Until she dumps him for Merle, eh?" Desiree elbowed Nora. "Is that the plan? I didn't mean to listen in, but Merle has quite the stage whisper." Desiree patted her middle and gave herself a once-over in the mirror. "Since we're reporting on our exes, mine and his girlfriend have a regular gig at Uncle Roy's now. Maybe they'll make the second act, but I'm not holding my breath." She stood up. "At least he's working, yah? Maybe he'll pay a little more child support."

"Shhhhhhh." Fred lunged through the doorway and glared, his eyes popping. He motioned wildly toward the stage. "Two minutes to curtain."

"Whoa, mister." Desiree held up her hands in surrender.

Nora giggled. Someone else besides Greta needed an herbal energy intervention.

Harriet secured her Elmira Gulch hat and gave Nora a meaningful look as she strode through the door to wait in the wings for her first appearance.

AFTER THE TORNADO SCENE, GRIFF WAS OFFSTAGE LONG ENOUGH to make his preparations. During his years in Vietnam he had perfected the art of blending in. Now, even out of the jungle, he could move among people without being noticed. Griff slipped past a group of Munchkins and townsfolk spilling out of Actors' Alley and through the basement door without attracting a single glance. He turned on his pocket flashlight and trained its beam on the Energy Center. Was it his imagination, or was the big tube humming louder than usual? Did It feel warmer? Was It summoning strength to do battle?

The side door was standing open. Sloppy. He pushed it shut and gazed around at the mess made by the stagehands. Couldn't be helped. The witch had to melt, and someone had to catch her. He would just have to work around the play. He was used to that. At least this was fairly predictable, not like 'Nam. In the jungle you never knew where the enemy was going to show up. Griff made his final adjustments and then turned to the Energy Center. He pulled out the bag he'd hidden behind It and double-checked his tools. Everything was ready.

❧

DESIREE LOVED HER FIRST ENTRANCE. EVEN KNOWING WHAT she had to do later didn't interfere with her pleasure. Her tooth-whitened smile dazzled as she descended in her glowing sphere, wand upheld. A disco ball danced light bubbles all around her.

"Are you a good witch, or a bad witch?" she trilled to Dorothy. She sensed the audience beyond the scalding brightness of the stage lights and felt a surge of energy. Everything was going to go her way tonight.

⤳

PATRICK EXCLAIMED, "WHOOPS. HA HA. THERE GOES SOME OF me again." Straw littered the stage. The hot lights beat down, and sweat dribbled down his back.

Dorothy looked sympathetic. "Does it hurt you?"

Patrick thought about the little pieces of himself he lost all the time. Was it too late to learn how to be more careful? Could he convince Cindy he deserved a second chance? He reached down and picked up some straw off the stage. "Oh no, I just keep picking it up and putting it back in." He stuffed the straw into his shirt and flopped around, a big smile on his face.

⤳

EVAN STOOD FROZEN IN PLACE, HIS ARM RAISED WITH THE AX held high. His muscles were starting to cramp.

"Why, it's a man. A man made out of tin." Dorothy's eyes grew wide.

That's me all right, thought Evan. Here for all to see. "Oil can," he grated. "Oil can." If only it were that simple.

After they oiled him up and he could move again, Evan danced his stiff jerky dance and sang his song about the heart. He thought of Luke sitting in the audience, the only person—besides Belinda, of course, and perhaps Harriet and even other onlookers (oh god, how many?)—who knew the truth behind the song.

Soon the Scarecrow and Dorothy invited him to come to Oz with them, and he wasn't alone anymore, stiff and stuck in the woods. Evan put an extra spring in his jerky step.

⤳

WHEN THEY REACHED THE "LIONS AND TIGERS AND BEARS" scene, Mahina was feeling relaxed and confident, fully immersed in her role. Ziggy was acting like a boss. Moku had put in extra time with him during Hell Week, and it showed.

The Cowardly Lion leaped out and terrorized the Scarecrow and the Tin Man. Then he pounced after Toto, growling.

She slapped his hand and he backed away, crying.

"Shame on you," she admonished. Dorothy's aggressive side came naturally to her.

The Cowardly Lion sobbed and writhed. Soon they all comforted him and invited him to come along to Oz.

Mahina had to work hard to put extra expression into Dorothy's generous side. She might be bossy, but she also made friends easily and liked to help people. Kind of a sap.

On to the poppy field, then intermission. She was starved. And she had a decision to make.

⤳

GEORGE HAD DECIDED EARLY ON THAT THE WICKED WITCH'S crystal ball scenes would take place offstage. The audience would only hear her voice. That was fine with Harriet.

As Glinda sent the snow to wake Dorothy from her poppy-induced sleep, Harriet raged, "Curse it. Curse it! Somebody always helps that girl. But shoes or no shoes, I'm still great enough to conquer her. And woe to those who try to stop me."

What was it she wanted to conquer? Not Howard's little bride. He was here now, wasn't he? Certainly not Dorothy. Her own fears? Inertia? She threw back her head and let out a long cackle, feeling the power surge through her.

﹀

DESIREE HAD TO WORK FAST AFTER THE POPPY FIELD SCENE where she rescued Dorothy. Intermission would last only twenty minutes, which gave her twenty-five minutes tops to rescue herself from the mess she'd landed in. Her heart pounded in her throat. If Kapili didn't catch her "gang," she would have to go into hiding.

She was glad her children had a refuge with their father, especially with police oversight. That was one good thing about the inclusive nature of home in these big extended families. Children moved around among their relatives, and no one thought anything of it. Life in the 'ohana could make them nearly untraceable for an outsider like Hunter. If by any chance he got close, Makani's cousins would smack him down, no problem. She had more confidence in them than in the police, especially since the older brother, Denello, had the hots for her. She didn't need Miss Makani to tell her she could still pull the men.

Desiree had forced herself to be nice to Hunter since her session with Moses Kapili. No complaints about the meeting places or Clownface or anything. Bastard. She'd even been flirtatious when she invited him to opening night. "We're all excited about your mysterious donor," she said.

The clincher had been a call earlier that afternoon, as instructed by Kapili. She told Hunter she'd heard something. She was worried and needed to talk to him. Not over the phone, in person. She would meet him during intermission.

Desiree raced into the single bathroom stall backstage to strip off her dress and face mic unseen. George and Fred would have a fit if they saw her, and Kapili had told her to leave everything in place. But she couldn't go out and mingle with the audience in costume, and Hunter might think the mic was a wire. She pulled on stretchy capris and a long loose top, which hid the wire and battery pack. She hoped she hadn't dislodged anything.

Someone pounded on the door.

"Almost done." She looked at her face in the mirror, garish with stage makeup. One of her false eyelashes was coming loose. She closed her eyes and pressed with her fingertips. Deep breaths.

She opened the door and whooshed through, her glittering dress bunched in her arms. "My back teeth were floating—whew." Her smile dazzled.

Harriet raised her eyebrows and shouldered past her into the bathroom.

Desiree hung her dress on the rack, mic pack tucked inside, and slipped out of the dressing room into the alley. She passed the smokers and the homeless guys, who whistled at her. Out of costume she was nearly incognito, except for the hair and makeup. Oh well. She hurried across the uneven pavement alongside the theater to the lights of the road ahead.

Hunter was easy to spot. He stood at the end of the alley, his arms crossed.

"This had better be good." He grabbed her by the elbow and marched her down Haili Street toward the water.

"Not so fast, soldier, I have to get backstage in a minute." Desiree tried to pull away and he backed her against the wall. She leaned forward to avoid contact with the battery pack.

"So, what is it?" Hunter's eyes were flat, like hard blue pebbles.

"I heard Iris's police boyfriend talking to her last night at dress rehearsal. I heard my name and then yours. And I heard him say 'ice' and 'crackdown' and 'Hawaiian Beaches' and something about opening night. I think he's planning a raid." Okay, say something incriminating quick. She dug her nails into her palms.

Hunter's breath reeked of vodka.

She tried not to breathe in through her nose. Disgusting. His drug of choice was legal, unlike the one he sold.

A grating sound came from Desiree's left, on the ocean side, and then a sharp scent that seemed familiar. Bleach? What was going on? She turned to look but Hunter grabbed her face in his hand and turned it back toward him.

"Well, this is very interesting." He smiled and leaned closer. He jerked up her shirt before she could react. "No wonder you're only in community theater, baby." He ripped the wires and tape off her skin and she winced, trying not to panic. "Not a very convincing actress, are you?"

Desiree was about to retort when a terrible pain shot from the back of her head through her whole body, a burning river.

Clownface. Her vision narrowed and everything went dark.

CHAPTER 30

Patrick took a long drag on the cigarette. Just one. Cindy was in the audience tonight, with one of her regular clients, Mariko. He'd spotted them near the front. They must have arrived early to get such good seats. He was surprised Mac had let her go out without him glued to her hip. Maybe she'd broken up with him and was ready to reunite with Patrick. He intended to catch up with her after the curtain call and press his advantage.

Patrick stood near the chain-link fence at the edge of the parking lot. Sharp rocks dug into his feet through the thin soles of his floppy Scarecrow shoes. The backs of the other old buildings surrounding the Palace rose against the sky, their corroded plaster and peeling paint softened in the darkness. He'd quit smoking years ago, but every now and then he gave himself a treat. He deserved one, considering all the recent shocks to his system. Now he should drop the butt and step on it. But how? His shoes might burn. He'd have to crush it with a rock.

"Patrick?"

Shit. He turned around and grinned. "Hey Belinda." Patrick had been stalling on their lunch date, since he seriously doubted a middle-aged man could really just be friends with a pretty woman twenty years younger, especially when she was looking for a relationship. He would have to let her down easy.

"You smoke?" Her eyes were wide and accusing. Here was his chance.

"Sometimes." He lifted the cigarette and took another drag, blowing the smoke to the side. "I find it calms me down. Centers me." He smiled and held it out to her. "Here, give it a try."

Her mouth tightened, and she backed away. "No thanks." She whirled and stomped back to the theater.

Patrick watched her go, feeling a pang of guilt, but a greater sense of relief. Young people were so full of judgment.

He and Cindy had seen each other's faults and hurt each other, and yet they could still choose to forgive, he hoped. A lifelong relationship would require tremendous generosity of spirit.

He dropped the cigarette and ground it out with his heel. Warm, but not painful. He looked down the alleyway. What was Desiree doing out of costume?

⌣

IRIS NEEDED SOME FRESH AIR AFTER THE MUGGY, BODY-PACKED theater. She stood out under the blazing marquee in the cooler night air and fanned herself with her program while Moses walked up the car-lined street, away from the chattering crowd, to call the station. He said he hoped to retrieve some officers from the Royal Gardens scene for backup at the Palace.

She exchanged greetings with clients, colleagues, and parents of Mahina's classmates. Hilo was such a small town, everyone so connected. She had chosen well, making a home for Mahina here rather than in vast, soulless L.A., where her past was waiting to strike.

Community theater shows drew so much support on the Big Island at least in part because there were no professional drama productions. Musicians of all stripes blew through town regularly, to and from their more lucrative engagements in Honolulu, but no one brought theatrical shows to the neighbor islands, except for an occasional one-person act. Community theater did very well as a result. People were hungry for live performances, even if they didn't always recognize their hunger, trying to feed it with inane TV shows and predictable blockbuster movies. They needed real sound waves and vibrations moving through the air, and real bodies full of heat.

She walked a little way down Haili Street toward the water, away from the milling crowd talking, smoking, laughing. She stopped. Weren't those three children from the play? Munchkins dressed in flying monkey suits now. What were they doing out here?

Through years of conditioning as a stage mother, Iris moved to shoo them back into the theater. She stopped when she saw what had drawn them out.

Farther down the block an overhang shadowed the sidewalk from the streetlight's orange glow. In the gloom beneath, she saw a person who resembled that man Moses had spoken about. Desiree's boyfriend. Something about the back of his head and his general build, the way he was dressed. He was talking to a woman. Then he pushed her against the wall.

Was it Desiree? If so, she wasn't in costume. Iris caught a glimpse of blonde hair—was that the gleam of a tiara?

The windows of the abandoned building behind them were black pools. No wonder her clients had backed off when she'd tried to rent them office space there. She started forward, and then the woman fell—and disappeared underground.

The man jumped after her into what must literally be a manhole, and the sidewalk slid back over both figures. What?

The monkeys yelled and raced forward, with Iris right behind them.

"The tunnels," Iris heard the bigger monkey yell. "He's taken her underground." She recognized Desiree's daughter and Nora's twins.

The sidewalk looked smooth. She couldn't see where it had opened.

"Wait," she called. "We need to tell the police so they can find your mother."

But the children dodged around her and raced back down the alley, gravel flying.

Iris turned and trotted back up the hill, jostling through the crowd to find Moses.

⌣

PATRICK JUMPED BACK AS THREE FLYING MONKEYS BOLTED PAST him down the alley and pelted up the stairs into the theater.

Harriet caught one of them in the doorway, while the other two slipped past.

Patrick moved closer.

"Wait just one minute, young man." The boy, a red-haired twin, struggled in her grasp. "You slow down. What's going on?"

"It's Glinda. That man took her into the tunnels." He tried to twist away. "I have to help Kolea and Miri."

"What man? What tunnels? What are you talking about?" Nora emerged onto the landing from backstage, her Ozian headdress quivering as she held on to another red-haired monkey.

The twins moved together, their green eyes glowing like cats in the dusky light.

"Can I help?" Patrick asked. Cindy would be a good mother, like Nora. He imagined her shining head bent over their small, misbehaving son or daughter.

"Kolea's mom—we saw her. That man pulled her under the sidewalk. We have to go help her!" The twins' spoke alternately, almost in unison, their bodies crackling with excitement. A spark flew between them and Patrick.

Adventure and rescue. Ah, to be young again. And just think, he could experience that energy vicariously for eighteen years with a child of his own.

"I swear they're telepathic." Nora turned to Patrick with a tense smile. "I'm always three steps behind these two." She took each twin by the arm. "Come on, then, let's tell someone who can help."

As Patrick watched them go, a wave of loss washed over him. Would Cindy choose him to be a father, or would he be judged and found wanting?

～

IRIS SEIZED MOSES BY THE ARM, PANTING. IN A LOW VOICE, SHE told him what she'd seen, and he immediately made another call.

He clenched his fist and punched downward. "What do you mean they'll be tied up for another two hours? I need them here *now*." He turned and strode back into the theater lobby.

Iris followed.

His police radio crackled, and he stopped. "I'd better take this outside. Don't want people to panic."

There was a scuffle in the curtain leading from the auditorium to the lobby and Nora—in brilliant green Ozian attire—appeared with her twins, the flying monkeys.

Theatergoers stared, holding their drinks in the air, then turned back to their conversations.

Iris put her hand on Moses's arm and he turned back. "I think they're looking for you."

Nora's headdress waved in the air as she hurried over, pulling the reluctant twins behind her. Moses drew them into a corner.

"I don't know for sure what's happening." Nora spoke in a rush. "But Oliver says he saw Desiree—you know, Glinda the Good?—disappear underground with that man, her friend from the workday. And her oldest daughter Kolea has disappeared too, down in the basement. She's trying to find Desiree." Nora shook her head. "Something about tunnels?"

Moses thanked her and said he was already on it, and she should by no means try to help. All civilians should stay above ground and leave matters to the police.

"Now may not be the time," Nora hesitated. "But I had a disturbing phone call at my place of work this morning. A man who mentioned the theater and threatened my children. I called the police afterward. Maybe it's related to all the other incidents: the ghost, and now this?"

"Nothing is irrelevant." Moses nodded. "Stay calm and keep your children close."

Iris could see the tension in his face and upper body. His aura was a muddy red, unlike its usual pure golden glow.

His police radio crackled again, and he murmured into his phone as he stepped back outside.

Iris followed him, feeling superfluous but unwilling to stay behind. It dawned on her that Moses had become her safe place as the threat of exposure approached. She couldn't ignore the physical pull, as though they were connected by a cord of flesh.

◡

GRIFF TRIED TO STOP THE FLYING MONKEY AS SHE HURTLED INTO the basement and through the open door, but her gauzy wing came off in his hand. It was time to go in. He switched on his headlamp and plunged into the darkness.

◡

MAHINA CLATTERED DOWN THE BASEMENT STAIRS IN TIME TO see Griff pass through the door into the tunnel. She had brought a flashlight this time, just to have a peek. She told herself it was not procrastination. She was not afraid of learning the truth. She hadn't talked to the lawyer yet because she was too busy, and now it was far too late to call the West Coast.

She opened the door and before she could stop him, Ziggy darted through it, barking.

"Ziggy, come back!" She shone the beam on the rough walls, recoiling at the sour smell of underground air. Ziggy's yips grew fainter.

Mahina waited and called, but he didn't return.

Her heart surged as she realized she had no choice. She had to follow her little dog and bring him back to safety.

◡

"HEY." ALICE WAVED TO NORA FROM ACROSS THE CROWDED LOB-by. She stood in the long concession line with Giles and Amelia, who started prancing around in excitement when they saw the twins in costume. "Are you supposed to be out here mingling with the punters?" She winked. "You chaps are wonderful. Great show."

In a fog, Nora noticed Clyde and Greta standing nearby.

Greta's children, Hans and Karen, ran over to join the twins, spilling popcorn in their wake.

Well, Nora thought, no time like the present. She and Alice locked eyes. Let the smear campaign begin.

⌣

Two uniforms joined Moses in the alley. "You guys are it?" He barked orders, and they spread out. He turned to Iris. "I need to work now. I don't mean to push you away, but—"

"I know, I'm following you like a puppy. Just nerves." Iris laughed. "I'll go backstage and check on Mahina. I'm sure she's fine, but I'll feel better if I see her face."

"Good idea." Moses turned away.

She was already forgotten.

CHAPTER 31

DESIREE STRUGGLED BACK TO CONSCIOUSNESS AGAINST A sick pounding in her head. She panicked when she realized her mouth was duct-taped shut, her wrists and ankles also bound. Fuck. She lay on her side on a hard, cold floor, which felt gritty under her hands and cheek. A stale odor of dirt, mold, and decay lay over her like a shroud.

Oh, *hell* no. She blinked carefully. At least she wasn't blindfolded. She turned her head and almost passed out again as a blinding pain stabbed like an icepick.

That fucker Clownface must have climbed up through some kind of trap door in the sidewalk and bludgeoned her while Hunter was talking. But why? Where were they now? Most importantly, when would they be back—and what would they do to her then?

Desiree opened her eyes again, squinting against the pain. Walls and a table loomed above her. There must be a light source, however faint. She heard thumping overhead and a sort of echo.

She closed her eyes, fighting a surge of nausea.

Moses Kapili must have realized the wire was compromised. Someone in the play must have noticed she was missing. How long had she been unconscious? Had they started the second act already?

Desiree scratched her hand on something sharp. She smiled against the pull of the tape. Not dead yet. She sawed the tape binding her wrists back and forth against the edge, wincing when she gouged her own skin.

⌣

"IT'S A GREAT SHOW, GEORGE." CAL HAD THOSE LINES NEXT TO his mouth that always deepened when he was under strain. His eyes looked sunken. The group of nurses he was sitting with congratulated George, then gave him dark looks and moved chattering into the lobby.

George was still flying high from the sparkling, fabulous first act. The cast had never played their parts with such energy. Even Dorothy had come through with a show-stopping rendition of "Somewhere over the Rainbow." He had underestimated her.

The audience was buzzing. They loved it.

He and Belinda were sitting together in the premier row just above the walkway, and people kept stopping to pay their respects, like it was the royal box. The president of the Palace Friends had lingered for five minutes, raving. George was surprised the ever-present Phil wasn't hovering nearby, trying to horn in on the glory, Cheshire Cat grin in place.

Cal summoned a gallant smile. George could tell he was about to follow his friends and started to rise from his seat.

"George." Harriet stood before him in full Wicked Witch garb. He could only stare. "Desiree has disappeared and the police are sending reinforcements. We hope."

"What are you doing out here in costume?" he snapped. Then he sat back in his seat, absorbing the unbelievable news. Was this the ghost's work? Were people in danger? Right away his mind started to work. Without Glinda, the show would be ruined. Did they have another dress? Could someone step in?

"Her daughter is missing, too, and they think Desiree's unpleasant friend is responsible." Harriet looked excited.

What a ghoul. This was getting worse and worse.

George remembered his conversation with Hunter Craddock at the workday and his strange reappearance at the theater. Odd little man. Sinister and grandiose. Desiree hadn't seemed very fond of him. Now he was the architect of doom?

George let out a small moan. "Why tonight?" He pressed the heels of his hands against his forehead, holding back the screams.

A warm hand gripped his shoulder. "Let's go backstage." Cal ushered him out of the row.

Belinda followed. She'd been silent the entire time, her eyes wide like a horror movie heroine just before the psycho's knife slashes down and the shrieking begins.

Backstage, cast and crew scuttled back and forth like bugs whose rock has been lifted off.

"Look! The dress." Belinda whirled around and held it up. Her eyes locked with George's as they thought the same thing. "I can play Glinda—if it comes to that, of course." Belinda blushed. "I'm sure they'll find her."

Wordless, George squeezed her hand. The show must go on.

"Where's Mahina?" It was her mother, Iris, wild-eyed. What was she doing backstage? This was ridiculous.

George stepped forward. "My dear woman—"

"Don't you 'my dear woman' me," she shouted. "What have you done with my daughter?" She burst into tears and ran across the stage behind the curtain, calling, "Mahina. Mahina!"

Fred appeared on the other side and intercepted her. About time. Hysterical mothers were the stage manager's business.

George sank down on a nearby chair. This really was the end. No one could stand in for Dorothy. He looked up and saw Belinda calculating, but they both knew it was no good.

"Everyone, just stay calm." Harriet held up her hand. Some nearby Munchkins cowered. "I'm sure the police are searching, and we should keep out of their way. And we should stay together. We don't want anyone else to go missing, do we?"

"Where's Griff?" Cal held George down on the chair as he struggled to rise.

"I'm sure he's around," Cal's voice soothed, and suddenly George just wanted to melt back into him and forget about the show, forget about the theater, forget about everything. It was all going to hell in a hand basket anyway.

He reached up and put his arms around Cal. "Please stay with me. Let's call whatshername and have a baby. I'll do anything. Just don't leave me."

Harriet snorted. "Very touching, but we could use a little leadership around here, please." She motioned for everyone to gather around. "Perhaps we should call roll."

⌣

"WONDERFUL SHOW, NORA." CLYDE LEANED OVER TO PECK HER on the cheek. The lobby buzzed around them. He'd used extra gel on his ponytail tonight and his stubble had sharp boundaries defining it. Did he actually go to a salon?

"The children are loving it." Greta stuck out her hand and Nora shook it. Was she imagining it or was there a tic in Greta's cheek? Otherwise the woman's face looked like a mask. Botox injections? How old *was* she? Nora's heart beat a little faster.

"Merle is a fantastic actor." Greta's eyes lit up. They were only slightly dilated tonight. "Such a multi-talented man."

"Yes he is, and thank you." Nora beamed at them. "We're having a great time up there, and you're a very supportive audience." Never mind that the good witch has been abducted and the police are conducting a manhunt as we speak. At least we hope they are. Where are the sirens and flashing lights? She giggled, nerves bubbling to the surface until she tamped them down again. "Merle said how much he enjoys working with your energetic landscape, Greta." Nora sneaked a glance at Clyde, who stiffened.

They all stood there, smiling.

"You do seem much calmer, Greta." Alice patted her on the arm. "We were all so worried about you after the last homeschool group meeting. You know, when you couldn't find your pills." She slapped her hand over her mouth. "Oops. Not another word, I promise."

Greta shrugged. "You Americans think everything can be cured with pills. Merle has channeled natural energy into my auric body and washed my home with green serenity."

Alice mouthed, "Not an American," and rolled her eyes.

Nora looked around and her heart gave a sudden lurch. "Where did Oliver and Miri go?" She had thought they were with Alice's twins in the popcorn line, but now the lobby was monkey-free.

"They said they had to find their friend." Greta's daughter took her thumb out of her mouth. Her son slumped over his Gameboy, thumbs tapping.

"Attention, Palace patrons." The old loudspeaker crackled in the lobby. "We're experiencing technical difficulties. Intermission will continue for another ten minutes. Thank you for your patience and support."

Nora said Clyde's name, and he registered her look. Thirteen years of marriage had left their mark. "The twins may be in danger." Her voice shook.

Together they lunged toward the velvet curtain.

⌣

THE FLYING MONKEY HAD VANISHED, AND NOW GRIFF WAITED with growing impatience at the rendezvous point specified by his Guide. He swallowed hard. He was starting to get that twitch in his throat he always used to feel in 'Nam right before an ambush. Time to move. He glided down the musty passage.

Up ahead, he heard a scuffle. Griff backed against the wall as his Guide, X, clown mask in place, came out of another passageway holding two flying monkeys by the arms. He'd only seen one go in. They were struggling and kicking.

X shoved them up against the wall.

Griff felt a burning start in his chest. His muscles tensed, and he launched himself down the tunnel, yelling, his truncheon in hand.

X whirled around, loosening his grip on the children, who squirmed away. He reached into his waistband and pulled out a curved blade.

Pain seared through Griff's side as his body hit X's. Then everything went dark.

⌣

DESIREE HAD JUST SAWED HER HANDS FREE, RIPPED THE TAPE off her mouth, and was tearing at the tape around her ankles when she heard muffled shouts. Her head throbbed, and she couldn't control the nausea any longer. She freed her feet with one mighty wrench and stumbled into a corner of the room, ignoring the stabbing pains in her cramped muscles as she hunched over and threw up with as little noise as she manage. Her head was on fire. Maybe she should just lie there and die, after all.

She pulled a dirty tarp over her body and lay there panting, gathering her strength. From this new angle, she saw a stairway leading up to a door. Time to take a chance. She slithered out from under the tarp and had just mounted the stairs when she heard the pounding of feet and two little bodies hurtled into the room.

"Mom!" It was Kolea, her face streaked with dirt and tears. Her friend Miri was right behind her—strange to see her without her twin. "A clown hurt Griff." The girls' flying monkey outfits were dirty and torn, their eyes wide. "And we can't find Oliver."

"Come up here." Desiree pushed panic aside. "We need to get out of the tunnels."

The girls scampered up the steps, and the three of them pushed open the door at the top. To Desiree's surprise, they emerged into the candy store a block away from the Palace, with glass bins and barrels spilling over with every kind of sweet imaginable, their bright colors distorted in the orange glow shining through the glass from the corner street light. The girls looked at each other and then at Desiree. She shook her head and winced. They started grabbing handfuls of saltwater taffy and tootsie rolls anyway.

"Come on." Desiree moved toward the glass door leading to the bayfront. "We have to get out of here."

And then the door opened, its cheerful bell jingling.

"Well well well, is this a burglary in progress?" Hunter held a big gun, rock steady. "You bad girl. You didn't wait for me like you were supposed to. And now you're teaching your children to be thieving whores, too?"

"Fuck off, Hunter." He'd just said another of her trigger words. Desiree gave him the finger. Great final act, she thought. "I never took anything from you I didn't earn, and I wore the wire because I didn't have a choice. The cops caught me with the drugs because your buddy wasn't at home—too busy playing tricks at the Palace. You would have done the same." She braced herself for the bullet.

"Well sure I would, and I have, sweetheart. Why do you think I don't have a criminal record?" Hunter stepped closer, and she backed away, hoping the girls were behind her. Maybe they would have a chance to escape back down the stairs. She'd left the door wide open. "But that doesn't mean I approve, or that I'll forgive you for doing it to me."

"You have to be a grownup to be a whore, dummy." Desiree made shushing motions but Kolea didn't back down. She stood next to her mother, glaring at Hunter. "We're children."

"On the contrary, brat." Hunter gave her a greasy smile. "Children make very nice whores. In fact, I think you and your friend could be real money-makers, now that you mention it." He waved the gun at Desiree, who was ready to leap on him, her acrylic nails extended like claws. "Now now, Mom. Don't do anything foolish."

⌣

PEOPLE KEPT DISAPPEARING. GEORGE'S HEAD WAS SPINNING. From triumph to disaster in minutes.

When Harriet took roll, they found that Glinda, Oz, Dorothy, Toto, and three Flying Monkeys were missing. At least now a policeman was stationed in the basement to guard against both ingress and egress. What had taken him so long to get there? And why only one? George would have strong words for the police department after the final curtain tonight. If there was one.

Fred had come forward to say he could play Oz/Professor Marvel. He'd memorized the part following the script during rehearsals. He even had the makings of costumes, thanks to their tireless costume designer, Enid, who had brought all her goodies with her in case of repairs. She was already busy with a glue gun.

Griff had left his turbans and other accessories behind.

Belinda was making herself up as Glinda. The dress hung on the rack next to her, and the wand lay on the counter. "Where's Phil? I could use a little help with my hair."

But it was all a dead loss without Dorothy.

"George?" He turned to the source of the inquiring voice. It was Moku the stagehand.

"I can play Dorothy." Moku pursed his lips and tilted his head. He held up his long dark hair, which was usually pulled back in a ponytail or knotted in a bun. Enough for braids. "I learned the part for fun—good thing, yah?"

George stared at him. Was this kid for real? He bit back a retort as the loveliness of Moku's face registered in his director's mind. "Can you sing in falsetto?"

"Brah. When I'm not here I'm singing with my family over at the hotels Kona side, top harmony and 'ukulele." He broke into a soaring rendition of "Somewhere Over the Rainbow."

It was beautiful.

Moku curtseyed. "Mama's little *māhū*."

"You're hired." George shook his hand. "Go find Enid and get into costume. Tear down the curtain if you need to."

⌣

PATRICK, EVAN, HARRIET, AND MERLE COMMISERATED, SHAKING their heads. What a bunch of amateurs, running off in the middle of a performance.

Desiree had always been unreliable, missing cues, talking everyone's ear off, disappearing backstage, and now this abduction story. Obviously a child's fantasy.

Griff was a wacko and Mahina was a diva. Everyone knew children and animals were always more trouble than they were worth, and as for their parents. Well.

They congratulated each other on their professionalism, seasoned community theater thespians who would not abandon their parts, even when danger loomed and it seemed impossible that the show could go on.

"But I feel like such a coward." Merle chewed on his tail in frustration. "Nora gave me this look as she ran past with her ex-husband, and I just stood there in my Lion suit. She'll never respect me again."

"Relax, buddy." Harriet patted his furry back, adjusting her pointed hat with the other hand. "That ship already sailed. She knows about Robin—you know, your previous lover from the high school? And how do you think it looks that you're living in Valerie the medium's backyard? I don't think respect is even in the picture anymore. Time to move on. Don't you have a rich European on the string, too?" She gave him a scary smile.

Merle glared at her. "You're just a jealous old hag." He elbowed her in the ribs. "Just kidding." He danced around her, faking punches. "Put 'em up, put 'em up."

"Jesus, Merle, no one is in the mood for your Lion persona right now." Patrick gave him a disgusted look.

"Well, you should be," Merle retorted. "We're going back on in a few minutes."

"Luke said his dad is here staying with you." Evan looked at Harriet. She could see the hope in his eyes. He was still at the stage where he took solace in saying his beloved's name.

"Yes indeed." Harriet twitched her nose. "Howard and I have had a lovely time catching up. But no romance re-blossoming, if that's what you're wondering." She shook her head. "He's got a fiancée and new family now."

"He's made his bed and now he has to lie in it, right?" Patrick smiled. "Poor sod."

"Ah, the lure of young flesh." Merle shook his head. "So delicious, yet so treacherous—and so temporary. He probably never gets any now."

They all laughed, Harriet included.

"Poor Howard. Perhaps I should be kind to him." She smiled and gazed off into the distance.

They looked at her in surprise.

"What? Can't a woman have sex with her ex-husband if she wants to?"

Evan was actually blushing beneath his silver makeup, fortunately not the toxic kind that nearly killed the actor playing the movie Tin Man. Harriet felt sad every time she watched it, knowing his fate.

"I hope my ex-girlfriend shares your feelings," blurted Patrick. "She's here tonight, too. I'm trying to win her back."

"How could she resist?" Harriet batted her eyes at Patrick. "Brains, heart, and courage all in one package. The whole trifecta."

Fred, made up as the Wizard, wheezed at them from under his turban. "Places. We're on in five."

"Well, knock 'em dead, everyone. Let's send up a little prayer for our missing members, wherever they may be." Harriet reached out and they all joined hands for a moment.

"Amen."

They scattered to their positions in the wings.

⌣

"FOLKS, WE HAVE AN UNPRECEDENTED SITUATION HERE TO-night." George paused and smiled out at the faces of the audience as the house lights dimmed to a glimmer. They rustled and murmured, still annoyed by the long delay. "For the first time in Palace history, we have some new major players debuting in the second act. This shows how fabulous the East Hawai'i Community Players truly are."

Scattered cheers.

"Please welcome to the stage Fred Moon as Oz, Belinda Hudson as Glinda, and (drum roll), our very own Moku Jabilona-Poli'ahu as Dorothy."

Wild cheers and foot stomping broke out from the gallery, plus an ear-splitting whoop from an air-horn.

Moku had sent out a mass text to all his friends and family, who had converged on the theater in remarkable haste, only some of them bothering to buy tickets before they stampeded into every empty seat they could find.

"And now, ladies and gentlemen." George bowed and moved toward the stairs. "On with the show."

CHAPTER 32

MAHINA WAS LOST. SHE TRIED NOT TO PANIC, BUT SHE'D AL-
ways been a little claustrophobic and this was too much.
She'd dodged down a side tunnel when she heard shouting ahead.
Now she couldn't find her way back. Where had her little dog gone?
There were openings all around. Who would have thought Hilo had
catacombs? She half expected to stumble over a pile of skeletons
like the ones she'd seen on the History Channel. Spooky music
started playing in her head.

She sank down and put her head between her knees.

Then, out of the darkness, Ziggy trotted up. He whimpered and
licked her chin.

Her heart actually leapt with joy, just like they said in books.

"You are such a bad dog." She held him tight. "Why did you run
away?" She checked her cell phone. Still no signal. She tried to call
Keola anyhow, but couldn't connect. She hesitated, then tried her
mother, too. Nothing.

"I can see you, my pretty." An eerie voice echoed down the tunnel. BomBoy.

Mahina scrambled to her feet and switched off her flashlight. Ziggy let out a yip and Mahina held his muzzle shut. He wriggled in protest.

"There's no way out." The voice was stronger now. "You may as well walk this way and I'll be nice to you, and your little dog, too." The voice laughed in a definitely not nice way. "You didn't like the purple poof? How ungrateful."

Mahina turned on her flashlight again and ran the other way, stumbling over the uneven surface, but sure enough, the tunnel ended. She saw another passage to the left and dashed down that one, but it, too, came to an end. Laughter echoed behind her and she shivered. Then she saw a small opening, just wide enough to squeeze through. She shoved Ziggy into the gap ahead of her, then struggled against the rough edges until she popped out on the other side, feeling her clothing rip and warm trickles of blood on her arms.

Much wider now. She'd made it back to the main tunnel. Her little flashlight was yellowing, the battery nearly dead. Her heart pounded in her throat. Which way was out? If anything happened to her it would be all Iris's fault.

Up ahead, someone lay on the ground. Ziggy nosed the body and whimpered. Mahina hesitated, then crept forward.

It was Griff.

She knelt down and touched his face, then felt for a pulse in his neck as they'd learned to do in Health class. It was racing. He was alive.

⌣

Nora stumbled along after Clyde as he held up his cell phone to light their way through the tunnel. She felt a numb urgency bordering on mania. She wanted to pound on his back to hurry. They had to find the twins. Who had to be all right. Nothing else was possible. She heard a sound somewhere between a sob and a moan and realized it had come from her.

"Shhhhh." Clyde still had a snappy temper.

"Oh shut up," she muttered under her breath.

The wall felt slimy when she touched it. Of course. This was Hilo. She was surprised they weren't wading through knee or hip-deep water, actually. These tunnels must flood during heavy rains. They'd had a drought for a couple of months, people said. She wouldn't know, still not attuned to the subtle seasons and weather patterns of her new home.

Home? After this? Never.

This must be a bad dream, like she'd been knocked on the head during a tornado. Nora saw the events of the past year flash before her as she half-walked, half-ran through the darkness. The move to Hawai'i, divorce, forced exile in Hilo, the play, the psychic hotline, her brief romance with Merle—and now all life and hope narrowed to the size of this tunnel. She tripped and almost fell. Clyde didn't even slow down.

Nora made a vow. If they found Miri and Oliver—no, *when* they found Miri and Oliver—she would move heaven and earth to take the children and move back to Canada where they belonged. She pushed away the troubling thought that she would be found to blame for this trauma, an unfit mother.

Clyde stopped, and Nora almost ran into him. STOP. Her mind silenced itself in a red blare. Voices. Up above. A dim light slanted out from what looked like a doorway. They felt their way along the tunnel and peered through to stairs that led up to the source of light. Something moved in the corner and then a small form shot forward and grabbed Nora around the waist. Oliver!

"Oh, thank god," she whispered, holding him tightly. "But where's Miri?"

Oliver put a finger to his mouth and then pointed up the stairs.

"You tape up the others and then do your ankles again, like a good girl." A man's voice. "And then maybe I won't blow your head off."

Nora took one hand off Oliver and gripped Clyde's elbow so the three of them were connected. This time, he didn't snap or shake her off.

⌣

GRIFF CAME TO AS PAIN SLICED THROUGH HIS SIDE. SOMEONE was shaking him. His hand shot out and grasped an arm. A small, thin arm, like a twig he could snap.

"Griff, wake up. It's Mahina. We have to get out of here." She was sobbing.

Her hair brushed his face. It tickled and smelled of coconut. He let go of her arm and Toto's wet tongue licked his hand.

Griff sat up and groaned with the pain. He held his side. That bastard X had knifed him. Not too much blood. Must be a surface wound. Painful but not disabling.

The voices in his head started up: What did we tell you? Now the greys are going to eat you with their spiky teeth. Give them the girl, and maybe they'll let you go.

Shut up. Griff knew talking to them was a mistake. They just grew bolder and louder. His suspicion had been correct. X wasn't his guide, couldn't be. He saw it now. X must be BomBoy.

"Come with me." Griff lurched to his feet and headed back down the tunnel.

"Where are you going?" Mahina's voice was a mournful echo.

Griff just kept trudging.

"But that man is back there somewhere. He'll find us." Her footsteps followed.

He gave no answer. Each step required every shred of energy and will he still possessed.

⌣

EVAN HAD TO ADMIT THAT MOKU MADE A GREAT DOROTHY. THE boy was a natural. What was he, sixteen, seventeen? Evan felt a flicker of something as they cowered against the witch's castle walls and he held Moku close. The Tin Man was very protective of Dorothy.

The Winkies goose-stepped across the stage. "Oh-eee-oh, ee-ooohh-oh."

As he chopped down the door to rescue Dorothy, Evan hoped Fred upped his game when they came back to Oz with the broom. The stage manager knew the Wizard's lines, but so far he didn't sound convincing—and the next scene was a doozy. Oz had to have charisma. He had to really sell the concept. Griff had nailed it.

"How about a little fire, Scarecrow?" Real flame. How had the fire department ever approved that in this tinderbox? Evan was glad Harriet hadn't disappeared. Nothing to do with Luke. She was just a great Wicked Witch.

Moku threw the (pretend) water at her, from the conveniently placed bucket.

Evan watched in admiration as Harriet played her final scene, oozing bit by bit through the trapdoor.

"I'm melting. Melting! Oh, what a world. What a world. Who would have thought a good little girl like you could destroy my beautiful wickedness. Ohhh. Look out. Look out! I'm going. Ohhhhh. Ohhhhhh..."

Evan hoped she didn't have any clothing remnants stuck in the trapdoor like those times in rehearsal. The cape lay puddled over the door, hat on top, just as it should, the charred broom to one side.

And now, back to Oz for the denouement. The untying of the knot. Another "It pays to enrich your word power" winner.

‿͜

PATRICK'S SENSE OF URGENCY GREW AS THEY ENTERED OZ'S chambers, broom in hand. Would Fred be able to pull it off? It was George's fault for not finding a new Wizard after the séance. Of course Griff had flaked out. But beneath the immediate concerns onstage—and offstage with Cindy in the audience—he wondered what was going on underground. Where were Desiree, Mahina, and Griff? Was something actually happening, not just a hoax? This was the strangest experience he'd ever had. Talk about surreal.

Fred handed him his diploma. "Th.D. That's Dr. of Thinkology." He had just the right serious but goofy tone. Go, Fred!

Patrick spouted, "The sum of the square roots of any two sides of an isosceles triangle is equal to the square root of the remaining side. Oh joy, rapture! I've got a brain." He gave a little leap.

And thank god it kicked in. He grinned and mimed joy to the audience.

That was close. He thought he saw Cindy smile, and put an extra kick in his step.

‿͜

WHEN HARRIET MELTED THROUGH THE TRAPDOOR, NO SUPPORT-ing hands caught her, and her feet landed with a painful thump.

She stumbled backward on the rough floor below. What? She'd give those stagehands the rough edge of her tongue—when she found them. The dark was impenetrable. A hand clamped over her mouth, and an arm tightened around her throat. The smell of bleach was overpowering.

Harriet reacted without thinking. She fell backward and rammed her pointed heel into what felt like her attacker's instep.

Her assailant grunted in pain but hung on. Harriet was losing consciousness. She reached behind her and groped for his crotch. He punched her temple with his free hand and she almost passed out. But then she had him. She squeezed hard.

He squealed, and Harriet wrenched away with a savage twist. She stumbled toward where she thought the stairs must be, but tripped over what felt like a duffel bag and landed painfully on her hands and knees. What the hell?

⤳

NORA FOLLOWED CLYDE UP THE LADDER, MOTIONING TO OLIVER to go back and hide in the corner. She stopped as Clyde held his hand back in warning and waited, her heart pounding.

Everything happened very fast.

Clyde leaped up, grabbed Miri, and pulled her toward the stair opening. A gunshot hit the wall behind him and he froze, his arms clenched around Miri's waist.

A man's head peered down at Nora. Desiree's friend. Hunter, that was his name. His gun was pressed against Clyde's neck.

"Welcome to our little party," he said. "You don't want to leave so soon, do you? Your daughter is enjoying herself." He motioned at Nora with the gun. "Come on up, now, don't dilly dally. I won't miss on purpose the next time."

She started up the stairs, and Hunter hit Clyde across the temple with his gun. Clyde and Miri sprawled across the floor, knocking over a barrel of hard candies, which rolled and bounced in a bright spray across the parquet flooring. Nora gasped, and rushed to see if Miri was injured.

Her daughter's mouth was duct taped and her eyes looked scared, but she nodded at her mother.

Desiree was taped up in the corner. It was a fair guess Hunter wasn't her friend anymore.

Her daughter Kolea, also bound, was closer. Nora patted her shoulder.

Hunter lobbed a roll of duct tape at Nora and motioned to Clyde. "Tape him up, dearie, and then do yourself, nice and tight. Great outfit, by the way." Nora realized she was still wearing her Ozian costume: tight-fitting emerald green dress and sparkly headgear.

Nora complied, shaking, but took care to wrap the tape as loosely as she could without it looking too obvious. She even contrived to wrap her own wrists by flicking the roll of tape around them. She'd had a broken arm in junior high and remembered the tricks. Anything so that loathsome man wouldn't touch her.

Clyde groaned and moved on the floor next to Miri. Nora leaned against the wall and slid down with a thump on their daughter's other side, closer to the open door and the stairs. She hoped Oliver would keep quiet and stay hidden, and that Desiree's other children were safe with the rest of the cast back in the theater. They'd been giggling with the younger monkeys backstage, and Belinda had corralled the children with her arms to keep them from following Nora and Clyde as they'd raced past on their way to the basement.

Nora closed her eyes and breathed through her nose, trying to slow the rapid thumping of her heart. Adrenaline coursed through her body, fizzing in every cell. Well, she thought, for all your worrying, agonizing, and analyzing, you totally missed this one, sweetie. Some psychic you turned out to be. She kept her body tense, ready for whatever might come next.

~

HARRIET LAY IN THE DARKNESS, HER MOUTH PARTIALLY TAPED shut. Her assailant had done a sloppy job.

He had pounced on her while she was still stunned from her fall and zip-tied her hands behind her back, then taped her ankles together in spite of her vigorous kicking.

She squirmed and felt her limbs—nothing broken, just bruised, perhaps a sprained wrist. When she turned to one side, she saw a red light blinking.

"Care to guess what that is?" A flashlight beam shone from above. The voice was nasty and grating. "Oh, right, you can't talk."

"Is that a bomb?" Harriet tried to say, around the edges of her duct tape gag. It came out as slurred gibberish.

"Got it in one, witchy." He laughed. Not a nice sound. "You're not going to melt, you're going to explode. Serves you right. You may have damaged me permanently. But you'll be the first casualty." A pause. "Pity. I've had such fun being the ghost, watching all of you screech and fret. Blowing you all to smithereens will be sweet revenge for a lifetime of abuse from stuck-up thespians. I would have been a perfect Pirate King back in high school, and all those bitches in the drama club just snickered at me and made me do their hair. And this show? I should be playing the Wizard. Well, you can all rot in hell now."

Harriet rubbed her face against the dirty cement and freed one side of her mouth. "Don't be ridiculous. The police are everywhere.

They'll be down here any second to disarm your precious bomb." She fed her anger so fear couldn't take over. His voice sounded familiar. "Wait a minute, I know you."

"A little slow, aren't you? Right now I'm a clown, one of my many personas. And as for the police, I haven't seen many. I think they're all investigating my other bomb far, far away. That rookie they sent down here wasn't up to much." The voice laughed. "He and those two silly stagehands are trussed up under the stairs. As for disarming the device, I know a thing or two about bombs, witchy. Learned all about them from my brother after he served our ungrateful country in Vietnam. I'm an explosives expert. I doubt anyone here in Hilo can say the same." He laughed again, like a megalomaniac in a B-movie.

"I wouldn't be so sure, X. Or should I call you BomBoy?"

Harriet recognized the second voice. The line sounded like it came from the same bad movie. "Griff?" Her voice rose and she struggled to keep from shrieking. "Help! I'm tied up over here."

"You're still alive. How careless of me." BomBoy laughed. "So, you figured out my little ruse?" He added, "You can call me BomBoy, or X, or AdVisor. Yes, that was me, too, fool."

More bad movie lines, thought Harriet. What was this, a farce? This was not going to be the way she died. Absolutely not. She struggled to sit up and heave herself to her feet, but just fell back on her rump.

There was scuffling and thumping to the side, with grunts and a sharp cry of pain. A dog barked. Sounded like that annoying little rat dog playing Toto. Something heavy clattered onto the floor.

"Damn dog!" The voice sounded shrill. "Should've killed you, not fed you chicken legs and given you a free makeover. Lousy mutt."

"I won't let you destroy the Energy Center." Griff's voice sounded mechanical and disembodied. "Even if I have to kill you."

"Hold on, fella. No need for that kind of talk." The voice was wheedling now. "You were my brother's war buddy, right? These civilians don't know what you went through. Why should you care about them? They haven't taken care of you, have they? Put that down and let's leave them to their fate."

Another loud thunk—squelchy this time.

"I have duct tape in my bag." Griff's voice. "You tape him up while I work on the bomb."

Who was he talking to?

Grunting and thumping sounds came from deeper in the basement.

"The stagehands," Harriet called. "That maniac said they're under the stairs. You need to cut them loose. The policeman, too. And me!"

Someone clattered over to free the stagehands, who burst into tears and bolted up the stairs.

"That masked man shot me with a dart," the young policeman slurred. "I'll call for the bomb squad now. Anyone have a phone?"

Duct tape ripping. They must be immobilizing the attacker.

"Hey Harriet—sorry, Mrs. Furneaux—it's Mahina." The girl shone a beam on her own face. She sliced through the zip tie and then the duct tape, and Harriet scrambled to her feet.

Griff switched on a headlamp and examined the bomb.

The policeman said, "Hey, you shouldn't get near that thing."

Harriet grasped Mahina's shoulders. "You have to evacuate the theater. Right now. Don't wait for me, child. Run and tell the others." She infused her voice with the last vestige of authority she possessed.

In the dim light, Harriet limped over and tore off the rubber clown mask covering the unconscious man's face. The bare scalp wasn't shining and the wide white grin was missing, but it was Phil the Palace Friends board member all right. Alias the Palace ghost, alias BomBoy.

Harriet grabbed the policeman. "Why is there only one of you?"

"We're shorthanded tonight—explosion on the other side of town." He rubbed his neck. "I think I'm going to throw up."

"Everyone should go. Now." Griff turned. "I work alone."

CHAPTER 33

"HOLD IT RIGHT THERE, CRADDOCK." ANOTHER JINGLE, and the Policeman stood haloed in the doorway of the candy store, his big gun trained on Hunter's back. He flipped the light switch and the fluorescent tubes on the ceiling hummed and blazed bright.

Desiree blinked her eyes in the sudden glare. She had never been so glad to see a cop in her life.

"Put your weapon down, nice and easy, and back away."

Hunter just laughed. "Nice try, tough guy, but in case you didn't notice, I'm pointing my gun at Desiree here, your little stool pigeon. Big help she turned out to be, eh?"

"Actually, a great deal of help." Kapili's voice was calm. "We have your conversation recorded back at the station. You said some interesting things about your history in Las Vegas, your ties to the mob, and your current operation here on the Big Island. Also, your interest in child prostitution."

"Bullshit." Hunter's gun wavered. "I tore the wire off myself. You're bluffing."

"The wire you ripped off was a decoy." Kapili smiled. "We have new technology, old timer. That's no ordinary tiara."

Well I'll be damned. Desiree's eyes widened. Thank god I forgot to take it off.

Hunter's face flushed an ugly mottled burgundy.

Suddenly he dropped low and bolted for the stairs, dodging barrels of candy on his way to the open door. Kapili leaped after him, unable to shoot with all the bodies in his way. Desiree craned her neck to follow the lightning swift action. Ouch.

Nora was sitting closest to the stairs. As Hunter hurtled past, she slid down and kicked up her bound feet. He cartwheeled over them and sailed through the doorway, crashing hard at the bottom. After listening to the silence for a moment, Desiree tried to let out a whoop, but the duct tape stifled it and she almost choked instead.

Kapili shone his big flashlight down the stairs and spoke into his radio. "Suspect down at Kam and Furneaux lower level. Send backup to candy store. Five hostages recovered, may need medical care."

A flying monkey scampered up the stairs carrying Hunter's gun. Nora's other twin.

"Make that six." Kapili took the gun and shoved it under his belt, ruffled Oliver's hair, then cut their hands free and left the knife. He started down the stairs, then stuck his head through the doorway once more. "Stay put and wait for the uniforms. Others are still missing. This isn't over yet." He disappeared.

They ripped off their gags first and all started talking at once as they dispensed with the rest of their bonds.

"You shouldn't have come looking for me, cupcake." Desiree hugged Kolea. "You're a badass."

Nora and her ex embraced the twins.

The ex was good-looking in a yuppy sort of way, Desiree appraised. No island style about this guy.

"Nice move, Mom." Miri hugged her mother, and Nora broke into a huge smile.

"Yeah, Mom, you knocked out the bad guy," Oliver crowed. "Just like the movies."

"And you disarmed him, Oliver." Nora squeezed them tight. "You're both so brave."

Desiree didn't have time for a lovefest. "I have to find Nakai and Malia." She moved toward the door. "The uniforms can stuff it—if they ever show up. I'm outta here."

"So are we." Nora's short skirt had ridden up and she tugged it down. "Let's go."

The children scooped up fistfuls of candy, and Desiree grabbed a hunk of chocolate from a smashed glass case, picking off the shards. "For shock."

They tore off the remaining shreds of duct tape as they ran out the door, Desiree seized by an urgent need to make sure all her children were safe. They pelted down the sidewalk past the darkened storefronts of Kamehameha Avenue, Kolea, Oliver, and Miri in front, as if they really were monkeys in flight.

Desiree felt a fierce energy she hadn't experienced since she was a teenager sneaking out at night. The near-death rush was powerful, although she wasn't about to take up sky diving anytime soon.

Homeless people sheltering in the doorways called out as the ragtag company ran past, wings on their heels.

Desiree and Nora grabbed the children before they leaped straight into the sluggish Haili Street traffic, Nora's ex panting behind.

Obviously a desk jockey.

They crossed the road at a trot, motorists staring at their outlandish attire, then raced up the alleyway to the theater's side door and burst into the backstage area by the dressing room.

"Damn. You look like you've been dragged through a hedge backwards." Several Ozians stared with their mouths hanging open. "The show went on without you."

Nakai and Malia ran over and clung to their mother, and Desiree almost collapsed in sheer relief. She stumbled into the dressing room to find a chair before she fell over. All the adrenaline had drained away, and her legs felt like noodles.

Belinda turned and stared. Desiree stared back. "My god, you're me."

"Someone had to be," Belinda blurted. "Here, I can change out of your dress. There's still time for you to clean up and get ready."

Desiree sank into a chair, and Malia climbed onto her lap. The pain had rushed back in to fill her head, which felt like it was going to explode any second, and her vision was blurred. "Are you kidding? Look at me. You know the lines?"

Belinda nodded. "I've been running them madly."

"I'm pretty beat up." Desiree rested her forehead on her daughter's hair. "You go ahead and do it. You look great."

"Really?" Belinda beamed.

"Really."

"Can I have your tiara?"

Desiree looked up and winced. Belinda held out her hand.

Desiree felt the top of her head. She pulled the tiara out of her tangled hair and held it for a moment before she handed it over. Who would have guessed she had secret powers? It sparkled under the lights, only slightly bent.

⌣

WHEN MAHINA CRASHED THROUGH THE BASEMENT DOOR, scraped, tattered, and streaked with dirt and blood, the stage-hands and actors waiting in the wings just stared. Apparently the girls she'd cut loose hadn't delivered a convincing message. Idiots. Ziggy let out a few sharp yips.

She said, "Run! There's a bomb in the basement."

Then she ducked under the curtain and appeared onstage, the lights hot and bright.

Time slowed down. She was underwater, and the voices sounded like an old recording turned on low speed, deep and slow and wavery.

The Scarecrow, the Tin Man, the Lion, Oz (Fred? Really?), Dorothy (Moku? Nice dress.) and the Ozians stopped and stared at her through a shimmering haze. Muffled exclamations rose from the audience. Oz and Dorothy were in the balloon, the others waving goodbye. Moku/Dorothy turned his gaze away and gave stuffed Toto a discreet underhand pitch into the wings.

Real Toto, Ziggy, barked and squirmed out of Mahina's arms.

Time speeded up again. *Whoosh.* Moku, ignoring Mahina, hopped out of the basket and gave chase, calling, "Toto, come back." He turned back to Oz. "Oh don't go without me. I'll be right back. Toto!"

Mahina took a deep breath, faced the audience and yelled, "Fire!" Right from the diaphragm.

All hell broke loose.

She stood there in a daze and watched the wild stampede down the aisles. Audience members clambered over the seats, jumped, and fell over the center railing on top of other bodies as they streamed through the passage to the lobby. More people clogged the side exits, pushing each other in a bobbing river down the steps to the alley.

"Hey, I would have let you finish the part. All you had to do was ask." Moku put his hand on Mahina's arm. The rest of the actors still stood onstage, staring at the wreckage of the play.

"What?" She turned to him and snapped back to reality. "This isn't a joke. You need to get out of here, all of you. There's a bomb in the basement." Her voice rose to a screech.

The Cowardly Lion led the charge down the stairs, battling his way toward the side exit.

The Scarecrow followed on his heels, apologizing to people the Lion had shoved out of the way. He scooped a small, dark-haired woman into his arms and carried her to safety.

The Tin Man grabbed Moku by the hand, and they ran toward the backstage exit.

Mahina was suddenly enveloped in her mother's arms and scent. She felt her body loosen, all her strength gone. She began to weep. "There's a bomb in the basement," she sobbed. Then, "Why did you lie to me?"

"You're alive." Iris held her tight, then reached for her hand and looked into her eyes. "I'll explain everything, but now you have to run with me."

They bolted after Moku and Evan, Ziggy scampering ahead. Mahina saw Harriet running, too, an awkward figure in her black cape and hat.

Out on Haili Street, people streamed toward the bayfront. Two uniforms were cordoning off the building and speaking into radios. Police car lights flashed. Sirens wailed not far away.

"Where's Moses?" Mahina turned to look at her mother. "Why aren't there more police?"

"Budget cuts and misdirection." Iris's mouth tightened. "He's out chasing the bad guys himself, being a hero."

"Griff." Mahina stopped and looked around wildly. "Griff may still be in the basement—with the ghost. He was trying to defuse the bomb. Someone needs to rescue him."

Iris seized the arm of a uniformed officer, who looked at her in annoyance. "There's a bomb in the basement below stage. My daughter saw it. And there are still at least two people down there. You need to help them. Tell Moses Kapili right now."

"And who are you?" He raised his eyebrows. "Is your daughter the one who yelled 'Fire' in a crowded theater?" He shook his head. "That's a criminal offense, you know."

Iris snatched the radio out of his hand and pressed transmit. "Moses, I know you're out there. There's a bomb in the Palace basement. I have Mahina, but Griff may still be down there." She pressed receive.

Crackling and static, then a voice. "Roger that, Iris. Now get as far away from the theater as you can."

The officer stared at her, mouth open, and she shoved the radio back into his hand.

Iris pulled Mahina into the surging mob, leading her daughter to safety.

～

GEORGE SAT ON THE HARD CURB OF THE BUS STATION PARKING lot on Bayfront, where police were directing the evacuation. Cal's arm wrapped around his shoulder, warm and tight. A light breeze stirred up dead leaves and fraying paper wrappers and sent them skittering across the pavement.

"I should be back in the theater making sure everyone got out." George rubbed his face. "I'm the director. I'm supposed to look out for my cast and crew. The captain doesn't leave the sinking ship."

"You didn't have a choice," Cal soothed. "You did the right thing, leaving. The police are in charge."

George tried to rise to his feet, but Cal held him down.

"Look. The Cowardly Lion is making a move on someone from the audience."

Even in his distressed state George knew when he was being handled. Cal was distracting him like he was a two-year-old. He started to bristle and then thought, No. Cal's nursing experience will make him a terrific father.

"Isn't the Lion involved with a woman in the chorus?" Cal loved the theater gossip. It was one of the gifts George could give him. "Look at that."

Sure enough, Merle, still in Lion costume, was holding a lanky blonde woman who looked completely zonked out. Two blond children clung to her, and Merle patted them on the head occasionally.

Nora and her twins were redheads.

"Please come back to me, Cal." George held on tight. "I know I don't deserve you. I've been a brute and a cad. But I can change. And I need you."

"We'll talk about it." Cal held on, too.

GRIFF WAS GLAD FOR HIS HEADLAMP SINCE SOMEONE HAD SHATtered the fluorescent tube in the basement.

Harriet had clambered up the stairs to safety, pushing the groggy young policeman in front of her. She'd told Griff he was insane to stay. "Let the old girl blow."

She was a big bossy cow and he ignored her mooing.

X was already stirring. Hadn't hit him hard enough. But Mahina had duct-taped their adversary securely. If the bomb detonated, BomBoy would go, too.

It had been a long time since he'd disarmed a bomb. Griff slowed down his breathing and heartbeat, the way he used to do in Vietnam. He shoved the voices down as deep as he could and dropped a heavy block on top of them. He flexed his fingers, still strong and dexterous. This was an interesting one, but not beyond his skills. He'd seen bombs more complicated, more unstable, bigger. It was time to go in.

He hoped everyone was outside the blast radius, just in case. With an ordinary building, he wouldn't be as worried, but the Palace was ancient, termite riddled, fragile. Even a bomb this size could collapse the whole structure.

Griff never had broken the rusty padlock on the wooden cabinet against the basement wall. Like everyone else, he'd assumed it held cans of dried-up paint, rusted tools, defunct building materials. Now its doors stood open, revealing stacks of cash and bags of drugs, some of which had been transferred to a big duffel bag that gaped open on the floor.

Damning evidence. But it didn't interest Griff.

He pushed thoughts and judgments about his own ignorance and credulity away. Let the voices gibber. No time for that now. It was all down to him. Maybe he was the Guide himself and he just hadn't known it.

He turned his attention to the bomb. Four bunches of red, green, yellow and black wires connected to four homemade containers of explosive made up the bomb's four sectors. Drugs weren't the only useful substance you could buy at the feed store. His adversary had obviously stocked up on fertilizer.

All of the wires led into a central timer. Three minutes and ticking. Griff began to sweat.

He had to figure BomBoy would try to trick the bomb squad by changing colors. That's how he'd have done it. He'd have to disarm the sectors one by one. Which color was which?

Griff went into his senses and felt the wires in the first bunch. Yes. He carefully teased away the red wire and cut it. His hands were steady. One sector finished. Slow and easy.

He breathed, then started in again with the second bunch, trusting the feel of the wires in his fingers the way he used to in 'Nam. He'd never been wrong. Not yet. The timer's ticking was like a hammer hitting his head.

He heard movement up above. Mahina hadn't gagged the imposter—the clown mask had been in the way. No time now.

"Are you crazy?" BomBoy's voice was strangled with rage and fear. "You're going to get us both killed. Just like you killed my brother."

Griff ignored him.

Thumping and scraping, as the imposter rolled closer. "Cut me loose and I'll share the loot. You'll be rich! I have protection from the DEA—they wanted to nail Hunter Craddock." More sounds of struggle. "You *know* me. Phil. I got you permission to play your precious organ, remember?"

Idiot. The Energy Center had called him to the organ. And he could take the cash and leave right now if he wanted to.

"My brother was a crazy asshole anyhow." BomBoy/Phil was crying now. "We lost touch years ago and I don't give a shit that he's dead. I was just yanking your chain. I'll swear to everyone you're really him, I promise. Just let me go." More sobbing. "I only found out about you by accident," he wheedled. "I volunteered for the Palace board to get access to the tunnels, and there you were on the cast list. How many Griffin K. Petersons could there be?"

Phil's words swarmed around Griff's ears like buzzing hornets. He held the green wire in his fingers and paused. Sweat dripped off his forehead. He snipped it. Half the bomb disarmed.

He felt for the third bunch of wires. This time, the yellow one spoke to him.

Phil struggled noisily, but he couldn't get free. "Leave it. Just leave it." He was screaming now. "Help! Someone help."

The timer was almost at zero. Griff cut the yellow wire, then lunged across the floor and slithered around behind the Energy Center. One sector was still armed. He wrapped his head in his arms and pulled his knees in tight. A blinding light exploded behind his eyes like sound. He heard nothing.

The comet had arrived.

"I'm ready." His body floated through the dust and debris. "I've been waiting for you," he spoke without words. Griff opened his eyes as alien shapes reached out for him.

Gentle but insistent hands grasped his body, which was light as air.

"Take me to your leader." He laughed.

They raised him up and carried him into the sky.

PART FIVE
RUBY SLIPPERS

CHAPTER 34

Out on Bayfront, the explosion sounded like a muffled New Year's Eve firework. Every face swiveled back to Haili Street. The crowd cried out, and a few people screamed. The homeless folks who lived at the bus station rolled off their benches and staggered out to investigate.

Nora and Clyde held onto their children and stared back toward the theater. Was that a cloud of smoke rising against the orange glow of the streetlights?

It was a sign.

"Clyde, we need to go home." The words just came out, their truth as explosive as the bomb. Nora's heart thumped, and she clutched Oliver and Miri tighter. "I mean really go home, back to Canada where we belong. Please."

In all the violence and excitement, Clyde's sleek ponytail had come loose from the elastic band and now flopped around his face. He looked more like the man she had married all those years ago, straight out of college.

Clyde's mouth tightened, and Nora braced herself for an attack. But then he closed his eyes and let out a long breath.

"All right."

The children squirmed away to get a better look at the smoke, and Clyde put his arm around Nora's shoulders.

"What?" Nora couldn't believe what she was hearing. She pulled away to face him. "Do you mean it? You won't try to stop us from leaving?"

"No." Clyde shook his head. He looked deflated. "The Big Island isn't big enough for me after all, Nora. I think I will go to Australia. The twins will be better off with you. I'll come visit during the holidays so we can both be with them. And they can come to me for the summers."

Nora stared at him. "You've been thinking about this." She imagined her elderly parents' joy—their only child and grandchildren home again. She could rejoin her circle of friends, put Miri and Oliver back in their excellent public school. She could stop slathering on sunscreen and wear long pants and sweaters again. She wouldn't miss another ski season.

"I don't want that woman taking care of my children. Ever." A furious surge of energy swept through Nora, like the aftershock of an explosion, fire rushing in to fill the vacuum.

"Don't worry, I think Greta and I are through. She's crazy." Clyde pushed his floppy hair behind his ears. Definitely not the look he'd been after, nerdy and almost endearing. "But I *have* done a lot of thinking." He paused. "Maybe you and I should get back together, Nora. We could go to Australia as a family. Try again."

Nora bit back a sharp retort. He was trying, and it was rather sweet. "Oh Clyde." She gave him a squeeze. "We're still the same people. Let's not fool ourselves. And you know how I loathe the heat."

Clyde looked stricken, then rallied and took her arm. "Come. Let's walk. I can't just stand here."

They pulled the twins back in and strolled along past groups of excited theatergoers and costumed players as fire engines roared past on Bayfront, their sirens blaring. Nora felt a strange distance from the scene, even in her dirty Ozian outfit. She was part and yet not a part of this.

Tall palm trees rustled their fronds in a breeze that didn't reach the muggy air below. Beyond lay the deep, dark ocean she would soon travel across for the last time. She doubted she would ever return. She waved at Harriet, who stood with her son and a balding older man. The ex-husband?

Nora nudged Clyde. "Look." Together they stared at Merle and Greta. Clyde's erstwhile girlfriend sat on the Lion's lap with her head on his furry shoulder. He was stroking her hair with his paw.

"That didn't take long."

They laughed and shook their heads. Nora saw Alice and some of the homeschooling group huddled nearby.

Oliver and Miri slid their small hands out of their parents' and raced over to join the other children. They pointed toward Haili Street. Sure enough, arcs of water from the fire hoses sparkled above the storefronts.

"Thank god you're safe." Nora and Alice embraced, while Clyde stood to the side. Alice hugged him, too.

"But the Palace. I wonder how bad it is." Nora felt tears start to slide down her face, warm and wet. Her shoulders quaked and she gave a shaky smile. "Must be a delayed reaction."

Alice held her close and patted her back. "There, there, sweetheart. You've had a nasty shock."

Nora burst out laughing. "You sound like one of those British nurses in a WWII movie. Next you'll urge me to drink a nice hot cup of sweet tea."

"If only," Alice exclaimed. "I'm parched."

The scene was dreamlike, fuzzy around the edges. Groups of people shifted in waves and eddies. A breeze whipped up off the ocean and a light rain began to fall, spattering Nora's face and arms.

"I'll take you and the children home." Clyde took her arm and called to the twins. "We parked by Café Rialto and walked, so my car should be fine."

Nora thought about her dear old Volvo, companion of many years, which she'd parked behind the theater. No doubt totaled. Blown to bits. She felt a momentary sorrow, then set it aside. The children were alive. She was alive. And now they were free. Her head tingled.

"What about Greta and her children? You can't just leave them here." She turned to look.

"We'll drive them home. Unless your friend the Cowardly Lion insists on doing the honors himself." Alice grinned and gave her a little push. "You go on. You must be exhausted. I want to hear all about it tomorrow. Ring me." She waved and then turned to start rounding up her group.

Clyde and Nora called again to the children, who scampered over, their grubby faces glowing.

"Time to go home."

They walked down the street together, a family temporarily re-united by disaster.

⌣

IRIS AND MAHINA WATCHED NORA AND HER FAMILY WALK BY from their seat on the curb. The brief rain shower had passed.

"You'd better just tell me everything." Mahina still held her mother's hand. Ziggy had collapsed into a dingy pile of fluff on the grass next to her, exhausted from his adventures and fast asleep.

"I am so sorry, love." Iris's voice broke, but she carried on. Now or never. "I was so young, barely older than you are now. I was so angry and afraid. Not the best time or circumstance to make huge life decisions. And then it was done, and I couldn't see how to undo it. Cowardly and unfair to you, I know."

"I'm going to be mad at you for the rest of my life, Mom." Mahina squeezed her hand. "Keep going."

As the story poured out of the dark place where she had confined it, Iris remembered everything in vivid technicolor. It was that kind of story, clichéd and larger than life. She had been a beautiful eighteen-year-old girl, daughter of an undocumented housekeeper, seduced by her mother's rich, handsome forty-something employer. Her married employer.

"So he knocked you up?" Mahina looked sideways to meet Iris's eyes. "With me?"

"In a nutshell." Iris laughed again, but it felt looser. The tightness in her chest, in her whole body, really, since the letters had arrived, was unspooling at last. Mahina didn't hate her. "I thought he would leave his wife and marry me, which of course he'd said he would."

"But he didn't." Mahina tossed her head. "Pervy asshole."

Iris remembered her heartbreak, which had changed in a white-hot flash to fury. She had threatened to tell his wife, a perfectly nice woman who gave her mother hand-me-downs. He had bought her off.

"But what about your mother? Did she know?"

"She was furious, said I'd ruined everything for her, which I had, because he fired her right after he found out I was pregnant. I begged her to come with me to Hawai'i—we'd always dreamed of going. But she said no, she was going back to her family in Mexico. I was legal, since I was born in L.A., but she didn't have papers, and now, no references. When I tried to give her money she threw it on the floor and spat on it." Iris could see her mother's distorted features and hear her voice, railing at her in Spanish. "After all I've suffered and sacrificed, this is how you repay me?"

"I'm sorry I didn't tell you the truth, Mahina." Iris looked at her daughter. "And I'm so sorry your father didn't deserve you. I know it must hurt terribly. I didn't want you to grow up feeling unwanted, just because of him, so I made up a story instead."

Mahina was quiet for a few moments. Then she spoke. "So I have relatives in L.A. *and* in Mexico?" She put her face in her hands. "Wow. This is wild, Mom." She looked up and grinned. "You were a little slut."

Iris started to protest, but broke out laughing instead. She laughed and laughed until she rocked backward and lay in the patchy damp grass next to the bus station. Mahina joined her, and they stared upward into the lacy canopy of trees overhead. Stars twinkled through the leaves.

"We're probably lying in hobo pee," said Mahina, setting off another fit of giggles.

"I *was* a little slut," said Iris. "And I got very lucky anyhow. Go figure." She turned her head so she could see her daughter, the grass scratchy beneath her cheek. "I got you—and a big pile of cash." She touched Mahina's face. "We've had a good life together so far, haven't we? I haven't been a terrible mother?"

"Don't push it, Mom." Mahina snuggled into her mother's neck. Her hair tickled Iris's nose, and she stroked it down.

"I'm not sure what's going to happen with the trust now, but I've been saving money all these years, just in case." She kissed Mahina's head. "And I've made a pretty good living in real estate, too. So whatever the heirs decide, we'll be fine. We don't need their money anymore."

"So my biological father died of a heart attack, and my half-siblings just found out I exist?" Mahina pulled away again. "Do you think they'll want to meet me?"

"They're fools if they don't. But you don't have to do anything unless you want to, love. You're in charge."

"I don't know what I want to do." Mahina sighed and then stiffened. "So who's the man in your fake wedding photograph, the one I've always thought was my father?"

"Oh my lovely girl." Iris felt her eyes well up with tears. "Carlos was a friend, one of the gardeners at the estate where my mother worked. He had a crush on me."

"So you told him what happened even though you weren't supposed to?"

"Damn right I did." Iris smiled. Tears slid down her cheeks. "I needed someone on my side. And something to show you after you were born, even if it wasn't real."

"He's hot. Too bad he wasn't my real dad. Come to think of it, he looks kind of like Moses Kapili."

They started laughing again. Then Mahina sat up. The breeze had changed direction and a burnt, smoky odor wafted over the bus station.

"What happened to your mother, then? Did she stay in Mexico?" Mahina turned to brush the twigs off her back. Iris could tell she was trying to act like she didn't care.

"I sent her a photo after you were born. I thought she might relent when she saw her granddaughter. But my cousin wrote back instead. Your *abuela* was killed in a car crash." She steadied her voice. "I used that part of the story for your made-up father instead." Iris shook with unexpected sobs. Had she ever grieved properly for her mother? She'd been so intent on living a lie that the truth had seemed unreal. Until now. "I know she would have loved you."

Mahina stood up and held out her hand to her mother. "I want to learn Spanish. And I want to meet our Mexican relatives for sure, even if they disapprove of us."

"I never even knew who my father was." Iris let it all come out. "He was probably married, which explains why my mother felt so betrayed when I made the same mistake. She used to tell me stories about her childhood back in Mexico: the hard work, the celebrations, the big loving family. We were always going to visit, but we never did." She wiped her face with the backs of her hands and looked into her daughter's eyes. "No matter what you do, and I hope it won't be anything as foolish as I've done, I will always love you and take care of you. Okay? And no more secrets and lies, I promise."

"Okay Mom, but your credibility is shot."

Iris pulled Mahina in for a long hug. "I've probably forgotten my own Spanish. I left it behind with the rest of my life when I moved here to start a new one. But we'll learn together. And plan a reunion trip. Soon."

Mahina yawned and stretched, then wrinkled her nose. "God, I stink. Let's go home, Mom. I need a shower."

Ziggy woke with a yip, as if to second the motion.

CHAPTER 35

MAHINA STUCK HER HEAD THROUGH THE DOORWAY AND peered into the hospital room. The blue curtains on the railing around the bed were pulled back for visiting hours. Griff lay on the white bed, tubes running down into his arms and up his nose.

"Are you awake?" Mahina said in a loud whisper.

He lifted a hand, then dropped it back down.

"I brought you some flowers from our garden." She held out a bouquet of anthuriums. Their waxy red petals shone dully in the fluorescent light, yellow stamens jaunty. She saw a glass half full of water and plonked them in.

Mahina sat down in the chair next to the bed. The monitoring machine hummed and blinked its lights behind her, like a friendly robot.

"You should see the other guy." Griff let out a rasping grunt that must have been a laugh.

"They say it's a miracle you survived." She leaned forward. "The organ blower saved your life."

"Energy Center," Griff corrected, turning his head to look at her. His eyes were bloodshot and his face was puffy.

Mahina had told her mother about Griff's stories.

Iris said he must be mentally ill, and probably also had post-traumatic stress disorder. "From Vietnam, love, a terrible war."

Mahina didn't know what to think.

"You saved the Palace. Everyone says so. If the whole bomb had gone off, it would have just vaporized the entire building, like a death ray or something. Anyway, they've had to close it for repairs, so that's the end of our run."

She leaned back. Rain was falling outside the window, and the lush forest fell steeply away to the Wailuku River Gorge below. "George says an international news syndicate picked up the story, and now money is pouring in from all over the world. Everyone who's ever visited Hilo wants to help. The theater might be able to open again in six months!"

"Mmm."

"I'm so glad you're okay." Mahina felt tears prick her eyes. "I really do want to take organ lessons from you when you're well again. I wasn't just saying it."

"Organ?" Griff's hands clenched and unclenched.

"It's okay. The...the Energy Center, too. The metal casing is really strong, I guess, so it wasn't even damaged by the bomb." Mahina smiled. "George says that's a miracle, too, since it might be impossible to replace. I guess hardly anyone knows how to make them for old organs anymore."

Griff's hands lay still on the bed.

"BomBoy didn't make it. Turns out he was working undercover for the DEA the whole time."

Mahina paused to tear the wrapping off a box of chocolate-dipped shortbread cookies on Griff's bedside table. She bit one in half and her eyes rolled back in pleasure. "They caught the kingpin. It was Desiree's friend from the workday, the creepy guy, remember? She actually wore a wire—totally hardcore."

Mahina continued. Talking to Griff was so restful. "Moses, Mom's boyfriend, the Policeman, said they recovered half a million in cash blown around the theater by the explosion. Some of the bills are damaged but the bank will honor them. Normally the DEA would seize the money, but since their guy Phil caused the damage they've given it to the Hilo Police Department, and the police are donating most of the money to the Palace repair fund."

Iris had told her it was the least they could do since the Chief had bungled Moses's operation so badly, cutting his budget and then pulling all his officers and sending them out to Phil's decoy explosion.

Mahina held out the box. "Do you want a cookie?"

"Mmm." Griff's eyes were closed, his lids twitching a little.

"Moses and Mom are getting married—can you believe it?" Mahina went on, guessing the answer was no.

She ate another cookie. The buttery, chocolaty crumbs melted in her mouth. She'd stopped throwing up after Iris caught her and made her start seeing a geeky therapist who told her to love her body. Duh. "Next week we're flying to Oʻahu to meet his huge Hawaiian ʻohana. And I'm going to have a sibling!" She paused to swallow. "Mom thought she was menopausal, and she was really hāpai—that means pregnant in Hawaiian, in case you didn't know. Some example she's setting, yah? Turns out she was an unwed mother all these years with me. For real."

Mahina still could hardly believe any of it. She was surprised her mother's pregnancy and impending marriage made her happy instead of angry or jealous. In fact, anger, for so long her default mode, seemed to have eased into something else that felt almost like contentment. Maybe, she thought, feeling suddenly old and wise, now that her whole history had been rewritten over the past month, nothing would ever shock her again. It would actually be fun to have a little brother or sister. For one thing, her mom wouldn't be so clingy. And Moses had turned out to be pretty cool. He'd be her stepdad—now that she was too old for a dad. Weird.

Speaking of dads, her biological father's children had not dissolved the trust. Their mother had died a few years earlier from cancer, and they wanted to meet their younger half-sister. When she was ready.

Mahina had pushed the hurt of her father's rejection away. It had nothing to do with her, really. Iris had already done the suffering for her. In fact, Mahina and her mother were planning a trip this coming summer to look at colleges. Maybe she would apply to schools in California as well as on the East Coast. Maybe she would even consider Hollywood as an alternative to Broadway. She had plenty of time to decide.

Mahina brought her focus back to the present. "The drugs blew up completely. White powder everywhere." She laughed. "Moses said they keep catching the homeless guys from the alley in there licking the floor to get high."

Griff's chest heaved, and the rasping grunt came out again. Laughter.

Mahina had one more choice piece of news. "Guess what? Mrs. Furneaux—you know, Harriet the Wicked Witch—gave me an A on my final project in art class. She said I had real talent. I painted a big portrait of Aunty Em and the little ghost girl in the theater, and my perspective technique 'exceeded expectations.' When I showed it to Aunty Em—Aunty Keiko, that is—she loved it, even though she's screaming like the head in the Munch painting Mrs. Furneaux showed us. Mom said she's going to get the board to hang it in the Palace lobby when the theater reopens. I'll be a famous artist!" Mahina beamed at Griff, but his eyes were closed.

"Well, I guess I'd better let you sleep." Mahina stood up. Griff lifted his hand, and she grasped it and held on. "I'll come and visit again."

His hand fell back onto the bed.

Mahina tiptoed across the linoleum and out the door.

⌣

ONE MONTH LATER, THE EAST HAWAI'I COMMUNITY PLAYERS gathered at Harriet's house for the long-delayed after party. Most people swung past the Palace on their way, just to feel the theater's presence behind the chain-link fence and scaffolding that surrounded it.

It was the weekend before Thanksgiving and the crushing heat had abated. Late this year, they all said. Global climate change? Cast and crew embraced as though reunited after years of exile. Casseroles, salads and desserts crowded the long dining table, wine bottles uncorked and empty minutes later.

"Did you hear? Griff's out of the hospital." Patrick lounged against the wall, spearing cubes of *poke* off his loaded *lū'au* plate with a toothpick and popping them into his mouth. He kept staring over at his girlfriend, who was engaged in lively conversation with Harriet and Aunty Em/Keiko.

Probably about pregnancy, Desiree thought, given her obvious baby bump.

"George said Griff's cell phone has been disconnected, and no one knows where he lives." Patrick waved his *poke*-laden toothpick in the air. "I don't care what the purists say. Spicy ahi is the best."

Desiree shrugged and glanced over her shoulder at Iris and Moses Kapili talking to George out on the *lanai*.

Her concussion and abrasions had healed, but even more important, Kapili said she was free and clear now. He hadn't even asked her to turn in her drug money, and she wasn't about to. She had other plans.

There. Kapili was still talking to George, and Iris was heading to the drinks table. Ginger ale? Desiree's gaze lowered to the gentle swell of Iris's tummy. Well, well. She walked over to meet the other woman, leaving Patrick talking to the air, his mouth full of half-chewed fish.

"Hey, nice to see everyone, yah?" Desiree turned on her Glinda the Good smile and Iris smiled back. "Is Mahina here?"

"She's on her way with Keola, she says." Iris shrugged. "She's disappointed Griff won't be here. She says they bonded in the tunnels and they're war buddies now."

"He's an odd duck all right, but a real hero." Desiree leaned forward. "Listen, I'm interested in buying a house, so I thought I'd talk to you—to see if there's anything I could afford." She blushed. Iris must know where Desiree's money came from.

But Iris didn't miss a beat. "Sure. It's a real buyer's market right now. Lots of good deals since the housing bubble burst. Land speculators are looking to unload in a hurry before they go into foreclosure, so you don't have to feel bad about it." She took a sip of her ginger ale. "I know I don't. Just glad to be making a living."

"I have some money for a down payment." Desiree twisted her hands. "I'd like the kids to have their own rooms and a yard to play in?"

"I know we'll find just the right place." Iris dug into her tiny handbag and handed Desiree a card. "Call me and we'll set up a time to meet, look at some houses, and talk about the possibilities."

She handed Desiree another card. "This is a mortgage broker who won't scam you or get you into anything you can't handle. She's great."

Desiree felt wobbly. Her lips trembled. She straightened up. "Who'd a thunk, right? Me, a homeowner."

"Why not?" Iris beamed and put her hand on her stomach. A dead giveaway. "We all need a fresh start sometimes. Some of us more than once."

⤙

"So, I hear you're really doing it, Patrick, going back to school?" Harriet raised her glass to him. "Good for you. And congratulations on your expectant fatherhood, too. I found teaching and parenting a perfect complementarity."

Cindy waved from across the room. She and Iris pointed at their stomachs and gave a thumbs up.

Patrick beamed. "Thanks, Harriet." He shrugged. "Must be crazy to become a student again at my age—and start a family—but yeah." He set down his plate and picked up his beer bottle. "I'm actually really excited. Nervous, too. About both. What if I'm too old to learn? My brain may have atrophied too much. And what if my kid hates me?"

"Nonsense." Harriet fixed him with her intense gaze. "You'll sail through and then become the most popular teacher at the school. And a devoted father." She leaned closer. "And FYI, children have no choice about loving their parents, at least when they're young. Just think of it as a gift."

"I hope I can get a job teaching social studies." Patrick smiled. "I'll probably never get near an art room." He hesitated. "I found out the day after opening night that my mango bowl won first prize at the East Hawai'i Woodworkers exhibition." He spread his hands. "I owe it to Cindy. She jolted me out of my artistic block."

"Patrick, that's wonderful. Congratulations." Harriet gave him a hug. "And don't give up on the art room. I'll probably retire in a few years so I can spend more time making art myself. I actually have some projects going in my studio again after a long dry spell." She smiled ruefully. "At my age you hear the clock ticking, which can be great motivator. Plus, I'd like to do more traveling before I get too decrepit—in the off-season for a change, after a lifetime of crowded school vacations."

She poured herself another glass of wine, adding several ice cubes from the bucket. "I sent Howard home to his new family, poor dear, and Luke has a job offer in L.A., so he'll be gone soon." She looked at Patrick. "I'm feeling bereft in advance, but happy I'm here. My home is open. They can both come visit again, and I can visit them. We'll always be family." She chuckled. "Tiffany will just have to get used to it."

Patrick smiled. "Harriet, you're a constant inspiration."

She winked. "After I retire and you take over my art room, I'll come back and sub for you when I run out of money."

They laughed, clinked glass and bottle, and drank.

⌣

NORA AND THE TWINS ARRIVED LATE, KICKING THEIR SLIPPERS into the pile on the front welcome mat before they entered the house.

To Nora's joy and amazement, her faithful Volvo had survived the blast from the theater parking lot, sustaining surface wounds but no mortal blows. Lesser vehicles had been totaled by falling debris. Nora carried a bottle of Pinot Grigio, a six-pack of passion-orange-guava drink (pog for short), and a tub of Bag n Buy potato mac salad. Real Hilo potluck fare. She'd made an effort here at the end, now that she no longer felt compelled to resist.

Through the open sliding door to the *lanai* and back yard she saw Merle talking to Evan and Moku, and averted her gaze.

"Hey." Desiree gave her a hug, her long hair tickling Nora's nose. "I hear you're leaving us."

Nora smiled, her eyes hot. "Soon. Clyde wants the children for Christmas and then we'll both leave, he for Australia and the twins and I back to Vancouver." She shook her head. "It's all so strange. Like a dream. The kids can't stop talking about the kangaroos and koalas they'll play with when they spend the summer with their dad—which will be winter there. Unbelievable."

"Wake up, Dorothy." Desiree grinned. "You're going back to Kansas, sistah." She raised her arms and gave a little shimmy. "That's what you wanted, right?"

"Yes." Nora looked up, her eyes swimming. "I'm happy. It's just—"

"I know." Desiree hugged her again. "This place kind of grows on you—like mold."

Nora reached for a tissue in her purse and blew her nose, laughing. "Crikey, I'm a mess."

"Hello ladies." Merle's exuberant presence shone upon them from a foot away. He reached out and encircled them both with his long arms. Nora relaxed into his embrace. Why not? He was a lovely man if you didn't expect too much.

She smiled up at him. "I'll miss you, Lion." Then she dug her elbow in his side. "Are you actually dating Greta?"

Merle grinned. "What if I am? You left me brokenhearted, and even rich women with addiction issues need love, don't they?"

Nora snorted. "You're incorrigible."

"You know it, baby." He hugged her again. "Don't forget me."
Nora shook her head. "As if I could."

⌣

GEORGE STOOD IN HARRIET'S GARDEN, THINKING. HE WAS SURE
Cal would move back in soon. He was softening. They would have
a baby, and it could be friends with all the other theater babies.
Such fecundity. Life would change, but perhaps in wonderful ways.
Terrifying, certainly.

Work on the Palace was going well. The damage wasn't as bad
as they'd thought. His blood pressure still skyrocketed when he
thought about how thoroughly he'd been duped by friggin' Phil,
not to mention Hunter Craddock. Moses Kapili told him that
Phil, alias BomBoy, had been put in place by the DEA to infiltrate
Craddock's organization—unbeknownst to local law enforcement.
All the Palace mischief, including the bomb, was extracurricular.
Apparently he had a reputation as a malicious prankster. Well, he'd
gotten what he had coming to him, George thought, leaning over
to smell a spray of tiny white blossoms. Funny, though. Phil's last
name was Peterson, just like Griff's.

A week after the disastrous opening night—talk about a play
bombing—George had heard from his father's lawyer. Apparently
one of George Sr.'s investments was a valuable commercial property, and if his son and heir wanted to sell, there was a cash buyer
ready to sign. The lawyer could fax the prospectus immediately. George smiled. He could donate some of the proceeds to the
Palace in his father's name. Let the old bastard grumble in his
grave.

Actually, with the drug money and all the donations, from as
far away as Frankfurt in one direction and Singapore in the other,

the Palace Friends would have enough for repairs, the foundation work, and even a new roof. Evan was setting up a trust. Truly an embarrassment of riches.

George reached out and touched Harriet's rock wall, peeling back a little moss. It was cool, damp and spongy in his fingers. Living and persistent.

Maybe he would take up gardening. It could be a family thing.

⌣

EVAN SAT ON THE *LANAI* AND DRANK A BEER, SOAKING IN THE last rays of late afternoon sun just about to disappear behind the mountain. Belinda sat down next to him and sighed.

"What's the matter?" He slipped into a mild gay best friend mode. It was becoming a routine, but not a bad one.

"I'm so sick of men." Belinda flung herself back in the chair. "Look over there. Patrick got back together with his girlfriend and they're having a baby. Just like everyone else but me." She made a pouty face.

"He's too old for you anyhow, and a secret smoker. Eew." Evan patted her arm. "Although I have to say, carrying his beloved out of the burning theater was a pretty romantic gesture."

Belinda made a choking noise.

Evan held up his hands. "Sorry, sorry. Totally overdone."

"It wasn't burning," Belinda muttered, then gave him a sidelong glance. "How about you? Any progress with Dorothy?"

"Ha ha ha." Evan sat up. "Moku is a giddy young lad—a teenager—and I am a staid financial planner. Not going to happen."

"I don't see why not." Belinda winked. "And don't look now, but there's your old flame."

Evan's head turned in spite of himself.

Luke was talking to Harriet inside the door. He looked over and met Evan's eyes, then waved.

Evan waved back. "Shit." He set down his beer bottle.

"Go talk to him. He's probably here to see you." Belinda gave him a push. "He's going to tell you how wrong he was, how much he's missed you. Go on."

Evan stood up and stretched, trying to look casual.

"Hey." Luke had moved fast. "Glad I caught you. Just wanted to say goodbye. I'm off next week, back to the mainland."

"What about your big project?" Evan's heart flip-flopped in his chest.

"Client decided to build in Bali instead, but I've got a job in L.A." Luke shrugged. "Back to the smog."

"Well, that's great. Congratulations." Evan's whole being deflated. He smiled, but even his eyes felt droopy.

"You should come visit sometime, see the bright lights." Luke grinned and gripped his shoulder. "Hilo's great, but it's pretty quiet for guys like us. Right?"

Evan felt an expansion in his chest. "I don't know about that. I'm really a small-town boy at heart." He looked at Luke and laughed. "But who knows? Maybe I will come and visit."

Luke gave a little wave and turned back to the house.

"See?" Belinda nudged his back. "He's still hot for you, baby."

Evan just smiled.

‿

DOWN THE HILL FROM THE PARTY, GRIFF SWITCHED ON HIS headlamp and clamped down with his bolt cutters. No more padlock. He swung open the gate of the chain link fence erected around the damaged side of the Palace, which was covered neatly with house wrap. He opened a slit in the sturdy material with a large, wickedly sharp hunting knife, slipped underneath the flap and entered the debris field.

He flipped a light switch just to check. No power. A big chunk had blown off the stage, and the basement underneath was exposed in all its rawness. Chunks of plaster littered the ground, and Griff picked his way carefully. His knife wound burned.

He had checked himself out of the hospital against the doctor's recommendation. The beady-eyed goose had reached out his long, stethoscoped neck to honk his opinions at Griff. The nurses were ducks, paddling around in the hospital pond, waddling through the corridors, their quacking friendly but dictatorial. It was time for him to go. Birds of any kind made him nervous, and waterfowl were the worst. Their ability to fly and swim gave them an unfair advantage, and they liked to let you know it.

They hadn't bothered Mahina. She had just stared at them with her disdainful cat eyes and glanced away again, prowling past as though they didn't exist.

Griff walked downslope. No walls in the way anymore, no division between basement and auditorium. He stopped.

There it was, ahead. His headlamp beam glanced off the familiar curved metal structure, dented and pocked now from the explosion. The Energy Center. He felt the cylinder and It was cold. Lifeless. The Power was gone. They had taken It back, swept It into the burning comet as it blazed past. Griff moved to sit down but had to hold his side as pain shot through his body.

He had failed.

And yet. The comet had destroyed BomBoy and buried his secrets. Among them, his brother's stolen identity. Griff thought back to the morning he'd left the North Cascade Mountains to start his new life. The morning of The Transaction.

When he'd woken up, the fire was a heap of ash and frost covered the campsite, including the huddled form in the sleeping bag across the cold fire pit. Shivering, Griff had packed up his things, hoping for a clean getaway. He did not want a companion, especially not a blabbermouthed starling.

The other figure did not stir. When Griff leaned over to check, the vet's cloudy eyes glared back at him, his mouth frozen open in a grimace. Heart attack? Overdose?

He'd invited Griff to shoot up with him the night before, but Griff was already half asleep and had declined.

He hesitated.

Out of the silence, The Voice spoke. "Take what is given." He whirled around, but no one was there.

It was the work of a moment to exchange dog tags and rifle through the dead vet's backpack for valuables and ID. He didn't need them anymore.

And so, Griffin K. Peterson lived on.

Griff eased down and sat for a few minutes, leaning against the Energy Center. He looked up. The ceiling was barely visible in the dim light, high, high above.

As he shifted his weight, about to leave, he felt something against his back, a spark or jolt. Something alive.

They were here! They hadn't left him after all. The Power was dormant, but not gone—not vanished. Maybe next time They would take him for keeps.

The Voice spoke directly into his mind. "It will live again because of you."

Griff stood up and winced. He placed his hands on the curved metal casing. Did It feel warmer?

The Voice spoke again. "Go home and get some rest before you hurt yourself." It sounded kind of like Harriet.

He walked back out into the auditorium and felt his way up to where the organ sat on its pedestal, shrouded with a tarp. He would play again. He would fill the theater with music, giving voice to all that was within, all that was given. The Voice would sing through the pipes and reeds and chimes, bringing beauty into being.

All would be well.

Griff turned and walked back the way he had come, stumbling a bit. He pulled the gate shut and snapped on the new padlock he'd brought along, pocketing the key.

He would be back soon.

⌣

For months after the event, the town of Hilo was abuzz with stories about the Palace bombing. Drug rings, ghosts, madmen and heroes. Who could distinguish fact from fiction?

As time passed, the weather cooled and the trade winds eased. The volcano sent its smoldering breath down the mountain to shroud the town in a sulfurous haze of volcanic fog. The people of Hilo coughed and rubbed their eyes, attributing all maladies and misfortune to the vog, and praying the volcano would vent its fumes on the Kona side instead.

Teenagers sneaked into the theater and camped out on dares, setting small fires on the cement floor to roast marshmallows and hot dogs while they spun scary tales and half-hoped the ghosts would appear. Security guards finally had to set a nightly patrol around the building to keep them out.

During the day, construction workers rebuilt the damaged walls and stage. Geckos moved back in and laid their miniature ping-pong ball eggs in corners. Their chiding clicks merged with the co-qui frogs' chirping bells in the evening chorus. A few persistent minah birds tried to nest on the catwalks until they were driven out, shedding downy feathers and chattering in protest.

Rumors circulated about the grand reopening.

"Definitely this spring."

"Are you kidding? Next fall if we're lucky."

Speculation was rife about which musical the Palace Friends and East Hawai'i Community Players would choose to put on.

What could possibly top *Wizard*?

But on hot, still nights when the town had closed up shop and the gates were locked around the Palace, some people walking up orange-tinted Haili Street swore they could hear music floating out from deep within the old building. An organ playing.

The theater was stirring.

Soon the marquee lights would blaze, the doors would swing open, and the town would pour in and fill the Palace with life again. Music would roll out into the street and swell up to meet the night sky thick with stars, pulsing in time with the theater's beating heart.

THE END

ACKNOWLEDGEMENTS

I WROTE THE FIRST DRAFTS OF THIS NOVEL AS MY CREATIVE THE-sis for Goddard College-Port Townsend's MFA in Creative Writing. I am indebted to my faculty advisors, Victoria Nelson and Aimee Liu, for their sharp criticism, generosity, and astute guidance, to Rogelio Martinez, my second reader, for his keen insights and encouragement, to so many other faculty members for their readings and workshops during my Goddard residencies, and to then program director, Paul Selig, for his *Wizard of Oz* lecture, which lit an explosion in my brain.

I am very grateful to early readers Sara McKay, Lynne Walker, Lisa Bade, Gina Wackerbarth, Anitra Waldo, Jeri Gertz (musical theater expert extraordinaire), and Leslie Karst, for their helpful comments and enthusiasm. Thanks to Sandra Wagner-Wright, Emmeline de Pillis (Frankie Bow), Justina Taft Mattos, and Patti Panahi for sharing their publishing expertise. Thanks to eagle-eyed copyediting powerhouse Lorna Collins for calling me out on all my favorite verbal and punctuation tics, and to the folks at Palmetto Publishing Group for their beautiful book design, and for guiding me through the publication process. Thanks also to UH Hilo colleagues (and dear friends) Kirsten Mollegaard and Lauri Sagle for their support, and to my creative writing students, who surprise and inspire me with their stories. Many thanks to

UH Hilo Hawaiian Collection librarian Mary Louise Haraguchi for her good humor and patience with my questions—and for her deadly research skills.

Thanks also to Stu Dawrs and *Hana Hou* magazine (by way of Lauri Sagle) who gave me the opportunity to write "Pipe Dream," a 2006 feature article on the Palace Theater's organ, which planted the seed that sprouted into this novel. Thanks to Bob Alder (Hilo Theatre Organ Society) and Cheryl "Quack" Moore (former President of Friends of the Palace) for sharing their passion, and to Rick Mazurowski for an organ demonstration and tour of the Palace basement. The Friends of the Palace Theater rely on donations to keep this historic treasure alive in our island community, and would be grateful for your support (https://hilopalace.com/support/).

Many, many thanks to my sister, Lisa Bade, for her support and encouragement at every stage of the book, and for creating the original cover art and maps, to my niece, Nicole Bade, for her writerly feedback and tag-team back cover design with nephew Nate Bade. I owe everything to my wonderful parents, Judy and Dave Wackerbarth, who instilled a love of books and reading in all their children and created an environment in which our imaginations could run wild. My children, Peter and Laura Cellier, flood my life with love, delight and humor. Their enthusiasm, sharp analysis, unconditional support, and close readings of the manuscript have helped me make the book much better. Finally, thanks to my husband, Tim Oldfather, for his unquestioning support of my writing, and his many quirky ideas.

If I've left anyone out, I apologize. I appreciate you, too. Any mistakes of any kind, factual, historical, geographical, cultural, or linguistic, are all my own.

DISCUSSION QUESTIONS FOR READING GROUPS

1. All the point-of-view characters in *No Place Like Home* came to Hawai'i for a different reason. What brought each one to Hilo? Have they found what they were looking for? How has their new life changed them, and what problems do they face because of it?

2. Which character do you identify with the most? Why?

3. Several characters are part of disrupted families, and have to negotiate single-parenting and/or co-parenting issues. How do financial pressures, interactions with ex-partners, problems with children, etc., influence their lives and decisions? Would you have made different choices in their place? Why or why not?

4. To some extent, and in different ways, all the characters in this novel are searching for love and belonging—it is the human condition, after all. How does each one handle their desire for companionship, romance, friendship, and security? What problems does it create?

5. What does "home" mean to each character? Where does it reside for them? In a place? In family? In community? Does this

change for any of the characters over the course of the novel? What is home for you?

6. Most of the characters are dealing with realizations and life transitions: adolescence, divorce, midlife crisis, aging, professional identity, sexuality, whether to have children, and so on. Which of these situations can you relate to? What has your experience been?

7. At the center of this novel is the iconic American story, *The Wizard of Oz*. How do the roles the characters play in the musical—the Wizard, the Wicked and Good Witches, Dorothy, the Scarecrow, the Tin Man, the Cowardly Lion—connect with their own lives? How do these culturally symbolic figures also relate to other characters' lives?

8. This story is partly about the power of community art/theater to bring people from different backgrounds together across a city or town. What events have you participated in or experienced that have made you reflect on the value of the arts for this purpose? What play or creative event would you like to see in your community?

9. How does this novel's depiction of Hawai'i compare to your expectations or your own experiences of the place? If different, how did this affect your reading of the story?

10. Why do you think it was important to the author, a *haole* (white) person, to only write from the perspective of *haole* characters? What would or could have happened if she had chosen to write in the voice of characters with other racial, ethnic, or cultural backgrounds? Do you agree with the author's choice? Why or why not?

ADDITIONAL RESOURCES

Hawaiian Dictionary, Mary Kawena Pukui and
Samuel H. Elbert
Haoles in Hawai'i, Judy Rohrer
From a Native Daughter, Haunani K. Trask

CPSIA information can be obtained
at www.ICGtesting.com
Printed in the USA
LVHW041003061020
668075LV00001B/3